DESIRE UNLEASHED

Desire, Oklahoma 9

Leah Brooke

MENAGE EVERLASTING

Siren Publishing, Inc.
www.SirenPublishing.com

A SIREN PUBLISHING BOOK
IMPRINT: Ménage Everlasting

DESIRE UNLEASHED
Copyright © 2014 by Leah Brooke

ISBN: 978-1-62741-413-5

First Printing: November 2014

Cover design by Les Byerley
All art and logo copyright © 2014 by Siren Publishing, Inc.

Printed in the U.S.A

PUBLISHER
Siren Publishing, Inc.
www.SirenPublishing.com

DESIRE UNLEASHED

Desire, Oklahoma 9

LEAH BROOKE

Chapter One

Nat Langley turned from the kitchen sink, her stomach lurching at the sound of her husband's cell phone.

It was a sound she'd come to hate over the last several months.

It was a sound that could change Jake's mood in an instant.

And she didn't know why.

Secret calls. Secret text messages.

Calls and messages that he wouldn't discuss with her, and that widened the distance between them.

It scared her so much that she'd finally stopped asking.

And she hated herself for it.

He'd been getting text messages all morning, and the tension surrounding him seemed to be growing with each one.

His eyes, flat and cool as he read the newest one, lifted to hers again, his hard expression turning the knots in her stomach to ice.

Swallowing heavily, she turned back to the plate that she'd spent the last five minutes washing, fear and anger at herself igniting her temper. "Another one of the mysterious messages you don't want to tell me about?"

She wanted to call the words back as soon as she uttered them, but she couldn't stay silent any longer.

Something had to give—one way or another.

Expecting him to wave her question away, and tell her it was nothing the way he had repeatedly over the last several months, Nat stilled at the pregnant silence that followed.

She'd never been shy about confronting him in the past, and the fact that she was now infuriated her.

The distance between them had gotten worse in the last few weeks, making the tension even worse.

And it scared the hell out of her.

She loved Jake more than her own life, and the thought of losing him was more than she could stand.

Without answering her, he texted a short reply and set the phone aside, staring down into his coffee.

Taking the opportunity to watch him unobserved, Nat blinked back tears, the surge of love and desire nearly overwhelming.

God, she loved him so much.

Other than a few gray strands in his dark brown hair, he looked much the same as he did the day she'd married him. Regular trips to the gym kept him in shape, and the few gray strands at his temple only made him look more distinguished. His eyes, the color of dark chocolate, could go from loving and indulgent to sharp and possessive in a heartbeat, but now held a misery that tore at her heart. His unwillingness to confide in her left her feeling bereft and unsteady—her entire world off-kilter.

His confidence had always been a source of security and comfort and she hadn't realized just how much she relied on it.

His arrogance frustrated her at times, and aroused her at others, but the insecurity in his eyes now frightened her more than she wanted to admit.

It was as if her entire world and everything she knew had been yanked out from under her.

And she didn't even know why.

He'd always been a fantastic lover, and had introduced her to the world of dominance and submission many years ago.

With patience. With love. With tenderness.

He'd drawn her closer until they became like one.

Something tormented him, shaking the control she'd come to rely on, convincing her that whatever secret Jake had been keeping from her was significant, so significant that it would change their lives forever.

She was losing him—a little more every day.

And it terrified her.

He was her husband. Her lover. Her Master.

Her rock.

They'd become closer than she'd ever thought she could be to another human being.

He was a part of her, so much a part of her that it hurt her that he didn't confide in her.

He'd always confided in her.

He loved her.

She could see it in his eyes, feel it in his touch.

Even now.

Especially now.

She'd watched for signs that he no longer wanted her, but the opposite appeared to be true.

Jake's lovemaking had become more intense than ever, and his touch held a desperation she didn't understand. Each time he made love to her, it was as if it would be the last time.

Wiping her hands, she fisted them in the towel and turned away from Jake to stare unseeingly out the window.

As much as she tried to deny it, all signs pointed to either Jake having a lover, or some kind of illness.

She'd rather face the lover.

The fact that he wouldn't talk to her about it convinced her that it was bad.

Very bad.

Blinking back more tears, she swallowed heavily and turned again, her breath catching to find him watching her, his eyes unreadable.

With a sigh, he leaned forward, bracing his arms on the table, his hands fisted in front of him. "Sit down, Nat. We have to talk."

No! I don't want to know!

She wanted to scream it. She wanted to turn and run out the back door—to escape back into pretending that everything was okay again.

Once she knew whatever Jake had been hiding, she could no longer pretend.

Once he told her, things would never be the same again.

She didn't know if she could bear it.

She had to.

She had to face whatever happened, and with the strength Jake expected of her.

Too nervous to sit, Nat shook her head, bracing herself for the blow to come. Closing her hands on the edge of the cold granite countertop, she locked her knees when they threatened to give way, swallowing the huge lump in her throat. "So, you've finally decided to tell me?"

Jake stood and moved gracefully around the table toward her, every lean muscular line of his body tight with tension. Reaching for her hand, he brought it to his lips, his eyes flat and searching hers for something, but she didn't know what. "I'm sorry I couldn't talk to you about this sooner, but I've had a lot to think about. I don't like the distance between us." He lifted his other hand and pushed back a loose tendril of her hair, his eyes narrowing when she stiffened. "We've never had that before, have we? Distance. You and I have done well together, haven't we?"

Panic slammed into her—panic she struggled to hide even as bile rose in her throat. Taking a shuddering breath, Nat held herself stiffly, shaken by the uncertainty in his eyes, something she couldn't remember ever seeing before. "You caused this distance by not telling me what's wrong."

"I know." Jake gave her one of those fake smiles he'd adopted over the last several months, gripping her chin and keeping her gaze lifted to his when she would have looked away. "I had to get some things straight in my head. I also didn't want you to have to worry any longer than you have to." He smiled, another smile that didn't reach his eyes. "I know how you worry about things."

Fearing the worst, Nat hardly dared to breathe. Pressing her hand, still wadded up in the towel, against her stomach, she took a shuddering breath. "And it took you several months to get things straight in your head? I've been worried all this time, so you didn't do me any favors. Whatever it is, tell me. I'm strong. I can take it." Her voice cracked, terror gripping her by the throat and making it nearly impossible to speak.

Jake's lips curved in a semblance of a smile. "It appears I've run out of time."

Nat's knees turned to rubber, her stomach churning as the world spun around her. "No. Oh, God. Please, no!"

Reaching for him, she could feel the blood draining from her face. Her worst nightmare. A sob escaped, and then another. "No! Oh, Jake. Please, God. No!"

She fisted her hands in his shirt as her knees buckled, her world crumbling around her.

Please, God, no! No! No! Please!

Anything but this! She could handle anything but this.

Stop it, Nat!

He needed her now. She had to be strong.

She straightened, holding on to the countertop when her knees refused to support her. "You're dying. Tell me everything."

Jake cursed, catching her before she hit the floor and yanking her against him. "No. Oh, God, baby. No. There's nothing wrong with me. I promise." Rubbing her back with a firm caress, he held her tightly, his hold keeping her upright. "I'm so sorry. I didn't mean to scare you. Shhh. I never expected you to think something like that. I'm so sorry, baby. I wasn't thinking. Oh, God, baby. I'm so sorry. So sorry. I'm not sick. I swear to you, I'm not sick. Hell, I'm a fucking idiot."

He was sorry.

He wasn't dying.

He wasn't dying.

Thank you, God!

She tried to lock her knees, but they felt as though they were made of rubber, her entire body trembling in reaction. Gripping his shoulders, she took several shaky breaths, holding on to him like a lifeline. "You're everything to me."

Cupping the back of her head, he pressed her face against his shoulder, and she went eagerly, his low, crooning tone and clean, masculine scent starting to center her again. "You're everything to me, too, baby. You're the most important thing in my world. Christ, how could I have been so fucking stupid? I'm so sorry, baby. I'm so sorry. It never dawned on me that you'd think something like that. Please forgive me. I swear there's nothing wrong with me."

Clinging to him, Nat swallowed another sob and lifted her head, wiping away tears in order to see him clearly. "Are you sure? Don't lie to me. I know I fell apart, but I can handle it. We can handle it together." Her voice came out as little more than a ragged whisper, but she could tell by the flare of his eyes that he'd heard her.

His smile, filled with tenderness, began to warm her again. "I'm sure."

Holding her face between his large hands, Jake groaned, his eyes tortured. "I'm sure. Hell, baby. I'm sorry. I never dreamed you'd think I was sick." His smile held a hint of sadness. "I swear, I would never keep something like that from you."

He wasn't sick. He wasn't dying.

That only left one thing.

Another woman.

Taking a deep breath, Nat stiffened, locking her knees to remain upright.

The joy—the overwhelming relief—began to fade, leaving her feeling cold and bereft.

Knowing she had to count on her own strength, she straightened on shaky legs and gently pushed his hands away, bracing herself against the countertop at her back. Lifting her gaze to his, she took a deep breath and let it out slowly. "But you have been keeping something from me. What is it?"

She needed to hear him say it. She needed to hear from his own lips that he'd betrayed her.

She needed to hear him say that he didn't love her anymore.

Bracing herself to have her heart ripped from her chest, Nat forced herself to face him squarely. Sucking in a breath at the flicker in his eyes, Nat avoided his outstretched hands and stepped to the side. "Don't. Just...don't. Say it. Whatever it is, you're not looking forward to telling me about it. I see it in your eyes." The excruciating pain almost doubled her over, but she knew she couldn't let him see it.

She'd fall apart later—much later—when she was alone. Confused, she stepped closer to him and laid a hand on his shoulder, needing the contact, and despite her anger and fear, aching for him.

Pulling his arm until he faced her, she looked up at him, her pulse tripping as always at the flare of possessiveness in his dark eyes. "Tell me. I'm scared, and you know how much I hate that. If you're not sick, whatever it is, I can take it. Just tell me the truth. Dragging this out is killing me."

His handsome features, so beloved, softened as he trailed his fingers over her hair. "I'm sorry, baby. I sure as hell didn't mean to scare you. Keeping her hand in his, he turned away, leading her into the living room.

"I've been pretty scared myself. Give me a minute. I have no fucking idea how to begin."

Nat allowed him to pull her down to the sofa, but instead of snuggling against him the way she normally did, she slid to the opposite end and turned toward him, needing to see his face. "Well, you're going to have to figure it out. You're pissing me off."

Jake didn't smile the way she'd expected, and even more alarming, his eyes didn't light with anticipation the way they usually did when she confronted him with her temper.

Instead, he sighed. "I know, and I'm sorry for it. I haven't given you what you need from me these last few months, have I, baby?"

His lips twisted. "My only excuse is that I'm scared, Nat." Holding her gaze, he sighed. "I'm scared to death of losing you."

"That could never happen. I can't imagine not loving you." Too nervous to sit still, she started to get up, cursing when Jake grabbed her arm and pulled her to land heavily against him.

Overcoming her struggles with frustrating ease, Jake pulled her onto his lap. "You're not going anywhere. Let me finish, damn it!"

"Then finish!" Nat's temper dissolved at the anguish on her husband's face. "I'm sorry. Tell me, Jake. Please."

"Don't you think I'm trying?" He scrubbed a hand over his face in a rare sign of frustration. "I'm probably going to screw this up, but you're staying right where you are until I get it all out."

"Fine. Just do it." Shaken by her usually controlled husband's demeanor, Nat waited, her nerves stretching to the breaking point as she watched his inner struggle.

Jake sighed again, his sharp gaze holding hers. "Hoyt's retiring."

A gasp escaped before she could prevent it, and it took every ounce of willpower she possessed to show only mild interest.

At least she hoped she only showed mild interest.

The jolt to her system made her heart pound furiously and affected her breathing. She fought to hide it, ashamed of herself for still having feelings for the man who'd been out of her life for years. "Is that who all those private calls and text messages have been from? What the hell does that have to do with us?"

Hoyt.

Her first lover.

Her son's father.

The man who'd held a piece of her heart ever since he'd first captured it.

The image of the way he'd looked the last time she saw him rose in her mind—her stomach fluttering when she remembered the pain and resignation in his eyes.

Jake's eyes sharpened. "There it is."

Running a hand over her hair, he lifted her face to his, tightening his hold when she would have pulled away. "You would never have said anything about it, but it's there. It hasn't dimmed at all, has it, baby?"

Ashamed of herself, she averted her gaze, fighting the surge of panic that made her stomach roll. "I don't know what you're talking about."

Nothing mattered except what she had with Jake. Nothing could ever be allowed to come between them.

His lips thinned. "You know Hoyt and I have always been close. We've spoken on and off over the last several years, but much more in the last few months."

Nat frowned, fighting not to show any emotion as she struggled to understand where this was going. "Oh?"

Jake rubbed his hand up and down her back, the way he did when she was upset about something. Lifting her chin, he regarded her steadily, his hand still moving in a slow rhythm as if he worked to loosen the tight muscles in her back she hadn't wanted him to know about. "He used to come and visit every chance he got, but he stopped coming a few years ago." His eyes sharpened on hers. "You've never mentioned it—never asked about it. That's not like you. The more I thought about it, the more it shook me. You want to tell me why you never mentioned it?"

Sitting on his lap, she found it difficult to avoid his gaze—a maneuver she recognized well. Spinning her wedding ring around her finger, Nat shrugged, trying not to think about those visits from Hoyt—visits that had been both heaven and hell for her. "I figured he stopped coming by because he got busy. I assumed he had a girlfriend."

She'd lost a lot of sleep thinking about Hoyt in the arms of another woman, something that both shamed and infuriated her.

He used to visit every chance he got and especially made a point to visit at the holidays whenever possible. Over the last three years, he hadn't spent his vacation time with them, and had missed every holiday.

Holidays had been hell for her because she'd imagined him spending them with another woman.

Leaning forward, Jake took her left hand in his, staring down at it as he ran his thumb back and forth over her wedding band. "No. He doesn't have a girlfriend." Lifting his gaze to hers, he lifted a brow. "I think you know why he stopped coming around. The fact that you haven't discussed it with me has given me quite a few sleepless nights."

Her stomach fluttered, nerves making her too restless to sit still. Yanking her hand out of his, she jumped to her feet. "I have no idea why he stopped coming around. Hey!"

Jake tumbled her to the sofa, covering her body with his, and lying full length over her. "Be still." Using his weight to press her to the cushions, he ran his fingers through her hair, his eyes hard and cool. "We're not done here."

Nat knew that tone well, a tone that sent a chill of alarm up her spine. Her alarm intensified when he gripped both of her wrists in one hand and lifted them over her head, holding them there with a firm grip she knew she wouldn't be able to shake.

Dealing with Jake in this mood was dangerous.

The very real fear of revealing too much made her defensive. Knowing that the best defense was a good offense, she gathered every bit of anger she could muster. "Get the fuck off of me."

With his face just inches from hers, he stared into her eyes, his grip on her chin not allowing her to look away. "You're scared. Interesting." He ran his thumb over her bottom lip, making it tingle. "Hoyt stopped coming around because seeing you and not being able to have you hurt him too much."

The knots in her stomach tightened, her breath catching with both panic and exhilaration.

Heaven and Hell.

"No."

Jake's eyes flickered, telling her just how much she'd given away.

She should have known he'd see.

His sharp eyes missed nothing.

"Yes." Jake's smile held a hint of desperation that fueled her own. "He wants you, Nat. I've always known that, although both of you tried your best to deny what you felt and hide it from me." Running his thumb over her bottom lip, he sighed. "He knows about Desire, and he knows why I moved us here shortly after we got married."

Shaking everywhere, Nat swallowed heavily, struggling for composure. "Of course he knows about Desire. He's been here several times. What are you trying to say? I thought we moved here because you liked that people could live as they wanted, and it was a great place to relocate your store."

"We never discussed it, but you knew." Pressing his cock against her mound, Jake used his powerful thighs to push hers wider. "You knew why I moved us here. You knew that both of us loved you. You love both of us. You only married me because Hoyt had already signed up for the service and would be leaving."

Running his free hand over her hair, Jake smiled, the tenderness making her eyes sting with tears. "You and I talked about it. We've always been honest with each other, Nat."

Sliding his hand to her breast, he unerringly found her nipple, his smile widening when she jolted and cried out. "You also liked what I could do for you in bed. We clicked, didn't we? But I knew that Hoyt was devastated. I moved us here because I knew that one day he'd be back for you. I knew that he'd never be satisfied with another woman. I knew that one day we would share you, because I sure as hell wasn't about to give you up. The thought of sharing you with him even excited me—at first."

Trembling helplessly, Nat writhed beneath him, her mind spinning. "You never told me that, and I sure as hell didn't marry you just because you were good in bed. We didn't even have sex until after I had Joe. Oh!"

Digging her heels into the sofa cushions, Nat arched, pressing herself against him, the sharp pinch to her nipple making her clit swell.

Anger and fear became desire in a heartbeat. "What do you mean—at first?"

Jake fisted a hand in the hem of her sweater, stripping her out of it with a roughness that thrilled her and suited her mood. Holding her wrists above her head again, he tore open the front closure of her bra, baring her breasts to his gaze. Closing his thumb and forefinger over her nipple, his eyes narrowed. "I've always known that he was your first choice, but I was glad to have any part of you that I could get. The thought of sharing you with him excited me, especially when I thought about how much pleasure we could give you together."

Nat sucked in a breath at the sharp stab of lust, struggling to clear her head. "I love you, Jake. You know how much I love you, damn it!"

Jake smiled faintly, his eyes laser sharp. "Oh, I know you do. But I always knew that you loved Hoyt. You still do."

"No!" Panicked now, Nat began to struggle, too afraid of what he saw in her eyes. "You're wrong."

His eyes, dark with fury, narrowed to slits, his jaw clenching as his fingers tightened on her nipple. "Don't you ever fucking lie to me again."

Crying out, Nat writhed against him, the sharp pinch sending arrows of need clawing through her.

She'd never seen him like this before.

The power surrounding him, the power he'd always kept on a very tight leash, and that she'd only seen hints of over the years, broke free, the force of it nothing short of astonishing.

God, she wanted him.

Her pussy clenched in desperation, her panties already soaked. "Jake, please!"

Lust seemed too tame a word for what she felt now, need boiling inside her like a living, breathing thing that threatened to consume her.

Brushing his lips over hers, Jake slid his palm over her nipple, his eyes glittering with erotic intent. "Oh, I'll please you, my love. But, we're not quite done yet, are we?"

Nat couldn't stop shaking, her body screaming for release.

Jake knew her too well. He knew how to stroke her to make her mindless with need, and knew what the combination of silky voice laced with threat would do to her. He knew how his demanding touch ripped away her defenses, leaving her weak and trembling under his hands.

"Jake—" She sucked in a breath at the feel of his hand sliding into the front of her jeans, and with a hard pull, yanked them down to her knees.

"Hoyt wants you. He wants to share you with me. He wants you to belong to both of us."

Nat sucked in another breath when he ripped her panties from her, desperate for him to listen to her—desperate for him to take her. "Jake, I want *you*. I love *you*!"

Jake smiled, tossing her panties aside as he stretched out full length on top of her, leaning slightly to the side. "Yes, you do."

Running his hands over her breasts, teasing one nipple and then the other with a slow caress, Jake held her gaze. "But, you also love him." Shaking his head when she would have spoken, he smiled again. "Did you think I couldn't see it? I know you tried to protect my feelings by trying to hide it from me, but don't you know, my darling wife, that I know everything about you?"

Running a fingertip down the center of her body, he traced a pattern on her belly. "Did you really think you could hide anything from me?"

His fingers slid lower, the slow decadent caress over her bare mound sending trails of sizzling heat to her nipples and slit. In contrast to the havoc he created inside her, Jake continued to speak in a deceptively casual tone.

"I've always known you would have married Hoyt. I've always understood that. I've always known that you love him."

Nat couldn't hold back a cry when Jake ran a firm finger over her clit, her entire body shaking with the need to come. "I love *you*! Oh, Jake!" Groaning in frustration when his fingers caressed her mound again, she dug her heels into the cushions, desperate for his touch.

Jake gripped her jaw, turning her face toward his. "I won't let you go. You're mine, Nat. You're mine, and you're staying that way."

"Yes!" Relieved that she'd gotten through to him, Nat lifted her hips, silently begging him to take her.

Covering her body with his, he toyed with her nipple, his gaze steady on hers. "When Hoyt told me he was coming here to see if there was a chance that the three of us could build a life together, I told him to go fuck himself. All of this passion belongs to me."

His eyes narrowed and sharpened. "He wants the three of us to be a family, Nat. His family. We're the only family he has. He says he can't start the rest of his life without knowing. Now, I find that I have to know, too. I have to let this play out, or it'll always be between us, won't it? I won't allow *anything* to stand between us. Anything. Ever."

Jake unfastened his jeans and shoved them to his knees, fisting his cock as he looked into her eyes. "God help me, Nat, but I have to know if you belong to me no matter what. I have to know if you'd choose him over me."

Covering her body again, he forced her thighs wide and thrust his cock deep inside her with a force that stole her breath.

Thrilled her.

His tortured gaze tugged at her heart, his hold fierce as if he wanted to absorb her. "I always knew you loved him, and that one day this might happen, but now that it is, I'm scared to death of losing you." He took her hard and fast, the desperation in his lovemaking igniting fires inside her that only he could extinguish.

Crying out in pleasure, and elated that the emotional and physical intimacy had been reestablished between them, Nat wrapped her legs tightly around him to hold him to her. "Never. You'll never lose me. I'm yours, Jake. I'll always be yours. No matter what."

Staring down into her eyes, he took her with a fierce possessiveness that forced her over with a ruthlessness that sent her senses reeling.

His lovemaking fulfilled the primitive need raging inside her—the need to be *taken*.

Shaking with pleasure, she rippled around him as wave after wave of incredible bliss washed over her.

Jake always seemed to know just what she needed.

He continued to thrust into her, watching her face, his own features harder than she'd ever seen them. "Yes. Come for me. You're mine, Nat. Forever. I'll never let you go."

With a harsh groan, he tightened his hand on hers and surged deep, his cock pulsing inside her. Throwing his head back, he groaned again, surging impossibly deeper.

Fascinated and humbled by Jake's response, Nat arched closer, desperate for him to believe her. "I'll never let you go, either. We belong to each other."

With another groan, Jake released her hands and wrapped his arms around her shoulders. Lifting her against him, he buried his face in her hair, his big body shaking. "You're everything to me. Christ, woman, I'd die if I lost you."

Trembling, Nat held on to the only solid thing in her world.

Tears burned her eyes, and at that moment, she had a renewed appreciation for the close bond she shared with her husband.

Threading her fingers into his silky hair, Nat squeezed her eyes closed against the tears that threatened, ripples of both pleasure and nerves warring inside her. "Tell him not to come here." Her voice had a catch in it, and she had to swallow before she could continue. "We're perfect the way we are."

Jake lifted his head and pushed the damp hair back from her face. His eyes, always so dark and mysterious, had an uncertainty and distance in them that told her how badly this had shaken him.

Nothing ever shook Jake.

He brushed his lips over hers, his smile distant. "Are we? Will everything still be perfect with this cloud of doubt hanging over us?"

Sliding her hands to his biceps, Nat gripped the hard muscle, afraid that she wouldn't get through to him. "Jake, I love *you*. We don't need this."

Shaking his head, Jake sighed. "I think I do. I know Hoyt does. He needs to know if there's a chance that he could become part of a family with the only woman he's ever loved—with a woman he's never been able to get over. You love him, Nat."

Trailing his fingers over her cheek, he stared into her eyes. "And you miss him."

Knowing that Jake would see through any lie, Nat sighed. "I miss him, but nothing's as important as us."

Cupping the back of her head, he lifted her face to his and brushed his lips over hers again. "There's nothing more important to me than making you happy. I see your eyes when he visits and whenever we talk about him. I've never been able to deny you anything, and I won't be responsible for keeping you from Hoyt."

Sliding his cock free, he released her, got to his feet, and refastened his jeans. "I can't—won't—stop this. I *need* to know how this will affect us. I don't want anything between us. No secrets, Nat. Ever. No regrets. No recriminations. I couldn't stand it if you resented me for standing in the way of your happiness."

"No!" Nat jumped to her feet and gripped his arm again. "I won't resent you! You're not standing in my way. I want *you*! You *are* my happiness." She fixed her bra, glaring up at him. "I sure as hell wouldn't share you with another woman."

Jake threw his head back and laughed, running a hand over her bare ass. "That's not an issue. God, I really do adore you."

Turning away, she went to retrieve her clothes, shaking at the thought of seeing Hoyt again. Grimacing at her ripped panties, she tossed them aside before sliding her jeans back on. "Just call him and tell him that we talked about it, and I'm not interested."

Nat kept her gaze lowered as she fastened her jeans, fearing what Jake would see in her eyes.

She loved Jake—more than she thought she could ever love a man. A mature love, one that grew stronger every day, and she wouldn't risk it for anything.

"Nat." Jake lifted her chin. "If you didn't have feelings for him, I would turn him away. But that's not the case. He needs to know how this would play out, and so do I." His eyes narrowed. "If you're honest with yourself, you do, too. Besides, Hoyt has a right to know his son."

Nat stilled, her heart pounding furiously at the subject that she and Jake almost never touched on. "Joe's *your* son. *Our* son."

Jake smiled faintly. "And Hoyt's. We all know that the reason you married me so fast was because you were carrying his child."

Nat gaped at him, struck by the hurt in his tone. "You knew I was pregnant! That's how you talked me into marrying you, damn it!"

"You're right, love." Jake sighed. "And I've never regretted it."

Gripping his hand, Nat shuddered. "Tell him not to come."

Shaking his head, Jake blew out a breath. "No, you're going to have to face him, or this will always hang between us."

Lifting her chin, Nat nodded. "Fine. I'll tell him. When's he supposed to be here?"

Jake smiled coldly. "Tonight."

"What?" Nat gasped, her heart racing—fear and excitement warring for supremacy.

Jake smiled faintly. "I didn't want to tell you until he was already on his way. I didn't want you to worry about this until you had to."

Gripping her shoulders, he held her gaze. "He needs answers, Nat, and so do I. Just be honest about your feelings, and everything will work out— one way or another. I'm going to go check on a delivery at the store."

He gave her a long look, touching a finger to her lips when she would have objected. "I know you need some time alone to absorb all of this. I'll be home in a couple of hours. If you need me before then, all you have to do is call."

Gripping his arm, she swallowed the lump in her throat. "I'll always need you."

Jake smiled, but his eyes remained flat. "I'm betting everything that that's true."

Chapter Two

With a heavy heart, Nat watched Jake pull out of the driveway, turning away from the window when his car disappeared from view.

Pacing the living room, she wrapped her arms around herself to fight off the chill, struggling to come to grips with all that had happened that morning.

Drawing a shaky breath, she glanced at the clock on the wall, finding it hard to believe that it had only taken an hour for her world to be turned upside down.

She lowered herself to the large, overstuffed chair, dropping her head in her hands. "Oh, Hoyt. Why do you have to come back? How the hell am I going to be able to look you in the face and tell you I don't want you in my life?"

Memories of his last visit came rushing back.

Memories she wanted to forget.

Memories she cherished.

It had been over three years since she'd seen him.

Hoyt liked to spend every holiday he could with Joe, and he'd been really looking forward to Christmas.

After years of visits, Hoyt and Jake had already reestablished their friendship, and although a slight amount of tension lingered, they'd become closer than they'd been in years.

Hoyt had worked hard to develop a close relationship with Joe, and over the years, the three of them had become even closer.

She envied their ease with each other, because during Hoyt's visits, she'd been a nervous wreck. As long as they were all together, she could hide it, but one night during Hoyt's last visit, she found herself alone with him for the first time in years.

Jake had gone to close his store for the night, and Joe had gone out to a holiday party with some friends.

She'd been washing the dinner dishes, acutely aware of Hoyt's gaze raking over her as he sat at the table sipping coffee.

"Are you alone at night often?"

Nervous already, she immediately became defensive. Whirling, she glared at him. "Of course not. Look, just because Jake has to go to the store at night—"

"Easy, Natalie." The snap of his voice cut her off more than his words, the ice in it unmistakable. "I'm not criticizing Jake. I'm just concerned about your protection."

Turning back to the sink, she went back to washing the plate, her shaking hands making it a struggle to hold on to it. "I'm fine. You have no right to be concerned."

"I have every fucking right to be concerned about you. You may not be my wife, but you're the mother of my child."

Shaking even harder at the edge in his voice, Nat lowered the plate, afraid she would drop it. "There's nothing for you to worry about. This is a safe town."

Before she even realized that he'd moved, she felt the heat from his body against her back.

"You're shaking. You have no reason to fear me. I'd die to protect you."

Fighting the hunger she had no right to feel, Nat picked up the plate again and attempted a laugh. "I'm not afraid of you."

"Liar."

To her relief, he moved away, going to the coffeepot to refill his cup before turning. Leaning back against the countertop, he sipped his coffee, staring at her for several long seconds, the tension in the room growing every moment. "Maybe I should teach you some self-defense."

Swallowing heavily against the thought of Hoyt touching her, she rinsed the plate and set it in the drying rack with hands that shook. "No, thanks. That won't be necessary."

Hoyt's slow smile held a hint of mischief that she hadn't seen since they'd been lovers. "Scared to have me touch you? Don't worry. I have no desire to poach on another man's territory." His eyes narrowed. "You're safe—for now."

Turning to him again, Nat gritted her teeth. "Forever. Look, you arrogant—"

"I see that temper's only gotten worse over the years." Hoyt clicked his tongue. "A sure sign that you're in need of some attention."

"Why, you—"

"Behave yourself, brat. Let's talk about what you can do to protect yourself."

Nat smiled. "I can throw this plate at your head."

To her surprise, Hoyt grinned and nodded. "Very good. There are weapons everywhere, Natalie. You just have to be smart enough to recognize them—*and* have the courage to use them."

She couldn't help but smile at that. "You think I won't do it?"

Hoyt's lips twitched. "No. You won't do it. You're too afraid of how I'd retaliate."

She wanted to smack the cocky grin from his face, but she knew he wouldn't let her get away with that either.

Hoyt took another sip of his coffee, his eyes filled with amusement. "Your mind is your best weapon. You've already realized that throwing that plate at me would only get you into even more trouble."

Turning back, Nat shrugged and concentrated on keeping her hands from shaking as she washed another plate. "Maybe I just don't feel like cleaning up the mess."

The heavy silence that followed stretched her nerves to the breaking point. Unable to stand it any longer, and trembling under his stare, she turned to him again.

Whatever she'd been about to say died on her lips, her mind going blank at his long, searching look.

His gaze sharpened, his expression thoughtful. "I'd wondered."

Clenching her jaw, Nat went back to washing dishes, hoping he couldn't see how badly she shook. "Wondered what?"

"If you'd gotten over me."

She had to swallow before speaking, her throat clogged with tears that she'd vowed never to shed. "I have."

"Liar."

Wiping her hands, Nat lifted her chin, fighting back tears. "You left."

Hoyt's tender smile melted something inside her. "But, I always come back, and you know damned well that I'm never more than a phone call away. Joe calls me. Jake calls me. But, you never do. Not once."

Swallowing a sob, Nat shook her head, holding out a hand as she backed away from him. "Don't. Don't do this to me. Jake and I are happy. I love him. Don't do this."

Hoyt's eyes hardened, glittering with fury. "I would never do anything to hurt any of you." Shaking his head, he set his cup aside. "Everyone has a weakness. You just have to find it. It seems you've found your weapon after all. I just needed to know. Tell Joe and Jake that I got called away."

Minutes later, he'd walked out the door, and she hadn't seen him since.

In the months—the years—since then, she'd wondered if she'd ever see him again.

He's on his way.

Too nervous to sit still, she shot to her feet, grabbed her keys and headed out the door.

She needed to talk to her sister.

* * * *

Nat looked down at where her watch should be, grimacing when she realized she'd left the house in such a hurry that she'd forgotten it.

Hoping that she wasn't too late to catch Jesse before she left for work, Nat knocked on the front door of the house her sister shared with her two husbands.

Two husbands.

Shaking her head, she thought about the advice she'd given Jesse in the past, and how easy she'd assumed it would be to be shared by two men.

Not many women ever got the chance to love and be loved by more than one, and the ones that she knew seemed deliriously happy.

The thought of dealing with both Hoyt and Jake made her a nervous wreck.

Maybe it would have been different if she'd started a relationship with both of them at the same time the way Jesse had.

Everything would be on equal ground and everyone would have known what to expect from each other. Trying to juggle her marriage with Jake, and reestablish a relationship with Hoyt was more than she could handle.

As soon as she saw Hoyt, she'd tell him, and put everything back to normal.

In the meantime, she had to calm down, and hoped that a visit with her sister would help her.

She looked up as the door swung open, unexpected tears blurring her vision at the sight of Clay filling the doorway. She tried to speak, but the lump in her throat prevented it, nearly choking her.

His welcoming smile fell, his eyes sharpening. "Hi, honey." He reached for her, wrapping a hand around her upper arm and gently pulling her inside. "You okay?" His tenderness nearly undid her.

Nodding briskly, Nat tried to smile, but the look of concern in Clay's eyes told her she hadn't quite pulled it off. "I'm fine. I need to talk to Jesse. Is she still here?"

Frowning, Clay nodded. "Of course. It's still early. We were just having a second cup of coffee."

Finding it hard to believe that it could be early when so much had already happened that day, Nat allowed Clay to pull her into the living room. Looking up at him, Nat narrowed her eyes at the knowledge glittering in his. "You know, don't you?"

Clay dropped a kiss on her hair, running a hand over it as he turned her and guided her toward the kitchen. "Jake needed someone he could trust to talk to, just like you do right now." Stopping her with a hand on her arm, he turned her to face him, smiling encouragingly. "Jake loves you very much, and he's been in hell, wondering how all of this will affect you, and your marriage."

Nat's stomach clenched. "Did he tell you everything?"

Clay grinned and turned her back toward the kitchen again, smiling at the sound of Jesse's giggle coming from that direction. "How would I know that, if I don't know what *everything* is? You're really rattled today, aren't you, honey? Talk to your sister. Rio and I will get out of your way."

Lifting her chin, he smiled, a smile full of encouragement. "I'm here for you. If you need me, just call. If you need a night alone with Jesse, we'll clear out."

Nat sniffed. "If I need you to beat the hell out of someone, will you do that, too?"

Clay smiled and kissed her hair. "Of course. Come on. Have some coffee and talk to your sister. You'll feel better."

As they walked through the doorway, Rio whispered something in Jesse's ear, something that made Jesse giggle again, a sound that Jesse made often since marrying Clay and Rio.

Jesse was happy, and it showed.

Being married to two men worked for Jesse, but watching her sister, Nat realized with a sinking heart that she could never be so relaxed with Jake and Hoyt.

It would never work.

Never.

Trying not to imagine herself in the position Jesse was in now, Nat paused, fisting her hands at her sides, wincing in pain when her keys dug into her palm.

Sitting on Rio's lap, Jesse giggled again, leaning into his wide chest as Rio smiled down at her and cuddled her close. Her hand looked small and delicate in Rio's much larger one as he lifted it to his lips and pressed a kiss against her palm, his eyes lit with delight and a desire that never seemed to fade. Jesse hadn't noticed Nat standing inside the doorway yet, her attention centered solely on Rio, the intimacy surrounding them making Nat feel like a voyeur.

Instead of making a sarcastic remark the way she usually did, such as telling them that they ought to get a room, Nat turned her head, curious to see how Clay reacted to Jesse and Rio's display of affection.

Clay watched his brother and wife with an indulgent smile, his eyes glittering with love and satisfaction, his relaxed demeanor evident as he leaned back against the counter and sipped his coffee.

"Don't you ever get jealous?"

Clay blinked in surprise as Rio and Jesse both looked up and whipped their heads around to look at her. "Sometimes. Not enough to risk losing her."

Retrieving a cup from the cupboard, he went to the coffeepot, glancing at Nat over his shoulder as he poured. He smiled faintly, the knowing look in his eyes telling her that he understood why she asked. "I'm sure Rio does, too. It's only natural. But, I know Jesse loves me just as much as she loves Rio. I get a lot of pleasure from seeing my wife and brother happy. So does Rio. You've seen it often enough in this town to know it can work."

Rio's welcoming smile fell as he studied her features, his eyes narrowing with concern. "Good morning, honey. Are you okay?"

Forcing a smile, Nat nodded. "I'm fine."

Frowning, Jesse slid from Rio's lap and went to Nat, looking from Clay to her sister and back again. "What's going on? Something's wrong. What is it?"

Clay straightened and set his cup aside. "Rio and I have some things to do. We won't be back for a couple of hours."

Nat watched as Clay and Rio both took the time to kiss Jesse's hair and run a hand down her back, both men meeting her questioning look with a faint smile.

Clay patted Jesse's ass. "Talk to your sister. Call my cell if you need something."

Dropping into one of the kitchen chairs, Nat ignored Jesse's searching look as she watched Clay and Rio leave, folding her hands in front of her, only to unclasp them and start drumming them on the table.

She just couldn't seem to calm down.

Hoyt was on his way.

Dear God.

Wondering what it would be like to have Hoyt love her the way Jake did, and what it would be like to live with both men—sleep between them every night, Nat stared unseeingly at the wall.

She could imagine Jake looking at her with lust and tender indulgence in his eyes as Hoyt's hands came around her from behind. She could almost feel Hoyt's hard heat at her back, the firm body she'd known, a body that had gotten even harder with muscle.

Jake running his fist up and down the length of his cock.

Hoyt tugging her nipples under Jake's dark, watchful gaze.

"Nat? You okay? You look flushed."

Wincing at the sound of her wedding ring tapping against the wooden table, Nat jolted when Jesse placed a cup of coffee in front of her. "I'm fine. Thanks." Wrapping her hands around the cup to hide the fact that they shook, Nat shifted restlessly in her seat, the strength of her arousal stunning her.

Jesse pulled a chair closer and dropped into it, frowning as she ran a hand down Nat's arm. "Okay, spill it. What happened? Did you and Jake finally talk? You look shaken."

Blowing out a breath, she braced her elbows on the table, closing her eyes and shoving her hands into her hair. "Yes. We talked. We sure as hell did. Jesus, Jesse. You're not going to believe this."

Lifting her head, she met her sister's gaze, forcing a smile, while inside the combination of excitement and fear made her stomach flutter. "*I* still don't believe it."

Gripping her arm, Jesse leaned forward. "What is it, damn it? Tell me!"

Nat nodded and patted Jesse's arm. "I will, but you're going to have to be patient with me." She blew out a breath, startled once again by the sting of tears. "For this to make any sense, I have to start at the beginning." Smiling, she shook her head. "Now I know how Jake felt when he told me." Sitting back, Jesse nodded and folded her arms across her chest, clearly impatient. "Okay. I'll be as patient as I can be, but I have to tell you, you're scaring the hell out of me, Nat."

Smiling, Nat patted Jesse's hand again before pulling her cup of coffee closer. "I felt the same way when Jake started to tell me, but I promise, there's nothing to be afraid of. We'll be okay." She took a deep breath and let it out slowly, hoping it would help settle her.

It didn't.

"Do you remember the guy I used to date in high school? Probably not. You were too young to notice, and I kept him away from the house because of Dad. I kept him from both of you. I didn't want you to get attached to him, and I didn't."

Jesse frowned, uncrossing her arms to lean forward. "I thought you dated Jake."

Overwhelmed at the rush of memories, Nat shook her head, not looking her sister in the eye. "No. Jake and I didn't date. Ever. I'm talking about someone I dated in high school and into college. Hoyt Campbell. He was a couple of years ahead of me. He's the same age as Jake. They were best friends. Very close. You rarely saw one without the other."

She'd always wondered if things would have been different if she'd met Jake first.

Staring down into her coffee, Nat sighed, struggling to focus on talking to her sister instead of fantasizing about what it would be like to have the kind of relationship her sister had. "Hoyt worked as a mechanic in his father's garage. He hated it."

Remembering how miserable Hoyt had been at that time, Nat grimaced. "He and his dad never got along, and it was just the two of them. His mom died in a car accident when he was seven." Glancing at Jesse, Nat forced a smile. "He'd lost his mom early, just like we did, and I think that's part of what connected us at first."

Shaking her head, she shrugged. "I don't know. We just sort of clicked." She blew out a breath. "Hell, that's an understatement."

When their eyes had met across the room, the powerful jolt to her system had nearly knocked her off her feet.

"He was always so serious."

So tall. So handsome. So incredibly masculine.

"God, I loved him."

Surprised that she'd blurted that, Nat got to her feet, looking away from her sister's sharpened gaze. "He was damned good looking, too."

Jesse turned in her chair. "I didn't know that. I don't think I remember him, but then you didn't exactly bring friends home, did you?"

Nat grimaced at the memory of her drunk father berating every friend she brought into the house, and insulting her in front of them. She'd protected Jesse as much as she could, but after their mother died, their father had crawled into a bottle and never crawled back out again. "No. I didn't. Hoyt met Dad once when he came to pick me up, but I made sure that he never saw him again."

Jesse smiled, but looked a little stunned. "You *loved* Hoyt?"

With a shrug, Nat smiled back. "Madly. Nothing existed for me except you and Hoyt."

As the knots in her stomach tightened, Nat took another deep breath, blowing it out in a rush. Dropping back into her seat, she smoothed her hands over the placemat in front of her. "He was my first lover."

Jesse gaped at her. "Holy shit. I thought Jake was." Sitting forward, Jesse stared at Nat wide-eyed. "So, how did you meet Jake? What happened between you and Hoyt? Why haven't you ever told me any of this before?"

"It wasn't something I wanted to talk about. It was too raw at first, and then Dad got worse, and you got married straight out of high school. It never seemed to be the right time. Now, it is." Nat forced a smile, struggling with the emotions that her conversation with Jake had brought to the surface, emotions that she'd thought she'd buried deeply enough to forget, but obviously hadn't. "I told you that Jake and Hoyt were best friends. It was rare to see one of them without the other. I met Jake through Hoyt and saw him a lot when Hoyt and I were dating."

Shaking her head, Nat smiled. "I loved Hoyt, and felt guilty because I found myself attracted to Jake. Jake always had this way of looking at me that made me feel like he saw more than I wanted him to see. He always had a way of talking to me that made me feel special, as though I had his undivided attention. He was always somehow intense and playful at the same time, and had a way of looking at me that aroused me. It embarrassed me, and I tried to hide it, but he saw. He knew. Jake's always known."

She couldn't help but remember how it felt to be sitting in the front seat of Hoyt's sports car, wedged between them.

She'd been too young and innocent to fully understand the riot of sensation that had consumed her then, or to even imagine it was possible to want and love two men.

Aware of Jesse's impatience, Nat took a sip of coffee to ease her dry throat. "We double-dated quite a bit, and I don't think Jake even dated the same woman twice. There was a spark between us. We both tried to ignore it, but it wouldn't go away."

Tracing a pattern in the placemat with a finger, she sighed, remembering how hard it had been to hide her feelings for Jake from Hoyt. "I never would have done anything about it. I loved Hoyt so much, and couldn't understand why I was falling in love with Jake. I felt guilty as hell. How the hell could I feel that way about two men at the same time?"

Jesse's brow went up, her eyes glimmering with amusement. "Hmm. Hard to believe that kind of thing could happen." Her eyes narrowed, filled with sympathy. "I never could have imagined something like that before meeting Clay and Rio either, and I can only imagine what it would be like feeling something like that when you were so young." Shifting in her seat, she pushed her cup aside. "Keep going. What happened, and what does this have to do with the talk you had with Jake?"

Wrapping her shaking hands around her own cup, Nat sighed. "It was a crazy time. You were getting ready to graduate from high school, and I was trying to deal with Dad so he didn't ruin it for you. Hoyt hated working for his father. Those two never got along, and Hoyt was miserable. He wasn't just miserable with his job—that would have been easy enough to fix—but Hoyt wanted more. He wanted to get out. Travel. He was restless. Edgy. One day he talked to a recruiter who'd come to the campus, and all of a sudden, he started talking about joining the Navy."

Unable to sit still any longer, Nat rose and went to the window, taking a sip of her coffee as she watched Clay and Rio work with the horses. Memories flashed through her mind—the heat, the love, the anger and hurt. The tangle of emotions had been so difficult to sort through, and it had been such a confusing time that parts of it seemed like a blur now.

But her love for both of them remained crystal clear.

Aware of Jesse's rapt attention, and grateful for her sister's patience, Nat sighed again and blinked back tears. "All of a sudden, the Navy was all Hoyt could talk about. He became obsessed with it. Before I knew it, he'd signed up. Everything changed. We were in love, but wanted different things. God, it hurt." She set her cup aside, her hands shaking so hard, she was afraid of spilling it.

Blinking back tears, she went to the table again, her legs too wobbly to support her. "It hurt so much for both of us. Hoyt was going through hell with his father. He joined the Navy and was so excited about it." Nat wiped away a tear, the memory of what came next making her stomach clench.

Rubbing her arms against the chill that went through her, she forced a smile. "Poor Jake. He was my rock. Hell, he was Hoyt's rock, too. I don't know what either one of us would have done without him." Nat met Jesse's gaze. "Especially when I found out I was pregnant."

Jesse's jaw dropped. "What? Wait! Are you telling me that Joe is *Hoyt's* son?"

Nat couldn't help but smile at the look of astonishment on her sister's face. "Yes. He is. Looks so much like him, especially when he's being a smart-ass."

"Wow." Jesse shook her head before turning back to Nat, her eyes wide. "Oh, my God! Does Jake know? Does Hoyt? Does Joe?"

Nat nodded immediately. "Of course. All three of them know. I've always been up front about things. You know that."

Jesse blinked. "You never told *me*!"

Nat sighed and rubbed her forehead where a headache had started to form, looking up when Jesse went to the counter, dumped her now-cold coffee into the sink and poured her a new one. "I know. I didn't tell you at the time because I knew you'd be upset that I carried the baby of one man and married the other, and also because I felt an obligation to Jake."

Waving her hand, she cut off whatever Jesse was about to say and reached for the fresh coffee. "Let me finish."

Wrapping her hands around the cup, Nat took another sip and stared into the dark brew Clay and Rio drank by the gallon. "Jake was the first to know. Hoyt was excited about enlisting and already making plans for us, and I was scared. I just didn't know what the hell to do."

Wiping her eyes with her napkin, she laughed humorlessly. "I know that doesn't sound like me, but I was young, scared, and pregnant. I didn't want to leave. I *couldn't* leave town. You needed me, and I was scared to leave all I knew while I was carrying a baby. It was a mess. I needed someone to talk to, someone who could understand. So, I went to Jake."

Jesse got up and came back to the table with a box of tissues. "Oh, Nat. I wish you'd told me."

Smiling, Nat patted her hand and reached for a tissue. "You had enough on your plate, and I wanted you to finish school without worrying about me." She waved a hand dismissively, needing to finish. "Anyway, I confided in Jake. I didn't know what else to do. Hoyt had already enlisted, and couldn't change his mind. It was done. I was naïve and terrified and couldn't imagine leaving everything I knew with a baby on the way. I couldn't leave you with Dad. I couldn't leave and Hoyt couldn't stay."

Jesse's eyes went wide. "Oh, Nat. I can only imagine what you went through. Dad and I didn't know any of this."

Nat snorted, wiping her eyes. "Dad didn't know anything when he started drinking. If he'd known, he would have only made it worse."

Reaching out, Jesse touched Nat's hand, her eyes dark with concern. "What did Hoyt say when you told him?"

Pressing a hand to her stomach, Nat blinked back tears. "He went crazy."

Her stomach rolled when she thought about Hoyt's fear—the first and only time she'd seen him scared about anything. "He was so happy at first, but I could see that he was also afraid. He wanted me to marry me then and there. He wanted me to go away with him. I couldn't. I wanted to so much, but I knew that I couldn't leave then, especially because I suspected that the only reason he'd asked me to marry him was because I was pregnant. I was so scared. So young. I was too scared to go with him, and the thought of leaving me alone and pregnant tormented him. He was devastated."

Jesse reached out to grip her hand. "Oh, Nat. That must have been awful for both of you. I wish I had known. I feel so selfish for not being there for you. I can't believe that I was so wrapped up in myself that I didn't even notice what you were going through."

Shaking her head, Nat got to her feet, kissing her sister's hair on the way to the coffeepot. "You never had a selfish bone in your body. You didn't know because I didn't want you to know, and you were very supportive when you *did* find out about the baby."

Shaking her head, Jesse sat back again. "I can't believe that I didn't suspect anything. I thought all along that Jake was Joe's father. Why didn't you tell me later?"

Nat shrugged. "There was no point. You met Brian and got married, and after Joe was born, Jake wanted to move to Desire. I felt I owed both Jake and Hoyt to keep our secret, at least then. Telling the truth would have just made life more uncomfortable for everyone."

Jesse frowned. "So, you told Hoyt you were pregnant. What happened then?"

"Jake stepped in." Wiping her eyes, Nat squeezed Jesse's hand before pulling hers away, the knots in her stomach so tight, she thought she was going to be sick. "Jake told Hoyt that he loved me. Hoyt punched Jake in the face, and asked me if the child was his. He went crazy. He and Jake fought. God, it was awful."

"Oh, Nat!" Jesse rose from her chair and came toward her, but Nat waved her away. "No. Let me finish." She was afraid that if she really starting crying, she'd never stop.

Nat moved to the counter and leaned back against it, swallowing the lump in her throat, and couldn't seem to stop shaking. "Between us, we finally got Hoyt calmed down. We stayed up all night, just the three of us, just talking. Hoyt was torn. Heartbroken. But, he had to leave. He'd already signed up, and there was no turning back. *I* was torn. Heartbroken. I couldn't imagine leaving, especially with a baby on the way, and Hoyt knew I was worried about you. He was worried about *me*."

Shrugging, she met Jesse's gaze. "We both understood each other's position. We both blamed each other. We both felt guilty for what we were doing to each other."

Taking a shuddering breath, she set her cup aside. "Jake told Hoyt that he wanted to marry me." She shook her head, Nat's pulse tripped as she remembered. "I'll never forget the way Jake looked at me that night—as if all the need for pretense had been ripped away."

Meeting Jesse's look, Nat smiled and shook her head again. "Shocked the hell out of me." With a shrug, she leaned back against the counter. "He told Hoyt that he would take care of us and encouraged him to visit us anytime he could. I fell asleep while they were still talking, so I don't know everything that they talked about that night, but in the morning, everything was settled. Jake and I would get married."

Blowing out a breath, Nat turned to stare out the window again, almost buckling under the memories. "Hoyt had always been so serious, but after that, he was even worse. He made me promise to put his name on the birth certificate, and promise to send him pictures and update him all the time. He was so happy when Joe was born and constantly begged me for information about him. Anything. Everything. Jake sent him pictures all the time, and we both wrote to him."

Staring at the opposite wall, Nat thought back to that time. "Jake was wonderful. We got married and then Hoyt left. Jake took care of me all through my pregnancy. He fussed and coddled me and basically spoiled me. He wouldn't let me worry about anything. I fell madly in love with him. We've been so happy all these years. He's been everything to me. Jake's always been my rock."

"I know." Jesse came forward to hug her. "He's madly in love with you, too. Anyone can see that. You two were made for each other." Leaning back, Jesse frowned again. "You said Joe knows that Hoyt's his father?"

Nat turned back to look out the window. "Of course. We told him as soon as he was old enough to understand—on one of Hoyt's visits."

"How did he take it?"

Nat shrugged, remembering how Jake and Hoyt had been with her son. "He was a little upset at the time, but Hoyt had established a relationship with him right from the beginning. Jake and Hoyt spent the entire day with him. They came home laughing and joking." Her love for all three of them made Nat smile. "Joe considers both of them his fathers. Hoyt and Joe have remained very close over the years. I don't know how they did it, but they worked everything out, and somehow became closer than ever."

Leaning on the counter next to her, Jesse stared out the window, smiling as Clay and Rio came into view again. "I'm so glad that Joe's close to both of them." Turning, she frowned at Nat. "But I've never met Hoyt, have I? I haven't seen him or even heard about him since I moved here."

Nat sighed. "And now we get to the heart of the problem."

A mental image of the way Hoyt had looked the last time Nat saw him brought a lump to her throat. "Hoyt used to visit all the time, and for every holiday he could, but he hasn't been here for three years now. He talks to Jake and Joe over the phone and through e-mails, but he hasn't contacted me. At all. Now, I know why."

Jesse straightened, wrapping an arm around Nat and leading her back to the table. "You're pale. Have you eaten anything?"

Lowering herself into her seat again, Nat waved a hand dismissively. "I had some toast before Jake and I had our talk. Right now, just the thought of eating makes me feel sick." Nat smiled reassuringly at her sister, recognizing Jesse's attempt to calm her. "I'm fine, Jesse. Stop fussing. I know you're dying to hear the rest. Just let me get through this."

Lowering herself into her own seat, Jesse reached for her cup again. "I assume this is where Jake dropped his bombshell."

Nat reached for her own cup, and just as quickly set it back down again. "You assume right. Son of a bitch, Jesse. I wasn't expecting this." She started tearing her napkin into little pieces. "When Hoyt stopped visiting, I ignored it. I missed him, but I didn't want to upset Jake or make him suspicious by asking about him. I've never gotten over Hoyt. He's a hard man to get over, but I sure as hell didn't want to hurt Jake."

Blowing out a breath, she tore another strip of napkin. "It turns out that Hoyt stopped coming because of me. Jake said that Hoyt still loves me, and it got too difficult to keep coming around."

Jesse stilled, her eyes going wide. "What? Wait a minute. Hoyt's still in love with you? Holy hell! Is that what's been bothering Jake? Is he mad? Did he have a fight with Hoyt? Why the hell is he taking it out on you? Is he jealous? What's he going to do?"

Despite her anxiety, Nat couldn't hold back a laugh. "Wait. I'm not finished. You've been so patient—a hell of a lot more patient than I was when Jake talked to me. Just bear with me. I'm all scrambled up inside and I'm trying to tell this in a way it makes sense."

Leaning back in her chair, Nat stretched her hands toward the ceiling in an effort to work out some of the kinks in her back, but it did nothing to settle her nerves. "Oh, Jesse." Blowing out a breath, she got to her feet again, too restless to sit still. "Jake's been talking to Hoyt for months, and I didn't know about it. Evidently, they've been having some intense conversations. Hoyt's retiring and he's coming here."

Meeting Jesse's stunned gaze, Nat smiled, her stomach fluttering with nerves and excitement. "He told Jake that he hadn't gotten over me, and he wants the chance to spend time with his son. He says that he can't go on with his life without knowing if we can all be a family."

Jesse shot to her feet. "Oh, my God! I can't believe it. What does Jake think about all this?"

Thoughts of Jake's mood that morning made Nat's pulse trip. "Jake understands Hoyt and his motives. He misses him. He's also afraid that not knowing if things could have worked out for the three of us will always stand between us. He doesn't want to be blamed for keeping Hoyt away when we live in a town where the three of us can be together."

Running her hands through her hair, she groaned and stretched again. "What a mess. Jake's scared of losing me. He knows that I would have married Hoyt if he hadn't joined the Navy."

Remembering the anguish in Jake's eyes, Nat faced Jesse again. "Jake refused at first. I can only imagine *that* conversation. But, Hoyt assured him that he had no intention of coming between us. He also asked Jake why the hell we moved to a town where ménage relationships are accepted if he hadn't been expecting it."

Jesse's brows went up. "Good question. What did Jake say to that?"

Blowing out another breath, Nat started ripping another napkin. "Jake admitted to me that he'd done it because he knew Hoyt would be back one day, and that if we lived in Desire, they could share me and Jake wouldn't lose me." Nat grinned, her pulse racing again at Jake's other admission. "Jake also told me that the thought of sharing me with another man excited him."

Her smile fell, her stomach knotting. "At first. That was a long time ago. After all these years of having me to himself, the thought of sharing me with another man is hard for him."

Jesse frowned. "So why didn't he just tell Hoyt to stay away?"

Nat jumped up again, "Because my husband's too damned observant and too fucking noble for his own good. He said that he could see that I still love Hoyt." She rubbed a hand over her stomach. "That's on me. I tried not to love him, and I certainly never would have done anything about it. I tried to hide it, but obviously I wasn't successful. Jake saw it, and wants me to be happy. He's seen enough relationships like yours to know it can work, but I still can't believe he'd be willing to go through this to make me happy."

Laughing and crying at the same time, Nat went to the refrigerator and helped herself to some of her sister's always present apple juice. "I love that man."

Jesse grinned. "It sure as hell can work. I never could have imagined how well it would work." Touching Nat's arm, she frowned again, her eyes filled with concern. "It works for me, but what about you? You haven't said how you feel about all of this."

"Scared spitless. Embarrassed. Ashamed."

After pouring herself and Jesse each a glass of juice, she went back to the table. "It might have been different if the three of us had been together from the very beginning like you, Clay, and Rio, but Jake and I have too much history together. We know each other well. We know each other's moods."

Despite her heavy heart, Nat forced a smile, not wanting her sister to worry. "But, we'll never know if it would work for us."

She'd made her decision.

She couldn't have made any other choice.

Determined to make this up to Jake, she pushed aside the yearning for something more. "Having both of them in my life wouldn't work, and even if I thought it would, I don't want to take the chance of hurting Jake. He's been there for me for all these years, and there's no way I'd ever do anything to hurt him. I told him that Hoyt could never come between us, but I don't know if he believes that." Shaking her head, she reached for her glass. "I won't do anything to jeopardize what I have with Jake."

Jesse bit her bottom lip, clearly unconvinced. "So what are you going to do?"

Restless again, Nat jumped to her feet and poured herself another cup of coffee she didn't want, just for something to do. "I'm going to have to talk to Hoyt. I'm going to be honest with him and tell him that I don't want to hurt Jake. He'll go away, and that'll be the end of it."

She could only hope.

Jesse's brows went up. "I've never met this man, but Hoyt doesn't sound like the kind of man to walk away. If he's loved you all these years the way you love him, I think it's obvious that it's not just going to go away—and neither will he."

Nat kept her back to her sister, not wanting Jesse to see the tears stinging her eyes. "Why not? He did it before."

Hoyt wasn't the type to settle down. He lived for excitement, and the kind of adventure that he would never be able to find in Desire.

Jolting at the slide of Jesse's hand on her back, Nat carefully schooled her features. "It'll be fine. I'll talk to him and take care of it. Then, everything'll be back to normal." She gulped apple juice to ease her dry throat.

Frowning, Jesse refilled her glass, eyeing her skeptically. "Nat, you might fool him with that, but you're not fooling me. If you've loved this man all these years, especially after not seeing him for months, even years at a time, it's not going to go away just because you want it to."

Nat gritted her teeth. "It doesn't matter. I won't hurt Jake."

Gripping her arm, Jesse turned Nat to face her, smiling faintly. "Do you really think you're going to be able to fool Jake into believing that you don't want Hoyt around? He's already proved that he knows you too well. You're never going to be able to lie to him."

Grimacing, Nat took another sip of juice. "I have to. Jake's always done everything he can to make me happy. I'm not going to be selfish about this. Jake deserves to know that I'd do anything for him. I don't need Hoyt. I need Jake."

Shaking her head, Jesse clicked her tongue. "I might not know Hoyt, but I know Jake well enough to know that he's never going to let you get away with it. You all have to know if this can work. None of you will be happy until you know for sure."

Grinning, Jesse hugged her. "I've always wondered what it would be like to see you rattled. Having two men in your life ought to do it."

Leaning back, she smiled, her eyes shimmering with tears. "Oh, Nat. I just want you to be happy."

"I will be, honey." Swallowing the lump in her throat, Nat turned away. "I just need to face Hoyt again. Once he leaves, everything will work out just fine."

She'd never see him again.

Somehow, she had to learn to live with that.

Chapter Three

Hoyt hadn't been so nervous since his first day of basic training.

He could fight his way out of any situation, disarm a man with his bare hands, had the patience to remain motionless for hours as he waited for an enemy to show himself, and lead a mission into the most hostile situation with cold, calculated precision.

His men claimed he had nerves of steel and ice in his veins.

His hands shook, though, and he'd broken out in a cold sweat at the thought of facing Natalie again.

Looking at Jake, he made a conscious effort to sit still, but knew he didn't fool Jake for a minute. "So what did Natalie say when you told her that I wanted to be a part of her life again?"

Jake's hard expression softened slightly, his eyes lit with amusement as he ran his thumb up and down the neck of his beer bottle. "She told me to tell you that she's not interested. She doesn't want to do anything to hurt me."

Hoyt hadn't expected anything less.

Natalie had always been fiercely protective of the ones she loved—and would sacrifice her own happiness for theirs.

He hoped like hell he could convince her to give him a chance.

His entire future was at stake.

Careful to keep his expression cool despite the war raging inside him, Hoyt raised a brow. "And you? Have you changed your mind?"

He'd made it clear to Jake that he had no intention of trying to come between him and Natalie, but he couldn't go on with his life without knowing if it was possible to have his son, his best friend, and the only woman he'd ever loved in it.

Jake's lips twitched. "That wouldn't do any of us any good, now would it? I can't go through life wondering about her any more than you can. I've always known that she would have married you if you hadn't gone in the Navy." Jake shrugged, the tension surrounding him tangible. "She loves you. I don't want her staying with me if she'd rather be with you. She knows that I'm fully aware that a ménage relationship can work, and I'm not going to be the one to blame if it doesn't."

Amused despite the tension, Hoyt couldn't hold back a smile, shaking his head. "And you think I'm going to be the one to do something to mess it up?"

Jake's confident smile, full of challenge, reminded Hoyt of the competitive friendship they'd shared long ago, but this time, neither one of them could afford to lose. "I know it's not going to be me. I'm not going to lose Nat by making a stupid mistake."

Hoyt raised a brow, knowing that they'd have to stick together to make this work. "And you think I will?"

Jake's lips curved. "I'm sure both of us are going to end up fucking this up. We're going to have to trust each other more than we ever have before. We're going to need each other's help to handle her and guide her through this. We can't go against each other, or let jealousy get in the way." His eyes hardened, the warning in them unmistakable. "Her happiness is my priority, and I'll do my best to make sure this works out for the three of us, but if you try to undermine me, I'll hang you out to dry."

Hoyt allowed a smile. "Understood. I know how hard this is for you. I'll never be able to repay you for letting me have this chance." Shaking his head, he sucked in a breath and blew it out in an effort to rid himself of some of his anxiety. "I love her. I've never stopped loving her. God knows I've tried."

Too restless to sit still any longer, Hoyt got to his feet and moved to the kitchen window, looking out into the backyard. Fisting his hands on the counter on either side of the sink, he bent his head, his stomach churning. "I have to know, Jake. I'd never do anything to come between the two of you, but I've learned a lot about ménage relationships on my visits here. It's been in the back of my mind for years, ever since the first time I came to visit right after you moved here. I'll never be able to live with myself if I don't take the chance that we can all be a family. I have a lot to make up for. To you. To her. To our son."

Jake slammed his bottle on the table, startling Hoyt into whirling to face him. "You don't owe me a damned thing!" With a sigh, Jake picked up his bottle again. "I got what I wanted. I've been happier than I ever thought I could be. Nat and I have built something wonderful together, and I got a chance to be a father. I owe you for trusting me to take care of both of them."

Hoyt knew that Jake's sterility had always been a sore subject for him. Straightening, he smiled and shook his head. "I owe you more than I could ever repay. Because of you, I know my son and I've always had contact with Natalie. I've always known that she and Joe were well taken care of. That's been a hell of a relief to me over the years. I'd never do anything to betray you. I've been up front about everything, and I have no intention of changing. I want everything out in the open."

He'd never been comfortable talking about his feelings, but knew that Jake deserved the truth. "I love her so damned much. I can't even think of starting a life anywhere else. Everyone I care about is here."

Jake took another sip of his beer. "You and I used to be really close, but I have to tell you, I'd throw you out on your ass if she didn't love you."

Hoyt's heart stopped, and then began to pound furiously, a smile spreading over his face, one he didn't even bother to hide. "She does. Thank God."

Dizzy with relief, he moved back to the table and dropped back into his seat across from Jake, wondering what his men would think if they saw him nearly taken to his knees at the knowledge that Natalie loved him. "Thanks for telling me. I'm sure that wasn't easy for you."

Jake shrugged again, his lips twitching as he continued to run his thumb up and down the neck of his beer bottle. "When Nat loves, she loves hard." A small smile played at his lips. "She still won't risk what we have, though. She's determined to get rid of you."

Hoyt took another sip of his beer to ease his dry throat, eyeing Jake. "The three of you are my family—the only family I have. I wouldn't do anything to hurt any of you."

He'd die—or kill—to protect any one of them.

To his relief, Jake chuckled. "If I thought any differently, you wouldn't be here. Like I already told you, I can't say that I never expected this. Nat doesn't love lightly, and I could see that she wasn't getting over you, but you've got an uphill battle ahead of you."

Hoyt shrugged. "I've never been afraid of battle, especially since I have no intention of losing this one. I'm not giving up, and if it takes the rest of my life, I'll have her again."

Jake smile wasn't quite steady. "I know."

Hoyt smiled back, grateful that some of the tension between them eased. "Which is why you moved here when Joe was a baby? I have to admit that when I first came to visit and checked out the town, I was surprised at the things I discovered. I never brought it up to you, but I had the feeling that you moved here because you knew that one day I'd want to be a part of their lives."

He met Jake's steady stare. "Thank you for that. It gave me a lot of hope and kept me going for years. I have to salute you for finding such a town. I wouldn't want Natalie to be the subject of ridicule because of me. I couldn't live with that."

Jake's eyes narrowed. "She'll likely be the topic of conversation now. Everyone in town knows her, and we all watch out for the women here."

"That's one of the things I like about this town." Leaning forward, he met Jake's gaze squarely. "I've also learned how the men stick together to keep them safe. That was a great relief to me."

"You don't think I can keep her safe?"

"I never said that."

Something flickered in Jake's eyes that had Hoyt stiffening again. "Problem? This isn't going to work if you and I aren't on the same page."

Scrubbing a hand over his face, Jake surprised Hoyt by cursing and jumping to his feet. "I know that, damn it!" Jake blew out a breath, his struggle to get himself back under control obvious. Finally, he turned. "I have to know if she still wants me with you in the picture, but I have to tell you, I'm not handling this as well as I'd hoped to. The thought of losing Nat scares the hell out of me."

Hoyt shook his head. "That won't happen. Neither one of us will let that happen. I know damned well that Nat loves you. She'd never forgive me if I came between you."

Jake shrugged and stared out the window. "And she loves you. What if she decides she loves you more, and she and I are no longer as close as we are now? You know the lifestyle we lead. She's been my submissive for years. Do you know how long it took me to establish the kind of trust that requires?"

Hoyt jumped up, slamming his hand on the table in frustration. "I'm not trying to take anything from you, and I'm sure as hell not here to cause trouble. Damn it, give me some fucking credit."

Fury and nausea at all he'd missed rose up inside him. "Do you think it was easy for me to walk away from the woman I love and my unborn child?"

Dropping back into his seat again, he fisted his hands on the table and struggled for control. "I wanted her with me. I *begged* her to marry me and come with me, but I understood how scared she was. I handled her badly. I handled the whole situation badly."

Memories of that time tied his stomach up in knots. "She was so young then—so scared to leave everything she knew, especially since she'd just learned she was pregnant. I knew she was scared to leave her sister, especially with her father drunk more often than not."

He looked down at his hands, knowing that only sheer will kept them from shaking. "I pleaded with her, but she thought I only wanted to marry her because she was pregnant. She wasn't about to leave Jesse and hook herself to me when she didn't believe I really wanted a future with her."

The knots in his stomach tightened. "No matter what I said, I couldn't convince her." Shrugging, he picked up his beer. "It's true that I hadn't planned to marry her that soon. I wanted to get some money together first so that I could support her. That's why I joined the Navy to begin with. I could never have given her the life she deserved on what I made working in my father's garage. It was my only chance to get out and make something of myself. I wanted to be good enough for her."

Hoyt stilled, tensing as the back of his neck tingled.

Natalie.

He felt her presence just a second or two before the intoxicating scent of cinnamon and vanilla wafted to him.

Before he heard her—before he saw her—he was already hard.

"So why didn't you come home when your time was up? Why the hell did you reenlist?" The challenge in her sarcastic tone made him even harder.

Bracing himself, he rose to his feet and turned, facing the woman he couldn't stop loving.

The woman he couldn't stop aching for.

Everything inside him wanted to run to her, take her in his arms and lose himself in the feel of her.

Instead, he forced himself to remain where he was, and drank in the sight of her.

She wore her shiny, thick brown hair shorter than the last time he saw her, but it still hung several inches past her shoulders. She used to wear it much longer, so long that used to brush the upper curve of her ass and draw his attention there, sparking all sorts of erotic fantasies.

Those fantasies had grown and matured over the years, and he'd spent many hours imagining fulfilling each and every one of them.

Her eyes, several shades darker than her hair, had always looked too big for her face.

Narrowed now, they glittered with emotion—and tears.

There was nothing like a strong woman with tears in her eyes to bring a man to his knees.

Forcing himself to meet her gaze squarely, he carefully hid how much he wanted to run to her and wipe away her tears—to hold her and promise her that everything would be all right.

Knowing that words would be useless until he could back it up with action, and that any sign of weakness would only jeopardize his plans for her, he lifted a brow and gave her his most arrogant look. Bracing his hands on his hips, he let his gaze rake over her, inviting her anger, knowing that they wouldn't be able to move forward until they'd cleared the air.

Her curves, more womanly than they'd been when he'd held her last, made his palms itch with the need to explore them.

Knowing that her lips, now thinned in anger, would be incredibly soft against his, he let his gaze linger on them, hiding a smile when she frowned and shifted restlessly.

He couldn't wait to taste them again, and taste the passion that would have matured into something even more magnificent over the years.

Just the thought of it inflamed him.

She got to him as no woman ever had, and he wanted her with a fierceness that didn't allow for failure.

The years since he'd held her last hadn't diminished his need for her. They'd only made it stronger.

Fisting his hands on his hips to keep from reaching for her, Hoyt smiled and inclined his head. "Hello, Natalie. You look as beautiful as ever."

Natalie glanced at Jake before looking at him again, lifting her chin, her eyes shooting sparks. "You didn't answer me."

Hoyt sighed, knowing the woman he loved never beat around the bush about anything. "What was I supposed to do, Natalie? Come back here? You and Jake were happy, and it would just have confused Joe. I couldn't do that to any of you."

He stepped closer, hiding a smile when she took a hurried step back. Pleased to see that she wasn't as unaffected as she pretended to be, he took another step closer, the determination in her eyes to remain still delighting him.

He had a long way to go and each small victory would take him closer and closer to his goal. "You love Jake and were happy with him. Jake loves you and he loves Joe. If I thought otherwise, I would have taken you and Joe with me and never looked back."

He smiled coldly. "Kidnapped you if necessary, and I wouldn't have given a damn about any of your objections."

Natalie gaped at him, but he didn't make the mistake of letting her recover. He had to stay on the offense, knowing that in dealing with a woman like Natalie, he would need every advantage he could get.

He took another step toward her, the beast inside him roaring with satisfaction when she took another step back. Crowding her, he leaned closer. "I was suddenly the outsider. I reenlisted because I didn't have anywhere else to go. I checked to make sure you and Joe were okay. I made sure Joe knew me. I made damned sure he knew that I was his father, and that I love him. He knew that he could count on me, and I've stayed in touch with him. I've kept tabs on both of you."

Natalie glanced at Jake again, the connection between them more pronounced than ever. "Of course we were happy."

Crossing his arms over his chest, Hoyt allowed a small smile. "So I did what I thought was best for everyone."

She lifted her chin, a warning and a sign that she felt vulnerable. "And now?"

He'd expected the question—a question he'd asked himself a hundred times. Smiling faintly, he answered honestly.

"Now, I'm here, and I plan to stay here. I want my family."

* * * *

Nat slid a glance at Jake, her heart pounding so hard that she wondered if both men could hear it.

The reassurance and love shining in her husband's eyes comforted her, and gave her the confidence she needed to deal with Hoyt.

Bracing herself for the impact, she turned to face Hoyt fully, schooling her features to hide the rush of hunger, love, and excitement. Smiling sarcastically, she crossed her arms over her chest. "*Your* family?"

Hoyt had always been an intimidating man, but years of training and deadly missions had turned him into six feet four inches of barely leashed power.

Raw, intimidating power that both alarmed and excited her.

His shrug drew her attention back to his wide shoulders, every shift of muscle a sharp reminder that she no longer dealt with a young man, but a mature and overwhelmingly masculine one.

His eyes, sharp and narrowed, held hers, a possessiveness in them that made her heart beat faster. "My son, my best friend, and the woman I love. *My family*. Does that spell it out clearly enough for you?"

Forcing a smile to hide the turmoil raging inside her, she stepped farther into the room, giving him a wide berth as she made her way to the table. "You always were blunt."

Shifting his stance, he leaned back against the counter, his eyes—so much like Joe's—steady and searching. "I've always been honest with all of you. I see no reason to stop now." Scowling, he studied her features. "You used to be blunt, too. Now it appears you want to skirt around the issue. Scared?"

Glaring at him, she dropped into her chair. "Kiss my ass."

Jake moved to the sink, filled a glass of water and set it in front of her, his sharp gaze missing nothing. Caressing her shoulder, he dropped a kiss on her hair before moving away again to pour himself another cup of coffee.

"Honesty between us will be more important now than ever. You know that."

Frowning, Nat gestured toward her glass. "I wanted coffee."

Jake turned to look at her over his shoulder as he refilled Hoyt's cup. "No. You were with Jesse, which means that the two of you sat at the table drinking coffee for hours."

Indignant, she pushed the glass of water away. "I didn't drink coffee the whole time. I had apple juice."

Turning to face her fully, Jake leaned back against the counter and raised a brow. "Why? Your stomach start to get upset from all the coffee?"

Nat glared at him, furious that her face burned. "Shut up."

He knew her far too well.

A pregnant silence followed, her anger dissolving under their steady stares.

With a sigh, she looked from the man who'd been her rock for years, and who knew her better than anyone else to the man she'd never been able to get out of her system. Suddenly, the thought of kicking him out made her sick to her stomach.

If she tried to kick Hoyt out, Jake would always wonder about her feelings for Hoyt, and would consider himself second best.

She couldn't do that to him, but she sure as hell didn't plan to fall all over Hoyt. "I hate being put in this position. I don't know what either one of you expect me to do."

Hoyt's smile appeared strained, his gaze steady on hers. "I expect you to take this seriously. I expect you to give this a chance before you reject it out of hand."

Allowing a small smile, she propped her head on her hand. "You expect a lot."

Hoyt inclined his head. "Perhaps." He took the seat next to her and reached out to grip her chin, turning her face to his. "Is it really going to be so hard for you to accept having me in your life?"

Jake straightened and set his cup aside, glancing at Hoyt. "I'm going to the club for a little while. I think the two of you need a chance to talk alone."

"No!" Nat jumped to her feet in a panic, instantly regretting it when she saw the look of shock on Jake's face, and the glint of anger on Hoyt's.

The tension in the room could be cut with a knife, making Nat feel even more foolish for overreacting.

Jake's small smile of encouragement provided the calming influence she needed. "Nat, you're stronger than this. You're just panicking because you think you're going to hurt me. You need to settle down. I have no intention of letting you go without a fight. If I can't trust you alone with him, this is going to be a real problem."

Hoyt's jaw clenched, his eyes flashing with impatience. "I have no idea what the hell she thinks I'm going to do when we're alone." A muscle worked in his jaw as he searched her features again. "I have no desire to take you away from Jake. You'd never be happy without him in your life, and you'd blame me forever for losing him."

Jake reached out to take her hand in his, sending a familiar and always exciting electricity up her arm. "You and Hoyt need to talk. Alone."

His eyes held hers, a seriousness in them that instantly got her attention. "You and I both know why Hoyt's doing this. In his shoes, I'd do the same damned thing. If this doesn't work out, it doesn't work out, Nat, but all three of us need to know. We can't have *what could have been* haunting us the rest of our lives. Hoyt can't live with that. *I* can't live with that. Can you?"

Tightening her fingers on his, Nat lifted her chin and swallowed the lump in her throat. "I love you. I don't want you to get hurt, and I won't lose you."

Turning her head, she met Hoyt's hooded gaze straight on. "I won't let that happen."

Hoyt inclined his head, silently acknowledging the warning.

Jake tugged her hand, shifting her attention back to him. "Then face this squarely, Nat. Hiding your feeling for him from me hurts me worse than anything, as if you can't trust yourself to still love me if you love him. Don't you think we're strong enough for this?"

His eyes narrowed. "I can't live with the knowledge that you love him and feel you have to hide it from me. Are you scared to show me what you feel for him? Embarrassed? I can't live with the uncertainty. One way or another, this needs to be settled. None of us will be able to move on until it is. I'll be back in two hours."

Bringing her hand to his lips, he kissed the backs of her fingers before releasing it. "Talk to Hoyt." With a last look at Hoyt, he turned, grabbed his jacket, and walked out the back door.

Nat stared after him, swallowing heavily when he disappeared from view, aware of Hoyt's silent and watchful scrutiny.

Clearing her throat, she lowered herself into her seat before her knees gave out completely and reached for the glass of water.

Her hands shook so badly, she set it down again, glancing at Hoyt, who hadn't moved. "The way you stand there so still makes me nervous. Is that one of the things you learned in the SEALs?"

Hoyt's lips twitched. "One of them. I'll try to remember that. I don't want to make you any more nervous than you already are."

The scrape of the chair next to her made Nat jump, her shoulders so tense that they started to ache.

Hoyt paused, pulling the chair out slowly. "Sorry. I didn't mean to startle you. I guess it's going to take some time for us to get comfortable with each other again."

Moving with slow deliberation and a graceful power that the years in the Navy had honed to a razor-sharp edge, Hoyt lowered himself into the seat next to her again. "You're even more beautiful than the last time I saw you. I didn't think that was possible."

Shaken, Nat fisted her hands on her lap so that he couldn't see how badly they trembled as memories from their time together assailed her.

Hoyt had always told her she was beautiful, and the love and masculine appreciation in his eyes had always made her feel that way.

But, that was a long time ago, and she'd almost forgotten how his silky words and appreciation in his eyes warmed her all the way through.

Pinpricks of awareness broke out all over her skin, the knowledge that they would become lovers again hanging heavily in the air between them.

No.

She couldn't let it happen. She couldn't hurt Jake. It would be far too complicated.

But, God, what she wouldn't give for another chance to have his love again.

It had been so long since she'd felt his arms around her—so long since he'd touched her in passion.

What she felt for Hoyt had an edge now, one that hadn't been there before.

She wanted to know what it would feel like to be in his arms again.

She *ached* to know.

Damn it!

Jumping to her feet, she walked around him to the counter where the coffeepot sat, her hands itching to caress the T-shirt stretched tautly over his wide shoulders.

Keeping her back to him, she retrieved a cup and reached for the pot, struggling for something to say that would change his mind. "I'm not the same woman you knew before. I'm older and don't have the body I did before. I can be cranky, and I'm a hell of a lot more opinionated than I used to be."

Turning, she leaned back against the counter and sipped her coffee. "In other words, I can be a bitch and won't take any crap from you."

Hoyt turned in his chair, his eyes lit with anticipation. "I'm not the same man, but some things never change. There's always been something between us. You've felt it every bit as much as I have. There hasn't been a day that I haven't wanted you. There hasn't been a day that I haven't wanted you and my son with me. We know each other, Natalie. It's not as if we haven't spent time together over the years—both of us trying to pretend there was nothing between us. I'm tired of pretending." Although he kept his voice low, it carried easily, the deep timbre of it seeming to vibrate over her skin and set off little explosions of awareness through every erogenous zone.

Hooking an arm over the back of his chair, Hoyt let his gaze rake over her before lifting it to hers again. "In case you haven't noticed, I'm more opinionated, too, and I'm more than capable of handling your attitude." Grinning at her glare, he reached for his cup. "A hot ass should take care of any bitchiness."

Unable to hold back a gasp, Nat stared at him in shock. Alarmed at the surge of lust and rush of heat, she glanced at his lap, the mental image of being forced over it and spanked rising up and refusing to be pushed back. "You would hit me?"

Hoyt's smile fell, his eyes narrowing and darkening with anger. "I would cut off my hands before I hit you, but baring your ass and turning you over my knee sounds very appealing. I'll do it, Natalie. Make no mistake about that. I've never lied to you, and I sure as hell don't plan to start now."

Nat gulped, unable to do more than stare at him, the truth of his words glittering in his eyes.

Still holding his cup, Hoyt rose to his feet and strolled toward her. "You're not a scared girl anymore. You're a mature woman, who knows what she wants." His gaze sharpened as he moved close, close enough for her to feel the heat from his body. "I know that Jake's been teaching you the pleasure of submission for years."

Nat tried to move to the side, but Hoyt braced a hand on the countertop on either side of her, blocking her in. Shaking so hard that she knew she didn't stand a chance of hiding it from Hoyt, she lifted her chin, struggling not to look at his magnificent chest. "You're a Dominant?"

Memories of the past threatened to consume her, stolen moments of hot, sweaty sex, and cuddling in the dark as he whispered words of love to her. She tried not to imagine what he'd done with other women, but jealousy ignited her anger.

"You weren't before."

Hoyt leaned closer, his lips hovering over hers. "You were too naïve to recognize the signs." He followed her as she leaned back, his mouth dangerously close to hers, so close that his warm breath brushed over her lips with every word he spoke. "I was easy on you, and I didn't have the experience or maturity that I have now."

His lips touched hers, brushing back and forth with slow deliberation. "Thoughts of pleasuring you, teasing you, tormenting you have kept me awake at night for years. I want you, Natalie. I want you to be mine. I want to love you. Pleasure you. Cherish you. I want to possess you in ways I never have before—in ways I've only dreamed about."

A whimper escaped at the feel of his chest brushing her nipples, her heart pounding furiously when he scraped his teeth over her bottom lip. Hardly daring to breathe, Nat let her eyes flutter closed and parted her lips in anticipation of his kiss.

It had been so long since she'd felt his lips against hers, his nearness much more potent to her senses than she remembered.

Her pulse tripped, her hands going to his shoulders, her fingertips digging into hard muscle as she waited.

And waited.

Swallowing another whimper, she opened her eyes, startled and embarrassed to find Hoyt watching her.

His eyes, hooded and dark, and only inches from hers, flared with heat and satisfaction even as his features softened with emotion. "There it is. Yes, you still belong to me. You still want me, and I swear, if you try to deny it or push me away, I'll turn you over my knee so fast your head'll swim."

Mortified to have shown such weakness, she pushed his arm and moved away, putting several feet between them before turning to face him again. The knowledge that she'd escaped only because he'd allowed it added fuel to her anger. "You can't just push your way into my life and expect me to accept it."

Straightening, Hoyt reached for the coffeepot, glancing over his shoulder at her as he poured. "If you didn't love me—if you didn't want me—things would be different. I'd leave and not bother you again. But, that's not the case now, is it?" Setting the pot back on the warmer, he picked up his cup again, and turned to face her fully. "We have enough obstacles to overcome. I'm not about to let you create ones that aren't there."

His smile sent a thrill through her, one she struggled to hide. "It's not like I'm asking you to strip, jump up on the table, and spread your legs, baby."

The thought of it sent a flare of heat to her clit, making it throb.

Hoyt's eyes narrowed on her features as though he'd seen something she hadn't meant to reveal. "Yeah, it's there." Lifting his cup, he took a sip, watching her over the rim. "I'm not going to rush you, but I'm sure as hell not going to let you push me away."

Retrieving the cup she'd left on the counter, he brought it to her, placing it in front of her. "I'm sorry, baby. I don't want to scare you or cause any trouble for you and Jake. I just want to be a part of what you have here."

He reached out to play with the ends of her hair. "I've missed you so damned much. There hasn't been a single day that I haven't ached for you."

He smiled faintly. "The night Joe was born, I got drunk as hell and cried like a baby."

Gulping, she stared down into her coffee cup, tears stinging her eyes. The flood of emotion made it difficult to breathe, the years of yearning for him, coming back in a rush. "The night I gave birth to Joe, I wanted you with me. I cried for you."

The words she'd never meant to say poured from her, and disgusted with herself, she set her cup aside again and backed away to put some distance between them. "Look, I'm older now. I have stretch marks. Wrinkles. I don't need fancy words or flattery. I much prefer honesty."

Glancing at him out of the corner of her eye, she took a deep breath and let it out slowly, forcing back tears she couldn't afford to shed. "I couldn't bear it if you changed your mind about me and walked away. I can't trust you not to walk away, Hoyt. You're asking me to risk my marriage, and everything Jake and I have built together on the chance that you'll stay."

"I've never lied to you, Natalie. About anything." His voice had an edge to it that hadn't been there before.

Grateful for the surge of anger that kept her from sobbing, Nat stormed back to the counter, staring out the window over the sink. "How about the time that you told me that you hadn't asked me to marry you because I was pregnant?"

She didn't even get the chance to turn before he closed in on her from behind. Bracing a hand on the counter on either side of her, he pressed his hard body against hers. "I never lied to you about that. I never would have taken your virginity if I hadn't planned to marry you."

Struck by the feel of his body pressed against hers, a feeling so new and exciting, and yet so familiar, Nat stiffened.

He was even bigger now. Harder. Hotter.

A commanding presence that couldn't be ignored.

Her feelings for him had matured over the years, making her desire for him even stronger now. Richer. More intense.

Fighting it would be the hardest thing she'd ever done, but love for Jake and anger at Hoyt demanded that she try. "If that's true, why didn't you ever ask me before? Why didn't you ever—"

In a rare show of temper, Hoyt slammed a hand on the countertop. "Because I couldn't support you on what I was making while I was working for my father!"

Stunned by the bitterness and anger in his tone, Nat fisted her hands on either side of the sink and stiffened again. "I didn't need money, Hoyt. I had a job, too."

Leaning so close that she could feel his warm breath on her cheek, Hoyt closed his hands over her fists, his body tense against her back. "It was my job to support you. I didn't want you to have to work. I wanted to take care of you. I couldn't afford college, and knew that I could learn a trade in the Navy."

For the first time on over twenty years, his hands closed over her waist, sending a wave of longing through her—one so intense that it terrified her.

Sexual awareness gripped her, travelling in decadent bursts from the hard hands at her waist and the soft lips that touched her neck and flowing to every erogenous zone in her body.

Her mind fought the hunger—a hunger she'd spent years struggling to suppress, but her love and need for him proved overwhelming, and her body refused to listen.

She trembled helplessly, her breath coming out in short, desperate whimpers at the slow, upward slide of his hand.

Gripping her jaw, he trailed his fingers over her neck. Tilting her head back, he scraped his teeth over the ultrasensitive spot between her neck and shoulder, a spot he'd exploited often in the past, and one he obviously hadn't forgotten.

"I've missed this spot. So soft. So sweet. I want you so damned much. *You.* I've never wanted another woman the way I want you. You've ruined me for anyone else. There hasn't been a fucking night that I haven't lain in bed wanting you."

He slid the hand at her waist to press against her belly, pulling her firmly against him. "There hasn't been a day that I haven't loved you."

Moving the hand at her belly in a possessive caress, he tightened the hand at her jaw, pressing his face against her neck. "I'll love every stretch mark you have. They're *my* marks on you, marks from giving birth to my son. You wear my brand, and I can't wait to explore each and every one of them. I wanted you with me so much, Natalie, and it ripped my heart out to watch you marry Jake. It nearly killed me to leave you behind."

Swallowing a sob, she fought her hunger for him, and the memories that created an empty feeling in her stomach, one that she remembered well. "But, you still left."

Lifting his head, he turned her face to his, the torment in his eyes tugging at her. "I *had* to leave. I'd already signed up. I'd already made the commitment. I wanted you with me—where you belonged—but I saw the fear in your eyes. I know you were afraid of leaving. I know how you felt about leaving Jesse with your father. You were carrying my child, and I wanted what was best for you. For both of you."

He scraped his teeth over that sensitive spot again, nuzzling it as though he couldn't get enough. "But, there hasn't been a day since then that I haven't considered you—both of you—mine."

Nat shook her head, jerking away before she came completely undone. "I'm Jake's."

Tightening his hold on her jaw, he turned her face toward his again, holding her head tilted back against his shoulder, his eyes glittering hotly. "Yes, you're Jake's, but a part of you has always belonged to me. I was the man who took your virginity. I was the man who gave you a child. You love me. You always have, just as I've always loved you."

The hand at her waist slid higher, settling right below the lower curve of her breast. "Part of you will always belong to Jake, but part of you also belongs to me. You know it as well as I do. I want what's mine, Natalie—what's always been mine."

Her ragged breathing became even more pronounced as the heat from his hand burned the underside of her breast, making her nipples bead so tightly they ached. She shivered at the huskiness in his voice as he said her name.

No one else called her Natalie.

No one but Hoyt.

God, she wanted him.

"I can't do this." She shoved at him, but she couldn't move him the slightest bit.

"Yes, you can." Hoyt nipped her earlobe. "You're the strongest woman I know. If any woman could handle two men, it's you."

She sucked in a breath when the hand pressing against the lower curve of her breast shifted slightly and his thumb slid back and forth over the sensitive underside, alarmingly close to her nipple. Little sizzles of erotic electricity raced from his fingers to her nipple, making it bead impossibly tighter, the ache for his touch overwhelming. "Hoyt. Oh, God." Shaking like a leaf, she gripped his forearm with the intention of pushing it away, an intention forgotten as soon as the first surge of white-hot lust hit her system.

Hoyt's lips moved over her jaw, sending waves of heat racing through her. "Yes, love. It's not too late for us. It's never too late. I can't forget you, Natalie. I've tried. I can't get you out of my head. Thoughts of what I was missing have driven me crazy. I gave in to you when you wanted to stay here. I only wanted you to be happy. I've given you everything you've ever asked me for. I let you have your way when it damned near killed me."

Wrapping his arms around her waist, he cuddled her close and buried his face against her neck again. "Now, I need this from you. I have to know, Natalie. I have to know if there's a chance for us. I would never be able to live with myself if I didn't do everything I could to get you back into my life."

His lips moved over the spot that rendered her weak and turned her knees to rubber. "I need to know if I can fit in here. I want my family, Natalie. The way you respond to my touch, and the love in your eyes—the love you try so hard to hide—convinces me that I'm right where I belong."

Spinning her to face him with a speed that made her dizzy, he fisted a hand in her hair and tilted her head back, using his other hand to hold her against him. His hooded gaze held hers for several long seconds before a slow smile of satisfaction curved his lips. "Yes, Natalie. I'm right where I belong."

She barely managed a gasp before Hoyt took her mouth with his in a searing kiss filled with an emotion and possessiveness that melted the last of her resistance. It had an edge to it now that hadn't been there before, one that seemed to reach inside her and draw every bit of yearning and love she felt for him to the surface, leaving her feeling vulnerable and exposed.

His kiss, so familiar and yet so different, had a dangerous feel to it now, an erotic sexuality that had been honed to a razor sharp edge.

Some of the tenseness left Hoyt as he eased his hold and lifted his head slightly, sipping at her lips as if to prove to her that he didn't need to hold her to keep her there.

With his lips hovering over hers, he ran his hands through her hair, bringing back memories of how much he'd always liked to play with it. Smiling, he gripped her chin, holding her gaze with eyes that glittered with emotion. "Admit it, Natalie. You need to know, too. We can have it all. You only have to give us a chance."

Staring into light brown eyes with flecks of gold that seemed to glitter, Nat swallowed the lump in her throat, trembling with excitement for what could be, and struggling against the fear of what could happen. "You're right. I *do* need to know, but more importantly—Jake does. I'd like you to have time with Joe, and I know that Jake's missed you over the years."

Running his thumb over her still-tingling and moist bottom lip, he watched her intently. "And you?" His eyes narrowed. "Have *you* missed me?"

Knowing a lie would probably choke her, she nodded. "Yes." She shook her head, wishing she could shake off her nerves as easily. "But Jake's my husband. What's done is done. We've all made our choices, and I've grown to love Jake. More than I ever thought I could love. I love him so damned much that losing him terrifies me."

Meeting his gaze squarely, she took a deep breath and let it out slowly, desperate to make him understand her position. "Jake is my husband. He raised Joe as his own. He's always been there for me. We've built a great life together. I love him so much, and would do anything for him. He's a part of me. I know he feels the same about me. I won't hurt him, Hoyt—not even for you."

Chapter Four

Nat's hands shook as she washed the dishes, the events of the day leaving her unsettled and nervous. Aware of Hoyt's scrutiny as he dried the plate he held, and Jake's sharp attention on both of them, she fought to appear as normal as possible, but she didn't remember what normal even felt like anymore.

Everything had changed, the excitement in the air tangible even as her unease around Jake grew.

Afraid of hurting his feelings, she didn't want to show how much Hoyt affected her, or how much she craved the relationship they'd both proposed.

Jake had come home shortly after she'd told Hoyt that she wouldn't hurt Jake for him, and aware of his sharp attention, she'd tried to keep as much space between her and Hoyt as possible.

Hoyt thwarted her at every turn, crowding her and touching her often, and doing it under Jake's watchful and enigmatic gaze. Hoyt had suggested going out to dinner, but Nat didn't feel like dealing with all the questioning looks, and needed something to do, hoping that staying busy cooking the meal would help her shake some of her nerves.

It hadn't.

Having both of the men she loved talking about mundane topics like bills and chores that needed to be done around the house intensified the reality of the situation.

They made it sound so *permanent*.

Hoyt opened a cabinet and slid a plate inside, the realization that after years of visiting, he already knew where everything belonged adding even more of a sense of permanence. "I have to get to the bank and open an account here."

Jake got up to help himself to another cup of coffee, patting Nat's bottom as he passed her. It was something he did often, but not in front of others, and *never* in front of Hoyt.

A small thing, but it served to emphasize the difference in their relationship now, something she suspected had been Jake's intention.

Both men seemed to be doing their best to keep everything as normal as possible, but even the smallest thing took on greater significance.

Jake turned to look at Hoyt over his shoulder as he refilled his cup. "Did you bring everything with you?" The camaraderie between them seemed to grow by the hour as though the two of them had come to some kind of understanding.

Not knowing what went on between them made her even more uneasy.

Hoyt chuckled softly and reached for another plate to dry. "Except for the Mustang, everything I own is in the truck. I've lived on base most of the time, and travel light. I have some more computer equipment being sent to me, but other than that, I have everything with me."

Turning at the waist to set a plate in the drying rack, Nat caught a glimpse of Hoyt and Jake standing together. Stilling at the picture they made, she sucked in a breath, her pulse tripping.

Love for both of them—memories, both good and bad—hit her like a sledgehammer, the rush of emotion so intense that she actually gasped, jolting at the sound of the plate she'd been holding crashing to the floor.

This was really happening.

Her head spun, making her dizzy, the humming in her ears blocking out their voices. She gripped the edge of the counter for support, distantly wondering why both men looked so concerned.

Jake cursed and swept her up in his arms, breaking her out of her trance. "What's wrong, baby? Are you all right?" He dropped into one of the kitchen chairs and settled her on his lap, holding her face lifted to his, the fear in his eyes bringing her back to the present.

Feeling like a fool, Nat nodded and smiled reassuringly to ease the concern in his eyes, reaching up to lay a shaking hand on his cheek. "I'm fine. Just clumsy." Inwardly cursing, she sat up, trying to hide her unsteadiness. "Don't make a fuss. I'm all right. Just let me up."

Hoyt knelt at her feet, taking her foot in his hand and yanking off her sock, and then doing the same with the other. "She okay? I don't see any cuts."

Forcing a smile, Nat swallowed heavily, the surge of love for both of them making it difficult to breathe. "I'm fine. I promise. I just dropped a damned plate. Don't make such a big deal out of it."

Jake tumbled her back. "I saw your face. Do you feel okay?"

Hoyt shoved her socks back on, his features hardening. "I don't like it. She looks too pale. Let's get her to the hospital."

"Oh, for God's sake!" Feeling like a fool, Nat tried to jump up, but Jake's hard arm around her waist kept her from getting to her feet. "I'm fine. I swear."

When they shared a look, Nat sighed, knowing that unless she did some fast talking, she'd end up being looked at by a doctor. "It just hit me, okay? Let's not make a big deal out of it. I feel stupid enough as it is."

With a hard arm around her back keeping her in place, Jake turned and lifted her face to his, frowning as he studied her features. "What hit you, baby?"

Threading her fingers into his thick, silky hair, she leaned in to him. "Just how much I love you. The relief of knowing that you're not sick and haven't found someone else. Having Hoyt here. I looked up and saw the two of you and everything just hit me at once."

Delighted at the relief and flash of emotion in his eyes, Nat wrapped her arms around his neck and brushed her lips over his strong jaw. "I love you so damned much."

The slide of his hand over her waist warmed her and left a trail of heat in its wake. "And I love you—so much that it hurts at times. I can't live without you. I know how hard you love, baby."

Hoyt straightened from where he'd cleaned up the glass. "I'll go out and start unloading my truck."

Lifting his gaze, Jake glanced at Hoyt before giving Nat a meaningful look and releasing his hold on her.

Understanding that he wanted her to go to Hoyt, Nat nodded and got to her feet, blocking Hoyt before he could leave the room. "Just because I love you doesn't mean I'm comfortable with it."

Hoyt stopped abruptly and blinked, staring at her for several heart-pounding seconds before a slow smile lit his features. "Loving you isn't exactly what I'd consider *comfortable*."

Jake rose and approached Hoyt, slapping a hand on his back. "I'll help you unload everything. The sooner we get you settled, the better."

Wrapping his arms around her waist, Jake hugged her, pulling her close. "I love you, baby. Just relax. Everything's going to be just fine."

She leaned back into his embrace automatically, the way she had a thousand times before over the years, but this time with the knowledge that Hoyt watched. Patting the hand he pressed against her stomach, Nat forced a smile, her breasts and clit tingling for his touch. "Of course it will."

Knowing that if they'd been alone, he would have slid his hands up her sweater to cup her breasts, Nat stiffened, tense with anticipation. She wanted his hands on her, needed the closeness and connection that their lovemaking created, but was uneasy at the thought of him touching her intimately in front of Hoyt.

As Hoyt moved away, and went out the front door, Nat looked up at Jake over her shoulder. "I wouldn't hurt you for the world. One word from you and all of this ends."

Jake smiled, a genuine smile that made his eyes sparkle in the way she loved so much. "You're giving me a safe word? That's quite a switch for us, isn't it, baby?"

Rubbing her forehead against his jaw, Nat smiled. "Yes, and I'll honor it every bit as much as you do."

Closing his hands over her waist, Jake pressed his lips to her temple. "I love you, baby."

Hoyt reappeared, carrying a box under each arm. "Is it all right if I take the guest room I always used when I visited?"

Jake cursed. "This is your home now, too. This isn't going to work until we get comfortable with each other and you stop acting like a guest here." He slapped Hoyt on the back, the tension from him still palpable. "Come on. Let's give Nat some time alone. I think she's a little overwhelmed."

Nat snorted. "Yeah, yeah, yeah. Go play with your toys and let me finish."

Watching them go, Nat smiled, amused at herself. She understood now how Jesse got so rattled at times.

Dealing with one arrogant, domineering, and possessive man had always been an adventure.

Dealing with two would take a hell of a lot of stamina.

She had a feeling that the rewards would be worth it.

If only she could settle, maybe she'd be able to handle the situation a little better.

With that thought in mind, she sat at the table sipping coffee as Hoyt and Jake carried Hoyt's belongings inside, taking a great deal of satisfaction in just relaxing and listening to their voices. Their laughter rang out with increasing frequency as they talked about some of the crazy things they'd done in the past.

They'd always been close. Even when Hoyt came to visit, he'd usually spent almost as much time with Jake as he had with Joe, while she'd floundered, Hoyt's presence making her too nervous to join in.

Getting up, she refilled her cup, pausing at the realization that they'd stopped making trips in and out of the house. Hearing them speak in low tones from the room Jake had cleared for Hoyt's office, Nat found herself lonely for their company and anxious to see them together again. On shaky legs, she made her way down the long hallway, her steps slowing as she approached the smallest bedroom—the room that her son, Joe, had used to store all of his sports equipment.

The door had always been kept closed, so she hadn't even known that Jake cleaned it out.

He'd obviously made up his mind to allow Hoyt into their lives quite a while ago, proof that the distance between them had been even wider than she'd suspected.

Holding her cup in both hands to warm them against the sudden chill, Nat leaned against the doorway, drinking in the sight of them working together to unpack and set up what would be Hoyt's office.

Both men glanced up at her from where they knelt on the floor amid several pieces of computer equipment and wires, once again proving that they were both highly attuned to her.

Apparently satisfied with what they saw, both Hoyt and Jake smiled at her and turned back to work.

Watching Jake, she sipped her coffee, thinking about how much her life had changed since he married her.

He'd led her slowly, inexorably into the erotic world of domination and submission, a world that had seen her through dark times, especially when she'd been missing Hoyt. His level of caring, his unwavering patience, and the trust needed for such a relationship had strengthened the bond between them.

Over the years, that bond, forged in love and trust, had strengthened even more and grown.

His love had given her the security she'd needed—like a warm blanket that she could wrap herself in.

The last several months of secrecy had frayed that bond, but it hadn't broken it.

Her heart swelled as she watched him with Hoyt.

Over the years, her love for both of them had driven a wedge between them. Blaming herself for Jake's insecurity, she vowed to herself to do whatever she could to make a relationship with both of them work.

Determined to make an attempt to appear relaxed, Nat gestured to the assortment of boxes around the room. "Hoyt, I thought you retired. What are you going to do with all this stuff?"

Hoyt surprised her by turning away from what he'd been doing to give her his full attention, his eyes glittering with hunger. "I retired, but I'd go crazy with nothing to do." Smiling faintly, he looked away and tore open another box. "Years ago, I found out I have a knack for computer viruses. I was on medical leave—"

"Medical leave?" Nat straightened, glancing at Jake as a strange sensation settled in the pit of her stomach. "What medical leave? I didn't know about any medical leave. What happened?"

Looking back down into the box he was in the process of emptying, Hoyt waved a hand negligently. "Gunshot. Just a shoulder wound. Anyway, I was going stir crazy and found myself in the computer lab, bugging a friend of mine for something to do. I had quite a bit of training with computers, and with the time I had, I started tinkering with a virus they couldn't get a handle on. I was surprised to find I was good at it. I worked on computers until I could get back in the field. They asked me if I wanted to freelance for them once I retired. With the number of viruses popping up all the time, they need all the help they can get. I knew I would go nuts with nothing to do, so I said yes." Glancing up, he flashed a smile. "They're going to send them to me here, so if you get a disk in the mail, *don't* put it in your computer."

Nat straightened, swallowing heavily, her stomach knotting so tightly, she thought she might be sick. She took several deep breaths and struggled to keep her voice steady despite her fear and fury. "You were shot?"

Jake stilled and turned, eyeing Nat before lowering his head to deal with the cables in front of him. "Uh-oh."

Hoyt glanced at Jake before shrugging and looking up at her. "It's only happened a couple of times, and it was never any big deal." Opening the box in his hands, he produced a brand-new laptop, which he set aside.

Nat cringed and began shaking. She'd known the dangers involved with his work, something she tried not to think about too often. She'd taken a long drive by herself, crying in relief when she'd learned he would become an instructor, and would no longer be going on dangerous missions.

He'd been hurt and she hadn't even known it.

He hadn't cared enough about her to tell her.

Pain sliced through her, stealing her breath, the euphoria that had been building over the last several hours dissipating and leaving her feeling hollow.

Her stomach churned at the thought of Hoyt lying alone in a hospital bed, fear for what might have been igniting her temper. Careful to keep her voice low, Nat clenched her jaw, the roaring in her ears making her a little unsteady. "And you didn't think it was important to tell us that you'd been shot?"

Jake picked up the box he'd been working on and got to his feet, placing the box on the desk they'd already set up and perching a hip on the edge of it. After sharing a look of understanding with Nat, he turned to Hoyt and frowned. "She's right, Hoyt. Someone should have let us know."

Hoyt sighed and stood, looking from Nat to Jake as he dropped into the desk chair that had been pushed back out of the way. Frowning as if he didn't understand the problem, he eyed both of them. "I listed both of you as my emergency contacts. You would have been notified if I'd been killed in action. I wasn't, so you weren't."

He turned to Nat, his eyes hooded. "Natalie and Joe are listed as my beneficiaries."

Gritting her teeth, Nat exploded with hurt and anger, the emotion she tried hard to contain spewing out of her. "You cold son of a bitch! Do you think that makes it okay? I don't want to be the fucking beneficiary of a man who doesn't care enough to let me know when he's hurt. I don't want a fucking thing from you!" She didn't even think about it. She threw her almost empty cup at him.

Hoyt blinked, his hand snaking out to catch the cup in midair. Frowning, he stiffened. "What the hell?"

"Bastard." Nat spun away, not wanting him to see the tears in her eyes. "Get out."

Swallowing a sob, she made her way to her room, slamming and locking the door behind her. Leaning back against it, she let the tears flow.

"Damn it, Hoyt. Why the hell did you have to come back?"

Chapter Five

Jake winced at the sound of the bedroom door slamming, and turned to meet Hoyt's dumbstruck expression. Struggling between concern for his wife and amusement at Hoyt's obvious confusion, he sighed. "Well, now you've done it."

Shooting to his feet, Hoyt stared at the doorway where Nat had been standing. "What the hell was that all about?"

Even though he felt a little sorry for his friend, he couldn't hide his anger. "She loves you, and you hurt her feelings by dismissing hers. Nat's not a naïve woman anymore, Hoyt. She's an opinionated, confident one now and her feelings—and temper—are not to be trifled with, something you're about to learn."

A muscle worked in Hoyt's jaw, his eyes narrowed. "I wasn't trying to hurt her. I know exactly how Natalie is. I've been in love with that woman for most of my adult life. Don't you think I've noticed the changes in her over the years? You've given her a confidence that makes her even more exciting. She's a hell of a woman."

Unsurprised by Hoyt's defensiveness, Jake smiled faintly. "Then you know she's a headstrong woman who loves fiercely, and with the same passion she puts into everything else—including her temper."

Blowing out a breath, Hoyt dropped back into the chair, scrubbing a hand over his face. "I didn't want anyone to worry. There wasn't anything to worry *about*." He glanced again toward the doorway. "I didn't mean to hurt her. I just didn't see the need to worry her unnecessarily. I could see that she was scared about what I did, and I hated that."

Amused to see a man who went into deadly missions without a qualm get so rattled when dealing with Nat, Jake decided to confide in him. "You know, she cried like a baby when she heard that you weren't going on missions anymore." Meeting Hoyt's incredulous look, Jake smiled. "She doesn't know that I know, but right after I told her that you would be training others instead of being in the middle of the action, she said she had to go shopping. She was gone for hours and came back with nothing. I could tell she was crying, and she did everything she could to hide it. When I pressed her, she got defensive. On a hunch, I mentioned you, and she started to tear up again."

Hoyt stared at the doorway, the dawning awareness of how his decisions affected all of them glittering in his eyes. "I never thought—"

Jake sighed, and faced his clearly distraught friend squarely, fighting his own need to go after his wife. "You've been alone a long time. You're used to thinking as part of a team, but not as part of a family, and certainly not as a man who has a woman to appease. If you want to be a family, you're going to have to start *thinking* like part of a family. Everything you do affects us. Anything that happens to you affects *all* of us just like it affects your team when you're on a mission. The difference is—on a mission, you don't have to deal with hurting anyone's feelings."

Hoyt dropped his head back, closing his eyes on a moan. "Hell. Christ, I love that woman more than my own life. I never stopped thinking about any of you, and I thought I was doing the best for everyone involved. I didn't want anyone to worry about me, when you had enough in your own lives to worry about that I couldn't help with. I never meant to hurt her."

"You're not alone anymore." Smiling when Hoyt met his gaze again, Jake lifted a brow, determined to make sure Hoyt knew what both he and Nat would expect. "Isn't that what you wanted?"

Hoyt glanced toward the doorway again, a small smile playing at his lips. "Yeah. Don't worry about me backing out. I've wanted this for too long. There's no way I'm backing out." He scrubbed a hand over his face. "Christ, If I fuck this up, I'll never forgive myself."

Relieved that Hoyt started to understand some of the emotion minefield he'd have to learn to navigate in order to keep Nat happy, Jake couldn't help but smile. "You've never had a permanent relationship?"

Hoyt shrugged, staring at the empty doorway. "I never wanted a permanent relationship with any of the women I met. I kept comparing them to Natalie. I didn't want a substitute. I wanted the real thing."

Running a hand through his hair, Jake sighed. "I know how much Nat means to you, and I'd rather have everything out in the open. It's all or nothing. If you're going to go into this thinking you can do it half-assed, you should know up front that neither one of us will put up with that."

Hoyt cursed again and nodded, leaning forward and fisting his hands as he glanced toward the doorway again. "You're right." He looked like he wanted to run after Nat, but held back, the effort it cost him hardening his features. Turning to Jake, Hoyt gestured toward the doorway. "Would she have walked away from you like that?"

Jake grinned. "She never would have made it through the doorway." Remembering how he'd dealt with his wife's temper in the past, Jake chuckled, feeling sorry for Hoyt, but knowing that his friend would have to develop his own relationship with Nat. "We might as well start as we intend to continue. You're the one who pissed her off and hurt her feelings, so you're the one who's going to have to fix it."

Hoyt nodded and jumped to his feet, clearly anxious to get to her. "I will. I'll fix things with her. Hell, if I don't get the upper hand with her, I'm going to lose her before I even begin."

Chuckling, Jake straightened. "Yeah, well having the upper hand with Nat is an elusive and deceptive concept. You'll learn soon enough that she's the one in charge."

Hoyt's slow smile was filled with memories. "She always was." Pausing at the doorway, he turned. "Got any advice?"

"Be honest. She'll see through a lie, and it'll only end up hurting her more."

Seconds later, Jake found himself staring at an empty doorway, and let his smile fall, his hands fisting at his sides. Retrieving the cup Nat had thrown from the desk where Hoyt had placed it, he stared down into it, his stomach in knots.

Letting someone else, especially someone who had been his wife's lover, go to her while he stood aside, went against everything he believed in—one of the adjustments he would have to learn to live with.

Looking around at the neatly organized clutter around the room, he couldn't help but smile. He'd missed Hoyt, and the friendship they'd had. It had been uncomfortable when he and Nat had first gotten married, but had gradually become close again, and when Joe came along, most of their conversations centered around him.

Until Hoyt's feelings for Nat kept him away.

Listening to Hoyt knock on the door to the Master bedroom, Jake cursed and started for the kitchen. Grabbing his coat and his keys, he went to the back door with the intention of giving the two of them the time alone that they needed, pausing with his hand on the knob.

He couldn't leave. Nat might need him.

If Hoyt didn't manage to calm her down, he would step in. He couldn't stand to see her hurting.

With a sigh, he hung the coat over the back of his chair, and tossed his keys into the basket on the counter before going to the coffeepot to pour himself another cup of the hot brew.

Hearing Hoyt plead with Nat to open the door, Jake smiled and went to sit at the table. He couldn't help feeling sorry for Hoyt, but if he planned to have a relationship with Nat, he'd have to learn how to deal with her in all of her moods.

"Open this door right now, Natalie, or I'll break it down."

Grinning at Hoyt's threat, he sipped his coffee, his body tight with anticipation at the thought of giving his wife an outlet for all that passion.

The image of Hoyt joining in made his cock stir.

He could use this new arrangement to reinforce his dominance over Nat, and ignite a new spark into their lovemaking—one that would reestablish the closeness they'd had before.

He'd bind her so closely to him that nothing would put any distance between them again.

* * * *

Standing at her bedroom window, Nat stared out into the darkness, unable to rid herself of the image of Hoyt lying hurt and alone in a hospital bed.

She couldn't help but wonder what she'd been doing at that time.

She couldn't help but wonder if he'd thought of her while he was lying there.

Had he wanted her near? Had he even thought of her at all?

If he'd died, there would have been so much left unsaid, so much between them that had never been resolved.

He would never have known how much she loved him. He would have never known what he meant to her.

Jolting at the knock on the door, she turned at the waist, wiping away the tears she didn't want him to see.

Another knock, this one louder than the last accompanied the jiggling of the doorknob. "Open the door, Natalie."

Turning back, she drew in a calming breath and let it out slowly, and stared unseeingly out the window again.

Picturing Hoyt lying in a hospital bed dispelled most of her anger, the thought of losing him without being able to let him know that she'd never stopped loving him dissolving the rest.

She'd hid her feelings for him for so long.

She didn't want to hide them anymore.

"Open this door right now, Natalie, or I'll break it down." Hoyt's icy command sent a shiver of apprehension through her.

She'd avoided him as much as possible over the years, nerves and her fear of letting her emotions show forcing her to keep a distance. Hoyt had also kept his distance, his cool politeness and quiet watchfulness making her more nervous by the minute.

It would be different now, and making the adjustment proved to be harder than she'd expected.

"I told you to leave."

"And I told you that I'm not going anywhere. Open the fucking door, Natalie, or I'll break it down."

Feeling raw and emotional, Nat turned and started for the door, knowing that Hoyt never made idle threats, something he and Jake had in common. Clinging desperately to the small amount of anger she could muster, Nat raised her voice to be heard through the door. "Don't you dare start breaking my house!"

"Then open the fucking door. Now, Natalie." He kept his tone cold and steely, but she knew him well enough to detect the trace of frustration.

Feeling more in control, she unlocked the door and swung it open, leaning against it to block him from entering. "What?"

Hoyt's eyes narrowed, his rugged features lined with tension. "We need to talk."

Lifting her chin, Nat faced him squarely, determined to keep a tight rein on her temper—and the tears that threatened again. "So talk."

Hoyt's eyes narrowed at her tone. "I didn't want you to know that I'd been shot because I didn't want to worry you." A brow went up, his eyes flashing with anger. "Did you think I couldn't see it? Every time I left, I could see the look of desperation in your eyes. The fear. Each time I came back, I could see the relief. If you'd known that I'd been shot, you would have worried even more. Why would I do that to you?"

Nat nodded, trying to keep her eyes on his instead of allowing her gaze to drift lower to the muscles that flexed in his biceps as he crossed his arms over his chest.

What kind of lover would he be now?

The confidence and grace in every movement added to the aura of danger surrounding him, and over the years had been honed to a razor-sharp edge.

Aroused despite her hurt and anger, Nat nodded, struggling to hide all emotion. "Fine. Then I don't see any reason to tell you anything that would worry you. Glad we got that worked out. Anything else?"

A muscle worked in his jaw, and Nat could see that it wasn't the answer he'd expected. His eyes narrowed again, the anger and frustration in them giving her a small amount of satisfaction. "I want to know every damned thing about you. Is there something wrong that I don't know about? I swear, Natalie, you'd better not try to hide anything from me!"

Nat raised a brow, allowing a small smile. "So you can keep things from me, but I can't keep them from you? No, that doesn't sound fair at all, and it certainly doesn't sound like any kind of relationship I want to be part of. I think I'll pass." She started to close the door, jumping back in surprise when he hit it so hard that it slammed back against the wall.

"Damn it, Natalie!" Running a hand through his short hair, he closed the distance between them. "Fuck, Natalie, sometimes you piss me off. I won't keep anything from you again, okay? Damn it. Don't try to create obstacles. This is going to be hard enough for all of us. I did what I thought was best at the time. I won't keep anything from you anymore, and you'd better not even think about trying to keep anything from me."

He started to reach for her, the hunger and desperation in his eyes thrilling her, but he pulled his hands back at the last second as if not trusting himself.

With a sigh, he scrubbed a hand over his face. "We didn't have that kind of relationship before. I want it now. I thought I'd made that clear."

Confident that she'd made her point, she nodded. "As long as we understand each other. I want your promise that you won't keep things from me. Jake kept the conversations he'd had with you from me because he didn't want to worry me, and I ended up thinking that either he was having an affair, or he was dying and didn't know how to tell me."

Hoyt's eyes widened. "Oh, Christ, Natalie. I'm sorry."

Turning away, she put several feet of distance between them, the temptation to thrown herself into his arms almost irresistible. "I want the truth. If we're not honest with each other, or I can't trust you, then none of this is possible. I'm a strong woman, Hoyt, and I expect to be treated with respect. That includes being honest with me. Intimacy is a two-way street. So is trust." She found herself holding her breath, glancing at him over her shoulder to see his reaction.

Hoyt stared into her eyes for several long seconds as the tension between them built. Finally, he inclined his head. "For you, I'll try." Smiling faintly, he leaned against the doorway. "If I fuck up again, just talk to me. Don't throw things at my head and run away."

Insulted, Nat lifted her chin. "I didn't run away. I left before I gave in to the urge to smack you. Think about how you'd feel if I kept things from you because I didn't want you to worry, or because I thought you couldn't handle it."

A muscle worked in his jaw. "It would piss me off."

Nat nodded and turned away again, hoping he'd go and give her a few minutes to compose herself. "Good. I'm glad we got that settled. I'll be out in a few minutes."

Closing the distance between them, he took her hand in his and turned her to face him. "I don't believe this. You're scared to fight with me. You're scared to lose that temper. Unbelievable."

Nat gaped at him, and tried to shake off his hand. "I—what?"

"You heard me." Pulling her toward him, he bent, pressing a shoulder to her belly, and lifted her over it so fast, it made her head spin. "We can't have that, can we?" He strode down the hallway, carrying her as though she weighed nothing. "You don't want me to hide anything, but you're mad as hell. I can see it in your eyes. I've already told you that if you try to hide something from me because you think I can't handle it, it's going to piss me off."

A hard slap landed on her ass. "You think I can't handle that temper of yours, honey?"

It took several seconds before she recovered from the shock enough to struggle. "I'm not afraid to fight with you. Damn it, Hoyt. Put me down. Right now!"

He ignored her, overcoming her struggles with ease and carrying her to the family room. Bending at the waist, he lowered her to the sofa, standing directly in front of her so that the only way to escape would be to scramble away from him—the amusement and challenge in his eyes daring her to try.

She glared up at him, not about to give him the satisfaction of overpowering her—something that she knew would excite her even more.

"Problem?" Jake's deep voice, filled with amusement, came from somewhere behind Hoyt.

Hoyt smiled and moved to the side, dropping to the sofa next to her. "She just lectured me about honesty, and then when I accused her of being afraid to fight with me, she denied it. An obvious lie. Look at her eyes. She's mad as hell, but she's trying to pretend that nothing's wrong."

Laying his arm across the back of the sofa, he ran his fingers over her hair, a habit he'd had when they'd been lovers. "Or she doesn't care enough to fight with me. Either way, I don't like it. If she doesn't care enough, I need to walk away now. If she's trying to hide her feelings, she has to learn right from the beginning that I won't tolerate it."

Stiffening at the feel of his hard, hot body pressed against hers from shoulder to knee, Nat turned to glare at Hoyt. "If I didn't care about you, the three of us wouldn't be in this predicament, now would we? Jerk."

Jake lowered himself into the overstuffed chair close to the side of the sofa where Hoyt sat. "You want to explain yourself, honey?"

Gritting her teeth, she lifted her chin, wondering what it was about a domineering, arrogant man that sent her pulse racing. "There's no point in arguing about something that none of us can fix. He was wrong and he knows it. We've already discussed it. End of story."

Jake's eyes narrowed, a warning flickering in them that excited her even more. "Discussed it how?"

Aware of Hoyt's steady look, Nat shrugged. "He says that he considers us his family, but then doesn't let us know when he gets shot. I told him that if that's the way he wants it, that's fine—as long as that's what he's willing to accept in return. If he doesn't want to tell me things that might worry me, I won't tell him things that might worry him. He got the message." Moving away from Hoyt, she curled up on the end of the sofa and reached for the remote. "There's nothing else to say."

* * * *

Hoyt wanted to shake her.

Seriously considering how much satisfaction yanking her pants to her knees and turning her over his knee would give him, he grabbed the remote and tossed it aside, not even attempting to hide his anger. "Don't make the mistake of trying to shut me out. I told you that I wouldn't keep things from you anymore, but that fake nonchalance pisses me off."

She gave him another one of those fake smiles that made his hand itch to connect with her well-padded bottom. "Too bad."

Hoyt leaned back to study her, not missing her nervousness that showed itself in her inability to keep her hands or feet still, or the arousal that beaded her nipples and gave her a slightly dazed look. "I told you that I want a different kind of relationship with you now. You're aroused, nervous, and mad as hell, but seemed determined to hide it from me."

He spared a glance at Jake before focusing on her again. "I can't go back and change the past, but I can promise you that I won't keep things from you in the future. I can sure as hell promise that I won't let you keep things from me."

Too restless to sit still, he got to his feet, hoping that by opening up to her a little, she would open up to him. "I'm sure I'm going to fuck up." Turning to her with his hands on his hips, Hoyt allowed a small smile, knowing that it would take time to build the trust he needed from her. "You and I are going to both have expectations and demands from each other. We've got a lot of things to work out together, and I'm not about to let you shut me out, or treat me like a guest. We need everything out in the open."

Jake inclined his head. "I agree."

Natalie stiffened and turned her head, her eyes narrowing, the suspicion in them making his cock stir. "What kind of demands are you talking about?"

Pleased to have her full attention, he sat back and crossed his arms over his chest. "Oh, there's going to be quite a few, but we'll start with communication. Hoyt settled back, delighting in the flare of desire in her eyes. "Do you think you're going to get away with running away from me whenever you're pissed off? If you've got something to say, say it, and don't try to keep me at arm's length. I never would have taken you for a coward, Natalie."

Her eyes widened and glittered with fury. "Kiss my ass, Hoyt."

Hoyt's cock jumped, his heart pounding furiously with anticipation as he reached for her. Gripping her wrists, he hauled her over his lap and delivered several sharp slaps to her well-rounded ass, the Dominant inside him thrilling at her cry of outrage. Using a forearm across her back to hold her in place, he grinned at her curses even as she lifted her ass in invitation.

Having her over his lap satisfied a need inside him, her struggles intensifying his pleasure. Holding her firmly, he glanced at Jake as he ran a hand over Natalie's ass, knowing that it would keep the heat in and spread it. "You have to push it, don't you? That's twice that you've told me to kiss your ass. Trying to find out how much I'm going to tolerate, baby?"

Thankful that she couldn't see his hands tremble, he reached under her and unfastened her jeans, yanking them down to her knees and exposing her soft, luscious ass. "Beautiful."

When Natalie screamed Jake's name, Hoyt glanced up at him, surprised to see the lust in Jake's eyes. "Damn it, Jake, are you going to let him do this to me?"

Jake shared a look of understanding with Hoyt before meeting Natalie's gaze. "Yes. You belong to him now, too, and you have to admit, you've brought this on yourself."

"Hoyt! You son of a bitch! How dare you?" Wiggling on his lap, Natalie kicked her feet, stilling when Hoyt bent and touched his lips to her warm ass.

Heaven.

Moving his lips over her smooth, scented skin, he slid a hand between her thighs to press at her slit, delighted to find her hot and wet. "You'll find that I dare quite a bit when it comes to you. You told me to kiss your ass, didn't you, honey?"

"Bastard!" She started wiggling again, only to stop with a gasp as her wiggling moved her slit against his hand.

Unable to resist, he pressed a finger against her clit and began stroking. "What's the matter, baby? Bite off more than you can chew?"

Twisting, Natalie looked at Jake. "Aren't you going to do something?"

With a smile, Jake squatted next to her hip, reaching out to run a hand over her pink ass. "I don't know what you're getting so indignant about. You told Hoyt to kiss your ass and he did. Do you think I would have let you get away with running away from an argument, or putting up with you telling me to kiss your ass without doing something about it? Hoyt's got to handle your temper and your defiance. Looks like he's making a good start."

* * * *

Nat gritted her teeth, mortified that another rush of moisture escaped to coat Hoyt's fingers. "That's different."

Oh, God. She was going to come!

Jake chuckled, a low sound filled with wicked intention that she recognized well. "It won't be from now on. You have two men in your life, and you're going to have to learn how to deal with Hoyt, too."

Hoyt slid his finger over her clit again, sending another wave of exquisite pleasure through her that she struggled to hide. "I don't have a hell of a lot of patience with walking on eggshells. You tell me to kiss your ass, Natalie, and I'm going to assume you mean it literally. You get sassy, and I'm going to assume you're in need of some attention. Are we clear?"

Turned on by his uncompromising manner, Nat clenched her jaw, fisting her hands at her sides as he moved his finger again.

The combination of his attitude, the heat from his slaps, and the slow strokes of his finger over her clit had warning tingles sizzling in her clit and driving her wild.

She felt so exposed, and for the first time in her life, could feel the gaze of two men on her naked flesh.

She couldn't believe Hoyt had actually spanked her, and realized that she'd grossly underestimated him.

It made her wonder just how deep his dominant nature ran.

Sucking in a breath when his finger moved again, she squeezed her eyes closed, fighting with every ounce of willpower she possessed to keep from coming.

Every slow, deliberate glide of his finger over her clit threatened her control, forcing her to keep her head down so he couldn't see her face.

If she came now, especially in front of Jake, it would embarrass the hell out of her, and Hoyt would become even more arrogant.

God, it felt so good.

The forearm against her back slid lower, and another sharp slap landed. "I asked if we were clear."

That cold steel in his tone did things to her that made her insides flutter and had her lifting her ass for more. "I'm not one of your men."

Hoyt laughed, obviously enjoying himself. "No, you're not." His finger slipped into her pussy. "You're my woman, something I've been dreaming about for a long time." Moving his finger of his other hand slowly up and down the crease of her ass, he loosened his hold, his tone deepening. "Jake, what was she like when you took her ass for the first time?"

Jake sighed and came to kneel beside her, smiling down at her as he ran a hand over her back. The heat in his eyes told her that he remembered that night as well as she did and even now, replayed it in his mind. "It took a long time to work up to that. Didn't it, baby? She was scared, but I could tell that she enjoyed the attention there. I sat right where you're sitting now, with her draped over my lap the way she's draped over yours."

Jake's lips twitched. "She'd been daring me for days, saying and doing things to piss me off, and to see how far she could push me. I could see that she enjoyed it, so I let it go for several days, curious to see how far she'd go."

Nat blinked up at him. She hadn't known that he'd figured out what she'd been doing. Snorting inelegantly, she shook her head. "I did no such thing."

Hoyt's finger pushed deeper into her pussy as he pressed a threatening thumb against her puckered opening, the threat sending a thrill of alarm through her. "She's quite a liar, isn't she?"

Jake patted her ass cheek as Hoyt withdrew his finger from her pussy and started to stroke her clit again. "She gets that way, and temperamental when she needs attention. I'm afraid over the last few months, I've been distracted, and haven't given her the attention she needs from me."

Nat inwardly cringed at the apology in his eyes, and tried to get up, but both Jake and Hoyt tightened their hands on her back. "That's bullshit. I didn't need that kind of attention. I just knew that something was wrong and you wouldn't tell me. Oh, God!" Sucking in a breath as Hoyt pressed his finger deep into her pussy again, Nat tightened her hands into fists on the carpet, her pulse tripping as Jake pulled her jeans and panties off and tossed them aside. "And I don't lie."

Brushing his finger over her forbidden opening, Hoyt groaned. "Damn, her ass is gorgeous. She's squirming like crazy and I'm only touching her. I'll bet she goes wild when she's breached."

Jake slid a hand over Nat's hair as he stood. "I'll get the lube and you can see for yourself."

Nat stilled, shaking by the intense rush of arousal. "What?"

Jake frowned down at her, his eyes gleaming. "You got yourself into this."

Pressing his arm at her back, Hoyt spread his fingers over her bottom and parted her cheeks wide, exposing her puckered opening. "Do you have any idea how many times I've imagined having you this way?"

His touch, more confident than it had been in the past, thrilled her, her ass and pussy clenching as sensation layered over sensation. "I know it'll take time, but I'll have your trust."

Jake came into the room and knelt beside her, handing the tube of lube to Hoyt. "That ass is mine, and I can share it as I choose."

Stunned by Jake's steely tone, colder and firmer than she'd heard in months, Nat gasped at the surge of heat and whipped her head around to stare at him. "Jake!"

A dark brow went up, his eyes moving over her, gleaming with pride and possessiveness. "You gave yourself to me a long time ago, my little sub. That ass is mine. I own it, which means that I can share it. Just because I haven't in the past, doesn't mean that I can't. You want to use your safe word?" Reaching out, he cupped her breast, unerringly finding her nipple. "You've never used it before. You gonna use it now?"

The lust and ownership in his dark eyes made them appear lit from within. His obvious excitement fueled her own, and she realized that this was a fantasy of his that she'd never been able to fulfill in the past.

How could she deny him, or herself the pleasure?

Determined to make his fantasy come to life, she arched, pushing her breast more firmly into his hand. "Not a chance. I never go back on my word." Smiling, she threw her head back with a moan at the light pinch to her nipple. "I gave myself to you." Turning her head, she looked into his eyes. "I trust you. Completely. With everything."

Jake smiled. "Good girl. Now, spread those legs wider and let Hoyt lube that ass so he can explore it. Don't resist him. I'm going to be watching, and I won't be happy if you resist him. I brought your punishment plug as well, so Hoyt can see how beautifully that ass stretches. I hope he gives you the spanking you deserve."

Her puckered opening tingled with awareness, her pulse racing. Moisture trickled down her inner thighs even as she spread them, something Hoyt would notice right away.

She hadn't been so excited in a long time, forced by her own needs and her love of Jake to turn herself over to a man she wanted so badly she ached with it.

Jake always understood her.

With a hand on each cheek, Hoyt spread her wider, so wide that her opening stung. "A punishment plug? Very nice. I'm sure her spankings are much more effective with her ass filled, and I have to say, this is a good sized plug to get her attention."

A moan escaped before she could prevent it, the sharp awareness in her bottom so extreme that she could almost feel his touch there. The tension in the air mounted as she waited for Hoyt to lube his finger, heightening impossibly when the tube hit the sofa above her.

Shaking uncontrollably, and feeling both of their gazes on her forbidden opening, Nat jolted when Hoyt's finger, coated with cold lube pressed against the sensitive puckered skin.

Nat gasped and automatically arched and tried to close her legs, but a hard slap on her bottom prevented it.

"Keep those fucking legs right where they are." Jake's icy tone aroused her even more, the heat from his slap spreading with alarming speed and seeming to center around Hoyt's finger. "Don't you dare embarrass me by acting up."

Hoyt's arm firmed at her back, keeping her in position, his fingers splayed over her bottom to keep her cheeks parted as he pressed a finger of his other hand against her opening, forcing the tight ring of muscles to give way.

"Oh! Oh, God." Sucking in breath after breath as he forced her to accept more and more of his finger, Nat groaned and squeezed her eyes closed against the decadent sensations. Being overpowered only excited her more, along with the knowledge that both men loved this as much as she did. Knowing that she had to behave herself in order to show Hoyt how well Jake had trained her only added to her excitement.

Hoyt tightened his hold on her bottom cheeks, forcing them wider. "Beautiful. I swear, I could sit here and play with this ass all day."

Nat shivered, her ass clenching around his finger as he withdrew until just the tip of his finger remained inside her before surging even deeper.

"That's it, baby. Clench on my finger. Very good, baby. You've trained her well, Jake. I envy you." The underlying steel beneath his gentle tone sent another wave of lust through her, making her skin prickle with sexual awareness.

Sucking in a breath when he withdrew, she curled her toes, trembling harder as Jake pushed her hair back, fisting a hand in it to turn her face toward his.

His expression remained hard and cold, a sharp contrast to the heat and pride in his eyes. "Keep those thighs spread and lift that ass up to Hoyt. Show him how much you want that sweet ass filled, and show me how much you want to please me." His eyes narrowed as he ran his thumb over her cheek. "You get to have Hoyt in your life because I allowed it. You have your fantasy. Now, I want mine. I'm going to demand even a deeper submission from you. You're going to show to me that you're grateful for what I'm giving you—the chance to have both of them men you love in your life. Understood?"

Nat loved him in this mood. "Yes. Oh, Jake. I know you let Hoyt come here because you know how I feel about him. I know you did it for me. I'll do anything for you. I love you so much."

Jake's slow smile made her heart beat faster. "I know you do, and I love you, too. I want you to do something for me, something that will excite me even more."

Stiffening when Hoyt pressed cold fingers against her puckered opening again, Nat curled her toes and instinctively lifted her ass in invitation. "Anything."

God, she wanted this. It felt so good. So naughty and so primitive and sexual to be used in this way. "Oh, God. I'll do anything you want."

"Good girl." Jake's smile and the flash of amusement in his eyes told her that he knew just how much being in this position excited her. "When Hoyt breaches your ass, I want you to call Hoyt Master."

She gasped, her pussy clenching and leaking more moisture as she stared at him. "You're kidding. Jake, I—"

Several sharp slaps landed on her ass in rapid succession. "Do I look like I'm fucking kidding?"

Shaken by the disappointment and anger in his eyes, and embarrassed that she'd questioned his command, Nat felt her face burn. "I'm sorry." Need clawed at her, his harsh tone, filled with excitement throwing fuel on the fires raging inside her. "I'm so sorry. I'll do whatever you want. I promise. Anything." It came out in a breathless rush, the need to come overwhelming.

With each ragged breath, she found herself slipping into the dark, erotic world he'd shown her—the world she loved.

Unnerved by Hoyt's chuckle, she looked down at the floor again and struggled to remain still for Jake, a struggle she lost when Hoyt pushed two fingers into her bottom. "Oh, God!"

Jake nodded once, silently accepting her apology, his expression hard and cold even as his eyes gleamed with heat. "I'll be watching."

Moving his fingers, Hoyt pressed against her anal walls, while loosening his hold on her back. His hand moved up and down her back in a gentle and alarmingly possessive caress, his voice low and sinfully intimate. "Draped over my lap, and unable to prevent me from doing whatever I want to you. Given to me like a beautiful gift to enjoy."

Unable to resist challenging him, Nat gritted her teeth and glanced over her shoulder at him. "I can stop you. I just have to use my safe word."

"Hmm." Hoyt spread his fingers, making her puckered opening burn. "You would disappoint and embarrass your Master—after all he's done for you? He puts your happiness above his, and yet you would deny him the pleasure of seeing you this way?"

Feeling Jake's stare, she avoided looking in that direction, turning her head to look down at the floor again and fighting not to beg Hoyt to push his fingers deeper. She wouldn't embarrass herself—or Jake—by saying the wrong thing again. "No."

"It looks to me as if you have two fingers up your ass, Nat. How are you supposed to address Hoyt when your ass is filled?" Jake's icy tone sent a shiver through her.

Fuck.

He was actually going to make her say it.

More shivers raced up and down her spine as Hoyt moved his fingers in slow, deliberate strokes as if she needed to be reminded that, at least for the moment, she belonged to him.

Gulping in air, she trembled helplessly with a need so strong that she had to swallow a whimper. "No, *Master*."

Hoyt's sharp intake of breath both surprised and thrilled her. Bending low, he touched his lips to her shoulder. "I like the way you say that." Scraping his teeth over sensitive flesh, he pushed his fingers deeper while running the other hand over her hair. "Look at me, Natalie." The low silkiness in his deep voice did nothing to dilute the steel in his command.

Aware of Jake's watchful gaze, and unable to resist the chance to see Hoyt's eyes, Nat turned her head, her pulse tripping at the tenderness in Hoyt's expression. Swallowing heavily, she bit back a moan when he reached a hot hand under her to cup her breast.

Staring down at her, he teased her nipple, sliding his fingers from her bottom, only to press them against the slick opening again, sliding the tips of his fingers in and out of her as if to emphasize the fact that he could. "Do you know what it does to me to hear you call me Master? It's like a hot, silky mouth closing over my cock. Do you like having that kind of power over me?"

The thought that she could have that kind of effect on Hoyt had lust slamming into her. Hard. Sucking in a breath, she pushed her breast more firmly into his hand and found herself lifting into his slow thrusts for more. "Yes."

His eyes narrowed. "Yes, *what*?"

Some inner vixen inside her wanted to drive him as wild as he drove her. Batting her lashes, she pouted slightly, thrilling when his eyes narrowed in suspicion. "Yes, *Master*." It came out as a breathless plea, one that caused a rush of moisture from her pussy and a flare of heat in Hoyt's eyes.

His lips curved slightly, his cock pressing insistently against her hip as his body tightened. "The contrast of that soft, submissive tone and hint of daring in your eyes suits you, and makes me crazy for more." He applied pressure to her nipple, rolling it between his thumb and forefinger. "You're magnificent, better than any fantasy."

Smiling at her cry, he released her nipple, running his fingers over her breast as if he owned her. "But, you know that. You know how much pleasure Jake gets from dominating you, and you know damned well how to get to me. I'm going to have to take my time getting to learn you all over again." Flashing a grin, he pushed his fingers into her ass again, a smile of satisfaction curving his lips when she cried out and bucked her hips. "You're being so good. Jake's watching and waiting for me to push that punishment plug up your ass and spank you for trying to avoid talking things out with me. I won't let you get away with that, and I think it's important to drive that point home as soon as possible."

Tugging at her nipple, he moved his fingers in her ass again. "You ready, baby?"

Unable to hold still, and too aroused to be embarrassed, she flattened her hands on the floor and arched, giving him better access to her nipple while rocking her hips, desperate to take his fingers deeper.

"Yes, damn it."

Other than raising an arrogant brow, his expression didn't change. "Is that how you're supposed to address me?"

Nat turned away from him as the pleasure built, her inner thighs soaked with her juices. Frustrated that he held her in a way that prevented her from rubbing her clit against his pant leg and getting the friction she needed, she groaned in frustration and bucked harder, the need to come overwhelming.

"We can do this all night, Nat." Jake's deceptively mild tone didn't fool her at all, the icy intent sending a shiver of apprehension through her, something he would know well. "If you want to come after your spanking, you're going to have to start behaving yourself. This is your last warning. I really have been too soft with you. Apologize right now."

Trembling with need, she couldn't help but remember the times he'd punished her by not letting her come at all, and the agony it had caused her.

He'd teased and tormented her with her own hungers, hungers he knew well.

Already her pussy and ass clenched incessantly with the need to be filled, her clit tingling and feeling swollen and heavy.

Gritting her teeth, she kept her face averted. "I'm sorry, Master."

"How sorry?" Releasing her breast, Hoyt slipped his fingers from her ass and reached for the lube and the plug, making sure that she saw them before he moved them behind her back and out of sight.

Her bottom clenched, already anticipating how the plug would feel going into her.

How it would stretch her.

How it would send her reeling even deeper into the dark, erotic world of submission.

"Jake. Don't leave me." She wanted this. She wanted to lose herself in sensation, and give herself over to Hoyt with abandon, but she'd never submitted to anyone but Jake. Finding herself suddenly apprehensive, she looked up at him for reassurance.

Jake smiled, his eyes gleaming with possessiveness and pleasure. "I won't leave you. I'm right here. Now, tell Hoyt how sorry you are." Sliding a hand under her, he cupped her breast, running his thumb back and forth over her nipple and sending sharp spikes of hunger to her ass and clit.

Hoyt squeezed her bottom cheek. "This time with a little sincerity."

Comforted by Jake's presence, Nat gripped his forearm and pressed her breast more firmly into his hand while turning to glare at Hoyt, unable to resist provoking him. "Jake always accepts my apologies without being an ass about it."

Jake sighed, removing his hand from her breast. "When she gets aroused, she gets angry, and uses sarcasm to get me to be rougher with her."

He ran a hand over her hair, chuckling softly. "I'm going to leave it up to you to deal with her."

His fingers trailed over her shoulder. "I have a feeling that this time, she's trying to test you."

Nat stilled, whipping her head around to look at him, once again stunned by just how well her husband understood her.

Jake met her gaze with a knowing smile, one that held both amusement and anticipation. "Our little sub often tests my control, and it appears she wants to test yours."

Chuckling softly, Hoyt patted her bottom. "I expected that. I look forward to her little tests. It means she's starting to accept that I'm here for good. I can't have her thinking that I can't handle that attitude, now can I?"

With firm pressure, he ran his fingers over her puckered opening, his fingers massaging the tight ring of muscle there and pushing slightly into her on each pass.

A moan escaped and then another, each harsher and more desperate than the last. She swallowed heavily, groaning at the thought of the plug going into her, spreading her thighs even wider and lifting into Hoyt's touch.

"That's a girl. Lift that ass up. Do you know how much it's going to excite me to see this plug going into your ass, or how much I'm going to enjoy seeing it there while I give you the spanking you deserve?" Running a hand over her bottom, Hoyt bent to kiss her shoulder. "A spanking you're looking forward to as much as I am."

He knew. Of course, he would know.

She began to realize that he would understand her dark needs as well as Jake did.

"Are you ready to have that ass filled, baby?" The tension in his deep voice had become even more pronounced, his touch even more possessive.

"Oh, God. Oh, God." Shaking even harder, she let out a harsh moan as his fingers splayed over her bottom cheeks and he lifted and parted them, exposing her bottom hole.

Her toes curled, the anticipation making her breathing ragged as the plug touched her sensitive opening. Being over his lap in the position where she couldn't see either of their faces made her feel even more defenseless.

She loved it.

Knowing that fighting him would make him even more aggressive, she closed her legs and tightened her bottom against him, something contrary inside her needing to be overpowered.

Hoyt's growl thrilled her. "You don't really think you're going to be able to keep me out, do you?"

Wrapping his arm around her, he lifted her hips and pushed the tip of the plug into her, pausing at her pleasure-filled cry. "Yeah, that's it. You know you need this. Yes. Jake, look at her tight little ass taking the plug."

Running his hand over her thigh, Jake wrapped a hand around her knee and gently pulled it toward him, effectively spreading her even wider. "I never get tired of seeing it. I usually do it really slow, the way you're doing now, and drag it out as long as possible." He chuckled softly. "It drives both of us crazy, but I can't resist. Her thighs are soaked, so she's enjoying this almost as much as you are."

"Not even close. I've been fantasizing about being with her for years." Running his hand over her back and bottom, the affection and possessiveness in his touch unmistakable, Hoyt withdrew the plug slightly and then pushed it a little deeper. "Reality is much better, especially since she pushed me into dealing with her defiance."

As their voices got lower and more intimate, she struggled to bite back her cries and whimpers, not wanting to miss a single word.

Whimpering as Hoyt continued to work the plug into her, she rocked her hips, crying out as each inward stroke took the plug deeper. The relentless pressure forced her bottom to stretch to accept it, sending chills of delight up and down her spine.

She wanted more. She needed all of it inside her, the awareness he'd created in her ass making her inner walls clench with need.

"That's my girl. Jesus, I never expected her to be this way. Damn it, Jake. How the hell do you leave for work in the morning?" Still easing the plug into her, he ran his hand over her back. "I could spend all day just like this. She submits so beautifully. So sweet. I know that she's doing this for you, but just the thought that she can be this way makes me even more determined to earn her trust."

Groaning as the widest part of the plug went into her, she threw her head back, crying out as the plug narrowed and she felt the flat base press against her.

Driven by her own hungers, she found herself slipping deeper into the world of submission, craving the unwavering strength and dominance of a Master who could guide her.

Instinctively looking toward Jake, she rocked her hips and kicked her legs, moaning in agony as the hungers took over. "Please. I need to come. I need it bad."

Jake ran a hand over her hair. "Already, love? Hoyt's barely gotten started. You really like having the attention of two men, don't you?"

Thrilling at the feel of four hands moving over her, Nat couldn't stop rocking her hips, desperate for friction against her clit. "Please." Tears stung her eyes as the need for relief overwhelmed her. "I need to come. Let me come. Please. Please." Her clit throbbed, but Hoyt held her in a way that made it impossible for her to get the friction she needed.

Aware of their low conversation, she tried to be quiet, but moans and cries poured from her, her pussy and ass clenching and her clit and nipples aching for attention. Each time she clenched, the plug in her ass felt bigger, the full, stretched feeling sending her senses reeling.

Her body took over, releasing her mind from anything except the need for release.

The need to please her Master in order to get it.

"Please. I'll be good. I'll do whatever you want. Please let me come." Begging for a release she wanted more than her next breath, Nat spread her legs wider and gave herself completely over to them.

Hoyt's low curse, filled with sexual tension, had her focus shifting to him, sharpening to a razor edge. "She's a fucking fantasy come to life."

Bending over her, he touched his lips to her ear, his breathing ragged. One hand slid under her to cup her breast, while the other slid over her warm bottom in a light, threatening caress. "Are you ready for your spanking?"

"Yes, Master." Her bottom clenched, shivers racing up and down her spine. She'd do anything to be allowed to come.

Hoyt groaned. "You're determined to drive me crazy, aren't you, baby? My cock's hard enough to pound nails, and we're not even close to being done. Do you like knowing that you do this to me?"

"Yes! Please. Spank me so I can come." She could tell by his touch—by his voice—that this affected him as strongly as it affected her, but she still found herself needing to push him farther.

She needed a Master who could give her what her mind and body craved.

Without warning, several sharp slaps landed in rapid succession, no two landing in the same place. "Do you think I should let you come after what you did?"

A current of apprehension raced through her—the thought of being forced to endure such an intense arousal sending her into a panic. "Please!" Writhing on his lap, she fought to get free, the heat from his slaps spreading into wildfire and making her clit burn. "Let me up. Let me up. I'll do it myself. I need to come. I need to come."

* * * *

Hoyt nearly came in his pants.

Holding her firmly in place, he tore his gaze away from the delectable sight of Natalie's pink ass wiggling on his lap, lifting it to Jake's.

The same fascination and hunger he saw in Jake's eyes coursed through his own veins, a desire unlike anything he'd ever experienced.

He'd wanted women before, but nothing in his past had ever prepared him for what he felt now.

Love slammed into him, a deeper more intense love than he'd ever thought himself capable of feeling.

Christ, she was in his soul.

Looking down again, he ran a hand over her glistening skin, his heart pounding furiously—love for her threatened to choke him. He lifted his gaze to Jake's. "I never knew…"

Jake smiled, a slow smile filled with understanding. "You haven't even touched the tip of the iceberg." Inclining his head toward where Natalie writhed delightfully on his lap, her tortured cries filling the air, Jake ran a hand over her thigh. "She needs your strength now. Don't disappoint her."

Lust, love, and the need to possess combined into something so strong that it made him dizzy, her response to his touch making him feel ten feet tall. His chest nearly burst with excitement, joy, and love. "I won't."

Wrapping an arm around her waist, he lifted her slight weight and turned her, settling her on his lap.

He resented—but understood—that she looked toward Jake for guidance, and vowed to himself that one day she would look at him in that same trusting way.

Grateful for Jake's understanding, and humbled by his friend's compassion and generosity, Hoyt watched Jake move to a seat behind Natalie and out of her line of sight.

Determined to get her to focus on *him*, he stroked her back, grabbing her wrist before she could reach for her clit. "No. When—*if*—you come, it's going to be at *my* hand."

Her flushed face lifted to his, her eyes wild and unfocused. "Please, Hoyt. I can't stand it anymore."

Fighting the need to give in to her, Hoyt gathered both of her wrists in one hand and held them at the small of her back. "Is that how you address me?"

He knew he was torturing himself, but the need to hear her call him *Master* again in that low, silky voice, filled with need, proved irresistible. To his delight, she leaned into him. "I'm sorry, Master. Please let me come."

Such a strong woman, and she's looking toward me for guidance and relief.

His cock jumped, his need for her so strong that moisture leaked from it. Only willpower and the need to prove himself strong enough to deserve her kept him from coming in his jeans. Sliding a hand over her breast again, he took her nipple between his thumb and forefinger and applied light pressure. "Very good."

Injecting an ice into his voice that he was far from feeling, he let his fingers trail from one nipple to the other and down the center of her body, delighting in the way her muscles quivered beneath his touch. "You threw a coffee cup at me."

Looking up at him, her face flushed, she sucked in a breath when he ran a finger over her mound. "I'm sorry."

He hid a smile when she parted her thighs wider in invitation, an invitation he couldn't refuse. Slipping his hand between them, he forced them wider. "I can't let you get away with that, now can I?"

With his fingers flat, he delivered a sharp slap to her inner thigh, his cock leaking more moisture at her desperate cry. "Spread those thighs wider. We have a few other things to address."

Spurred on by the flash of heat in her eyes he'd been looking for, Hoyt kept his expression stern and uncompromising. "I can put up with your little fits of temper." Hiding a smile at her sharp intake of breath, and the glitter of insult in her eyes, Hoyt tightened his hold in her wrists and pulled them slightly, forcing her to arch her breasts toward him. "But, I won't tolerate it when you walk away from me instead of saying what you need to say."

He delivered another sharp slap before gripping her thigh to keep her in place. The Dominant inside him roared as she bucked her hips, crying out and begging for release.

So small. So delicate, and yet so strong.

Natalie tested his control as no other woman ever had, and he couldn't wait any longer to have her.

Releasing her wrists, he delivered another slap, his blood boiling with need for her when she cried out and began to shake harder. "That's my girl. Those little orgasms aren't enough, are they?"

Her ragged cries, each like a stroke to his cock, threatened to undo him. "That hot, swollen clit is just begging for attention, isn't it?"

Lifting her from his lap, he stood and lowered her to the sofa, drinking in the sight of the woman he loved—wild with need—a need *he'd* created inside her. "If you ask me nicely, and part your folds, I'll use my mouth on you and suck that pretty red clit and make you come."

* * * *

Another rush of heat went through her, the sharp sizzling stabs of pleasure only making her more desperate for release. "Please, Master. Suck my clit. Suck my clit." She could only imagine how she looked, lying there with her legs spread, holding her folds parted wide and begging for Hoyt to use his mouth on her, but she didn't care. Mindless with need, she cared about only one thing—and she knew by the way Jake had stepped aside, she had to count on Hoyt to give it to her.

"Please, Master." Thrilled at his low growl each time she called him Master, she did it again and again. "Please, Master. Help me."

She would swear she could almost hear Hoyt's control snap.

With a harsh curse, he reached for her, spreading her thighs wide and burying his face between them.

His hot mouth moved on her clit with a rough possessiveness, one that suited her mood perfectly. Licking and sucking her clit, he gave her just what she needed—the friction against her sensitive and tender bundle of nerves almost more than she could bear.

Between one harsh breath and the next, the pleasure inside her exploded.

Crying out at the intense rush of heat, Nat rode the waves of release, arching into Hoyt's touch, her entire body trembling with sensation.

Lifting his head, Hoyt looked down at her, his eyes seeming lit from within. He continued to manipulate her clit, the slow, gentle slide of his finger over it dragging her orgasm out and leaving her weak and breathless.

She'd come at his hand, and while Jake had been watching.

Oh, God.

Blinking back tears, Nat tried to curl into a ball, feeling more vulnerable than she could ever remember feeling.

"Hey, you don't have to hide from me." Before she knew it, Hoyt lifted her, turned her in his arms, and settled her on his lap, wrapping both arms around her and pulling her close.

Pushing her hair back from her face, he smiled down at her. "You've always been beautiful—so beautiful." Running a hand up and down her back, he pulled her closer with a hand on her thigh. "When you let yourself go, you were stunning. I knew from the first time I kissed you that I was in big trouble."

Surprised that someone like Hoyt would not only feel such a thing, but admit it to her, Nat stared up at him in awe. "Hoyt—"

Bending, he touched his lips to hers, effectively silencing her. His eyes gleamed with lust and satisfaction, the love in them and in his smile making her pulse trip. "Now, Natalie, you take my breath away."

Nat swallowed heavily and glanced at Jake, her eyes welling with tears. "I can't believe you said that. I can't believe you feel that way. Shit, I hate when I'm mushy like this. Let me up."

"Not yet." Smiling at her, Hoyt nuzzled her hair, his hands moving over her trembling body and warming her. "I want to hold you."

"I can't believe that just happened." Nat groaned and dropped her head to his chest, looking toward Jake, who approached and knelt at her side.

* * * *

Hoyt took her hand in his and lifted it to his lips, willing his cock to behave. "Believe it. It wasn't the first time I put you over my knee, was it, honey?" Memories of the light, playful spankings he'd given her in the past paled in comparison to what had happened tonight.

Shaken by the depth of emotion he felt for her, Hoyt cupped her jaw and lifted her face, his chest swelling at the love shining in her dark eyes. "You were so surprised that it excited you." Touching his lips to hers, he ran his thumb over the palm of her hand. "It excited me, too."

With a small smile, Jake slid his fingers over her hair. "So that's why she objected so much the first time I spanked her—and why she got so aroused."

To Hoyt's delight, Natalie's face turned beet red. Lifting the hand he held, he wrapped her arm around his neck. "Were you thinking of me?"

Nat slapped at both of them, backing away, her eyes darting back and forth between them, a slightly desperate look in them. "Please don't do this."

Cupping her face, he lifted it to his, searching her eyes for a clue to what made her uncomfortable. "Do what, baby?"

The sparkle of tears in her eyes weakened his knees. "I'm so scared of hurting either one of you. I'm scared of messing this up. I'm scared you're not going to stay. I'm scared that you are."

Pushing out of his arms, she got to her feet, wrapping her arms around herself as if needing comfort.

He started to get to his feet to go to her, but she shook her head and moved away.

"I'm sorry. I'm just a little shaken. Having both of you here…" Her gaze kept sliding to Jake's.

Hoyt's hands trembled as he struggled to suppress his own fears. "There's nothing to be sorry about. I think we're all a little overwhelmed, but I sure as hell wasn't going to let you get away with avoiding a fight with me as if you're afraid of driving me away. I can handle your temper, Natalie, and all of your moods—as long as I know that you love me. You're going to have to deal with my moods, too, and I don't want to feel like I'm walking on eggshells around you."

Humbled by the tears brimming in her eyes, and wondering just how many people knew what a softie she was underneath her usual brass, Hoyt got to his feet and went to her, pleased that she didn't back away. Not wanting to alarm her, he ran a finger down her arm, instead of gathering her close the way he wanted to. "There won't be any more secrets between us. Jake and I didn't handle this as well as we should have, but we didn't want to bring you into it until we'd settled things between us."

Jake closed in on her from behind, his lips against her neck making her shiver, much to Hoyt's delight. "We begin here and now."

Fisting a hand in her hair, Jake pulled her head back, exposing her vulnerable and extremely delectable neck. "Deal?"

Natalie's eyes closed on a moan, but not before Hoyt saw the hunger swirling in them. "Deal."

Hoyt's cock stirred again at her husky tone, but the need for relief was secondary to caring for Natalie.

His sub.

His woman.

His life.

To his surprise, he got a great deal of pleasure watching Jake arouse her. Following the slide of Jake's hand to her belly made Hoyt's cock's thicken and lengthen even more.

Tilting her head back, Jake scraped his teeth over her neck, making Natalie cry out and shiver again. "And no more yelling at Hoyt for not telling you he'd been shot, or at me for not telling you about this sooner. We've both apologized. Repeatedly. Unless of course, you don't want me to accept your apologies in the future."

Hoyt watched in fascination as Natalie's eyes flew open, the slight edge of alarm in them a direct contrast to the renewed need that darkened her eyes and had her arching her breasts higher in invitation.

To his further surprise and delight, she reached up to wrap her arms around Jake's neck, leaning back against him as she stared up at Hoyt, her submissive posture so arousing, it stunned him.

Her smile, filled with challenge, taunted him. "No. I accept your apology."

Jake slid his hand higher, lifting her sweater out of the way, and tugging at her nipples, eliciting a cry from her that made Hoyt's cock leak moisture. "And no sulking."

Hoyt couldn't resist. He reached out to slide a finger down her jaw, his breath catching at her low moan.

Staring up at him with eyes slightly unfocused, Natalie moaned again. "No sulking."

Fascinated by her response, Hoyt shifted restlessly, his cock pressing painfully against his jeans.

"I guess that's settled, then." Jake met Hoyt's gaze, his own laced with amusement and dark with desire. "Our Nat needs a firm hand."

Hoyt gripped her chin, running his thumb over her bottom lip. "She always did."

Wishing he could spend the night making love to her, but knowing that it wasn't the right time, Hoyt grimaced and released her. "It's been a long day. I'll see both of you in the morning. I think she needs *you* now."

He had a lot to think about, and needed some time to come to grip with his own intense feelings for her.

Pleased by the disappointment in Natalie's eyes, Hoyt made his way to the bathroom, hoping that after a long shower and the chance to give his body the relief he needed, he'd be able to sleep. He'd had so many sleepless nights in the last several weeks, the anticipation of seeing Natalie again and her reaction to his presence making him too restless to relax.

His future with Natalie seemed even brighter than ever, and he found himself looking forward to tomorrow in a way he hadn't for a long time.

Finally, the woman he loved was back in his life.

And she loved him.

With a sigh, he stepped into the shower.

He'd made progress with her, but his own feelings stunned him.

She was in his life again, but he still had a long way to go toward the life he wanted with her.

Chapter Six

Supporting his wife's slight weight, Jake cupped her breasts from behind and bent to scrape his teeth over her soft neck, breathing in her sweet scent. "Hoyt's in the shower, probably jerking off. It won't do him much good, though."

Sliding a hand down her body, he parted her folds and tapped her clit, smiling at her soft, hungry cry. "He won't be able to forget the sight of that gorgeous, plugged ass draped over his lap. Nothing will satisfy him except having you."

Wrapping an arm around her waist, he continued to manipulate her clit, carefully keeping his touch light and slow—enough to arouse her, but not enough to allow her to go over.

The need to have his wife's attention focused on him—to hear her cry his name—wouldn't be denied.

Her quivering body rubbed against his, her moans of pleasure and growing arousal making his cock so hard it hurt. "Why didn't he take me then?"

Chuckling softly at her indignant tone, Jake nipped her earlobe. "That's something you're going to have to ask him. You're going to have to develop your own relationship with Hoyt, without my interference."

He'd seen the look of awe and stunned amazement on Hoyt's face, the shock as the sharp possessiveness hit him hard.

It amused him to see his usually hard and controlled friend flustered as he realized that loving his submissive was nothing like just dominating a woman.

Nat had already begun to draw Hoyt in, something that Jake understood very well.

He'd long ago discovered how loving a woman who had the strength and trust to submit could turn a man's life inside out.

Jake found himself attuned to her in ways that he'd never imagined, and had a feeling that Hoyt had begun to realize just how deeply loving Nat would affect him.

Having the chance to watch them together had also taught Jake a few things. He'd been able to watch his wife, and had an unobstructed view to every inch of her while Hoyt spanked her.

Nat's eyes had been wild with pleasure before she lowered her head and let her hair hide her face from view. Being over Hoyt's lap, and unable to see what went on behind her kept her on edge more than he'd expected. When he and Hoyt began talking about her, she raised her head, biting her lip to hold back her cries in an obvious attempt to hear them.

More aroused by the minute, he'd watched her, learning more about her with every second that passed, things that he hadn't had a chance to see in the past.

She wiggled against him, crying out softly with every movement. "Jake, I need to come again. Oh, God. Please. Take me. Please."

Delighted with her, he pressed against the base of the plug. "Every time you move, this plug's shifting inside you. I know how much you like having this ass filled."

Christ, he wanted her.

He knew how tight her pussy would be with the plug inside her ass, and couldn't wait to take her with Hoyt, knowing it would be even tighter.

Holding her close, he pressed again at the plug while slipping a finger into her slick pussy. "You know that Hoyt and I are going to take you together, don't you?"

His cock jumped when she clenched on his finger and cried out again. "Don't you, baby? A cock up your ass and one in your pussy. Both fucking you."

"Oh, God!" A shiver went through her, and she slumped against him.

Nuzzling her neck, he kept his voice low and even, knowing what she needed probably better than she did.

His control.

"You like that. You like the thought of being helpless while we take you."

Trembling, she spread her legs wider and started to lower her hands. "Yes, damn you. You know what I need. Don't make me say it."

"Put your fucking hands back up." He could feel the excitement flowing through her veins, her need to feel vulnerable and helpless in this aspect of her life as she would never allow in others.

She obeyed him, but more slowly than he could accept, her need to be overcome showing itself in her defiance. "If you're not going to make me come, I'm going to do it myself."

Her insolence, especially so soon in the aftermath of watching Hoyt discipline her had Jake wild to possess her.

Recognizing her attempt to provoke him for what it was, Jake chuckled softly and slapped her still warm ass. "You trying to top from the bottom again, baby? I'm in charge here, not you."

The Dominant inside him roared, demanding satisfaction.

He knew what she wanted—knew that she wanted him to overpower her.

What *he* needed, however, was to hold her.

Pulling her tightly against him, he moved to the chair closest to the sofa and lowered himself into it, settling her across his lap. Urging her to lay her head over the padded arm, he parted her thighs and pressed his hand against her slit.

"You'll get to come, but my way. First, we need to talk."

* * * *

Nat blinked, not sure she heard him right. "Talk? I don't want to fucking talk!"

The plug in her ass drove her wild, shifting inside her every time she moved.

She bucked against his hand, moaning harshly at the pleasure from the plug moving inside her and the friction against her sensitized clit.

Feeling Jake's eyes on her only increased the pleasure, a pleasure that proved short-lived when he moved his hand away from her clit and pressed it against her abdomen to keep her from moving.

Knowing he'd keep her that way until she complied, Nat gritted her teeth and glared at him, struggling to remain still. "Fine. Talk."

The tingling in her clit drove her crazy, the air moving over it torturing her so much that she tried to close her legs against it, but a sharp slap on her inner thigh stopped her.

"Open. Now."

A shiver went through her at the ice in his command, the heat from his slap spreading to her clit and making it tingle even hotter.

Forced to keep her thighs wide made the sensation even more intense, and made it nearly impossible to stay still. She did it, though, knowing Jake wouldn't begin until she did.

Thinking of all the ways she could pay both Jake and Hoyt back for tormenting her, she fisted her hands at her sides.

And waited.

To her surprise, Jake didn't make her wait long. "How did it feel to have Hoyt touching you again?"

She studied his features, searching for any signs of anger. Finding none, she took a shuddering breath and tried to ignore the heat from his hand against her clit. "I l–liked pleasing you."

Jake's lips twitched. "You pleased me very much. Did you like knowing that I watched Hoyt put that plug in your ass and spank you? Did you like knowing how much it aroused me?"

"Um—oh!" She jolted at the slide of his finger over her clit, groaning in frustration when he stopped. "Damn it, Jake. Don't stop. I'm trying to concentrate, but my clit's driving me crazy."

"You're gonna have to try harder, then, aren't you? Focus, Nat."

She cried out when he thrust a finger into her pussy, the sharp, tingling sensation getting even stronger. "I can't take much more. I need to come."

Touching his thumb to her clit, Jake tapped a nipple, his gaze sharpening when she cried out again. "You got to come once already. You should be able to hold back a little longer."

Gripping his shirt, she lifted her head with a growl. "You know damned well I can never resist you. You know how to touch me to make me crazy."

Jake chuckled. "That I do. Now, answer my question. Did you like knowing that I watched what Hoyt did to you?"

"Yes, damn you! Yes. I liked when he touched me because I know you wanted him to and because I knew you were watching me."

Jake stroked her clit as if rewarding her. "You liked that, did you? Did you like having Hoyt see you that way?" His eyes narrowed on hers, the desire in them unmistakable. "Did you like submitting to him and letting him see just how much you like being dominated?"

"I um…" God, it was hard to think when he stroked her clit, each slow slide of his thumb taking her closer and closer to the edge.

Clenching on the plug in her ass, she swallowed heavily, struggling to gather her thoughts. "Jake, I can't think."

Gripping the base of the plug, Jake slid his finger over her clit again. "Focus. Did you like showing Hoyt what a good little submissive you are?"

Gritting her teeth, she clenched on the plug, moaning at the full, stretched feeling. "Yes! Happy?"

She couldn't take much more, her entire body shaking with the effort to remain still. "Please, Jake. Please. I'm begging."

Moving the plug from side to side, he slowly pulled it until the widest part stretched her puckered opening, raising his voice to be heard over her cries. "Hoyt liked it, too. So did I."

His strokes to her clit came faster. "You've been so good. Come for me, baby."

He'd barely gotten the words out before her body tightened, the sharp pleasure consuming her.

Stiffening, she cried out his name, clenching on the plug as he worked it free. The strokes to her clit drew her orgasm out. It went on and on, leaving her trembling and weak. Ripples of heat continued to wash over her as the strokes to her clit slowed, and with a moan, she curled against him, needing his warmth. "Jake."

Sighing his name, she let her eyes fluttered closed. A moan escaped when he murmured softly to her, wrapping his arms around her and pulling her close, enveloping her in warmth and surrounding her with his strength.

"That's it, baby. You're so sweet. So good. I love watching you fall apart in my arms."

Still trembling, she buried her face against his throat, soothed by the familiar scent of him. "I love you so much." Weak and trembling, she gripped his shirt. "So much."

"Hmm." His lips touched her hair. "I love you, too, baby. You're my life."

Flattening a hand on his chest, she opened her eyes and stared at the far wall. "Are you mad at me?"

"For what?"

Smiling at the confusion in his voice, she tilted her head back to look up at him, grateful for the strong arm supporting her. "For responding that way to Hoyt."

Shaking his head, Jake smiled and ran a finger over her shoulder. "Of course not." Lifting her chin when she would have lowered her head again, he stared down at her, the love and indulgence in his eyes easing the knot in her stomach. "You haven't done anything wrong."

Pulling her close again, he sighed. "I have to admit that I'm a little surprised at how you respond to Hoyt."

Stiffening, Nat jerked upright, her stomach knotting in fear. "Jake, I knew this would happen. I—"

"Shh." Jake pulled her close again. "I'm also surprised at how much satisfaction I got from seeing you with him. It wasn't just physical for either one of you, and both of you included me." He blew out a breath. "Jesus. The way you looked at me when he touched you…"

Smiling, he urged her back to look down at her, taking her hand in his and running a finger over her wedding band. "You're a constant delight to me." He flashed a grin. "A pain in the ass at times—but a delight."

He caught her hand in his before she could smack him, his soft laugh like music to his ears. "Behave, brat. You've had enough tonight."

Running a finger over his soft bottom lip, Nat swallowed the lump in her throat. "Is that why you didn't make love to me, either?" Shifting restlessly, she forced a smile, searching his eyes for any sign of disapproval. "I'm beginning to think there's something wrong."

"Just the opposite." Pulling her close, he buried his face against her throat. "It looks like everything's working out just right. Just don't stop loving me."

"Never." Gripping his hair, she sighed, blinking back tears. "Nothing could ever make me stop loving you. Not even death."

* * * *

After washing his wife's back and settling her in a perfumed bath, Jake made his way to the kitchen, unsurprised to find Hoyt sitting at the table, staring down into a cup of black coffee. "I figured you'd want a beer after that."

"Coffee sounded better. Besides, I don't need anything else muddling my brain." Looking up, Hoyt glanced toward the doorway. "Is she okay?"

Turning to pour himself a cup of coffee, Jake smiled. "She's fine. I held her for a while and we talked some. Washed her back." Facing Hoyt again, he leaned back against the counter. "She was a little surprised that neither one of us made love to her, and she thought I was mad at her for responding to you."

Hoyt stiffened. "Are you?"

Shaking his head, Jake frowned. "Of course not."

With a shrug, Hoyt relaxed slightly. "I didn't know how you'd feel actually seeing me touch her. I didn't plan on it happening so soon, but I couldn't let her get away with that." Blowing out a breath, he stared at the far wall. "I was very afraid that I'd made a big mistake with her."

Clenching his jaw, Jake pushed back the anger. "I didn't make this decision lightly, Hoyt. I know having both of us in her life is better for her." Looking toward the doorway, he smiled. "I learned something, too. I got the opportunity to watch her with you, and I saw things I wouldn't have ordinarily seen. You should have seen her face when you first turned her over your lap. The excitement. The anticipation."

Shrugging, he straightened. "Watching you with her and seeing just how much you care for her was very enlightening." He sipped from his cup, wincing at the taste of the strong brew. "Christ, it's a wonder you have any stomach lining left."

Hoyt's lips twitched, but it was apparent by the way he kept glancing toward the doorway, that his mind was on Nat. "I love her. Jesus, she's something." Hoyt scrubbed a hand over his face and stared down into his cup again. "I didn't expect it to be like that." Lifting his head, he met Jake's gaze. "Thanks for taking care of her afterward. Hell. It hit me hard."

Amused, Jake smiled and dropped into the seat across from his friend. "My pleasure. You looked a little shaken. Not quite the same when you love the woman you're dominating. It's a little more intense, isn't it?"

"That's putting it mildly." Taking another sip of coffee, Hoyt glanced toward the doorway again, smiling faintly. "She likes her baths, huh?"

"She does, especially since she got involved with Jesse's business. She loves experimenting with all the scents, and she gets a kick out of the fact that I can't stop touching and sniffing her." He shrugged, his cock twitching in anticipation of his wife joining him again. "It also relaxes her." Taking another small sip of the strong coffee, he watched Hoyt over the rim. "Something on your mind?"

Smiling, Hoyt shook his head, turning back to him. "Natalie packs quite a wallop." Spreading his hands on the table, he sat back. "Look, I'm not used to sharing what I feel. I've never been good at that kind of thing, something that the women I was involved with complained about ad nauseam. I wasn't good at it when Natalie and I were together before—and I've paid dearly for it. I sure as hell don't want to make the mistake again."

He looked toward the doorway again. "I love her. I can't be happy without her. I don't want to fuck this up."

Jake smiled and got to his feet. "Then don't." Dumping his coffee into the sink, he turned. "If you love her, it'll all work out."

He hoped like hell it did. He'd taken a gamble of a lifetime, one he couldn't afford to lose.

Chapter Seven

Nat woke with a sense of anticipation, and before she even opened her eyes, her heart pounded with excitement.

Seconds later, she remembered, and knew why.

Hoyt was here.

Turning her head, she frowned, disappointed to find Jake's pillow empty.

Sitting up, she listened for any sounds that would tell her where Jake and Hoyt were, her heart beating faster when she heard their deep voices coming from the kitchen.

She smiled at the low chuckle of laughter, relieved that they seemed to be on friendly terms again. Wrapping her arms around her legs, she listened, enjoying the sounds of the voices.

She blinked back tears that would only upset them, and with an angry swipe, wiped away one that escaped. She hated crying, but she seemed to have done little else since Jake told her that Hoyt was on his way.

She definitely had to get it together.

Knowing that she'd need to be wide awake to deal with both of them, she threw the covers aside and sat up, shivering at the chill in the room against her naked flesh.

She reached for her fuzzy socks at the foot of the bed, and pulled them on before getting to her feet and reaching for her equally fuzzy robe.

The robe and socks weren't sexy, but they were warm, and that was all she cared about at the moment.

Hoyt would just have to get used to the fact that comfort was more important to her than looking sexy.

After she washed her face and brushed her teeth, she left the bathroom and started for the bedroom door, drawn by the intoxicating scent of bacon and coffee.

She scuffled down the hall, smiling as she listened to their beloved voices.

Once she got to the kitchen, she paused to lean against the doorway, her pulse tripping at the sight of both of the men she loved turning to smile at her.

"Good morning, baby." Sitting at the table sipping coffee and already dressed for work, Jake smiled, the flash of delight in his eyes thrilling her.

That look alone made her feel special every single day, and she wouldn't risk losing it for anything.

Smiling, she straightened and stepped into the room. "Good morning."

Gathering the lapels of her robe together, she held them closed in her fist as she turned to face Hoyt, who stood at the stove cooking eggs. She searched his features for any sign of tension, breathing a sigh of relief when she found none.

His smile, filled with warm indulgence raked over her before lifting to hers again. "Good morning. I heard you moving around. Your coffee's on the table and your breakfast is almost ready."

Nat grunted and made her way to the table, her sleep-deprived brain too sluggish to attempt conversation until she poured some coffee into her.

Lifting the cup to her lips, she took a sip, coming awake with a grimace as the strong coffee hit the back of her throat. "Ugh!" Setting her cup aside, she looked at Hoyt. "Your coffee's deadly."

She pulled out her chair and started to plop into it, pausing when Jake's dark brow went up.

"Where's my morning kiss?"

Nat blinked, narrowing her eyes at the amusement in his. "I woke up alone this morning. Do you really think you deserve one?"

His lips twitched. "Of course."

Hoyt turned, setting the spatula aside, a faint smile curving his lips. "Morning kiss? I want in on that."

Warmed by their teasing, she kept her expression cool, raising a brow. "Neither one of you deserve a kiss. I didn't even get fucked last night, and I had to sleep alone."

Setting his coffee aside, Jake leaned back in his chair, smiling in that coldly erotic way that sent blood rushing to every erogenous zone. "You didn't sleep alone, and you got to come. Twice. Now, I want my kiss."

When she hesitated, glancing at Hoyt to see him watching expectantly, Jake pushed his cup aside. "Now."

Nat shivered at the steely tone, knowing that Jake didn't issue idle threats, and that he would make her pay for disobeying him.

The glint of anticipation in his eyes told her that he would enjoy it—especially now.

So would she.

Her abdomen tightened, her breath catching as a rush of erotic need swelled inside her. "The two of you sat up last night talking. I couldn't hear what you were talking about, but if you've made plans that involve me, I'm not going to be as docile about them as I was before."

Jake's dark brow went up. "We talked about you, and discussed the way we're going to handle you." Smiling at her gasp, he let his gaze move over her, leaning back and sipping from his own cup. "You know, Hoyt and I have both always fantasized about sharing a woman, but we're both selfish bastards and didn't want to share."

He glanced at Hoyt, who stood watching her, his eyes sharp with hunger. "We're very much looking forward to loving you—dominating you—together."

Nat reached for her coffee cup, taking a sip of the strong brew to ease her dry throat. Finding it easier to swallow this time, she took another, needing the jolt of caffeine. "So, you're not worried about me swooning in Hoyt's arms and ditching you?"

Jake's lips twitched, his eyes steady on hers. "I was, but I realized that what I was most afraid of was the secrecy. I couldn't stand that you hid your feelings for him from me, and it drives me crazy when you get that guilty look on your face every time he touches you."

Hoyt sighed. "I can't say that I'm crazy about that either. I don't like that she hides bits and pieces of what she feels, and I sure as hell don't want her to feel guilty when she's in my arms."

Jake's eyes narrowed. "I won't tolerate your shyness or embarrassment in coming to me in front of Hoyt. You know how much I hate repeating myself, Nat. I want my kiss. Now."

Obeying him when he spoke in that low tone came as natural as breathing.

So did the rush of heat that dampened her thighs and made her nipples bead.

Never looking away from his steady gaze, she set her cup aside and took a step closer to him, and then another, her nipples tight and achy against the plush material of her robe. Moving slowly to tease both of them, she smiled and trailed her fingers over the table, aware of Hoyt's gaze raking over her as she approached Jake.

The sexual tension in the room could be cut with a knife, but it felt different than the night before. There was a playfulness and camaraderie between them that hadn't been present the previous night.

She paused in front of Jake, her pulse tripping at the dare in his eyes.

Nat lowered herself to his lap, her body's response to his mood sending another rush of moisture to coat her inner thighs. Eager for his kiss, she gripped his wide shoulders and stared at his mouth as she leaned forward and touched her lips to his.

The hands at her waist tightened, the hunger in his touch fueling her own.

Years of experience had taught her just what Jake wanted, and she did it without hesitation, pouring herself into her kiss and slipping her tongue into his mouth to tangle it with his.

As usual, he took control of their kiss almost immediately. His hands shifted and pulled her closer, readjusting her position on his lap until she straddled him.

He kissed her with a heat and desperation that made her head swim, her heart pounding furiously when his hands slid higher and inside her robe.

The feel of air on her skin only made her hotter as he loosened her belt and parted her robe.

Lifting his head, he stared into her eyes as he cupped her breasts, running his thumbs over her nipples. "Who do these beautiful breasts belong to?"

Trembling, she sucked in a breath, knowing her husband's dominant nature well. Despite his claim, she knew he would need reassurance—a reassurance she would happily give. She licked her dry lips and swallowed heavily, stiffening when she heard Hoyt move behind her. "You."

Jake smiled, rewarding her by sliding his thumbs over her nipples, and drawing a gasp from her as sharp arrows of need shot to her clit. "That's true, but now they also belong to Hoyt, don't they?"

The slide of Hoyt's hand down her back added an edge to the erotic tension, the reality of having both men touch her like something out of a dream.

A fantasy.

And she was living it.

Jake tightened his fingers on her nipples just enough to startle her. "You're not focusing. It's not like you to get flustered so easily. Answer my question."

Staring into his eyes, Nat gulped, the rush of emotion and lust making it difficult to breathe. "Yes!"

Hoyt's hands tightened on her shoulders as his lips touched her hair.

Jake smiled and tugged a nipple. "But you've been mine for so long, I think I should be the one to give them to him. Don't you agree?"

Nat blinked. "I thought you did that last night."

Jake's hand clenched on her waist. "No. Last night was about something entirely different. It was about Hoyt letting you know that he wouldn't let you get away with avoiding issues. But, he touched you because I was there. That's why he brought you out to the living room. This is about giving you permission to let him touch you when I'm not around. I know you're struggling with it."

Nat shivered in erotic delight as Jake turned a morning kiss into a decadent assault to her senses. Staring into his eyes, she saw the thrill it gave him to do this, along with the slight edge of concern as he watched her steadily, as though braced for any sign of discomfort.

Smiling reassuringly, and once again humbled by how much the wonderful man she'd married loved her, Nat ran her hands over his chest, loving the familiar feel of heat and hard muscle. "Whatever you say."

Aware of Hoyt's stillness behind her, and elated at the feel of them surrounding her, Nat smiled, clenching her hands on Jake's chest. "Master." Smiling at Hoyt's sharp intake of breath, Nat arched her back, the glint of possessiveness and power in Jake's eyes enticing her to press her breasts more firmly into his hands.

He slid one hand up to cup her cheek, his eyes flaring with heat and satisfaction when she automatically turned her face into his palm. Massaging her breast with the other hand, Jake smiled. "You're both uncomfortable touching the other in front of me, and you'd both be consumed by guilt if you did anything while I wasn't around. We need to fix that."

Nat turned her head to look at Hoyt, her stomach clenching at the look in his eyes.

His eyes seemed to gleam with a combination of love, heat and possessiveness as his gaze lowered to the hand Jake held on her breast.

"She's skittish around me. I thought last night would have settled that, but I don't want her worried that she'd angered you by getting pleasure from my touch." His eyes lifted to hers. "I can't stand the look of guilt in her eyes when I touch her."

Jake chuckled. "I'd take off her robe, but she always gets chilled in the morning."

Hoyt smiled. "I'll remember that. I'll do whatever necessary to keep her nice and warm."

Turning her face toward his, Jake ran his thumb over her bottom lip, branding her with every touch. "I've fantasized about sharing you in the past, but I was always too possessive. I could never share you with anyone but Hoyt. Hoyt tells me that he feels the same way. Now, we both have you. Now we can show you how it feels to be loved by two men. Are you going to let us have our fantasy, baby? Are you going to let us give you yours?"

Her own need to please Jake would have been enough incentive for her to say yes, but her love for both of them, and the excitement of living her own fantasy brought tears to her eyes.

She'd never loved him more.

Smiling, she cupped his jaw. "I'd do anything for you."

The flare of heat and possessiveness in his eyes thrilled her. "Good girl."

He ran his hand over her hair, the other at her breast. "Look at Hoyt." His tone brooked no argument.

Sliding a hand under her robe to her back, Jake pulled her closer, his other hand still massaging her breast. "Hoyt, you really didn't get to see too much of her last night. Would you like to see her breasts?"

Hoyt's eyes narrowed, his lips curving in a slow, tender smile. "I'd like nothing more."

Exposing her breasts to Hoyt's heated gaze, Jake ran his fingers over the upper curve of her left breast, smiling at her moan. "Her breasts are very sensitive."

Hoyt's eyes warmed, filled with tender indulgence. "I always had to be very careful with her nipples."

Sliding a hand to the underside of her breast, Jake cupped it, his eyes on hers as if daring her to object. "Would you like to touch them?"

Hoyt's eyes narrowed, dropping to her breasts again. "Absolutely."

Trembling, Nat tightened her hands on Jake's shirt, her nipple tingling in anticipation.

Her own sexuality stunned her.

She'd always loved the way Jake made her feel, the way his eyes glittered with delight as he explored her making her feel ridiculously feminine.

Desired, but more.

Owned—but in a way that made her feel like a valued possession.

Seeing that same hunger in Hoyt's eyes, Nat gulped in air, her entire body tingling with pinpricks of awareness.

Watching Hoyt's hand move closer, she stiffened, sucking in a breath and jolting at the first touch of a finger against her beaded nipple.

"Be still." Jake's low growl, accompanied by a sharp slap to her bottom, sent another surge of hunger through her as Hoyt smiled and closed his forefinger and thumb on her nipple.

The slight pinch sent a wave of electricity through her, a burst of sizzling sensation that centered at her slit.

Hoyt's eyes narrowed at her soft cry, the heat in them making them gleam. "Keep your hands on Jake's chest." Watching her eyes, he tugged at her nipple. "I've watched her grow from an insecure, frightened young woman to a confident, self-assured one. Every time I saw her, I wanted her even more."

Jake pushed her hair back and toyed with her other nipple, the dual sensation making it increasingly difficult to remain still. "When her mother died, and her father crawled into a bottle, it shook her, especially since she felt responsible for Jesse."

Uncomfortable with their conversation and reminder of that time, Nat opened her mouth to change the subject, but a sharp look from Jake had her snapping it closed again.

"Not one word. Be still." Stroking her nipple, he continued on, the knowledge of what their touch did to her darkening his eyes. "Now, she's strong enough to be a remarkable submissive, something that she fought for years until she realized she couldn't fight her own body's needs."

Hoyt tapped her nipple, seemingly enthralled each time she moaned or cried out. "I always knew she would be a good submissive, but you've given her a confidence that makes her a magnificent one."

Fisting her hands on Jake's chest, she fought not to move as the tingling in her clit became almost unbearable.

Hoyt grinned and lightly caressed her nipple. "She's too passionate to deny herself. Controlling her with her own pleasure has always been a dream of mine. She fights it." His eyes narrowed, glittering with challenge. "It's in her eyes. She doesn't submit easily at all, does she?"

Jake chuckled. "She's learned that I won't let her get away with defying me. When she gets in a mood, she fights the pleasure and tries to top from the bottom." Shrugging, he smiled as he ran a fingertip over her nipple. "I never let her get away with it, but it's fun when she tries."

Hoyt glanced at Jake. "When she fights the pleasure, do you make her come until she begs you to stop?"

Jake grinned. "And beyond. Of course, the threat of not being allowed to come at all is what's keeping her still right now."

Glaring at him, Nat dug her short nails into his chest, smiling in satisfaction when he winced.

With a cool smile of his own, he retaliated by closing his finger and thumb on her nipple. "Brat. She dug her nails into my chest, and if I allowed her to speak, she'd use the excuse that she was so overwhelmed, she didn't know what she was doing."

Hoyt chuckled softly, his eyes never leaving hers. "Oh, she knows what she did all right, and she did it on purpose." He tugged her nipple. "Those expressive eyes have driven me wild for years. She can't hide anything, can she?"

Closing a hand over her breast, Jake massaged gently. "No, to my unending delight."

Nat arched into their touch, the slide of Jake's hand up and down her spine, and the firm pressure of their fingers on her nipples making her pussy clench as the hunger grew.

Jake's hand settled on her bottom, squeezing gently. "Over the years, I've managed to work up her tolerance for pain in her nipples. I have several sets of nipple clips for her, and have adjusted them so that the pressure is firm enough to keep them on, but not to hurt her too much. A little pain there drives her wild, but I always have to be careful with her."

Hoyt pursed his lips, his gaze focused on her nipple as if imagining the clips on her. "I'd like to see that for myself. She's always been so sensitive there." Hoyt applied more pressure, the slight pain sending a rush of need to her slit. Lifting his gaze to hers, he smiled when she moaned and arched her back to thrust her breasts out. "She's delicate, but doesn't see herself that way, does she?"

Lifting a hand to her cheek, Jake locked his gaze with hers, his eyes warm with appreciation. "Not at all. I've always found the combination of sweet femininity and strength irresistible."

Hoyt slid his hand over the outer curve of her breast, the awe and wonder in his eyes bringing tears to hers. "Definitely irresistible." Closing his hand over her breast, he squeezed gently, running his palm back and forth over her nipple, his eyes narrowed on hers.

"Oh, God." She threw her head back, crying out at the feel of both of their hands on her breasts. Fisting her hands tighter in Jake's shirt, she rocked against him, desperate for friction against her clit.

Another sharp slap on her ass made Nat jolt, the tug at her nipple sending another wave of erotic heat through her.

Jake's eyes glittered with a possessiveness and excitement she hadn't seen in a long time. "I trained you better than that. I told you to be still. It looks like we're going to have to intensify your training again so that you can show Hoyt what a good girl you can be. Don't embarrass me by disobeying me again."

Shocked at Jake's dominant demeanor, Nat realized how easy he'd been with her. Delighted with the thrill in his eyes, she wanted desperately to fulfill the hunger she saw in them and surrender to him in ways he hadn't demanded in a long time.

Her face burned at her lapse, and she found herself drifting in to the world he'd created for them so many years ago, slipping into the submissive role that now fit her like a glove. She smiled at him, letting her love and trust in him show in her eyes.

After giving her the chance to have it all, he deserved that and more from her, but the knowledge of all the pleasure she'd receive in return made it an irresistible lure. Arching to give Hoyt better access, she met the flare of heat in Jake's eyes and gave him an impish grin. "I'm sorry. I won't embarrass you."

The glitter of relief and possessive hunger in Jake's eyes told her she'd said the right thing.

"Whatever you want is yours. *I'm* yours."

Jake rubbed her bottom, his slow smile filled with deep satisfaction. His eyes never left hers as he slid his hand from her breast, clearly enjoying himself. "And now you're going to belong to both of us. I'm sure Hoyt's anxious to see the rest of you. I want you to be a good girl for me and show him that sweet pussy."

Nat bit her lip to hold back a moan, her stomach clenching in excitement. The robe still covered her abdomen and mound, but she knew that it wouldn't stay that way much longer.

Hoyt gently massaged her breast, his eyes taking on a possessiveness that made her wonder again just what kind of lover he would be. "Very anxious. Her breasts are beautiful. Soft. Firm. So sensitive. Like her ass. I can't wait to explore the rest of her."

Leaning closer, Hoyt cupped her other breast and toyed with her nipple. "She used to get aroused when I spanked her, but nothing like last night. Is that usual?"

Jake chuckled softly. "Yes, she loves her spankings. She gets sassy when she wants one or feels neglected."

Nat smiled. "You never neglect me. Sometimes I just want to get your attention."

Jake smiled, watching Hoyt's hands move over her breasts. "You always have my attention, baby."

Hoyt leaned closer, sliding his thumb back and forth over her nipple. "And you have mine." Smiling, he tapped her nipple, his jaw clenching at her soft cry.

Jake shook his head. "She needs a firm hand, though. I give in to her too often."

Hoyt pressed a thumb against her bottom lip, forcing her to part them as he moved closer. "I can't say that I blame you."

He brushed his lips against hers, lifting his head to stare down in to her eyes again. "I never got a chance to take her very far. She was so young and inexperienced. A virgin. Taking her virginity was the most exciting thing I've ever done. I wanted to take her further, but we ran out of time, didn't we, love?" The fascination in his eyes sucked her in, the memories of the time they'd spent as young lovers rushing back with a speed that made her dizzy.

Lifting her chin, he held her gaze. "She's had some time to think about the implications of belonging to both of us. I need to hear her say that she still wants this."

Licking her lips, she stared into his eyes, love and need for both of them making it difficult to speak. "Yes." It came out as a hoarse whisper, but she knew they both heard her.

Hoyt smiled, his eyes hooded and dark with emotion as his rough palm moved over her breast again. "A new beginning." Lowering his head, he took her mouth with his in a gentle kiss, but one that still held the mark of possession.

Forcing her lips to part, he swept his tongue inside, the taste of coffee and Hoyt so familiar and yet so new and exotic. Swallowing her moan, he deepened his kiss, his hand moving softly over her breast, the friction of his rough palm over her nipple intensifying the ache that heated her slit.

Through it, she felt Jake watching her, felt his touch as his hand moved up and down her bottom with a warm, firm caress filled with possessiveness and encouragement.

Hoyt explored her mouth with a thoroughness that left her senses reeling, and with an erotic edge that hadn't been there before.

A hunger stronger and more potent than it had been in the past.

A strong, masculine possessiveness that pulled at something deep inside her.

Lifting his head, he stared down at her. "I didn't think it could be any better than before, but it is."

Jake grinned, no longer as tense as he'd been earlier. "It's going to get even better." Jake slid his hand higher to capture her hair in a fist and pull her head back, her position arching her breasts out to both of them. "Last night, Hoyt didn't get to explore you the way he wanted. Just relax and let him get reacquainted with your body. Let him see how beautiful you are."

A moan escaped at the feel of both of their hands sliding over her skin, the anticipation in both of their sharp, hooded gazes sending her arousal soaring. "Yes."

Hoyt grinned as he straightened, circling the table, and helping Jake turn her to face him.

With his chest hot against her back, Jake pressed a hand to her belly, surrounding her with heat. "Lean back against me. I want to see everything." Kissing her temple when she obeyed him, Jake parted her robe, baring her mound to Hoyt's gaze, running his hand over it possessively. "Isn't she beautiful?"

To her surprise, Hoyt knelt in front of her, running his finger over one of the stretch marks on her belly. Glancing up at her, he swallowed heavily, a look of awe in his eyes. "I left my mark on you, didn't I, love?"

Jake cupped her breast, massaging gently. "I used to put cream on her breasts and her belly while she was pregnant. That's how I got her accustomed to my touch."

Hoyt ran his fingers over each pale line, looking up at her as he bent to kiss each one. Glancing at Jake, he smiled faintly. "Thank you."

Jake nuzzled her temple. "Thank you for giving her to me."

"And now we both have her." Hoyt ran his fingers over her waxed mound, sending a sharp jolt of electricity straight to her slit. "I like her bare. Thank God I didn't know about this. I never would have gotten any sleep." Lifting his gaze to hers, he kept his fingertips moving over her mound. "So soft. How does it feel to be bare, Natalie?"

Fisting her hands at her sides, she moaned and arched, her thighs trembling. "It feels good. It's very sensitive. Jake makes me stay waxed and I love it." Not until Hoyt's brow went up did she realize the defensiveness in her tone.

His smile fell, his eyes narrowing with intent. "I love it, too. Let me see you."

Nat stiffened, wondering if he could mean what she thought he meant.

Jake's fingers tightened on her nipple. "Open those legs and spread your folds. Show Hoyt how beautiful you are. Show him that sweet pussy and clit."

Tilting her head, she looked up at Jake, studying his expression. "Jake, are you sure?"

Understanding her, Jake smiled, a slow smile filled with love and reassurance. Cupping her face, he ran his thumb over her lips. "I'm sure, baby. You trust me, don't you?"

"Always." She touched her tongue to his thumb, smiling at the flash of desire in his eyes. "I'd trust you with my life."

Touching his lips to her hair, he hugged her close. "Good girl. Now, spread yourself and show him that beautiful pussy."

Nat gasped at the sharp tug to her nipple, and with shaking hands, rushed to obey the husband she adored. Parting her folds, she looked into Hoyt's eyes, stunned by the appreciation in them.

Obviously enjoying her predicament as much as he enjoyed exploring her, Hoyt gave her a mischievous smile. "Wider, honey."

With the sense that she'd seriously underestimated him, Nat obeyed him with shaking hands, her clit screaming for attention.

Trailing his finger from her mound to her clit, Hoyt wrapped his other hand around her thigh, spreading her wider. "Hmm. Very pretty. You're drenched, darling. You like being explored, don't you? You like showing off this pussy. I don't blame you. It's beautiful."

He met Jake's steady gaze over her shoulder, the relief and emotion in his eyes like a powerful jolt to her system. "She's trembling under my touch." His voice broke, a muscle working in his jaw as he visibly fought for control.

The thought that a man like Hoyt could be so nervous that his hands shook when he touched her, and so moved that she wanted him, had Nat falling in love with him all over again.

Releasing her folds, she reached one hand back to cup Jake's jaw and the other toward Hoyt. "I want both of you. I love both of you. If we screw this up, I'm never going to recover from it."

Jake took her hand in his, kissing her fingers before releasing it. "Then we won't screw it up." His eyes glittered with tenderness. "Now, spread those folds and show Hoyt that pretty clit."

Obeying him, she parted her folds under Hoyt's watchful gaze, her clit tingling hotter. Crying out at the first touch of Hoyt's finger on the swollen bundle of nerves, she wrapped her legs around Jake's in an effort to remain still, pushing the tops of her feet against his calves. "Oh, God. Oh, God."

Holding her securely, Jake cupped both breasts, running his thumbs almost negligently back and forth over her nipples. "She loves being explored." He slid his hands lower, gripping her thighs and pulling them back against her chest and wide. "I want you to stay still and let Hoyt play with you."

Shocked at this new side to her husband, Nat sucked in a breath, her stomach and thigh muscles quivering with the effort to remain still as Hoyt continued to manipulate her clit. Staring down at Hoyt, Nat took several sharp breaths as his finger slid lower, her entire body shaking.

A cry escaped when he plunged it into her pussy and began to thrust it inside her, the friction against her inner walls almost more than she could bear. Clenching on his finger, Nat fought not to come, pushing her legs against Jake's hold.

Determined to prove to them and to herself that she could be what they needed, she bit her lip in an effort to hold back her cries, jolting when Hoyt slid a finger over her clit again.

"Oh, God." Shuddering with pleasure, she clamped down on Hoyt's finger, pushing back against Jake.

Hoyt grinned and withdrew, his gaze steady on hers as he circled her pussy opening before plunging his finger into her again. "I've had a lot of time to imagine the kinds of things I want to do to you." He withdrew and plunged his finger into her again, moving faster and with increased firmness, his watchful gaze narrowing at her hoarse cries of pleasure. "Ways I want to take you."

Bending his head, he kissed her clit, the sharp, hot tingling warning her that she couldn't hold back much longer. "Ways I want to take care of you." Looking up at Jake, he smiled. "I can understand why you spoil her. I have a feeling I'm going to be just as bad."

Jake nuzzled her temple. "Yes, I'm afraid I've spoiled her. She's easy to spoil. She's always so giving and as tough as she tries to make everyone believe she is, she's a softie underneath."

Nat groaned and sucked in a breath, gritting her teeth as she fought the pleasure. "I am not."

Jake sighed. "Yes, you're definitely spoiled. She's so unbelievably sweet."

Hoyt smiled and withdrew his finger. "I found out how sweet. The thought of it kept me up most of the night. I'd love to taste her again. I think I'm already addicted."

"Oh, God." A surge of sizzling heat went through her as a series of small orgasms made her senses reel.

Her toes curled at the effort to remain still under Hoyt's tongue's slow exploration of her slit.

So hot. So wicked. So intense.

His tongue moved slowly, tracing her folds and pussy opening, followed by sudden rapid flicks of it over her clit that threatened the small amount of control she had left.

He licked her as if he had all day to explore her slit with his devious tongue, and planned to enjoy every second of it.

Without warning, he focused his attention on her clit, the shock of sharp pleasure stunning her.

The quick flicks of Hoyt's tongue gave her the friction exactly where she needed it, and with the perfect amount of pressure.

Gasping, she stiffened, crying out in anticipation as the warning tingles grew hotter, crying out again in frustration when he lifted his head.

"No! Please don't stop. Please don't stop."

"Shh, baby. We'll get there." Hoyt ran his hands up and down her thighs. "Did you think I couldn't tell you were close? You really can't hold back at all, can you? Easy, baby. We'll make it even better. Now that you've had a minute to settle, we'll start again."

Moan after moan poured from her as the tension inside her built, each caress of Jake's hands over her breasts and stroke of Hoyt's tongue over her slit pushing her closer to orgasm.

Each time she thought one more flick of Hoyt's tongue would send her over, he paused and focused his attention on her thighs, pulling her from the edge just to start over again.

Each time, the need got sharper.

Hoyt nipped her thigh. "Stop squirming. You're not coming yet."

The heat, the dominance of it drove her wild.

God, she loved a man who wasn't afraid of going for what he wanted— a man in control.

"No, Natalie. Keep those legs spread." Hoyt kept his hand on her belly, holding her in place while thrusting a finger into her pussy. "She's soaked, Jake, and her pussy's milking my finger. I think our little sub's getting ready to come."

Hoyt slid his finger from her pussy and pressed it against her puckered opening. "I can't resist. Years ago, I didn't have the chance to work up to taking her ass. She was so skittish then that every time I touched her like this, she jerked away."

"She won't this time." Jake tightened the arm around her waist. "She's going to stay perfectly still and let you do whatever you want."

Nat's mind couldn't seem to process all of the pleasure, the physical and mental stimulation of their conversation overloading her senses.

A breathless whimper escaped, her breath coming out in sharp pants as Hoyt began to push his finger into her. The sharp sting had her tightening on his finger in an instinctive urge to close against him.

Hoyt's low chuckle excited her more. "You really don't think you're going to be able to keep me out, do you? I'm breaching this ass, Natalie." Although he'd barely raised his voice, the underlying steel in his tone spoke of years of being in command.

She'd be willing to bet that not many people had ever disobeyed him.

Whimpering with excitement and the effort it cost her to hold back her orgasm, Nat sucked in a breath, her stomach clenching when he ran his finger over her puckered opening, his gaze hot on her tender flesh.

"Very pretty."

Jake's lips touched her hair. "Isn't she? I love playing with that ass, and she's so tight. She's been trained to tighten on your finger or your cock while you're fucking her ass, and the feeling's incredible. Show him, baby." His fingers closed on her nipples, tugging lightly.

With no warning, Hoyt thrust his finger deep, and started fucking her ass with it, giving her no time to adjust.

She tried to clench on him, but the attention to her nipples made her movements clumsy, not nearly as graceful as Jake had taught her.

Jake sighed. "It seems she's going to need a lot of work on her concentration. It's something that hasn't been this much of an issue in the past."

Hoyt withdrew and added a second finger, pressing them deep and forcing her puckered opening to stretch to accommodate him, sending chills of pleasure up and down her spine. "I'm looking forward to it. Yes, that's a good girl. She's clenching hard. You've trained her well with that. Is she as good with her mouth? She and I never got that far."

Jake laughed softly and ran his hands over her, his tone filled with affection. "She's magnificent with her mouth. She tries to use it to get the upper hand. I've never minded, because it's so damned adorable, and it feels so good. She'll try with you, too. She never stops trying to take control."

"That won't be allowed with me." The icy steel in Hoyt's tone sent another shiver of delight through her.

"Good. Then we're on the same page with that." Jake ran a hand down her side. "What do you think of our baby's ass?"

"Fucking incredible. I thought I must have been mistaken about last night, but you're right. Whenever her ass is breached, she's damned near helpless." He withdrew almost all the way and surged his fingers deep again. "I can't imagine what she'll be like when I work my cock into her."

Hoyt thrust deep again, the force and fullness of it sending warning tingles to her clit.

Jake studied her features. "I know, baby. You want to come." Cupping her cheek, he ran his thumb over her bottom lip. "I know how hard it is for you to wait. It's my fault for spoiling you so much."

"I can't. Please." She started rocking her hips in time to Hoyt's thrusts, crying out as the pleasure sharpened.

Jake smiled. "Hoyt's really working that ass, isn't he baby? I know how much you like that. He couldn't believe how you responded last night."

As Hoyt slid his fingers free, Nat gulped and nodded, so close to coming that she could barely focus on Jake's words, her ass clenching at emptiness. "Please, Jake. I need to come. I can't stand it." The awareness in her ass still lingered, driving her crazy with lust.

Gripping her jaw, Jake tapped her nipple. "Behave. You've been getting away with a lot because I'm so much in love with you that I can't even think sometimes, but I can't let it get in the way of what you so obviously need. Stand up and show me that pussy."

On shaky legs, Nat slowly rose to her feet, stunned by the change in her husband. Spreading her legs the way she knew he wanted, she reached down and parted her folds, holding herself open and shivering at the feel of air moving over her clit. Holding her breath as he reached for her, Nat locked her knees, unable to hold back a cry when he plunged a finger into her.

"You're drenched. You obviously need this. I've been too lenient. I'm sorry, baby. I haven't given you what you needed, have I?"

Nat shook her head abruptly, sucking in a breath when he moved his finger inside her before withdrawing it, leaving her empty and needy. "No! You give me everything I need."

Jake shook his head, clearly not convinced. "Get up on the table, baby."

Hoyt and Jake helped her on to the kitchen table, laying her back against the hard, cool surface. As if they'd planned it, each man took one of her feet in his hand as they stood side by side between her legs, spreading her wide.

Excitement bubbled through her veins as their gazes raked over her, the thought of the pleasure to come making her knees weak.

Nat cried out at the first touch of Jake's finger on her clit, so aroused that the first warning tingles began almost immediately.

"Come, baby."

"Oh, God!" Nat screamed as it hit her, her body bowing as the strong wave of tingling heat washed over her. Another wave followed and then another, each less intense than the last, but lasting longer. Hoarse from screaming Jake's name, Nat bucked her hips, thrashing her head from side to side until his strokes slowed. Jolting at each slide of his finger over her too-sensitized clit, Nat whimpered and fought to close her legs against the too-intense sensations. "Please, Jake. No more. No more."

Lifting his hand, Jake smiled down at her as he lowered his head, flattening his tongue as he slid it over her slit. "Good girl. You be good today." He reached for her, but Hoyt stopped him with a hand on his arm.

"No. I want to take care of her." Running a hand down her back, he pulled her closer. "I need to hold her. I need this part, too."

After a slight hesitation, Jake nodded, picking up her coffee cup. "All of this before you even had your morning coffee." He dumped her coffee into the sink and poured her a new one, setting it on the table next to her before bending to touch his lips to hers. Running a finger down her cheek, he smiled. "I love you, baby. I'll see you later."

"I love you, too."

Turning as he shrugged into his jacket, Jake smiled again, his eyes filled with tenderness. "I know, baby. I know."

Nat watched Jake leave before turning back to Hoyt, her face burning under his unwavering stare. Looking away, she started to slide from the table, stilling when Hoyt tightened his arms around her. "Be still. Let me."

He bundled her back into her robe before lifting her from the table and sitting down, settling her on his lap and pulling her coffee closer.

"Here, baby. Have your coffee. As soon as you settle down, I'll fix you some breakfast." He kissed her hair, cuddling her against him.

Slumped against his chest, Nat sipped her coffee, hardly able to believe how quickly her life had changed.

Hoyt pushed the edge of the robe aside and slid a hand into it, caressing her breast and belly as if to remind her that she belonged to him now, too—as if, now that he could touch her freely, he couldn't stop. "You okay, baby? You're awfully quiet. Please don't tell me you're having second thoughts." Lifting her chin, he smiled down at her, but the tension in his eyes spoke volumes. "You wouldn't want to make a Navy SEAL cry, would you?"

Nat shook her head, laughing softly. "No. I wouldn't want to be the one to ruin your kick-ass reputation."

Hoyt ran a hand down her back. "Yeah, well I've always had a weakness. She stands about five four, can curse as well as any sailor I've ever met, has soft, shiny hair, a way of looking at a man that can make him forget his own name, a body that doesn't quit, and a hard, prickly shell that she thinks hides the core of sweet femininity underneath."

His soft words, so unlike him, made her nervous.

Frowning, she sat up, setting her coffee aside. "I'm not soft, and neither are you." Crossing her arms over her chest, she lifted her chin. "We're alone now. Do you want to tell me what you're really doing here? Is something wrong? Are you in some kind of trouble? Are you doing this because of Joe?"

Hoyt stiffened. "I've never lied to you, Natalie. I'm here because I still love you. I tried like hell to stop loving you, but I can't. You're the mother of my son. I belong here."

Alarmed at the cold anger in his voice, Nat shrugged and slid from his lap. She pulled her robe tighter, already missing his warmth. "You don't even know me anymore. If you want to be here for Joe, that's one thing, but—"

Hoyt moved so fast that she didn't have time to do anything more than blink before he reached her. Gripping her upper arms, he raised her to her toes, his expression hard with fury. "Damn it, Natalie! I told you why I'm here. Don't brush what I feel for you aside. If you didn't love me anymore, that would be different, but you do."

Wrapping his arms around her waist, he lifted her to the counter and pushed her thighs wide to make a place for himself between them. Holding her close, he shocked her by burying his face against her neck. "Thank God, you do. I don't know what I would have done if I came back to find you no longer loved me. The thought of it gave me nightmares."

Speechless, Nat could only hold on to him, her heart in her throat.

She really wanted to believe.

Wrapping her arms around his neck, she held him close, blinking back tears. "If you change your mind and decide you don't love the woman I've become, I'll kill you."

Lifting his head, he touched his lips to hers in a tender kiss that brought tears to her eyes. "I know you, Natalie. I know you. Every time I visited, I fell deeper in love with you. So strong. So sweet. So incredibly beautiful. You're everything I ever wanted."

Tears blurred her vision, the surge of love for him making it hard to breathe. Blinking them away, she sniffed, and hurried to lighten the mood. "You're turning me into a blubbering mess."

Hoyt smiled indulgently. "I'm honored that I'm one of the few people on earth who can do that." Touching his lips to hers again, he held her face between his hands, using his thumbs to wipe away the two tears that had escaped. "Since you're uncomfortable, and desperately trying to change the subject—are you ready for some breakfast? I make great omelets."

Nat couldn't even think about eating with the butterflies still fluttering in her stomach. Blinking the last of her tears away, she smiled in gratitude. "I'm not hungry. I'll eat something later with Jesse."

Hoyt frowned, lifting her face and studying her features critically. "You really should eat something. You hardly touched your dinner last night."

Shaking her head, Nat smiled and pushed his hands away. "You always did see everything. Jake's a lot like you in that respect, but I have to assume that being in the SEALs for all these years has made you even more observant."

Hoyt's lips twitched. "A bit, perhaps. I think I'm going to enjoy fussing over you, but for now, I'll give you the space you obviously need."

He moved the neckline of her robe aside and brushed his lips over her shoulder. "Why don't you go get dressed and I'll walk you to work? I'm not quite ready to let go of you yet, and I want people to see us together. I'm not going into this half-assed."

Chapter Eight

Nat walked down the street with Hoyt, and although the heat of his hand around her waist permeated her light jacket, it was the look in his eyes that warmed her all the way through.

Holding her close, he slowed his steps to match hers. "Jake's a hell of a man. He loves you so much that he'd do anything to make you happy."

Smiling at the affection in his tone, Nat nodded. "He's wonderful. I love him, Hoyt. So much. More than you can imagine."

"I know that, baby. You're everything to him." Hugging her, he studied her features. "You do realize that what happened this morning wasn't just about sex?"

Nat's face burned at the memory. "I know." Looking away, she scanned their surroundings, unsurprised to find the streets of Desire bustling with shoppers. "He wanted to make sure that I knew that he accepted the fact that we would be lovers. He knew I was embarrassed that I responded to you last night so easily. It wasn't easy for me to let him see that. I feel guilty about wanting you. I've felt guilty for years because I had a man as wonderful as Jake, and, no matter how much I love him, I still couldn't get over you."

Running a hand over her hair, he smiled down at her. "We stayed up most of the night talking about you."

"I know." Nat eyed him warily. "The last time the two of you sat up all night, you agreed that I would marry Jake." Shrugging, she looked away. "I've never regretted that decision, but if the two of you try to decide my fate again, I won't be so agreeable."

Chuckling, Hoyt pulled her closer. "Yes, baby. We know." Bending, he touched his lips to her temple. "Jake and I talked about the future. Evidently, you really shook him when you thought he might be sick. He's worried that something like that could happen, and he said it makes him feel better to know that you and Joe would be taken care of."

Nat blinked, pausing to stare up at him. "What? Oh, my God."

Hoyt rubbed her back. "It's another reason I didn't want to cause trouble between you and Jake, and why I agreed to let him marry you. I had a dangerous job, and knowing that Jake would take care of you and Joe was a great source of relief to me."

Shaking her head, Nat swallowed the lump in her throat. "I don't want to talk about it." She glared up at him over her shoulder. "I'm still mad at you for not letting us know when you were shot."

Hoyt shrugged. "I did what I could to protect you. I told Jake then that I'd always be part of your life, and would fight him tooth and nail if he ever tried to stop me." Meeting her look of surprise, he raised a brow. "Did you think I'd just walk away from you? I told him that I'd be back, but I think Jake hoped I'd fall in love with someone else. I couldn't."

He waited until another group of people passed them before continuing. "I knew that he wouldn't take it well, but we understood each other. Neither one of us is willing to give you up, and we're both desperately, hopelessly in love with you. Nothing's more important to either one of us than your safety and well-being, Natalie. Your happiness. We want this to go as smoothly as possible for you. I can't stand the thought of you being uncomfortable around me, and Jake doesn't like feeling as if you're putting on a show for his benefit. Just relax. The three of us can build a wonderful future together. Life's too short for regrets."

His eyes narrowed, his gaze lowering to her breasts, a small mischievous smile curving his lips. "The three of us can make a great life together, and have a hell of a lot of fun while we're doing it."

Snorting inelegantly, Nat turned to look straight ahead again. "Like this morning?"

Throwing his head back, Hoyt laughed out loud. "I don't know what you're bitching about. You got to come."

Enjoying herself, and thrilled to be in Hoyt's company, Nat laughed, feeling more lighthearted than she had in years. She couldn't remember ever seeing him so relaxed before, and it made her feel good to know that she'd played a part in it. "Yeah, I did. Felt great, too. Too bad you didn't fuck me when you had the chance. Poor baby. You still aroused?"

Hoyt gave her a playful glare. "I'm always aroused when I'm with you. It's made for some damned uncomfortable moments."Gathering her close, he bent to touch his lips to her ear. "I reach for you in my sleep."

Stunned, Nat turned to look up at him, struck by the love and hunger in his eyes. "Hoyt, I—"

Pressing a hand to her back to urge her forward, he sighed. "I just wanted you to know, Natalie. This isn't a whim for me. I've ached for you for years, baby."

"Hey, Nat!"

Nat spun toward the masculine voice, amused that Hoyt's protective arm around her waist tightened. Waving to Logan James and Beau Parrish, who stood across the street on the sidewalk in front of their stores, Nat smiled in greeting, keeping her face averted so that Hoyt couldn't see her blush.

Beau stepped forward. "Hey, is that you, Hoyt? I was beginning to think we'd never see you again."

Hoyt smiled, not easing his hold. "It's me. I'm here for good now." He lowered his voice, touching his lips to Nat's ear. "I'll bet Jake's going to be busy on the phone today."

Nat grimaced. "They've never seen me with anyone but Jake before. You know Logan and Beau?"

Chuckling, Hoyt ran a hand up and down her back. "I know both Logan and Beau very well. I sent Beau and his new bride a wedding present. They invited me to the wedding, but I was in the middle of something and couldn't leave. I've made it my business to know the people who live here. Where did you think I went when I used to leave the house to go walking around?"

Logan grinned. "Stop by when you get the chance, and we can catch up."

Hoyt lifted a hand. "Will do."

Looking down at her, he frowned. "You're blushing. Are you embarrassed to be seen with me?"

"No, it's not that." Nat rushed to reassure him, wondering how the hell anyone could handle two men and their egos. "It's just that I know they're all curious, and they'll be calling Jake. He's going to spend the day explaining that he's now sharing his wife with another man. It won't be easy for him."

Hoyt touched his lips to her hair. "I know, baby, but it's better to get it out in the open. I'll do whatever I can to help him, but they're his friends, and they're going to want to hear it from him. But, I'm not going to hide what I feel for you anymore. I've done it for too long."

Nat whipped her head around, struck by the hard edge in his tone. She knew Hoyt well enough to know that he wouldn't take any crap from anyone, and hoped like hell that no one was stupid enough to confront him.

"Nobody said that we had to hide anything. I just know that Jake's afraid that he's second best. He knows that I would have married you if you hadn't gone into the service."

Tilting his head, he regarded her steadily. "Would you have? I've often wondered."

Frowning, Nat looked up at him, surprised that he'd tensed. "What do you mean?"

Hoyt shrugged. "There was always an electricity between you and Jake." Shaking his head when she started to speak, he hugged her close. "I didn't really think either one of you would have ever done anything about it, but it was there. Yes, I had a few bad moments wondering if he was Joe's father, but once I cooled down, I knew neither one of you would betray me. I often wondered if you would have married me if I hadn't already signed up, or if you were using it as an excuse. You wouldn't believe me when I told you that I would have married you when I got enough money."

Nat shrugged, her stomach clenching as she thought back to those days. "If I hadn't been pregnant, and you hadn't been leaving, I probably would have married you. Eventually. Maybe." Blowing out a breath of frustration, she continued down the sidewalk. "I was afraid that one day you'd realize that you only married me because I was pregnant and blame me for not being able to have the life that you wanted. I knew you wanted to get away from your father, and I didn't want to stand in your way. I had to watch out for Jesse and I didn't want to be a burden to you while you started your new life."

Hoyt's jaw clenched. "Neither you nor my son could ever be a burden to me."

Looking straight ahead, Nat bit back a groan at the sight of Jared and Erin Preston approaching from the other direction. "We might as well meet this head-on."

Erin, dressed in a thick jacket that did nothing to hide her advanced pregnancy, blinked as she approached. "I wondered if being pregnant had ruined my eyesight." In her usual outgoing way, she extended her hand to Hoyt. "Hi, I'm Erin Preston. and this is my husband, Jared. Who are you?"

Hoyt shared a look of amusement with Jared. "Hi, Erin. I'm Hoyt Campbell. Jared and I already know each other." Shaking hands with Jared, Hoyt grinned, some of the tenseness leaving his body. "Congratulations on your marriage and your upcoming addition to your family."

"Thank you." Jared frowned when a cold gust of wind blew, and wrapped Erin's scarf more securely around her neck. "I didn't know you were coming back for a visit. You haven't been here for a long time."

He met Erin's glare with a raised brow, and continued to fuss with her scarf as he turned his attention back to Hoyt. "I thought you'd given up on us."

Hoyt pulled Nat closer, relaxed and smiling. "I haven't been back for a while because it was too hard to see Natalie." Looking down at her, he smiled and touched his lips to her forehead. "I love her too much, and walking away from her was getting harder and harder, but not as hard as seeing her and not being able to tell her how I felt."

Jared nodded, apparently unsurprised. "I suspected as much. I saw your eyes whenever you talked about her."

Erin just gaped at him. "Why didn't I know anything about this?" Turning to Hoyt, she scowled at him. "Did Jake know anything about this? Is that why he's been in such a bad mood lately?"

Hoyt smiled, nodding once. "Natalie and I were together a long time ago. Jake and I were best friends. That's how they met. I retired from the Navy this week, and wanted to come here to be with her again, but Jake and I had to work it out first."

Erin's jaw dropped. "So, the three of you are together now?"

Unable to hold back a smile at the shock dancing in Erin's eyes, Nat nodded, pressing a hand to her stomach and blowing out a shaky breath. "It looks that way." Her stomach fluttered every time she thought about it.

Jared extended his hand again, his eyes sharpening with interest. "Congratulations. I'll go see Jake later." He winked at Nat before smiling at Hoyt. "You two certainly have your hands full."

"Typical man." Erin wrinkled her nose at him, glaring at Jared as she defiantly loosened her scarf. "You're going to go see Jake? Don't tell me that you're actually going to leave me alone for five minutes."

Jared tapped her nose, his lips twitching at her resigned sigh as he adjusted her scarf again. "Duncan's waiting for me to bring you back home. He'll have lunch ready by the time we get there. Then you can take your nap."

Erin shook her head in exasperation, but it was obvious she adored her husband. Turning to Nat, she gripped her hand, grinning. "They're always trying to get us into bed one way or another, aren't they?"

"Very funny." Jared smiled indulgently, holding her close as he faced Hoyt. "Her sister, Rachel, had some issues with high blood pressure late in her pregnancy, and the doctor's watching Erin closely. He wants her to have a nice, leisurely walk in the afternoon, and for some reason, my darling wife doesn't understand why we want to watch over her."

Hoyt's arm tightened around Nat. "I don't think they realize just how fragile they are."

Nat snorted, but was inwardly thrilled at the way he held her close. "Please."

Erin grinned and gestured toward where Logan and Beau stood whistling appreciatively at her, yelling out admiring comments about rounded pregnant ladies, much to Jared's obvious amusement. "Idiots. I can't walk twenty feet without running into someone I know. What the hell do you think could happen to me here in broad daylight?"

Jared pulled her collar up against the sudden gust of wind. "We won't have the chance to find out, because you're not going anywhere alone. It's getting colder out here with this wind. Let's get you home so you can have your lunch and take a nap. You're getting grouchy again."

Erin grinned at Nat. "Whenever they can't handle me, I'm *grouchy*. He's cute, isn't he?"

Jared threw back his head and laughed, extending his hand to Hoyt again. "Now that you're living here full-time, I'm sure I'll see you soon. Welcome to Desire."

"Thank you." Once they said their good-byes, Hoyt chuckled and, with a hand at her back, guided Nat down the street. "I like her. She's a lot like you. Jared, Duncan, and Reese sure as hell have their hands full, too."

"So does she." Shaking her head, Nat smiled up at him. "Having three husbands would be a hell of a balancing act. I'm just realizing how hard having two men in my life will be."

As they made their way down the sidewalk toward Indulgences, the store Jesse and her friend Kelly owned together, Nat discovered a newfound respect for her sister.

When Nat had taken a shot at matchmaking and introduced Jesse to Clay and Rio, she'd liked knowing that her sister would have two delicious men madly in love with her. After a hellish marriage, Jesse deserved all the happiness in the world.

Nat sure as hell hadn't considered the complications involved with juggling two arrogant men.

Hoyt pulled her closer and bent toward her. "I'm going to be thinking about what happened this morning all day. I want to take my time with your breasts." He brushed his lips over her jaw. "And then your pussy." Nibbling at her ear, he tightened his arms around her when she shivered in delight. Raising his head, he pushed back a tendril of hair that the wind blew over her face. "I've got to make up for a lot of lost time. I'll never be able to make up for all of it, but I'm going to do my best."

Sliding his hand over her jaw, he lifted her face to his, his eyes hooded and filled with possessive heat. "When Jake and I take you together, you'll really know that you belong to both of us. Have you ever fantasized about it?"

Nat gripped his shoulders to steady herself against the wave of lust that slammed into her. "Damn it, Hoyt!" Looking around to make sure no one had heard his provocative statement, Nat blew out a breath of relief to find the sidewalk around them empty. "Hell, yes, I've thought about it. How can I not think about it? The two of you are going to drive me crazy."

Chuckling softly, Hoyt hugged her. "Poor baby."

Nat led Hoyt down the alley toward the back of Jesse's store, grimacing when she saw Clay's and Rio's truck parked in the parking lot.

Usually, they dropped Jesse off in the morning, and on occasion, came back to have lunch with her.

Apparently, this was one of those days.

"Shit."

Hoyt's brows went up. "Problem, honey?"

Nat sighed and gestured toward the truck. "It's almost lunchtime. I'm late, and Jesse didn't call to see why, which means she knows I got tied up with you and Jake. I forgot that Clay and Rio come on Saturdays. They're going to bombard you with questions, and give me weird looks."

Pausing, he frowned, gripping her arm and turning her to face him. "What kind of weird looks?"

Shrugging, Nat pulled away. "Like they want to make sure I'm okay because I was upset when I went over there yesterday. I hate getting those kind of looks."

She was a grown woman, for God's sake, not a child to be fussed over.

Hoyt smiled and hugged her. "They're just concerned about you. I wouldn't have expected anything less. They know me, but I'm sure they'll want to make sure I really care about you. You worried I can't handle myself, baby?"

Nat couldn't hold back a smile. Having Hoyt as her first lover had pretty much ruined her for weak men, and being married to Jake had cemented it. "I have no doubt that you can handle yourself in any situation." She hoped Jesse and Hoyt got along. She felt like she was bringing a boy home to meet her parents, which was ridiculous under the circumstances, but she couldn't help it.

Irritated with herself, she forced a smile. "I just want you to get along with Clay and Rio. We spend a lot of time with them."

Hoyt's lips twitched. "It's funny how you avoid whatever's bothering you the most. You're nervous about introducing me to your sister, aren't you?"

With shaking hands, she reached for the door handle of the back door, her face burning. "Yeah. Maybe. Stupid, I know. Hell, just forget it."

Chuckling, bent to touch his lips to her ear. "That's so sweet. You really are a marshmallow inside."

"Kiss my ass."

"Later, baby."

A giggle escaped. "Jerk."

As soon as they walked through the doorway, Clay and Rio looked up from where they sat at the table. Both men grinned, studying her features as they greeted them.

Jesse turned from one of the cabinets. "Hey! I wondered if you were coming in today."

Placing the bottles she held onto the countertop, Jesse turned to stare at Hoyt, her eyes narrowing. After several long seconds, she grinned, slapping her hands together. "I remember you! You had a red sports car that you'd rebuilt. Oh, my God. I can't believe it. I only met you once, but I remember you and that gorgeous car. Please tell me you still have it."

"It's on its way." Obviously pleased that she remembered him, Hoyt smiled back at her. "You were such a little thing, and so quiet. Unlike your sister."

"Hey!" Nat nudged him, while Clay and Rio got to their feet.

Extending his hand, Clay smiled and shook his head. "So you're the one we should thank for Jesse wanting a red sports car."

Hoyt grinned back. "Sorry. She's got good taste."

"See?" Looking up at Clay, Jesse nudged a smiling Rio aside and approached Hoyt. "You've filled out. You used to be skinny."

Hoyt lifted hand to his mouth to cover a smile. "I could say the same about you." Glancing up at Clay and Rio, he shook his head. "But I have a feeling I'd get my ass handed to me for saying it."

Rio laughed. "It's good to have you back. I was beginning to think we'd never see you again. Want some coffee?"

"Love some. It's damned cold out." He helped Nat remove her coat, hanging it up on one of the hooks on the wall before removing his own. With a hand at her waist, he led her farther into the room, his thumb moving over her lower back as if in encouragement.

When the bell in the front signaled the arrival of another customer, Nat breathed a sigh of relief, grateful for the excuse to escape. "Behave yourselves." She gave all three of them a cocky grin to hide the emotions raging inside her. "Some of us have work to do. You three just sit there and enjoy your coffee."

Turning away from their soft laughter, she went with Jesse to the store in the front room, taking several deep breaths to calm herself. Excited and nervous about the twist her life had taken, she moved restlessly around the store, her gaze drawn toward the back room where the men talked.

While Jesse went to greet the customer, Nat went behind the counter and began straightening things that didn't need to be straightened, unable to stop glancing toward the back room. Leaning against the counter, she tried to make out the men's conversation, but their low tones kept her from hearing them clearly.

When Jesse approached, Nat sighed and kept her voice low. "They're going to interrogate him, aren't they?"

From the other side of the counter, Jesse smiled and patted her hand. "I doubt it. They like Hoyt and they've missed him. Evidently they used to hang around with him at the club when he left the house to give you and Jake time together."

After greeting yet another customer, Jesse turned back to Nat, keeping an observant eye on the two women as they browsed. "They're going to tell him that they're available if he ever wants to talk. Both Clay and Rio know that sharing you is going to be difficult for both Jake and Hoyt, and for different reasons."

Smiling, she shot a glance toward the back room. "They understand some of the problems that come up, and are eager to share their newfound knowledge with anyone who will listen."

Nat sighed, and attempted to straighten a display of samples on the counter, knocking them over instead.

With a curse, she started to straighten them again, her hands shaking so hard that she knocked even more over.

Frowning, Jesse came behind the counter and reached out a hand to prevent a small tin of balm from falling to the floor. "Damn, you're jittery. Calm down. Clay and Rio just want Hoyt to know that they're on his side, just like they're on Jake's. They want to help."

Patting Nat's hand, Jesse grinned. "Just like you can come to me for advice—like how important it is to spend time alone with each of them, and how not to let their jealousy get to you and cause fights."

In the process of straightening the small plastic bottles she'd knocked over, Nat attempted to glare at her sister, shaking her head in amusement instead. "You're enjoying this, aren't you?"

Laughing, Jesse patted her arm. "Immensely. I've spent my entire life listening to advice from my big sister. It's kinda nice to be able to turn the tables, and I plan to savor every minute of it."

Unable to hold back a smile, Nat leaned back against the counter, rolling her shoulders to ease the tension there. "You always were a smartass."

Jesse giggled. "I learned from the best." After ringing up and bagging a purchase, Jesse thanked the woman, waiting until she left before turning back to her. Glancing at the remaining customers, she kept her voice low. "Since I moved here, I've gotten quite a bit of advice from you concerning my love life. You convinced me to go for the brass ring. You made me believe that, not only could I love again, but that I could love and actually be happy loving two men."

Glancing toward the back room, Jesse smiled, her eyes going soft and dreamy. "Now I can't imagine my life without either one of them."

Turning back, she reached out and touched Nat's arm. "The way I see it, you're already halfway there. You love both of them. They both love you. You have this chance—this *one* chance to have a life with both of them. Jake and Hoyt have to know if this can work, and so do you. Honey, I want you to be as happy as I am. I want *you* to go for the brass ring. I don't want you to spend the rest of your life thinking *what if.*"

Touched by her sister's concern, Nat nodded. "We're all determined to make this work. Christ, I love both of them, but I've been keeping how I feel about Hoyt hidden for so long, it's hard to relax." With a sigh, Nat glanced toward the back again. "I *was* happy. I *am* happy. It took years to build what Jake and I have together. We're not only lovers, but best friends."

Remembering how things were in the beginning, Nat swallowed the lump in her throat. "When Jake and I first got married, he was so sweet. So patient. He treated me as if I was the most precious thing in the world to him during my pregnancy. When I had Joe, he was so happy. So proud. So worried. He fussed over both of us and treated me like a queen."

She glanced around the store to see that the other woman had gone. Blinking back tears, she forced a smile. "I was already halfway in love with him when I married him. How could I not fall madly in love with a man like that?"

He'd been her strength when she needed it, and given her the confidence to become the woman she was today.

He was everything to her.

Jesse glanced around as another woman came through the door, keeping her voice low as she leaned toward Nat. "But you couldn't stop thinking about Hoyt, could you? I'll bet you even felt guilty for not marrying him and going with him."

Thinking about Jake's patience through that time, Nat nodded. "Poor Jake. He didn't mention it, but he knew. He waited, and was always there for me. He never pressured me, and when we finally had sex, it was because I'd initiated it." Laughing humorlessly, she shook her head. "It's hard to imagine that a man like Jake would wait, but he did."

Straightening, she blew out a breath. "I was a coward, Jesse, not something I'm very proud of, but if I'd gone with Hoyt, I'd never have had all these years with Jake, so I can't say that I regret it. Still…"

Jesse's eyes shone with understanding. "You've got a second chance with Hoyt. You have a chance to have it all."

Nat nodded. "I know, and I want it to work, but I feel like I have to walk on eggshells all the time. It's not like when you met Clay and Rio. Jake and I have a history, and Hoyt and I have a history, but those histories don't overlap. Now, everything has to come together in some fucking way that doesn't hurt anyone. It's driving me crazy. You know I'm not good with beating around the bush, but I feel like I have to weigh every word. Every look."

She snapped her mouth closed as the woman approached and set her purchases on the counter.

Waiting for Jesse to finish ringing up the sale, Nat glanced toward the back again, Hoyt's deep chuckle sending a shiver of delight up and down her spine. She waited until the woman left the store before leaning toward her sister. "Jake's even more intense now. You should have seen him this morning."

Before she knew she would do it, Nat blurted out what had happened in the kitchen.

Jesse's eyes went wide. "Holy hell! No wonder you were late coming in. I figured the three of you were working things out, but I didn't expect anything like that."

Nat grimaced. "Neither did I. Jake keep saying that he spoiled me, and is reverting back to the way he was when he first started—well, you know."

"You're blushing!" Jesse laughed delightedly. "I can't believe this. Now that Hoyt's back, even Jake's making you blush. Oh, to be a fly on the wall at your house…"

"Shut up." Looking toward the back, Nat sighed. "I was nervous about Hoyt seeing my stretch marks. I mean, I don't look like I did when I was younger. He actually kissed each one and told me that they were his marks on me. Idiot."

She still couldn't believe that he'd done such a thing. The memory of his obvious pleasure still warmed her.

Jesse laughed, patting her hand, straightening and moving away to greet another customer. "He seems like a good man, but I hardly know him. I can't wait to get to know him better, but if you love him, he must be really something. You're a tough nut to crack."

Rubbing the back of her neck where it tingled, Nat turned, her breath catching at the sight of Hoyt striding toward her, Clay and Rio right behind him.

Six feet, four inches of masculinity smiled, his eyes filled with concern. "Hey, baby. You okay?"

Nat nodded, pausing when she noticed that the woman at the counter smiled flirtatiously at Hoyt. Curious to see how he would respond, and pissed off at the surge of jealousy that knotted her stomach, she glanced at him, once again struck by his strong presence.

Although not as handsome as Jake, Hoyt had a masculinity about him that drew attention.

Smiling politely at the other woman, Hoyt wrapped a hand around Nat's arm. "I have to run to the bank. I need to open an account here, so I might be gone for a little while. I told Clay and Rio I'd bring back lunch." Leaning closer, he touched his lips to her cheekbone. "You okay, baby?"

Nodding, she smiled up at him. "Of course." Glancing at Clay, who watched her thoughtfully from the other side of the counter, Nat lowered her head, keeping her voice at a whisper. "Was it too bad?"

With a soft laugh, Hoyt lifted her chin and ran a hand over her back. "Good grief, woman. What did you think they were going to do to me?" Bending to touch his lips to her temple, he ran his hand down her arm in a gesture that she assumed had meant to calm, but instead sent a surge of awareness up her arm and to her nipples. "You're going to have to trust that I'm perfectly capable of taking care of myself." With a smile, he tapped her nose. "And you."

Leaning back against the counter across from them, and heavily against Clay, Jesse smiled at Hoyt. "Why don't you take Nat with you? While you're opening your account, she can make the deposit."

Nat frowned and gestured toward the big window where a number of people walked by. "There's a lot of foot traffic. Where's Brenna? I don't want to leave you here alone."

Hoyt glanced at Nat. "Brenna? I don't think I've heard that name before. Is that someone who works here?"

Nodding, Nat straightened as another woman walked in, her eyes going wide at the sight of Clay, Rio, and Hoyt. Amused at the other woman's reaction, Nat smiled. "Yes, she married King Taylor and Royce Harley several months ago, and wanted something to do while they were busy at the club. She's so full of energy. We hired her on the spot. She's been a Godsend, especially with Kelly out so much."

Hoyt chuckled and grinned at Clay. "Jake told me about the new baby. It's hard to believe Blade's a father now. Jake didn't tell me that Royce and King got married, though. I'd like to meet the woman brave enough to take on those two."

Nat muttered under her breath. "Nobody says anything about me being brave, and I have to deal with you and Jake."

Kissing her hair, Hoyt patted her ass. "You're very brave, baby." His solicitous tone wasn't lost on her.

Irritated that the other woman, a regular customer, continued to ogle Hoyt, Nat snorted. "Yeah. Yeah. Yeah." Nat watched the other woman out of the corner of her eye, cursing her own jealousy as she shifted her gaze to Jesse. "Is Brenna coming in?"

Shaking her head, Jesse waited until the other woman walked to the far side of the store before turning to smile at Nat. "No. I told her not to come in today. I figured you'd want to talk and wouldn't want an audience. When the guys leave after lunch, we can sit down and talk about them."

Rio's grin made him look impossibly young and devilishly handsome. Wrapping an arm around Jesse's waist, he yanked her to his side and looked down at her lovingly. "You women are all very brave when you're together, but tonight, I'm going to have you alone."

Poking him in the stomach, Jesse lifted her face, clearly expecting to be kissed. "You don't scare me, tough guy."

Rio obliged her, his eyes flaring as he bent and touched his lips to hers. "Brat. Just because you have me wrapped around your finger doesn't mean I won't paddle your ass."

Jesse sighed. "Promises. Promises."

Rio turned back and raised a brow at that. "Hmm. It appears you're overdue." He glanced at Nat, but immediately looked back, focusing his attention on his blushing wife. "We'll be here. Go do whatever you have to do. Clay and I will stick around."

Hoyt chuckled. "Do you know how to sell this stuff?"

Nat snorted, unable to hold back a smile. "You must be kidding. Sales go through the roof when these two are here." She gestured toward the two women wandering through the store, who keep sneaking glances toward all three men. "They can sell anything. Rio turns on the charm, and when he raves about how much he likes a particular scent, they buy *everything* in that scent."

Hoyt laughed softly. "Okay, now I'm going to have to come in and see f I can do that. I can't have Rio outdoing me."

"You do that." Nat struggled for nonchalance, but Hoyt's possessive, casual embrace felt so natural and yet so new.

A hand at the small of her back.

A slide of his hand over her hair.

Fingers tightening on her waist.

Little things—small touches that may have appeared insignificant, but that brought back memories of another time.

Even that felt different.

No longer a young man, Hoyt held her with the maturity of a man comfortable in his own skin.

So much like Jake's touch, and yet so different.

How could she love two different men so completely?

Drawing in a shaky breath, she ignored Hoyt's sharp look, and met Jesse's. "If Clay and Rio are going to stay here with you, I'll go make the deposit. We'll pick up lunch and get back as soon as possible."

Leaning back against the counter, Jesse grinned at Hoyt. "Take your time."

After giving Nat a searching look, Hoyt smiled back and took Jesse's hand in his. "Thank you."

Frowning, Jesse straightened. "For what?"

Hoyt released Jesse's hand and took Nat's in his. "For welcoming me. For trusting me to make your sister happy. Both mean a great deal to me."

"You're welcome. You can make it up to me by giving me a ride in the Mustang."

Hoyt's lips twitched. "Deal."

Grinning again, Jesse winked at Nat. "She's going to be a trial, though."

Hoyt threw back his head and laughed, but Nat sensed a tension in him that hadn't been there before. "She probably will be, but I think Jake and I can handle her."

Jesse poked Rio again. "That's what they all say."

Studying Hoyt, Nat found herself consumed by guilt for yet another reason. She reached up to cup his jaw, her heart lurching when he turned his face to kiss her palm. "I guess I haven't exactly made you feel welcome, have I?"

It was as if a shutter came down, removing all emotion from his eyes. "Oh, I don't know. At times, you can be very welcoming. Besides, I didn't expect you to act any other way." He winked at her before turning to Jesse again, his eyes considerably warmer. "I've never had a little sister before. I hope you'll bear with me while I get the hang of it."

Jesse giggled, earning indulgent smiles from both Clay and Rio. "Careful. Nat got younger than me about ten years ago. She's only my *older* sister when she wants to tell me what to do or give me advice."

Stiffening, Nat pushed at him. "Wait a minute! What do you mean—you didn't expect me to act any other way?"

She *hated* being predictable.

Chuckling, Hoyt patted her back. "Don't get your panties in a bunch. I knew you wouldn't swoon in my arms. You're very loyal to Jake, and I understand why you have to make him your top priority." Turning her in his arms, despite her struggle, he ran a thumb over her cheek. "I have only myself to blame, but I hope one day to earn that kind of loyalty from you."

Mesmerized by the love and sadness in his eyes, Nat grimaced, her anger dissipating. "Damn it, you always knew how to get around me. Look, Hoyt—"

Touching a finger to her lips, he shook his head. "It's not important. We'll work it out." Lifting his head, he nodded at the others. "We'll be back soon."

As soon as they entered the back room, Hoyt frowned, searching her features. "You okay?"

"Yeah." After letting him help her into her coat, she went to the corner cabinet. Yanking open the drawer that held the deposit, she stared down into it. "I want this to work more than I've ever wanted anything in my life, but I feel like I'm not giving my all to either you or Jake, and it makes me feel guilty as hell. I feel guilty for putting Jake in this position. I'm pissed at both of you for putting *me* in this position. I'm mad at myself for loving you so much that I can't resist having this time with you. I feel selfish. I hate feeling this way."

Wrapping his arms around her, he pulled her back against him. "You've never been selfish. You've always sacrificed your own happiness to do what was best for everyone around you. Face it. If Jake hadn't insisted on this, telling you that he needed it, you would never have even considered it. You have nothing to feel guilty about. I love you, Natalie. You love me. Everything will work out. You're trying to be superwoman and take on the world. Just relax and let Jake and I take care of you."

Nuzzling the sensitive spot behind her ear, he patted her ass. "Now, stop worrying. I'll tell you what. I'll follow you to the bank so you can keep wiggling your sweet ass at me."

A burst of laughter escaped before she could prevent it, and she found herself blinking back tears as he hugged her. Grateful that he'd known what she needed, and had lightened the mood, Nat looked over her shoulder at him and smiled. "I don't shake my ass at you."

Laughing softly, Hoyt turned her, pressing a hand to the small of her back as he guided her to the door. Reaching around her to open it, he winked at her. "Maybe it's just wishful thinking on my part."

Nat actually giggled, something she hadn't done in a long time. "Idiot."

Once they made their way through the alley and back to the front sidewalk, Nat glanced at him. "Cheryl was the one shaking her ass at you. She also batted her lashes and gave you several come-hither looks."

Hoyt tightened his hold, pulling her closer to allow the group of people approaching to pass them. "What the hell is a *come-hither* look, and who the hell is Cheryl?" The amusement in his voice, and his playful mood, so rare and so precious, meant even more to her because she knew he did it to tease her out of her mood.

Biting the inside of her cheek to keep from laughing, Nat tried to step away once the others had passed, but Hoyt tightened his hold on her waist, keeping her close against his side.

Smiling, Nat cuddled closer. "Cheryl was the customer in Jesse's shop that was practically drooling over you, and I'm sure you've been on the receiving end of come-hither looks often enough to know what the hell they are."

Hoyt leaned back to look down at her, a brow going up. "You're not jealous, are you?"

Lifting her chin, Nat stared straight ahead, inwardly groaning when she saw Dillon Tanner and Ryder Hayes approaching from the other direction.

Their new wife, Alison, walked between them, laughing up at something Ryder said.

Cursing herself for wishing she could avoid another round of interrogation, she lifted her chin and kept walking. "Should I be jealous?"

Hoyt laughed at that. "Do you think I'd risk losing you for a lay with someone else?" His brow went up again. "On the other hand, if you ever looked at another man, I'd beat your ass."

Watching the others approach, she glanced at Hoyt. "You always were possessive. How do you expect to handle sharing me with Jake if you—" Frowning when he tensed, his eyes narrowed in warning, Nat nudged him with an elbow. "Stop glaring at Dillon."

"No." His eyes glittered. "And I have no problem sharing you with Jake, but I sure as hell won't put up with anyone trying to move in on you, which is why I understand him so well."

Dillon and Ryder paused in front of them, Alison looking up at them in confusion when they deliberately blocked the sidewalk. Looking pointedly at the hand Hoyt kept at Nat's waist, Dillon frowned. "Hi, Nat. Where's Jake?"

When Hoyt tensed and started to pull her back, Nat patted his arm. "Down, boy. Hi, Dillon. Jake's at work. This is Hoyt Campbell. He's an old friend of mine and Jake's. He just retired from the SEALs and lives with us now."

Ryder and Dillon shared a look before both of them turned back to her. Dillon scowled, eyeing her and glancing at Hoyt. "Oh?"

Amused that she'd managed to surprise them and take the wind out of their sails, Nat smirked. "We're together now." Meeting his dumbstruck look, she shook her head, knowing that the best defense was the perfect offense. "I can't believe you would think I would cheat on Jake."

Ryder's brows went up, and he turned to Hoyt, eyeing him with renewed interest. His slow smile made him look even more devilishly handsome as he held out his hand. "Hi, I'm Ryder." His smile softened, the love in his eyes unmistakable as he wrapped an arm around Alison. "This is our wife, Alison. Don't mind my brother. Dillon's a bit of a hard-ass. So, you retired from the SEALs?"

Hoyt smiled, the tension easing from his big body as he greeted a beaming Alison.

Dillon stepped closer, his hands on his hips. "Damn it, Nat. How was I supposed to know?"

Nat narrowed her eyes at him. She hadn't been married for over twenty years and raised a son without learning a few things about how to make a man feel guilty. "You actually thought I would cheat on Jake. Shame on you."

To her delight, Dillon blushed. "Hell, Nat. I'm sorry. What was I supposed to think?"

Nat raised a brow, enjoying herself immensely. "Not that I'm some kind of whore."

Dillon's eyes went wide, and his glances at Hoyt changed from hostile to wary. "I would never think that! Oh, hell." Dillon scrubbed a hand over his face and offered a hand to Hoyt. "Get her to forgive me, for God's sake. Please. I'll be in your debt forever."

With a laugh, Hoyt shook his hand and grinned down at her. "I'll do my best, but she's a stubborn woman."

Running a hand over Alison's hair, Dillon sighed. "Aren't they all? Sometimes, it's hard to convince these women that this town works because the women are firmly under the men's protection." He glanced at Nat. "Under the protection of *all* the men who live here."

Alison sighed, her gaze going to Nat's. "They're driving me crazy, Nat. I'm just trying to help out in the shop, but they're afraid that everything I touch is going to hurt me. They get nervous when I'm out of their sight. It's really starting to piss me off. Are they all so arrogant?"

"Yeah, they are." Nat glanced at Hoyt. "They certainly are. I've come to realize that I could never respect a weak man, but this is what you get with the strong ones. I've learned how to get my way. Keeping them in line is a constant battle, but we women have to do what we have to do. Call me sometime, and I'll give you a few pointers." Glaring at Dillon, she raised a brow. "Unless you have a problem with me talking to your wife."

Hoyt cleared his throat, unsuccessfully disguising his chuckle. "On that, gentlemen, I think we'd better close the subject. We have to get to the bank. It was nice meeting you."

Eyeing Nat, Dillon opened his mouth as if he wanted to say something, but at a sharp look from Ryder, who shook his head imperceptibly, snapped it shut again. "Yeah. You, too. If you're staying, I'm sure we'll see you around."

Hoyt gathered Nat against his side again. "I'm staying."

Once they parted, Nat turned to Hoyt. "I expected you to say something about what I said back there. No comment?"

Hoyt smiled. "I know you think the men here can be too arrogant, but with all the crap that's going on in the world, I can't see it being a bad thing. Since the beginning of time, it's been a man's job—his duty, his responsibility, his *right*—to protect the women in his life. That's the way it's always been. Yes, I understand all about women's rights, and I agree with them, but most women just aren't as physically strong as most men. Sure, you have to buck against your restraints from time to time, but you know that nothing you can say or do will change anything about the way Jake and I protect you. With the other men in town watching over you, I always knew you were safe here. I already told you how much that meant to me."

Hugging her close, he kissed her hair. "You've been bucking Jake's authority for years, and it hasn't gotten you anywhere. I'm kind of looking forward to you trying that with me."

"What makes you think it hasn't gotten me anywhere?" Nat couldn't help but notice the way Hoyt constantly scanned his surroundings. "What the hell are you looking for? You act like you think someone's going to jump out at you any minute."

Glancing at her, he smiled, his gaze constantly moving. "Habit. Besides, it doesn't hurt to be aware of your surroundings. Surprise attacks are much more effective." As they moved aside for another couple to pass them, Hoyt frowned. "I don't remember it being this busy before. For a small town, there sure is a lot of foot traffic."

Looking around, Nat smiled. "Yes. The weekends are getting busier and busier around here. I know Ace'll be relieved when the new deputies get here. He, Linc, and Rafe are run ragged. The bank gets busy, too. Everyone tries to get there on Saturday before they close and make their deposits. Almost everything around here is closed on Sundays. Everyone gets change and makes deposits to get ready for the next week."

Hoyt paused, glancing at the bank bag she held. "Do you often carry large amounts of money around?"

Shaking her head, Nat frowned up at him. "No. Jesse usually makes the deposits, and either Clay or Rio go with her. We're not stupid, Hoyt."

As he wrapped an arm around her and started across the street to the bank on the corner, Hoyt sighed. "And everyone goes on the same day, and everyone *knows* that everyone goes on the same day."

An uneasy feeling tightened her stomach. "Relax, Hoyt. This is Desire. You're going to have to learn to relax." She went through the door Hoyt opened for her, stepping into the bank.

The uneasy feeling turned to mind-numbing fear, her brain unable to assimilate the scene in front of her.

"On the floor!"

Lifting her gaze to the masked man who'd shouted at her, she pressed a hand to her stomach, frozen in terror.

She couldn't see anything—couldn't comprehend anything—except three masked men, and the guns in their hands.

Fear clogged her throat, making it nearly impossible to breathe.

Hoyt's grip on her arm tightened. He pushed past her, shoving her behind him, putting his body solidly between hers and the three masked men.

"No!" Gripping his jacket, she tried to pull him back, but she couldn't move him at all. "Please, Hoyt. Be careful. Do what they say."

He turned his head slightly, his voice barely a whisper, but so icy cold that she almost didn't recognize it.

"Get down. *Now*."

Chapter Nine

As he stepped into the bank, Hoyt's senses went on full alert. He took in the scene at a glance, and shoved Natalie behind him, his heart pounding furiously with fear for her.

Years of training allowed him to do what he had to do, using the rush of adrenaline to sharpen his focus as he mentally weighed his options—and plan of attack.

Breathing a sigh of relief when she obeyed him and dropped to the floor, he concentrated on the scene unfolding in front of him.

Three men. One teller. Mentally filing away a description of each—eye color, height, weight, hair color, build—and identifying the guns the men held, Hoyt pushed aside the fear of what a bullet could do to Natalie.

The customers and all but one teller had been forced to lie facedown on the floor.

Hoyt saw the flash of alarm in the teller's eyes, and her quick glance at the masked man standing on the counter before lowering her head to fill the bags again.

Seven people on the floor, all men, including the guard, who lay unconscious about five feet to his right, and bleeding from what appeared to be a gunshot wound to the chest. The bank manager, whom Hoyt had met in the past stood pale and shaking across the small lobby, a gun pointed at his head.

"You, too! Get on the floor!" The man standing on the counter, the obvious leader, waved his gun wildly—an amateur, the tremor in his voice and his wild gestures giving him away, as well as the fact that the idiot hadn't even locked the front door.

He was scared, which made him unpredictable and dangerous. Taking another bag from the teller and tossing it with another the teller had obviously just filled, he pointed to the masked man standing closest to him.

"What the fuck are you waiting for? Get over there and get him on the floor."

Amateurs.

Training and years of experience enabled Hoyt to calculate options and scenarios as he watched the man closest to him approach, keeping the one standing over the bank guard in his peripheral vision.

Aware of the fear emanating from Natalie, he altered his stance slightly, redistributing his weight as the man waved his gun and rushed toward him.

Using the adrenaline pulsing through his veins to his advantage, Hoyt waited until the man came within striking distance.

Lifting his arm higher, the masked man waved the gun in Hoyt's face, his eyes wild with fear. "Get down on the floor. Now!" His voice shook. He took one step closer—and Hoyt made his move.

* * * *

Nat bit her lip to hold back a whimper as one of the masked men approached Hoyt, the wildness in his eyes the most terrifying thing she'd ever seen.

Please, Hoyt. Get down.

Nat watched in horror, her heart in her throat as the man yelled at Hoyt and started to lift the gun toward him.

Hoyt moved, and everything became a blur.

She jolted when shots rang out—one shot and then two at once.

Or was it more?

Everything seemed to happen at once, chaos erupting all around her—a chaos that only Hoyt seemed to control.

Scrambling to her knees, she called out his name in a raw, strangled cry, the roaring in her ears drowning out the sounds of her own desperate cries.

Before she could get to her feet, Hoyt gripped her by the arms and yanked her high against him, his arms closing around her in a fierce hug that made it hard for her to breathe. "Hoyt! Oh, God."

Throwing her arms around her neck, she tried to pull him down, but he held firm.

"It's okay, honey. They're all down. You're safe." Turning with her in his arms, he lowered her to her feet, keeping her face pressed against his chest. "Oh, Christ. You okay, baby?"

Fisting her hands in his jacket, Nat took a shuddering breath and turned her head to press her cheek against his chest. "Hoyt. Oh, God." She had to raise her voice to be heard over the noise and confusion as everyone raced around and shouted at once. "Are you hurt?" Lifting her head, she leaned back to look up at him, her stomach knotting when she caught a glimpse of the three masked men all lying on the floor.

Linc raced through the door, his gun drawn, his eyes hard as he flew past them. Ace came in right behind him, his features as hard and cold as if they'd been carved from granite.

Nat pushed against Hoyt. "Let me see you."

Tightening his hold, he pulled her back against his chest, his expression grim and colder than she'd ever seen it. "I'm fine. Stay put."

Nat turned her head, noticing for the first time that Hoyt held a gun. Blinking, she looked up at him again, following his gaze to the bank teller who remained behind the counter, a stunned look on her face.

Royce appeared at her side, visibly shaken. "You okay, Nat?"

Running hands that shook over Hoyt's chest and still looking for injuries, she nodded, looking him over for any sign of injury. "Yeah. You?"

"I'm fine." His gaze lifted to Hoyt's. "Christ, Hoyt. If I hadn't seen that with my own eyes, I never would have believed it."

Hoyt yanked Nat closer when she tried to turn again. "Be still. Hey, Ace. This gun belongs to this asshole right behind you. Royce kicked away the other two. One's in the corner over there, and the other's in front of the counter.

Ace nodded, taking the gun from Hoyt's hand. "I've got some questions for you."

Hoyt nodded once. "I figured you might."

Nat swallowed heavily, watching Royce and Ace move several feet away and begin speaking in low tones. Locking her shaking knees, she pressed her face against Hoyt's chest. "Are you really okay?" The enormity of what had just happened hit her hard, making it difficult to catch her breath. She started shaking everywhere, her throat clogged with tears. "Oh, God."

She gripped Hoyt's jacket as her knees gave out completely, but Hoyt caught her to him and held her upright and close.

Lifting her chin, he glanced down at her. "You're okay, baby. It's over. I've got you. Christ, I was scared to death that you were hurt."

Royce returned just as the sound of sirens split the air. "I heard you were back in town. Hell of a way to welcome you back."

Hoyt ran a hand down Nat's back, keeping her close. "I have all the welcome I need."

* * * *

Jake looked up from the jewelry case as King Taylor came rushing into the jewelry store.

Usually calm and controlled, King looked frantic, his face pale. "Jake, there's been an attempted robbery at the bank. Shots fired. Damn it, Royce is in there." He turned and ran back out, disappearing as quickly as he'd appeared.

A wave of panic washed over him, and another when he thought about who might be inside. Saturday was a busy day at the bank, and any number of his friends and close neighbors could be in there.

Jake shouted to one of his sales clerks to take over and headed out the door, his heart pounding furiously at the thought of Jesse being one of the people inside.

Rushing down the street, he saw several others closing their stores and running toward the bank, and mentally checked people off of his list, hoping like hell that Royce was okay.

He glanced down the street toward Indulgences, praying that Jesse had already finished her banking and was safely back in her store.

Seeing her running toward where several other people had gathered outside the bank, he breathed a sigh of relief, his relief short-lived when she spotted him and changed direction, racing toward him, tears streaming down her face.

"Jake! Jake!" He caught her before she could run out into the street, the momentum nearly knocking him over. With an uneasy feeling in the pit of his stomach, he looked toward the bank and saw Ace and Linc race inside, gesturing toward a clearly distraught Clay and Rio to keep everyone back.

Yanking Jesse out of the way, Jake pressed her up against the building, keeping his body between hers and the bank. "Easy, honey. Thank God you aren't in there."

Jesse sobbed. "Nat's in there!"

Jake's heart stopped as the horror of Jesse's words penetrated.

"No!" It came out as barely a croaked whisper, his throat too dry and tight to speak.

Everything went out of focus, his world crumbling all around him.

Nat. His wife. His *life*! *Please, God. No. Please don't take her from me.*

He had to get to her.

A strange numbness settled over him, and the voices around him faded. He turned, broke away from Jesse's grip on his shirt and raced for the bank.

He came to an abrupt halt, but couldn't figure out why at first, and then realized something was holding him. Fighting to break free, he cursed, stunned to see Rio's face in his.

Rio held on to him, putting his body between Jake and the bank. "No, Jake! You can't go in there."

Jake shoved at him. "Get out of my way!" Nothing mattered except getting to her. She was everything.

Rio stood firm, not letting him past. "Jake, damn it. Stop."

Jake shoved at him again. "What would you do if it was Jesse?"

Jesse pressed herself against his side. "Please, Jake. Please." She gripped the front of his shirt, another sob escaping. "It's all my fault! Hoyt was going to the bank and I asked Nat to go make the deposit."

Jake stilled, meeting Rio's gaze, once again becoming aware of his surroundings. "Hoyt's in there with her?"

Rio nodded, wrapping an arm around Jesse, his expression grim. "Yeah."

Knowing that Hoyt would do everything in his power to keep her safe, Jake took a deep breath and let it out slowly, fighting the urge to run in after her. "Hoyt will protect her."

He had to believe that, but he couldn't get over the feeling that she wouldn't be safe until she was in his arms again.

She could even now be lying on the floor in a pool of blood.

"Jake!" King's voice, filled with fear and sympathy, came from his right. "Christ, I'm sorry. I just found out Nat and Hoyt are inside, too."

Jake looked from the bank door to King, recognizing the fear in his eyes. "Hell, Royce is inside. You said that. Where's Brenna? God, don't tell me she's in there, too!"

Shaking his head, King looked in the direction of the club he, Royce, and Blade Royal owned. "I snuck out without telling her. I told Sebastian to keep her occupied until I found out what the hell was going on."

Jake nodded, running a shaking hand through his hair as he stared at the door to the bank. "Good."

King ran a hand over his face, glancing from the direction of the club to the bank and back again. "She'd be frantic if she knew Royce was in danger."

"Yeah, frantic." Frantic didn't even come close to what Jake felt. "What the hell happened?"

Rio grimaced. "Evidently a shot was fired several minutes ago, but no one could figure out where it came from. Hoyt and Nat walked in just as people started to realize it had come from the bank."

Running a hand over his face, he stared at the entrance to the bank. "Just before you got here, three shots were fired. That's when Ace and Linc ran inside."

No. Please, God. No! Don't let them be hurt.

The thought of losing his wife turned his stomach to ice and sent that strange numbness through him again.

The minutes dragged on, the tension building as the residents of Desire stood across the street from the bank on all sides, everyone speaking in low tones, their eyes trained on the door.

Jesse gripped his arm, trembling against him. "She's all right. I know she's all right. Nat can't be anything but all right. If she was hurt, I'd know about it. She won't be hurt. She *can't* be hurt. No. She's fine. She's okay."

"Of course she is." Hugging her close, Jake ran a hand down her back as the seconds ticked off with excruciating slowness.

"Hoyt's in there and Ace and Linc went inside. There's no more shooting. I'll bet Ace has whoever it is in custody."

"Then why the hell aren't they coming out?"

Good question.

He shared a look with King, seeing the same fear, and had to swallow the lump in his throat before speaking. "They'll be out soon, honey. Hang in there."

"Royce!"

"Damn it!" King turned just in time to catch Brenna against him. "Easy, honey. Easy." Lifting her high against his chest, he pressed her face against his shoulder.

"King, Royce is in there, isn't he?" Lifting her head, she wiped her eyes. "Is he hurt? What's going on?"

King blew out a breath, pulling her face against his shoulder again and sharing another look with Jake. "We don't know what's going on in there, honey. Ace and Linc just went in."

Lifting up again, Brenna stared toward the bank. "Why isn't anyone coming out? What the hell's going on in there? Oh, God, King. If he was okay, he'd be coming out, wouldn't he?"

Facing the bank again, Jake took several steps forward, needing to be as close as possible. Fear made him dizzy, his head spinning with thoughts of Nat lying in there injured. Or worse. It seemed like hours, but was probably only a few minutes before the sound of sirens split the air.

Jake watched in horror as three ambulances roared down the street toward them, their tires squealing as they braked in front of him, blocking his view of the door to the bank. Cursing, he raced around the ambulance, scanning the area in the front of the bank in case Nat had come out.

He held his breath as the door to the bank opened again, and a hush went over the crowd as everyone waited, the tension and fear in the air thick enough to cut with a knife.

Standing between Hoyt and Royce, Nat suddenly appeared, white as a sheet and clearly shaken.

She was safe.

Applause broke out as the people who'd been inside poured out—their friends and family rushing to them.

Blowing out a breath, Jake braced himself against a nearby car, relief weakening his knees. Straightening, he swallowed the lump in his throat and moved toward her, letting his gaze rake over her and checking her for any sign of injury.

She didn't appear to be hurt—just shaken—and clung to Hoyt like a lifeline, stumbling several times as they made their way across the sidewalk toward him.

Hoyt supported her with an arm wrapped around her waist, half carrying her. Bending low, he said something to her, his smile encouraging while his eyes glittered with ice. Others came out behind them, but Jake only had eyes for his wife.

Tears filled her eyes, and with a cry, she broke free of Hoyt's hold and raced toward him. Leaping the last couple of feet, she threw herself at him. "Jake! Oh, God!"

He gathered her close, tears stinging his eyes. Bending his head, he buried his face against her neck, breathing in the scent of her.

Each breath he took settled him a little more, easing some of the dizziness and loosening the hard icy rock in his stomach. "Thank God! Christ, I was so scared."

"Oh, Jake. You don't know how much I needed this." She buried her face against his neck, a sob escaping. "Hold me tighter."

Lifting his head, he saw Hoyt standing behind her, his hands clenched at his sides. "As tight as you want, baby." He ran a hand down her back. "Are you all right?"

Nodding, Nat took a shuddering breath. "Yes. I'm fine. Hoyt made me get on the floor and he shot all three of them."

Jake looked to Hoyt for confirmation, breathing a sigh of relief when Hoyt nodded.

"She's okay. Might have a couple of bruises on her arm from me picking her up. I wasn't exactly delicate about it."

Leaning against Jake's chest, Nat reached back to Hoyt, who immediately took her hand in his. "We have to go back inside for questioning. Ace knew he'd have a riot on his hands if he didn't let everyone out so that you and the others knew we were all okay."

Hearing a squeal, Jake turned his head to see Jesse pushing out of Rio's arms and racing toward them. Reluctantly setting his wife on her feet, Jake met Hoyt's gaze over the two women's heads, the horror of the past several minutes passing between them.

Love for her, the horror of what could have happened united them like never before.

The relationship between them suddenly became more intense, the sobering experience they'd just had a sharp reminder of the responsibilities they would share.

After today, things would never be the same.

Nat patted Jesse's hand. "You shouldn't have worried so much. I just stayed behind Hoyt. What's the point in putting up with these big lunks if you can't use them as a shield when you need one?"

Everyone around them laughed, some of the tension easing as Jake suspected Nat had intended.

Clay and Rio looking relieved, smiling indulgently as the two women hugged.

Rio yanked Jesse against him. "Come on, baby. Let's get that lunch that Hoyt and Nat were supposed to get for us. Now that I'm not scared shitless, I'm hungry again."

Flattening a hand on his chest, Jesse looked up at him adoringly. "You're always hungry."

Hoyt tugged Nat's hair playfully as he pulled her back against him. "Is that all I am to you? A shield? I'm just glad that you're smart enough to follow orders." Pushing her hair back from her forehead, he touched his lips to hers. "You did just what I told you to do and didn't distract me. I'm proud of you."

Blushing, Nat shrugged. "Yeah, well don't get used to it. Doing what you tell me to do when guns are pointed at us is one thing. Don't expect it again."

Hoyt's lips twitched. "We'll see. Ace is over there gesturing for us to go back inside. Come on. Let's get this over with so you can go home with Jake."

Nat frowned. "What about you?"

Wrapping an arm around her waist, he steered her toward Ace. "I shot two people, Natalie. They're going to have a hell of a lot more questions for me. Come on. The Feds and state police are on their way, and they won't take kindly to Ace letting us out before we've been questioned."

Nat nodded, leaning into him. "Ace understands the way this town works. They don't."

Their ease with each other shocked Jake, and fighting jealousy, he stared after her, surprised when Nat turned back to him.

Although she looked better, she was still a little too pale for his peace of mind. "Do you have to go back to the store, or can you wait here for me?" The haunted look in her eyes made him want to run after her and carry her home.

Humbled by his wife's unusual display of neediness, Jake smiled, some of the tightness in his chest easing. "Of course, I'll be here. Nothing's more important to me than you are."

Her shoulders relaxed, the tension in her body easing. "Thanks." She winked at him, a smile playing at her full lips. "You're always there when I need you."

Jake smiled, his smile falling as soon as she disappeared back into the bank. "I always will be, baby. I always will be."

Chapter Ten

She'd avoided looking at the injured men being taken outside, but walking back into the bank, Nat automatically looked at the floor where they'd been, grimacing at the blood left behind.

With a hand at her back, Hoyt urged her along. "Keep going, and just look straight ahead."

They made their way to the manager's office, where Ace waited, his eyes glittering with barely repressed fury.

Nat knew that as sheriff, Ace would take the attempted robbery as a personal insult.

He took great pride in protecting the residents of Desire, and didn't take kindly to troublemakers.

What happened today would have him ready to chew nails.

Frowning, Nat dropped into one of the office chairs while Hoyt closed the door behind them. "How's the guard?"

Ace leaned back in the chair behind the desk and sighed. "He's alive, but that's all I know right now." Sitting forward, he eyed Hoyt, folding his hands on the desk in front of him. "The state police and the Feds should be here soon. I wanted to talk to Hoyt first and find out what happened before they get here. The Feds and state police are going to want to question him, too." His gaze met Nat's, softening. "Are you okay, honey?"

"I'm fine." Surprisingly, she was. Shaky, but calmer than she'd expected.

Hoyt took the other seat, reaching out to take her hand in his, running his thumb over the tops of her fingers, the comforting gesture also a protective one. "You can question her now. Jake's waiting to take her home. If anyone has any other questions, they can ask her there."

Nat blinked at his arrogance, his hard, cold demeanor so chilling that she shivered. To her further surprise, Ace's lips twitched.

"I'll do my best, but the Feds might feel differently." Sitting forward, Ace picked up a pen. "So you want to tell me what happened here? Nat, you start."

Shrugging, Nat glanced at Hoyt. "Hoyt was coming to open an account, since he'll be living here now. I came with him to make the deposit." Her stomach clenched. "Oh, shit. I dropped it on the floor."

Ace held out a hand when she started to jump up. "The bank manager has it. He'll take care of it for you. Tell me what happened." His sharp demand didn't surprise her. He would be mad as hell, and she would bet he'd be in a mood for weeks.

She tightened her hold on Hoyt's hand, her heart racing again at the memory. "We walked in, and I saw everyone lying on the floor, and those three bank robbers. It didn't really hit me at first. I saw masked men with guns, and at first, I thought someone had to be playing some kind of joke. Things like that don't happen in Desire." Her voice broke. "I thought we were dead."

She didn't think she'd ever forget the horror of that moment.

Gripping her hand, Hoyt wrapped his other arm around her and began rubbing her back. "Take a couple of deep breaths, baby. It's over. You're safe."

Nodding, Nat swallowed heavily, a little surprised that some of the panic she'd felt when she'd walked into the bank came rushing back. "I'm okay. It's over. I don't know what's wrong with me."

Frowning, she looked at Ace. "I swear, Ace, I stood there like an idiot. It was like my brain couldn't wrap itself around what I was seeing. I mean, that's not what I expected to see when I walked in. This is Desire. Nothing ever happens here. I've never been that scared before. I couldn't think. I couldn't move. I couldn't stop staring at the guns."

Shaking the mental image away, Nat blew out a breath and squeezed Hoyt's hand. "Before I could really process it, Hoyt told me to get down, and I did. I guess I did, but to be honest, I was on the floor and didn't even remember getting down there. The guy standing on the counter yelled something at one of the other masked men—the one closest to Hoyt. The other guy came rushing up to Hoyt, screaming at him to get down. He lifted his gun, and—" Irritated that her voice broke, she waved off Hoyt when he leaned closer. "I'm okay." Lifting her gaze to his, she smiled tremulously, shocked at the sting of tears. "He lifted the gun toward Hoyt, and I thought he was going to kill him."

Uncaring that Ace watched, she leaned toward Hoyt, thrilling at the feel of being gathered into his warm, secure embrace. "He just came back into our lives." Breathing in the scent of him, she lifted her head again, turning to frown at him. "You just grabbed my arms and yanked me right off the floor. How the hell did you do that?"

Hoyt smiled, bring her hand to his lips. "You don't weigh as much as the men I've had to lift."

Shaking her head, Nat smiled back, warmed by the way he kept her hand in his as she looked back at Ace. "Anyway, I was lying on the floor, but I watched the man rush up to Hoyt. I thought for sure he was going to shoot him. Then, Hoyt moved." Frowning, she tried to remember what had happened, but only remembered a blur of movement. "I swear, I watched it but I couldn't tell you what happened if I had to."

Turning her head, she looked into Hoyt's eyes. "Damn, you moved fast."

Nat jumped at the knock on the door, spinning around as the door opened to admit Royce.

Hoyt took advantage of the distraction to lean close to Nat, whispering against her ear. "And I can move just as slowly when it suits me."

Nat shivered as he straightened and sat back in his chair, the look of satisfaction in his eyes telling her he'd teased her on purpose to help her settle.

Surprised that after all the years they'd spent apart, he still could read her so easily, Nat smiled up at him, her breath catching at the tenderness in his eyes.

Royce shot a look of apology to Nat and Hoyt before facing Ace. "Sorry to interrupt you, but Linc asked me to tell you that Rafe's on his way to the hospital to talk to the guard and the other two men. Ace, you should have seen Hoyt in action. He was incredible."

Coming farther into the room, Royce began pacing back and forth behind Nat and Hoyt. "Even if you'd seen it, you wouldn't have believed it. I still don't know how he did it. Christ, those maniacs came in, shot the guard, and started waving those guns around. They had us all facedown on the floor before we knew it."

He kept glancing at Ace as he paced. "It all happened so fast. The next thing I knew, Hoyt and Nat strolled in. I was hoping that they'd just hit the floor so those assholes would leave without shooting anyone else. Hoyt shoved Nat behind him and said something to her over his shoulder, and thank God, she dropped to the floor. He didn't, though. Just stood there. Christ, I've never seen such a cold look before. Sent a fucking chill down my spine."

Pausing, he shook his head. "The one guy rushed up to him and Hoyt moved. Don't ask me what he did, because I couldn't tell you how he did it. He moved and everything happened at once. I think Hoyt's the only one who knew what the hell happened. Shots rang out and all three of those assholes were lying on the floor. I swear, it didn't take more than a second. He moved so damned fast. It was all a blur."

Nat turned to Royce. "You said that Rafe was going to talk to the guard and the other two men. There were three of them."

Ace nodded abruptly. "Thanks, Royce. I'll be out in couple of minutes. Take Nat with you. Jake's outside waiting for her. I want to talk to Hoyt alone."

Nat sat forward. "Why? What's going on? Ace, you're not going to arrest him for shooting those men, are you?"

Anger and fury combined, and without thinking, she jumped to her feet, waving a finger at him. "You heard what Royce said. Those men were waving guns around. Did you expect him to let them shoot us?"

Hoyt reached for her. "Natalie."

Shaking off the hand Hoyt laid on her arm, Nat leaned over the desk, getting in Ace's face, so angry she shook with it. So scared. "I can't believe you would arrest him for that! What was he supposed to do?"

Hoyt closed his hand over her forearm. "Baby, calm down."

Ace leaned toward her. "He could have just gotten on the floor like everyone else and waited until the guys left."

"Natalie—"

Nat shrugged off Hoyt's hand again, crossing her arms over her chest and raising a brow at Ace. "Is that what *you* would have done?"

Ace raised a brow as well. "No, but Hoyt isn't the law in this town, now is he?"

Fear that Ace would arrest Hoyt shook her to her core, and with a curse, she slammed her hand on the desk. "Damn it, Ace! You can't arrest him. Don't you pull that tough-guy stuff with me. How do you know those bastards wouldn't have shot all of us on the way out the door?"

With a sigh, Ace leaned back again. "Nat, I understand you're upset. I've got to question him, and then the state police and Feds are going to want to question him, too. We're going to have to look at the video and—"

Straightening, she avoided the hand Hoyt held out to her. "Good! Look at the fucking video and you'll see that he did what he had to do."

When Hoyt got to his feet and wrapped himself around her from behind, she elbowed him in his hard stomach before turning her head to look up at him. "Why the hell aren't you saying anything?"

Hoyt's lips twitched. "You're doing enough talking for both of us. Why don't you go with Royce and let me talk to the sheriff?"

Spinning to face Hoyt squarely, she shook her head. "I don't see how you can just stand there while Ace—"

Hoyt's brow went up. "While Ace—what? Wants to question me because I shot two men?"

"Why the hell do all of you keep talking about *two* men. There were *three!*"

Royce and Ace both stilled, Royce looking decidedly uncomfortable, and a far cry from the playful man she knew.

Ace sighed, running his hand through his hair. "Nat—"

Hoyt ran a hand over her hair. "The one that I grabbed died. I used him as a shield and the leader shot him while aiming for me. There was a death, Natalie. Ace just needs to ask me some questions about it. Now, go to Jake and I'll be there when I can." Meeting her frown with a smile, he tapped her chin. "Don't worry. If I'm arrested, you'll know about it. You can come visit me."

Nat poked his stomach, and scowled at him to hide her fear that he would be arrested. "That's not funny."

Hoyt bent to touch his lips to hers. "It'll be fine, honey. Go to Jake. I think you both need a little time together to settle."

* * * *

Hoyt waited until the door closed behind Royce and Natalie before taking his seat again and facing Ace. "The teller was in on it. The woman with the short blonde hair."

Ace stilled, his eyes hardening. "What makes you say that?"

Hoyt expected suspicion, but Ace displayed nothing except interest. Adopting a relaxed pose, he met the sheriff's gaze. "She and the man standing on the counter—the leader—kept exchanging glances. He also turned his back on her without thinking twice about it, and when he did, she didn't take the opportunity to hit the alarm. She actually looked worried about him."

Ace jotted down several lines of notes before looking up again. "You said that they exchanged glances. What kind of glances?"

"Intimate glances. It was clear that she was worried."

Ace's eyes narrowed. "Are you sure?"

"Yes." Hoyt sat forward. "Look, Ace, you know that I've been trained, as you have, to be observant. I see things a lot of other people might miss. I'm telling you what I saw."

Sitting back, he continued. "She's also the only one who screamed when I shot him and started to cry. She started around the counter before she remembered, and rushed back, but it was clear that she wasn't happy that it ended the way it did."

Ace took a few more notes. "What happened?"

Hoyt automatically adopted the tone he used when giving a report, keeping his expression emotionless. "I disarmed the target closest to me, and used him as a shield, while firing his weapon to shoot the leader before he could get off a shot. I then turned to the third target, the man standing over the guard, who'd already fired one round and hit the man I was holding. He shot again just as I shot, and that round went into the wall behind me. There were four shots, not three. I fired two of them."

He didn't tell Ace about his horror when he realized that Natalie had been trying to stand, or the mind-numbing fear he'd felt when he saw her on her knees and thought that the stray bullet had ricocheted and hit her.

Ace wrote several more lines, and looked up, his eyes searching. "Ballistics and the video will confirm that." Sitting back, he tossed his pen onto the desk, and for the first time since they'd walked into the room, Ace smiled. "I saw the video. It matches your story. Royce was right. Even watching it, it was hard to tell what happened. I had to watch it in slow motion to catch the details. I'll go back and look at it again, this time watching the teller."

Voices came from the other side of the door. "Feds are here. They're going to have questions, but it's nothing you should have to worry about. I have no doubt that ballistics, the video, and the eyewitnesses will confirm your story."

Getting to his feet, Ace held out a hand. "Anytime you want a job, there's a position open for you." Chuckling softly, Ace rounded the desk. "I've seen you in action. You're more than qualified, and sure as hell know how to handle yourself. You can ride with me to the office. They can question you there. I heard you didn't have lunch. I'll have some sandwiches brought in."

Amused, Hoyt grinned. "Do you know *everything* that happens around here?"

Ace grimaced, glancing out toward the lobby. "Sometimes, I slip up."

* * * *

Looking down at Nat as she whimpered and shifted in her sleep, Jake tucked the light blanket more firmly around her shoulder. He'd been holding her in his arms for the last forty-five minutes or so, just staring down at her, nestled safely against his chest. He pushed her hair back, studying her features, unable to get rid of the tightness in his chest.

He'd come closer to losing her today than he ever had, and he still hadn't stopped shaking.

Thank God Hoyt had been there.

Blowing out a breath, he scrubbed a hand over her face and went back to watching the late-night news. It didn't keep his attention for long.

He couldn't stop looking out her, his stomach still clenched at the thought of what could have happened.

Her features, flushed with sleep, still had a pinched look to them. She hadn't truly relaxed, and slept fitfully, whimpering periodically in her sleep, the sound ripping his heart to shreds.

Toying with the ends of her hair, he stared down at her, feeling like the luckiest man in the world.

This precious woman belonged to him.

The front door opened, startling him. Looking up, he saw Hoyt walking through the doorway, and glanced at the clock as Hoyt closed and locked the door behind him. "It's late. They must have had a hell of a lot of questions."

His friend looked beat, but there was a restlessness about him that Jake hadn't seen since the night he convinced Hoyt to let him marry Nat.

"They did. A lot of them." Hoyt's gaze swept over Nat, the concern in his eyes sharp despite his obvious fatigue. "Then we talked shop."

Glancing at Nat, Jake kept his voice low as he adjusted the blanket, running his fingers over the sleeve of her cotton nightgown. "We were worried. She wouldn't go to bed until you got home. She even called Ace to make sure you hadn't been arrested. I finally got her to sit down here about an hour ago, and started rubbing her back. She tried, but she couldn't fight it anymore. She went out like a light."

Hoyt shrugged off his coat, sat at the other end of the sofa, and pulled off his boots. "Ace told me she called. He thought it was funny as hell. The Feds didn't." Setting his boots aside, Hoyt leaned back, eyeing Nat as he lifted her feet to his lap. "She okay?"

Nodding, Jake ran a hand over her arm, unable to fight his possessiveness. "Yeah, but she can't quite settle. She keeps whimpering in her sleep and she's restless."

He reached for the hand she rested on his chest, running his finger back and forth over her wedding band. "She told me what you did." He glanced up at him, unsurprised to find him staring longingly at Nat. "The phone's been ringing ever since we got home. Everyone wanted to make sure that both of you were okay, to tell me that you and Nat looked pretty cozy walking around town, and to ask if the stories they were hearing about what you did in the bank were true. She must have told the story a dozen times. Jesse, Clay, and Rio came by a couple of hours ago, and Nat couldn't sit still. I think she finally wore herself out."

When Nat moved again, stretching her legs, Hoyt took the foot that peeked out from the blanket in his hand, running a thumb back and forth over her fuzzy-sock-covered toes. "Adrenaline crash, too. When I picked her up off the bank floor, she was as white as a sheet and shaking so hard that her teeth chattered." Hoyt sighed and stared down at her foot, apparently deep in thought.

Sensing that something bothered him, and knowing that Hoyt wouldn't talk about it until he was ready, Jake turned his attention back to the television, not really paying attention to it as he continued to play with Nat's fingers.

As the silence continued, Jake glanced at Hoyt to find him still staring down at Nat's foot. "Joe called."

Hoyt's head jerked up. "Oh, hell. He heard about the robbery. I didn't even think of that. Christ, I'm fucking this up."

Jake hid a smile. "It's going to take some time for you to get used to other people caring about you. Joe heard about the bank robbery on the news and wanted to know if anyone got hurt. When he found out you and Nat were inside and what happened, he freaked out. He talked to Nat, and she managed to calm him down, but he wants to talk to you. He wants to hear from you that you're okay, and he and his cousins want a blow-by-blow description of how you managed to take down three armed men without a weapon."

Hoyt's smile appeared strained. "I'll call him in a few minutes." Dropping his head back against the cushion, he blew out a breath and stared at the ceiling. "I was so fucking scared that the shot that hit the wall ricocheted and hit her. Every time I think about it, it makes me sick to my stomach. I was too damned slow."

Stunned, Jake whipped his head around. "What the hell are you talking about? I talked to Rafe. He said that you took those men out so fast that they had to slow the video to see how you did it."

Setting Nat's feet back on the cushion, Hoyt got to his feet. "Doing what I did at the bank was just years of training kicking in. Christ, Jake."

Blowing out a breath, he scrubbed a hand over his face. "I can handle any gun out there—shoot it, clean it, take it apart and put it back together with my eyes closed. I can handle myself in a fight. I can handle explosives, fly a helicopter, and not only plan a mission down to the last detail, but lead a team to carry it out."

Staring down at Nat, he shook his head, his expression softening. "But dealing with Natalie scares the hell out of me." Pacing back and forth, he couldn't seem to stop glancing at her. "When I first got here, and was talking to you, that's what I was thinking while we waited for her to get back from Jesse's. Today, when I thought a bullet might hit her, I realized that loving her is scarier than I first thought. I feel like all I'm doing is making mistakes—stumbling along and winging it."

Jake chuckled. "I have to say I've been there a time or two, especially when we first married." He glanced down at her, bringing her fingers to his lips. "I knew she loved you and that it was going to take some time for us to get comfortable with each other. For a long time, I woke up every morning with my heart in my throat, wondering if that was the day she was going to tell me that she'd made a mistake. The first time she told me that she loved me—Christ."

He could still remember that feeling in the pit of his stomach, the elation and dizziness that had him grinning like an idiot for weeks.

Hoyt turned away. "And now I'm in that position. I'm scared to death I'm going to fuck this up and I'll never get a chance to make it right. She deserves so much from me."

Shaking his head, he blew out another breath. "I'm starving. Ace got some sandwiches, but that was hours ago. Do you mind if I fix myself something to eat?"

Jake sighed, and shook his head, blaming himself for Hoyt feeling uncomfortable. He knew it would take time, but also knew that he hadn't done enough to make his best friend feel at home. "Hoyt, damn it, this is your *home* now. You can help yourself to whatever's out there, but Nat left a plate for you in the oven. You know she cooks when she's nervous. There's more in the fridge."

Glancing at Nat, Hoyt nodded, his eyes unreadable. "Thanks."

With another sigh, Jake eased his wife from his lap, placing a pillow under her head as he got to his feet. He couldn't let Hoyt go on this way. The tension in the house had all of them on edge, making it more difficult for everyone. Following Hoyt to the kitchen, Jake leaned against the doorway and watched his friend take a warm plate from the oven. "The only way you can fuck this up is by walking away."

Straightening, Jake went to the refrigerator and retrieved two bottles of beer. He handed one to Hoyt before twisting the cap from the other and tossing it into the trash can. "She finds it hard to believe, that after all these years, you still want her. She feels boring compared to what you're used to, and that living here will bore you out of your mind. She needs to know that you're not going to walk away again."

Hoyt's eyes flared, his grip on his fork turning his knuckles white. "Damn it, I had no fucking choice!" Glancing toward the doorway, Hoyt took several deep breaths, obviously struggling for control.

He leaned forward again, the anguish in his eyes making Jake feel even worse. "What was I supposed to do—kidnap her? I begged her to marry me and come with me, but she wouldn't. Leaving her here was the hardest thing I ever did. The only thing that kept me sane was knowing that you would take care of her. I knew you loved her, and I could see how much she cared about you. I came to see all of you as often as I could. I couldn't stay away—until it hurt too damned much to come back just for visits. I had to figure out how the hell I was going to approach you about letting me into your lives for good."

"I know, Hoyt. I know how much you love her." Shaking his head, Jake smiled. "I always knew. I just don't think she does." Jake pulled out a chair and sat across from him. "I understand that you had no choice. She understands it, too. Rationally, she knows you had no choice. *Emotionally*, though, she still has issues with it. You said it yourself—she's scared to fight with you. She's not secure enough to believe that you're going to stay."

Hoyt picked up his fork again, a faint smile curving his lips. "She sure as hell didn't have any trouble fighting with me when she thought Ace was going to arrest me."

Jake laughed, careful to keep his voice low so that he didn't wake his wife. "She told me about that as soon as she came out of the bank. She was sure wound up. Went on about it for twenty minutes."

Hoyt sighed. "I told her that I was staying. I don't know what else I can do to convince her."

Watching Hoyt dig into his food, Jake frowned and ran his thumb up and down the neck of the beer bottle. "Sleeping in the spare room probably isn't a good idea." At Hoyt's sharp look, Jake shrugged and picked up his beer again. "There are going to be times we're going to want to spend the night alone with her, but for now, she needs to know that we're both here for her. You're going to have to start acting like this is your home, and she's your woman, instead of acting like a guest here. Standing on the sidelines has never been your style, Hoyt. I think your hesitancy is making her nervous."

Hoyt lowered his fork and looked up. "I want her. I love her so damned much that it scares me sometimes. But, I don't want to come between the two of you. I'd hoped that you'd moved here, knowing that one day I'd be back for her. I'd hoped she knew that, too. I was arrogant enough to be surprised when I met resistance. I should have expected it. A lot of time has gone by. I just hope like hell it hasn't been too much time."

Jake smiled. "It hasn't." Raising a brow, he lifted his bottle. "You know she's going to test you, don't you? She's going to have to see how far she can push you before you throw in the towel and leave."

Hoyt grinned and started eating again. "I'm looking forward to it. She's not going to be able to get rid of me. I'm here to stay."

Jake nodded, grinning. "Good. You might not believe this, but I like having you around. I always had a feeling that you'd be back and want to be with her, but I have to admit, I never thought you'd want to share her."

Hoyt frowned. "You figured I'd try to take her away from you?" He shook his head. "First of all, that would never happen. She loves you too much to leave you, and I love her too much to try to make her choose."

Hoyt grinned. "Besides, I've missed you, too. We were always so close that we knew what the other was thinking. I've missed that."

Jake smiled, some of the tightness in his stomach easing. "We're going to need that, and need to stick together more than ever now." Gesturing toward Hoyt's plate, he got to his feet to get two more beers. "Eat up. You're going to need your energy. I think both of us are going to have our hands full with her."

Hoyt's slow grin reminded Jake of the young man he'd known years ago. "There's nothing I'd rather have my hands filled with."

Chapter Eleven

The warmth registered at first, followed almost immediately by the scent of delicious male.

Jake.

Firm muscle wrapped around her.

The familiar slide of hot, devious hands creating a light friction as they moved over her.

Gentleness. Tenderness. *Heat.*

She smiled, her body already trembling with the stirring of arousal. Running her hand over his chest, she kept her eyes closed, a soft moan escaping at the feel of his lips over her shoulder.

She treasured these quiet moments, the private time they carved out for each other before the day started.

Smiling at the feel of her husband's lips against her hair, Nat snuggled closer, sliding her hand lower to trace her fingers over the underside of his cock. "Good morning."

"Good morning, baby." His sleep-roughened voice never failed to thrill her, the gruff tone as potent to her senses as his silky drawl.

His cock jumped against her hand, and with a groan, he trailed his fingertips up her arm to her shoulder and down to the outer curve of her breast. "Soft. Pliant. Warm. Legs spread to make a place for me." He scraped his teeth over her jaw, sending a shiver through her. "The only thing that would make this more perfect is if you were naked."

Nat smiled as he rolled to his side, taking her with him. "Hmm. Wait a minute. I never wear a nightgown to bed."

Almost immediately, memories of the previous night came rushing back.

Jerking upright, she lifted her gaze to Jake's. Her heart skipped a beat to find him staring down at her, his hair disheveled and lying over his forehead, giving him a rakish look. "Hoyt? Did he come home?" She sucked in a breath when the bed shifted and a hard arm came around her from behind.

An equally hard body curled around her and pressed against her from her shoulders to the backs of her knees. "Yes, he did." With a hand around her middle holding her close, Hoyt pressed his lips against her neck, making her shiver under Jake's watchful gaze. "And he's already had his coffee and showered, and after lying next to you all night, has been waiting impatiently for you to wake up."

The rush of anticipation and awareness hit her hard. Her stomach muscles tightened under the hand Hoyt slid lower, a rush of moisture escaping to dampen her panties just as Hoyt slid his fingers into them. With a groan, she buried her face against Jake's chest, hiding a smile. "Oh, hell, another morning person."

Hoyt's hand slid over her mound, his breath warm on her shoulder. "You went to sleep so early last night that I thought you'd be up before now."

Jake stiffened and shifted beside her, rolling her to her back. Lifting her face to his, he studied her eyes, his gaze narrowed and sharp. "She hasn't been sleeping well. It's my fault. She's been lying awake at night, worried about the distance between us. I didn't know what to say to ease her mind, since I didn't know if you were really going to come here or not, and I didn't want to upset her more, so I said nothing."

Holding her gaze, he touched his lips to hers. "It was a mistake on my part, and one that won't be repeated. She slept like a baby between us, didn't she?"

Nat didn't get a chance to reply, melting under the heat of his kiss.

It was a kiss meant to overwhelm—and it did.

A kiss meant to possess, a kiss designed to brand.

And it did.

The kind of kiss that tore through her resistance with ease and made her soft and pliable under his touch.

Her Master's kiss.

Lifting his head, he studied her features, a small smile tugging at his lips when she lifted her head in an effort to close the distance between them again. With a hand pressed against her shoulder, he prevented it, his eyes filled with satisfaction. "I'm going to have to take better care of her in the future. Yesterday morning I saw that I've been too easy on her. I'm going to have to take her into the playroom more often, and be a little more demanding than I've been. To bring the edge back that she loves so much. To show her how much I need her. To remind her what she means to me."

Nat gulped, her clit tingling at the erotic threat—the erotic promise—in his eyes.

Desperate to touch her husband, she lifted her hand to place it on his chest, sucking in a breath at Hoyt's sharp tug to her nipple.

Jake took her hand in his and lifted it to his lips, his eyes flaring. "The three of us can spend the day together, exploring some of those needs."

"And see if we can create new ones." Hoyt worked the material of her gown over her head and tossed it aside, groaning and gathering her closer. "I've waited a long time to make love to her, and I can't wait any longer." His hand moved over her breast, her nipple beading under his palm. "God, she feels so good."

Jake smiled faintly and moved the covers aside, his gaze lowering to watch Hoyt manipulate her nipple. "I'm going to go get some coffee, and give the two of you some time alone."

Bending again, he touched his lips to hers. Tapping his finger over her other nipple, he lifted his head and smiled. "Stop looking so worried. I'm not going very far, and you're in safe hands."

Hoyt closed his fingers over her nipple just as the door closed behind Jake. "He's upset because he doesn't think he can protect you the way I did at the bank."

Nat stilled, concern for Jake mingling with the need Hoyt's expert fingers created. "How do you know?"

Hoyt's lips moved over her shoulder, a hard thigh pushing between her thighs and forcing them apart. "I could tell by the way he looked last night. The way he talked." Lifting his head, he pushed her hair back from her forehead and stared into her eyes. "Yesterday morning, I could see how much your response excited him. You excited both of us. He's going to expect even more from you now that he feels that he's been neglecting your needs."

Biting back a moan, Nat arched into him, rubbing her slit against his hair-roughened thigh and pushed her breast more firmly against his palm. "Jake has never neglected me. Never."

Turning her to her back, Hoyt rid her of her panties, covered her body with his and spread her thighs, making a place for himself between them. Staring down at her, he smiled, sliding his cock over her swollen clit. "Jake's going to need some reassurance from you. You're going to have to be a good girl and give him what he needs. *Everything* he needs. I'll do everything I can to make this work, including spanking that lush ass of yours if you defy him."

Wrapping her legs around him, Nat moaned and pushed against his cock, her pussy clenching with the need to have him inside her. "I always give Jake what he needs. He always gives me what I need, too. Are you going to take me, or are you going to talk all day?"

Hoyt's eyes narrowed, his eyes darkening. "Oh, I'm definitely going to take you. I need to wear a condom with you, remember? Or would you like to get pregnant again?"

The thought of having another baby, this time when Hoyt would be there to see her through her pregnancy sent a thrill through her, but reality had her shaking her head. "I'm too old to start over with diapers, and juggling you and Jake is going to take all of my time."

Bracing himself on an elbow, Hoyt slid his hand up her body to cup her breast, his eyes glittering with a combination of male satisfaction and hunger. "I'm fine with that. I want every minute with you I can get. I never thanked you for having my baby, did I?" Sliding a hand under her neck, he gathered her close. "Thank you, baby. Thank you for giving me a son."

Incredibly moved, Nat blinked back tears she hadn't expected. "You're welcome. You don't mind that we don't have another?" She hated the thought of what it might do to Jake.

Reaching over, he retrieved a condom from the bedside table, grinning as he ripped it open. "Not at all. Right now, I'm just grateful to have you back in my life."

He shifted slightly to roll on the condom, eyeing her steadily. "I'm not going anywhere." He covered her body with his again, fitting the head of his cock against her pussy opening. Fisting her hair in his hand, he pulled it aside and bent to nuzzle her cheek. "I've missed you so damned much. I've dreamed about having you just like this for years. Warm. Soft. Your legs wrapped around me. Heaven."

The desperation and hunger in his raw tone thrilled her, fueling her own desperation.

Pressing her heels to his tight butt, Nat lifted her hips, sucking in a breath when he thrust into her with one smooth stroke. "Hoyt!"

He paused, holding himself still as he studied her features. "Yes. It's me. After all these years, I'm inside you again. God, I've thought of this so many times. If I find out this is a dream, I'm gonna be mad as hell."

Nat's soft laughter ended in a moan. "You're not dreaming. You move differently. You feel different, but there's something so familiar about the way you hold me."

"I know what it feels like to lose you now." Twining his fingers with hers, he pressed the back of her hands against the pillow, his eyes daring her to object. The gentle dominance of the act, and the thrill of his slow, firm thrusts had her writhing beneath him, her excitement growing when he merely raised a brow, not budging at all. "I won't lose you again."

His eyes narrowed and sharpened, the anger in them stirring a primitive and raw edge to their lovemaking. "I spent years so furious with you for not coming with me—telling myself that if you'd really loved me, you would have married me and come with me without hesitation."

"What? You—" Nat tried to break his hold so that she could smack him, but he held firm, his eyes flaring with delight at her struggle as though he welcomed the opportunity to vent some of his frustration.

A muscle worked in his jaw. "I blamed you for a long time, and did whatever I could to get over you. Nothing worked. You were in my fucking blood. You've always been in my blood."

Struck by his admission, Nat stared up at him in wonder. "Hoyt, I never knew—"

He withdrew and thrust deep again, his entire body trembling. "Of course you didn't know. I couldn't let you see that just being in the same room with you was both heaven and hell." His deep, growling tone rumbled through his chest and vibrated over her. He withdrew until just the head of his cock remained inside her, and plunged deep again, stealing her breath. "I wanted to forget you." He plunged again.

And again.

"I wanted to stay away from you, but every time I could get away, I got here as fast as I could. I kept telling myself that it was to see my son, but I knew the truth. I couldn't stay away from you and it pissed me off."

Despite the gentleness of his lips moving over her face, the anger in his voice and in his movements couldn't be mistaken.

Tightening his fingers on hers, he slid almost all the way out of her, brushing her lips with his as he thrust deep again. "At times, I hated you." Another thrust. "I couldn't forget you." Another. "I couldn't stop loving you." Holding himself deep, he stared into her eyes. "I couldn't fucking stay away from you."

Touched, humbled, and feeling guilty for not realizing the pain she'd caused him, Nat rubbed her cheek against his jaw. "I'm so sorry. I didn't know. I never meant for you to think that I didn't love you. I've always loved you."

Looking up at him, she studied his features. "We both made mistakes, Hoyt. We were both young and stupid." Trembling with hunger and love for him, she took a shuddering breath, her heart pounding with something that felt suspiciously like panic. "Are you going to be able to get past all that? Are we going to be able to do this without the past getting in the way?"

A muscle worked in his jaw. "We have to." He released her hands and ran his fingers over her temples, his eyes darkening. "I can't live without you, baby. I've just been existing. I need you too damned much to let anything get in the way of having you in my life again."

Nat cried out at his rapid thrusts. "It'll work. We'll make it work. Oh, God!"

Every sigh, every breath, every soft groan was precious to her.

They'd been good together in the past, but the chemistry between them now stunned her. "Hoyt. Oh, God! I can't believe this. I can't believe you're here."

Blinking back tears at the rush of emotion, she dug her fingertips into his shoulders. "I can't believe we're together again."

She loved Jake and would never be happy without him in her life, but she'd yearned for Hoyt, a selfish fantasy she never would have asked for, or even admitted to.

To suddenly find herself with both men she loved seemed like a dream come true.

"Believe it." His low groan thrilled her. Sliding his hand under her, and between her shoulder blades, he lifted her against him, his light brown eyes appearing golden as if lit from within. "You're mine again, and you're staying that way."

Watching her face, Hoyt thrust deep, the possessiveness in his eyes sharper than ever. "After all these years, you're mine again, and I'm never letting you go."

"Oh, God." Tightening her legs around him, she rocked her hips in time to his thrusts, crying out as the tension and sizzling heat grew stronger.

So good.

So hot.

She couldn't stop clenching on his cock, her cries becoming more desperate as the warning tingles became stronger. Another cry escaped when he stopped moving, leaving her teetering on the edge. "No!"

Her eyes flew open, her first thought that he'd already found his release.

One look at the fierce hunger in his eyes told her that he hadn't.

Moving against him, Nat punched his shoulder, digging her heels into his butt to lift herself against him. "Move, damn it! I'm so close."

Hoyt's grip tightened, his eyes glittering. "Do you think I don't know that? Do you think I don't feel the way your sweet pussy quivers around my cock, or that you kept clamping down on me like you wanted to pull me deeper? I've dreamed of this for too long to let it end so quickly."

Fisting a hand in her hair, he pulled her head back, his expression hard as he began to move again. "I've spent years trying to forget you. Years!"

Staring into her eyes, he withdrew, and with a groan, slid deep again. "I teased and tormented other women the way I wanted to tease and torment you. I made them scream with pleasure the way I wanted to make you scream. I made them beg the way I wanted you to beg."

Fighting the jealousy she had no right to feel, Nat shoved at him. "I don't want to hear about your other women."

Nipping at her bottom lip, he groaned again, thrusting several more times. "But they weren't you. I wanted them to be you or to make me forget you, but nobody ever could. Nobody can satisfy me but you. Only *you* can make me feel this way, and I'm going to spend the rest of my life making you mindless with pleasure. It's going to take me the rest of my life to do to you the things I've been imagining doing to you for years. I'm going to make you beg. Plead. Cry out your pleasure. I'm going to hear those sounds from you that I've been fantasizing about all these years."

Nat hung on as his strokes came faster, thrilled and slightly alarmed at his anger.

"Hoyt, I've missed you, too." It felt so good. So right to be in his arms again.

To have him inside her.

The hard feel of him filling her—the feel of him all around her—had her frantic with need, the promise of release only a heartbeat away. "I thought it was over for us."

"Never. You and I will never be over." He stopped thrusting to look down at her again, easily subduing her struggles to get him to move again. "You want to come, don't you, baby?"

Fighting his hold, she bucked against him, frantic to ease the torment. "Please! Don't do this to me." Tears stung her eyes, the ache so intense, she would do anything to ease it. Thrashing her head from side to side, she closed her eyes and tried to buck against him.

"Look at me!"

Responding to the steel in his tone, Nat jerked, her gaze flying to his. Shaking with the need for release, surprising herself by whimpering. "Please."

Hoyt smiled, withdrawing and stroking deep again, his smile widening with satisfaction when she moaned and moved with him. "Say my name, and I'll let you come. I need to hear my name on your lips. I need to know that you know it's me that's pleasuring you."

Shocked by the torment in his eyes, Nat lifted her face to his, breathing his name against his lips. "Hoyt. Please."

His eyes flared, and with a groan, he pumped his hips, changing the angle of his thrusts slightly to dig at a place inside her that sent her over with a speed that sent her senses reeling.

Sliding a hand under her hips, he lifted her into his quick thrusts, his eyes flaring at her cry of release. "Yeah. That's it. Come for me." His deep groan washed over her. "Keep coming, damn it. More!"

Shaking, she reached for him, the hot waves of release holding her in their grip and refusing to let her go. Each swollen wave seemed to last longer, each rush of pleasure layering over the last.

With another groan, he thrust deep and buried his face in her hair. "Never like this. Only you. You're the only one who can make me feel this way. I'm going to do everything in my power to keep you."

Lifting his head, he brushed her hair back, staring into her eyes. "Jake's going to demand more of a submission from you than ever, and you'd better give him everything he needs from you. I don't want anything to get in the way of me having you. I won't allow it. Ever."

Chapter Twelve

Sitting on the deck between them, Nat sipped her coffee, wondering if she'd ever been so completely happy.

And yet, so emotional.

She wanted to cry as she listened with half an ear as they talked about things that Jake had been planning to do around the house—mundane things that seemed to interest Hoyt immensely.

They'd spent the entire day talking about unimportant things and doing yard work, as if by some agreement, keeping the conversations with her lighthearted and relaxed.

It made everything seem so normal. So *permanent.*

After dinner, they'd come outside to sip coffee and talk in quiet tones, but Nat had long since dropped out of the conversation, content to just sit there in the darkness and listen to their low, deep voices.

Looking from Jake, on her left, to Hoyt, on her right she sighed and sipped her coffee, letting their conversation flow all around her, warming her like a soft blanket. Staring toward the line of trees behind the house, she tried to make out the mountains, but the new leaves on the trees prevented it.

It had gotten dark about an hour ago, and the only light came from the kitchen window behind them, creating a warm glow all around them, which added to the intimacy.

The scent of spring perfumed the air, but the nights still held the brisk chill of a fading winter.

A few of her flowers had started to break through the ground, and soon the outside of her house would be a riot of bright colors.

Smiling, she leaned back. Both Hoyt and Jake had teased her often about her flowers, which included every color in the rainbow.

Hoyt nodded at whatever Jake said, his features barely visible in the faint light. "I can get some of that started." Reaching out, he took Nat's free hand in his. "I talked to Joe earlier. He's thrilled that the three of us are together. He actually got choked up when he talked about coming home at the end of the semester."

Nat smiled and turned her head to meet Jake's gaze. "I'm looking forward to having him home again."

Jake, who'd been unusually quiet all day, smiled as he looked at her, the glitter of erotic heat in his eyes making her pulse trip. "But, you're nervous about being around him when you're with both of us. It's something that all of us are going to have to get used to."

Nat nodded. "You have to admit, it's going to be a little strange." Looking from Jake to Hoyt, and smiling at each of them, she set her cup aside, attempting nonchalance she was far from feeling. "He's very lucky to have two such incredible fathers. I've always been happy at how involved both of you have always been in his life."

Hoyt brought her hand to his lips, the twinkling of mischief in his eyes visible even in the low light. "And you? Would you like to tell us how you feel about having two such incredible lovers in your life?"

Pursing her lips, Nat pretended to consider that. Struggling to keep a straight face, she looked out into the night. "Well, let's see. Incredible, huh? I know that I have two extremely *arrogant* lovers." She glanced at each of them, careful to keep her expression bland. "Yes, I would say arrogant."

"Arrogant?" Jake's smile flashed in the darkness. "I think it's more like confident." Leaning close, he reached under her sweater and tapped her nipple. "I can, and have made you beg—repeatedly."

Tightening her hand on his, Nat leaned toward him. "Is that why you've been so quiet today? Because Hoyt made me beg?"

Hoyt chuckled. "You always were direct."

Jake stared at her for several long seconds as if mentally weighing his words. "Okay. We promised honesty." With a sigh, he dropped his head back. "It was...uncomfortable knowing that you and Hoyt were making love this morning. It was different than being in the same room. When you came out, the intimacy between you sort of knocked me off kilter for a while." Turning his head, he smiled faintly. "Not the honesty you expected? It won't work any other way. We knew that this wouldn't be easy. You've been mine for so long that it's hard to see you with another man. Even Hoyt."

Hoyt got to his feet and strolled to the edge of the patio. "I know that feeling well. That's how I felt when you married her, and each time I came to visit." Turning, he smiled at her. "She loves both of us, though. We're damned lucky to have her. Now, if another man came along and wanted to edge in what's ours, I would not be happy."

Nat laughed out loud, grateful that he'd once again managed to ease the tension. "Christ, I can hardly deal with the two of you! What the hell would make you think I'd want another one?"

She squeezed Jake's hand, adopting a thoughtful expression. "Wait a minute. I don't know about that. Having a nice quiet man might be nice."

She turned away from Hoyt's sharp look, afraid she wouldn't be able to hold back her laughter. Staring out into the night, she sighed and leaned back, folding her hands over her stomach. "A man who would want nothing more than to please me. A gentle man who'd give me everything I want, one who would sit with me at night and give me a foot rub instead of copping a feel."

Hoyt spun, his eyes narrowed. "Excuse me?"

Lifting her hand to his lips, Jake chuckled softly. "You'd be bored out of your mind with a man like that."

Nat shrugged, and continued as if neither man had spoken. "Someone who would worship the ground I walk on. Someone who would bring me breakfast in bed." With another deep sigh, she dropped her head back. "A simple, uncomplicated man who'd—oh!"

Her eyes flew open as she found herself upside down over a wide, muscular shoulder.

"Someone who wouldn't paddle your ass for being such a brat?" Hoyt's deep baritone mingled with her laughter.

Reaching for Jake, she kicked her feet, unable to stop laughing, sucking in a breath when Hoyt slid a threatening hand over her ass.

"Jake! Aren't you going to help me?"

Grabbing her coffee cup, he followed close behind as Hoyt carried her into the house, pausing to close and lock the door behind them. "Nope. You asked for it. You wanted to egg him on, and you're going to have to deal with the consequences."

Running a hand over her hair, he smiled, the heat in his eyes sending an erotic thrill through her. "You dared him and you know it. That can only mean one thing—you're in need of some attention."

Lifting her head and blinking against the light, she braced a hand on Hoyt's back, knowing exactly what buttons to push to get a reaction from her husband. "Since when did you become a pussy?"

His eyes flashed. "A pussy?" Fisting a hand in her hair, he reached out to cup her breast. "Maybe a trip to the playroom would be more beneficial."

The knock on the door startled her, and with a curse, Hoyt lowered her to her feet, slapping her ass just hard enough to sting. "To be continued."

Wondering who could be at the door, Nat curled up on the end of the sofa while Jake went to answer it. Surprised to see Linc standing in the doorway, she got to her feet again, her smile falling when she saw the look in his eyes.

Jake looked equally surprised. "Hey, Linc. What's going on?"

Linc sighed. "I need to talk to Hoyt."

Hoyt shrugged and took a seat, not appearing the least concerned. "So talk." When Linc hesitated, Hoyt smiled, a cold smile that sent a chill through Nat. "We have no secrets here."

Nat shared a look with Jake, curious to know what made the usually even-tempered deputy look so furious and unsettled.

Jake gestured toward the kitchen, keeping his arm firmly wrapped around her. "Come on into the kitchen. Have a cup of coffee."

While Jake poured the coffee and Nat put out cookies, Hoyt sat at the table, never taking his eyes from Linc.

Linc thanked Jake and sipped his coffee before setting it aside. "We had to let Debra Smith go." At Hoyt's frown, Linc sighed and glanced at Jake and Nat. "The teller. We can't find a damned thing to connect her to the robbery. Ace, Rafe, and I have been pouring over every piece of information we can dig up. We've questioned the manager and her coworkers. No one's seen her with any of them. We're checking on family and friends, but so far—nothing. Her mom and dad are both gone."

Hoyt's eyes narrowed. "She's in on it."

Nodding, Linc reached for a cookie, clearly frustrated. "I believe you. Ace and Rafe believe you, but we can't *prove* it. We've had Lucas, Devlin, and Caleb watching her and she hasn't even gone near the hospital to visit them. I don't know if you've ever met them, but they have a security business here in Desire."

Hoyt's expression never changed. "We've met. Tell me about the leader."

Linc's eyes narrowed, and he studied Hoyt with renewed interest. "His name is John Engels. The man who got killed was his brother, Henry. The other man in the hospital, the one who shot Henry when he was aiming for you is Clyde Johnson. Clyde grew up with the Engels in Albuquerque. It seems that they worked their way through New Mexico and part of Texas committing robberies. Liquor stores. Convenience stores. Gas stations. They've all got warrants for their arrest. This is the first time they'd tried robbing a bank, though."

Hoyt reached for his cup again, his eyes hard, his voice clipped, and all business. "Where's she from, and how long has she be living here?"

Nat frowned, and allowed herself to be pulled onto Jake's lap. "She doesn't live here, does she? I never see her around town, just in the bank."

Linc nodded. "That's right. She doesn't live here. She lives in Cushing. She lives alone in a small apartment that she rents month to month. She doesn't appear to have any friends there, and her landlord says that she pays the rent by sliding an envelope under the door. She never even sees her."

Hoyt continued to sip his coffee, but his entire demeanor had changed.

Nat couldn't put her finger on exactly what was different, but suddenly he seemed colder. Harsh. Uncompromising.

It was almost as if a mask had come down on his features, changing them subtly, but in a way that she would have never been able to put into words.

Hoyt inclined his head. "So she's someone who has to be watched. She was in on it."

Linc nodded. "Lucas agrees. He looked at the tape and dug up some background information on all three of them, but focused on John Engels, the one in charge. He's petty ante. Lucas said that there's no way Engels would have escalated to bank robbery if he hadn't been sure that he could get away with it. She's the key and she's being watched closely, but right now, Ace doesn't have enough to pick her up."

Nat stiffened, glancing at Hoyt. "So she's just going to get away with helping them?"

Linc shrugged and sat back in his chair. "If they don't talk and we can't prove it. The weakest link was the younger brother, Henry. Neither John nor Clyde is talking." A slow smile transformed his features, showing a side to him that had women all over Desire chasing him. "Yet. We're watching Debra, though. Closely. The bank manager knows about our suspicions, and since he has no proof that she did anything wrong, he's keeping her on. It helps us keep an eye on her. Her phone calls are being monitored at work and Ace is trying to get her phone records."

Hoyt paused with the cup of coffee halfway to his lips. "You said she's being watched at work. What about her home? Has it been searched?"

Linc met Hoyt's look with a smile. "We can't do anything without a warrant, and we don't have one. If her apartment is searched, it's not something I would know about."

Lifting his coffee cup to his lips, Jake hid a smile. "It looks like we might want to go have a talk with Lucas and the others."

With another shrug, Linc lifted his own cup to his lips. "I don't want to know about it." Finishing his coffee, he got to his feet. "I just stopped by because Ace wanted me to come talk to you. He didn't want you to think he didn't take your claim seriously, or that he was brushing it under the rug. He believes you, but believing and proving are two different things. That doesn't mean that we're giving up, though. We don't need any troublemakers in this town."

Jake lifted Nat from his lap to show Linc to the door. "The three of you can't keep up this pace forever. When are the new deputies supposed to be here?"

Linc sighed. "At the end of the month. I can't wait. For a small town, we're dealing with trouble more and more. It puts everyone on edge. I can understand now why this town was set up the way it was and why the founders of Desire were such hard-asses. There's another seminar at the club starting soon. I just hope there isn't any trouble from that. Their new bartender seems to be more than capable of taking care of things there, but you just never know. I'll see all of you soon. If I hear anything else, I'll let you know."

After Linc left, Nat sat in the kitchen with Hoyt and Jake, sipping coffee. Eyeing Hoyt, she reached for another cookie, promising herself that this would be her last. "Hoyt, are you sure about her?"

"Positive." Hoyt smiled at her speculative look. "When your life depends on judging a person right, you learn how to do it quickly." Reaching out, he touched her hair. "That's why I know you're the only woman for me."

Nat shook her head, recognizing Hoyt's attempt to ease the tense atmosphere. She didn't want to think about how many times his life had been in danger over the years, or how many times only his instincts had kept him alive. "What was the thing you were doing when Linc was here?"

Frowning, he pushed his cup aside. "What do you mean?"

"You know. That look you get. It's scary."

Hoyt grinned and leaned forward, taking her hand in his. "If you want to see a scary look, wait until we get you into the playroom."

Chapter Thirteen

Jake let his gaze rake slowly over his wife, wondering if she'd ever know just what she meant to him—wondering if she'd ever fully understand just how happy she made him.

Since learning that Hoyt wanted to come to Desire, Jake had second-guessed himself many times, wondering if he'd ever really showed her.

He vowed to himself to spend the rest of his life showing this magnificent woman just what she meant to him.

Her blush after all these years never failed to arouse him.

Since Linc left, she hadn't stopped pacing, and after a shared look with Hoyt, the two of them stood in her way, their arms folded across their chests. Frowning, she turned from Hoyt and faced him, stopping abruptly when she saw that they'd blocked her in.

Determined to get her mind off of the bank teller, Jake raised a brow at her look. "Go get undressed and put on your robe. Wait for us in the bedroom." Jake's cock hardened at the flash of arousal in his wife's eyes, his body tense with anticipation at her response to the steel he'd injected into his tone.

The thrill of knowing that she would be used for their pleasure, and would have no say in what they did to her shone in her beautiful eyes.

She wanted this, and he suspected she *needed* it just as much.

She needed time with him and Hoyt together, to see them as a united front. She needed it for her own sense of security, and for her own peace of mind. She needed to know how much they both wanted her.

She needed to think about something other than the bank robbery.

He watched the sway of her ass as she left the kitchen, meeting her cocky look with an icy one, while inside his blood boiled with hunger for her. Once she disappeared from view, he turned to Hoyt. "You know, I don't remember you being into dominating women before. As many times as we've been to the club together, I don't ever remember you talking about it."

Hoyt shrugged and got up to set his coffee cup in the sink before going to the refrigerator for a beer. "I'd dabbled a little shortly before I met Natalie, and the deeper I got into it, the more I enjoyed it. Then, I met Natalie. She was a virgin and very skittish, and I loved her. I didn't want to take my demons out on her. I told you that I started to experiment with her, but I ran out of time."

Jake blinked. "Demons?"

With a sigh, Hoyt dropped into his chair again. "That's how it felt to me, especially when I was younger. I found that dominating women was sort of therapy for me—a release from my father's bossiness—from my frustration." His lips twitched. "It made me forget, and put all my focus into the woman I was with. The more pleasure I could give, the more she'd give up control, and controlling a woman with her own pleasure was a high I couldn't resist. The more control I had, the better I felt. The more pleasure I got out of it. It was another world, a world I couldn't resist."

His smile fell, a muscle working in his jaw. "When I left Natalie behind, the need became worse. Every woman had Natalie's face. I wanted them to depend on me for the pleasure. I wanted to make them beg."

Struck by the hint of desperation in Hoyt's tone, Jake nodded. "Like you wanted Nat to beg."

Shaking his head, Hoyt cursed and shot to his feet, going to the refrigerator for a bottle of water. "No matter how far I went, it was never enough. It never gave me the satisfaction I wanted. It wasn't about the control anymore. It was about *her*." Smiling faintly, he stared out the window. "I love her so damned much. I didn't even realize how much."

Turning, he leaned back against the counter and sipped his beer. "I was furious with her for years, and dominated other women in an effort to forget her. It was heady, and addictive. I couldn't stop thinking that the more I learned, the more prepared I'd be for her." His lips twitched as he looked down at his hands. "Now my hands shake at the thought of having her."

Jake chuckled, feeling better than he had in months. "I can't say that I blame you for that. She's an exciting woman." Getting to his feet, he refilled his coffee cup and turned, leaning back against the counter. "The only way this can work is if we stick together. One sign of weakness will shake her security. She has to know that we're united in rules for her, in protecting her, in seeing to her needs." Grinning, Jake sipped from his cup. "And she'll make mincemeat out of both of us if she senses any weakness."

Hoyt looked toward the doorway and sighed again. "Do you really think she's up for this tonight? She looked a little unsettled."

Pleased to see Hoyt's concern for Nat, Jake smiled. "She's restless because of the bank robbery. She's scared that they really *are* going to lock you up, and she's worried that she's going to get used to the three of us being together, only to have the rug pulled out from under her. I can't do anything about the first two, except try to distract her enough to stop worrying about it. A trip to the playroom should do that. The time we spend together with her should also go a long way to showing her that we have every intention of making this work. If we take her to the playroom together and are united about the way we handle her, it should ease some of her fears."

Hoyt grimaced. "I hated that she looked embarrassed after we made love this morning. It pisses me off that she feels uncomfortable facing you after she's with me."

Jake inclined his head. "I agree, but it's something that only time and our attitudes about it will resolve. I didn't help with it today, but seeing her come out of the bedroom all flushed, and seeing the developing intimacy between you hit me harder than I thought it would." He took another sip of coffee before putting it aside, smiling faintly. "I also think she's embarrassed for you to see how she responds in the playroom. She's not used to submitting to you, and I think it has her shaken."

Hoyt's mischievous smile reminded Jake of the man he'd known years earlier, and told him that he was very much looking forward to the challenge. He set the bottle aside, grinning. "Then this trip to the playroom should be *very* interesting."

* * * *

Wearing only her satin robe and slippers, Nat paced back and forth across the bedroom, her heart pounding with anticipation.

She couldn't imagine what was taking them so long—the thought of them devising plans for her making her heart race even faster.

She'd slathered on the new body butter she and Jesse had created, every inch of skin glistening, scented, and tingling with sensual awareness.

Her silky robe brushed her nipples with every step, inflaming her even more. She knew she looked good, but she still had to admit to being a little nervous about Hoyt's presence in the playroom.

Pausing, she pressed a hand to her stomach, the slight edge of panic still strong enough to shake her. She was scared of doing anything to hurt Jake—scared that Hoyt would decide that sharing her with another man wasn't all he'd imagined.

When he saw the way she was in the playroom, would he realize that she wasn't the woman he'd fallen in love with?

Straightening, she stilled at the deep silkiness of Jake's voice.

"Even when I'm pushing her boundaries, she eggs me on, but her eyes are too expressive to hide what she's feeling. That's why I never blindfold her when I'm taking her out of her comfort zone. In all these years, she's never used her safe word. I think it's a matter of pride for her, so I have to watch her carefully."Jake sighed. "We're going to have to keep her in line, especially now that she's going to have *both* of us spoiling her."

Nat raised a brow at that.

She'd never considered herself spoiled.

She just tricked Jake into giving her what she wanted.

Hoyt laughed. "Oh, I don't think we'll have any trouble keeping Natalie in line. There are two of us now. That should even the odds a little."

Nat smiled at that, anticipation bubbling through her veins.

Their possessiveness and protective natures could be a pain in the ass at times, but she could never respect a weak man and knew enough about herself to know that she would end up walking all over one.

Her heart swelled with love at the appreciation and emotion in their eyes as they both appeared at the doorway and smiled at her.

Her pussy clenched at the erotic intent in their eyes as they moved closer.

Jake went straight to the playroom door, unlocking it and pushing it open. "Come here, baby."

Shooting a glance at Hoyt, she crossed the room to Jake on shaky legs. As always, a thrill went through her when his arms came around her.

Wrapping her arms around her neck, she leaned into him, looking up into his eyes. "I love you, you know."

Jake smiled, lifting a hand to her face and pushing a tendril of hair from her cheek. "I know." Slipping his hand inside her robe, he cupped her breast. "Nothing in the world gives me more pleasure."

Nat pushed her breast more firmly into her hand and wiggled against him. "Nothing?"

Watching her closely, Jake smiled and pushed the edge of her robe aside, baring her breast. "Some other things come really close. Hmm, you feel and smell delicious. Makes me want to take a bite out of you."

Hoyt strolled closer, reaching out a hand to caress the outer curve of her breast. "She's always been that way. Drove me nuts." His eyes, hooded and filled with anticipation, held hers. "Do you know how many nights I lay awake remembering the scent of her? The feel of her?"

Moving in behind her, he slid his hands to her waist, making short work of unknotting the belt to her robe. Sliding his hands inside, he cupped her breasts, touching his lips to the top of her head. "I still can't get used to the idea that I can run my hands over her and breathe in the sweet scent of her whenever I want. I want to reacquaint myself with every inch of her."

Gulping in air, Nat flattened her hands on Jake's chest and leaned back against Hoyt, the feel of his hot hands moving over her breasts creating a stirring in her clit that had her shifting restlessly. Arching her back to push her breasts more firmly into his hands, Nat stared into Jake's eyes, thrilling at the heat in them and his obvious enjoyment in watching Hoyt touch her.

Gripping her chin, Jake kept her face lifted to his, his gaze raking over her. "Sometimes, I can hardly believe it myself. I watch her when she's sleeping. I stand and just stare at her when I have her spread and restrained in the playroom, and think—*she's mine*."

With a faint smile, he ran his fingertips down her abdomen and to her mound. "Every inch of her to use as I please. Hmm, interesting. She looks a little too smug tonight."

Hoyt chuckled against her ear as a hard arm wrapped around her from behind and lifted her against an equally hard chest. The hard cock pressing against her ass added to the unyielding wall of iron heat behind her. "Let's see if the two of us can't wipe that smug look off her face."

With a hand at her back, he urged her forward. "Come on, little sub. Let's see how smug you look once your Masters have their way with you."

Nat trembled with excitement, looking up at each of them and struck by the combination of lust, love, and indulgence shining in their eyes.

Jake guided her to the center of the room where two leather straps hung from the ceiling. Tracing his fingers over her abdomen, he lifted her chin, his steady, watchful gaze giving her a warm sense of security that reinforced her confidence. "You know what to do. Hoyt wants to explore you and doesn't want your hands in the way. Lose the robe."

Pinpricks of awareness broke out all over her skin as she obeyed him, the slide of the silky material over her back and bottom intensifying the sensation.

Jake's gaze sharpened as he watched the robe fall from her to puddle at her feet, the appreciation in his eyes making her feel very feminine and desired.

"Good girl. You look beautiful, baby." The affection and hunger in his eyes flashed briefly, the remnants still lingering as a cold mask came over his features. "Lift your arms above your head and stick those pretty breasts out."

A shiver of delight went through her at her husband's icy tone—a tone that never failed to arouse her.

Her nipples beaded tight under his gaze, her inner thighs slick with her juices.

She couldn't see Hoyt, who'd moved behind her, but when she turned her head to see him, a sharp reprimand from Jake had her turning back again.

"Nobody said you could turn around."

The brush of denim-clad muscle against her bottom made her jolt, the sense of vulnerability growing stronger at the reminder that she stood completely naked before them while they both remained fully clothed.

Jake did this often to her, knowing that it made her feel even more exposed and helpless—knowing how much she loved it.

"Let's get these hands out of the way." Hoyt caught her wrists in one big hand and lifted them, while Jake watched, his eyes narrowed on her unprotected breasts.

Stepping forward, Jake reached out a hand, cupping her breast and sliding a thumb over her nipple. "All on display, and there isn't a thing you can do to cover yourself, or protect yourself, is there, darling?" To reinforce her helplessness, he closed his fingers on her nipples, lifting them slightly away from her body until she cried out. "You're going to let Hoyt explore you. Tease you. Torment you. You belong to him now, too. Every sweet inch of you."

He released her nipples, the remnants of sensation sending stabs of pleasure to her slit.

The click of the locks above her head sounded loud and ominous in the tense silence, intensifying the sexual tension in the room. Tugging at her bonds experimentally, Nat swallowed heavy and nodded, her toes curling at another tug to her nipple. "Yes. Oh, God, Jake."

Nat shivered, her head falling back on a moan at the slow slide of Hoyt's fingertips from her wrists to her elbows, and then to her shoulders.

"Naked. Restrained. *And* at my mercy." Hoyt's lips brushed her ear. "I've dreamed of having you this way for years." Nibbling at her earlobe, he slid his hands up her arms again and closed them over hers in an affectionate gesture that threw her off-balance. "It didn't even come close to reality."

His fingertips danced back down her arms again to her shoulders, pausing here and there to circle around to the underside of her arms and leaving little sizzles of electricity everywhere he touched—sizzles that all seemed to gather at her nipples.

His hands moved lower, electrifying every nerve ending along the way.

Slow seductive currents of sizzling heat.

Over her shoulders. Down her back.

Sharpening at her slit and her nipples.

Throwing her head back, she moved restlessly in an attempt to ease the aches his touch and Jake's gaze created, but no amount of squirming helped.

Hoyt's hands slid over her hips as he knelt behind her. His lips brushed over her bottom, over one cheek and then the other. "So soft. So firm. So beautiful."

Crying out at the scrape of his teeth over her bottom, she twisted under Jake's watchful gaze, the heat of it exciting her.

Hoyt's lips moved down her legs and back up again, over her bottom and to her shoulders. "Delicious. I don't think I could ever get enough of you. Of this."

Straightening again, he pressed his body against hers, sliding his hands from her waist around to her belly, the light caress making her stomach muscles quiver.

Her unprotected breasts felt swollen and heavy, her nipples aching for Hoyt's attention, pebbling even tighter under Jake's intense gaze.

Hoyt caressed the sensitive underside of her breasts, his breath warm on her temple as he looked down at them over her shoulder. "Those pretty nipples look like they need some attention."

Yes!

His fingers moved back and forth, closer and closer to her nipples, but not quite touching them. "I can't wait to stroke them, tug them, pinch them."

"Yes." Arching, she moaned, her stomach clenching tighter when Jake moved closer.

Hoyt cupped her breasts, still avoiding her nipples. "I can't get enough of you." His lips brushed her arms. "You're like a drug in my system."

Nat shivered when his teeth scraped over the sensitive spot on her neck, lifting to her toes to try to get the friction she needed against her nipples. "If you change your mind, I'll kill you."

Hoyt groaned and pushed his cock against her lower back. "Never. I'm in this forever. I've waited too long for this. Ached for you too many nights. Loved you for too many years to ever think about walking away from the only chance I'll ever get to have everything I've ever wanted. Do you belong to me now, baby?"

Biting her lip, Nat rubbed her thighs together, gritting her teeth. "Yes, damn it—as long as you belong to me, too."

Hoyt's touch firmed, becoming more insistent. Possessive. "I've always been yours."

Jake's eyes narrowed in warning. "Thrust those breasts out. Offer them to Hoyt."

Shaking with arousal, Nat obeyed him, a low moan escaping at the slide of Hoyt's warm hands closing on her waist.

"Very nice. I think I'll accept your invitation." Sliding his hands higher, he traced patterns over the underside of her breasts. "You're being such a good girl. Now, be really still for me."

Holding her nipple between his thumb and forefinger, Hoyt tugged, making her squirm at the sharp ribbons of pleasure to her clit. "Be still. I won't tolerate being disobeyed any more than Jake does."

Her toes curled at the rush of heat at her slit, her breath coming out in harsh gasps as she struggled to calm herself. "Sorry."

Hoyt released her nipple, tapping it lightly. "Very good. Jake's here with you. He's still your Master and he's watching out for you. You're going to have to learn to accept me as your Master, too."

Nat smiled, sharing a look with Jake as she leaned back against Hoyt. "I might not be as submissive as you expect. Jake likes it when I resist."

Hoyt nipped at her earlobe. "You can resist me all you want. I'll get you to submit. Now, be still so I can explore you the way I want to." His voice lowered, becoming a soft caress. "I want to take my time. I want to learn every inch of you." Closing his thumbs and forefingers over her nipples, he rolled them gently, but with enough pressure to bring her to her toes again and sending another rush of pleasure to her clit.

Nat sucked in a breath and pulled away from him, not to escape, but to increase the pressure.

Chuckling softly, Jake stepped closer—close enough to reach out and touch her. "She likes it rough, although she won't admit it. You'll see for yourself soon enough that she provokes it."

"Likes to dare you, does she?" Hoyt released her nipples, pressing his hands against her waist to hold her against him as the feel of the blood rushing back into her nipples made her squirm. "If she behaves herself, I'll give her what she wants. For now, she's going to have to be patient and still while I explore her a little more."

Jake reached out to tap a nipple, smiling at her cry of pleasure. "Our Nat's not real good with patience."

Lifting her chin, Hoyt stared into his eyes. "Too bad. I don't plan to rush this. I plan to savor every moment." He moved around to stand in front of her. Caressing the underside of both breasts, Hoyt stared into her eyes. "I'd almost forgotten the effect such softness and responsiveness had on me. It's damned irresistible."

Trailing his fingers over the upper curve of her breast, he smiled. "She's even more compelling and beautiful than she was before. I didn't think that was possible."

Jake ran a hand over her hair as he circled her, the small gesture filled with adoration. "She's incredible all right. Her strength makes her even more compelling." He stopped behind her, moving so close that she could feel the heat of his body against her back.

Placing his hands on her shoulders, he massaged gently and bent to kiss her hair. "She can be a handful." The pride and love in his voice sent a thrill through her. "A strong woman with strong passions. A woman who isn't afraid to explore."

Staring into her eyes, Hoyt smiled as he ran his hands over her belly and abdomen. "Right now she seems pretty docile to me."

Her stomach muscles quivered, her pussy leaking more moisture at the feel of his fingers sliding lower to lightly caress her mound.

Hoyt's eyes narrowed, filled with challenge. "I want to see how she does with the nipple clips on while I explore the rest of her."

Nat gulped and stared down at the clip Hoyt held in his hand, her breathing ragged as he moved it closer to her nipple.

Jake's hands closed on her waist, his breath warm against her temple as he watched Hoyt over her shoulder. "Thrust those breasts out, baby. Show Hoyt how brave you are."

Hoyt rolled her nipple between his thumb and forefinger, his eyes hooded as he pulled it slightly away from her body and attached the clip, the sharp pain making her clit throb and sending another rush of moisture to coat her inner thighs.

"Oh, God. Oh, God." Fighting her bonds only excited her more, her movements sending the clip swaying and making the pull even more intense.

"That's it." Hoyt tapped the clip, sending the small chains dangling from it swaying. "Breathe through it. Look at me."

Staring into his gleaming eyes, she moaned, pressing back against Jake's warmth as he attached the other clip. "Hoyt. Oh, God!"

The dual sensations drove her wild, the pain easing to an unrelenting pressure that sent her arousal soaring.

Her clit throbbed with every beat of her heart, feeling so swollen and heavy that she couldn't help but rub her thighs together to get some relief. A fine sheen of perspiration broke out all over her skin, every nerve ending in her body screaming for relief.

Straightening, Hoyt toyed with the clips, intensifying the pressure and making her clit ached even more. "Damn, she's beautiful."

"That she is." Jake's hands tightened on her waist. "It took me quite a while to work up to the clips. I had those made specially for her. They're smooth and padded so they don't hurt much. I also had a matching clit clip for her. The small chains dangling from it drive her crazy."

Hoyt tugged at the clips, his eyes flaring at her cry. "I can imagine what that would be like on the day after her clit's had a taste of the whip." Squatting down in front of her, he ran his hands up and down her thighs. "Her clit's beautiful."

Oh, God!

Hoyt's fingers danced lightly over her mound, making her clit throb even harder. "It's just begging for attention."

Jake's hands slid higher, tugging the chains on the clips. "It always is. She's so passionate. Ask Hoyt nicely to touch your clit."

Sucking in a breath, Nat locked her knees against the incredible pleasure, lowering her head to look down at Hoyt. "Oh, God."

Hoyt ran a finger over her mound and down to trace her folds, raising a brow again in that arrogant way that drove her wild. "I'm waiting."

Gritting her teeth, she threw her head back against Jake's shoulder, stunned at the eroticism. "Hoyt, p–please touch my c–clit."

Hoyt's big hands closed on her hips. "If you want attention to that clit, you're gonna have to spread those thighs wide, darlin'."

A moan escaped when Jake starting playing with the chains on the clips again. Conscious of the moisture on her inner thighs, Nat parted her legs about shoulder distance apart, not willing to appear too desperate.

"You're trying my patience. If I have to stop to discipline you, I will." Hoyt tapped her inner thighs. "Wide, Natalie. You've been doing this long enough to understand how to follow directions. Would Jake let you get away with this?"

Scraping his teeth over her shoulder, Jake tugged the clips. "She knows damned well that I don't let her get away with that. I told you she'd try to test you."

Gasping at the tug to her nipples, and unsettled by the threat in Jake's voice, Nat looked down at Hoyt, thrown further off-balance by his disapproving expression. Watching his face, she took a deep breath and parted her legs a few inches wider.

Looking straight ahead, she closed her eyes and waited for him to touch her, her clit tingling harder in anticipation. She couldn't rub her thighs together to ease the ache, and even the brush of air against her slit tormented her.

Her thighs trembled with the effort to remain still, her nipples aching. Fisting her hands, she waited breathlessly for Hoyt's touch, groaning in frustration when it didn't come.

Opening her eyes, she lowered her head, alarmed to find him staring up at her, his brow raised again as he waited. "We can do this all night, baby."

Glaring at him, she widened her stance another inch.

Hiding a smile at his sigh, she looked straight ahead. She knew she wouldn't be able to defy him for long. Her own need wouldn't allow it, but she'd given in to him so easily so far, and she couldn't resist the opportunity to frustrate him.

To her surprise, Hoyt rose to his full height in front of her and reached above her, wrapping a hand around her leather-covered wrists, while gripping her chin with the other, holding her head high. "You want to play games, darlin'?"

Melting under his steady stare, and shaking even harder, she leaned back against Jake, grateful for his support as Hoyt lowered her arms several inches before securing them again.

Raising a brow, he gripped the clips, applying more pressure. "Spread those legs as wide as they'll go. Jake won't let you fall. Bend those knees outward. You've got more room now. I want them as wide as they'll go."

Sucking in a breath, Nat stared up at him in disbelief. "What?"

Applying pressure to her nipples, Hoyt raised a brow. "You got a problem with me inspecting my property? That pussy and ass belong to me, too."

"Property?"

Jake had used that term many times over the years, sometimes playfully, sometimes in an icy tone in the playroom—but this was the first time she'd ever heard Hoyt use it.

She sucked in a breath, astounded by the increasing level of dominance Hoyt displayed, and her response to it.

Somehow, though, something inside her had known.

Leaning close, Hoyt tugged the clips, his eyes seeming to glow from within. "*Property*—especially when we're in this room. Do you have a problem with that?"

Nat gulped, struck by the excitement in his eyes—humbled at the trace of uncertainty. Determined to let him see that he had no need for concern, she smiled saucily. "You think you can handle your *property?*"

His eyes flared. "Oh, yeah." He released the clips and ran a firm finger from the base of her throat to her chin, lifting her face to his again. "Say it."

Lifting her chin higher, she met his gaze squarely. "When we're in this room, I'm your property. Outside this room, we'll see."

His eyes glittered with anticipation. "That'll do for now. Now, bend those knees."

Shivering at his steely tone, Nat bit back a moan, and bent her trembling legs, effectively spreading herself wide. "Oh, hell."

Jake chuckled softly, sliding a hand down to caress her ass. "Looks like you're in trouble now." Curving an arm around her waist, he held her against him. "Just lean back on me. I'll take the pressure from your arms. Keep those thighs spread for Hoyt."

Kneeling in front of her again, Hoyt smiled and parted her folds. "Don't look so scared, baby. What could I possibly do to you?"

Gritting her teeth, Nat groaned at the slide of his finger over her clit, her knees giving out at the intense pleasure. Grateful for Jake's hold, she let him take her weight. "Christ, I'm gonna come."

"No, not yet, you're not." Hoyt plunged a finger into her pussy, fucking her hard and fast with it. "You're not coming until you have a cock in your pussy and one in your ass."

"Oh, God!" Just thinking about it made her ass and pussy clench.

Thick. Hard. Hot. Filling her completely.

Hoyt withdrew his finger with no warning, leaving her pussy grasping at emptiness. "Keep those legs spread while I get the lube."

Having her ass breached never failed to startle her, the first touch—the first moment that something entered her there, stealing the fight out of her.

Jake knew it, and now Hoyt knew it.

Holding her with a hard arm around her waist, Jake buried his face against her neck and kissed her throat, sliding his other hand to her breast. "Do you know how fucking hard I am at the thought of taking you with Hoyt?" Cupping her breast, he toyed with the clip, groaning at her soft cry. "Knowing that you're going to be experiencing this for the first time excites the hell out of me."

With a moan, Nat turned her head to look up at him over her shoulder, a thrill going through her at the heat in his eyes. Smiling, she dropped her head back against his shoulder watching Hoyt approach out of the corner of her eye. "I've been fucked in the ass before, Jake."

Jake grinned. "And you've had a plug in your ass while I've fucked your pussy, but it's not the same as having two cocks fucking you at the same time."

Hoyt stopped in front of her, a tube of lube in his hand. Reaching out, he turned her face to his, the sexual tension emanating from him wiping the smile from her face. His eyes held a sharp possessiveness and hunger—a man who wouldn't be denied satisfaction. "I want her ass. I want all of her to belong to me."

Hoyt looked so hard. So big. Formidable.

Something must have shown on her face because Hoyt's eyes warmed as he bent to touch his lips to hers. "I promise that you're going to love it. I'd never hurt you."

Jake stripped out of his clothes and cuddled her from behind, his cock hard and hot against her lower back. "And you know damned well I never would. I'm going to be watching those beautiful eyes the entire time."

Wrapping his arms around her from behind, he parted her folds with one hand while stroking her clit with the other. "Nice and wet."

Each stroke of his finger took her closer to the edge, each like little bursts of electricity through her clit.

Tears blurred her vision, and she knew she couldn't hold back much longer. "God. Please. Please, Jake. Please let me come. I can't stop it."

A sharp tug to her nipple forced a cry from her, the effort to hold back overwhelming. "You'd better stop it." Moving around to stand in front of her while Hoyt circled her to press against her back, Jake continued to slide a fingertip back and forth over the sensitive bundle of nerves, his eyes hooded and searching. "Yes, I've been far too soft on you. You're going to have to learn to focus." He tapped the underside of her chin, forcing her to lift her head. "I want you to keep your eyes on me. I'm going to slowly stroke your clit while Hoyt lubes that tight ass and gets you ready for his cock. Don't you dare come."

Gritting her teeth at the friction against her clit, Nat nodded. "Okay, damn it. Hurry up."

The rustle of Hoyt's clothing heightened the erotic tension in the room, and just seconds later, she sucked in a breath at the feel of his hot, hard nakedness pressed against her back.

"Temper. Temper." Hoyt slapped her ass once, a slap just sharp enough to renew the heat, and bent to touch his lips to the underside of her upraised arm while caressing the spot he'd just slapped. "Be a good girl while I take my time lubing this sweet ass. Jake's finger on that clit feels good, doesn't it, baby? He knows just how you like to be touched, something that I'm going to take great pleasure in learning."

She didn't see how his touch could get any better, but she had to admit that Jake's had a familiarity to it that inflamed her.

Her husband knew just where, and how to touch her to give her the most pleasure.

To drive her wild with need—or to keep her poised on the edge for longer than she thought possible.

She needed to come.

Badly.

Every delicate stoke of Jake's finger threatened to send her over, and when Hoyt wrapped a muscular arm around her from behind, it got even worse.

Her bottom clenched, the tight ring of muscle tingling as Hoyt lifted her several inches off of the floor and bent her over his arm.

Don't come. Don't come.

Hoyt ran a hand down her bottom, parting her cheeks and pressing a finger against her puckered opening. "Do you ever whip her clit?"

Just the thought of it threatened to send her over.

Don't come. Don't come.

The cold sensation at her sensitive opening seemed even colder on her overheated body, making it feel even more intense.

Her clit burned, feeling ten times its normal size, her muscles quivering at the effort it cost her to hold off her orgasm.

Jake smiled and gripped the clips on her nipples. "Only for discipline. Her clit's too sensitive to handle it very often. A few strokes of the whip keeps her clit sensitive for days—so sensitive that the slightest touch drives her wild." Bending low, he cupped her jaw and lifted her face to his, smiling coldly. "The threat of another keeps her in line very nicely."

Nat glared at him. "Very funny. Oh!" The feel of a cold, lubed finger plunging into her ass stole her breath, and as she started kicking her feet against the sensation, Jake removed both clips at once, sending the blood rushing back into her nipples.

"Oh! Sonofabitch. Sonofabitch."

She was going to come.

She couldn't stop clenching as she moved herself on Hoyt's finger, the need to come like a living, breathing thing clawing at her insides.

Hoyt withdrew slightly before pushing his finger into her again, moving it in slow circles, the pressure against her inner walls heightening the awareness there. Raising his voice to be heard over her desperate cries, he lifted her ass higher. "I envy you, Jake. I envy the closeness you have with her. I envy how well you know her. Physically. Mentally. Emotionally. I want that."

Gritting her teeth, she clenched on his finger, and turned her head to snap at him. "Really? You want to have a conversation about this now?" Her juices ran down her thighs, the hunger so intense it brought tears to her eyes.

Hoyt's chuckle sounded strained. "She does have quite a temper when she's aroused. I understand why you don't want to break her of it. Christ, my cock's throbbing."

Thrilled that he ached as much as she did, she pressed her face against Jake's chest, loving the feel of his hand moving over her hair as he pulled her closer.

Trying to close her legs proved useless, her position allowing Hoyt full access to her vulnerable ass—access he exploited.

He moved his finger inside her, spreading the lube around her inner walls with a thoroughness that made her toes curl.

Groaning in frustration when he withdrew his finger, she pulled against her bonds, wild for release. "No! Please. Please. Please." She watched in anticipation as Jake squirted more lube onto Hoyt's fingers, sucking in a breath when Hoyt's hand disappeared again.

He ran a finger over her bottom hole, the cold lube making her gasp. "I had to get more lube, darlin'. Now, two fingers. That's a girl. Keep those legs spread for me."

"Oh, God! Fuck. Oh!" Chills raced up and down her spine as he worked two fingers into her, the erotic fullness too decadent to resist.

Overwhelmed with sensation, Nat lowered her gaze, taking in the sight of her husband's hard cock. Fascinated by the drop of moisture at the tip, she licked her lips, wishing she could reach it.

"Look at me, baby."

Jake unfastened the leather cuffs, allowing her to lower her arms and lifted her against him. "That's my girl. Put your arms around my neck and hold on to me."

She did it automatically, slumping against him. "Oh, God. I need to come. Jake, I can't wait. This is too much. Oh, God, Jake. I ache everywhere." She couldn't stop moving, the demands of her body desperate for satisfaction.

Everything sizzled. Her sensitivity to every touch had heightened, but nothing ever seemed to be enough.

She wanted more.

Moaning as Hoyt slid his fingers free, she held on to Jake as he carried her to the low bench they'd used hundreds of times.

This time, though, they weren't alone.

Instead of lowering her to the padded bench as he usually did, Jake sat on the end, adjusting her so that she straddled him.

Lowering her gaze to his chest, she stroked the hard muscle there, conscious of Hoyt moving in behind her.

Lifting her chin, Jake held her gaze, his eyes narrowed. "You're going to have to wait. You're not coming until both of us are inside you. I told you to look at me. I want to see those beautiful eyes when we take you."

Gripping his shoulders, Nat held on while he lifted her by the waist and slowly lowered her onto his cock, a moan escaping at the feel of his hard, steely heat filling her pussy. "Jake! Yes. Hard. Fuck me hard."

She didn't want gentleness now. She needed to be taken hard and fast.

Jake groaned. "Yeah, baby. You're soaking wet. So good. Damn, I love the way your pussy clamps down on me. Hang on, baby, and Hoyt and I are both going to fuck you senseless."

From behind her, Hoyt cursed as he rolled on a condom. "Just the thought of working my cock into that tight ass has me ready to explode. With your cock already inside her, it's going to be even tighter."

Sliding a hand around her neck, Jake leaned back and pulled her down for a kiss, his other hand tightening on her hip as he took her mouth with his.

Hoyt bent over her, brushing his lips against the back of her shoulder. "Hang on to Jake, baby."

Her ass still tingled from Hoyt's ministrations, and she could only imagine how it looked to him to see her ass spread wide and glistening with lube. She sucked in a breath and started to shake in earnest when Hoyt flattened a hand on her back. She stiffened at the strength and heat of his touch, the pressure making it hard to move.

He trailed the head of his cock down the crease of her ass and pressed it against her puckered opening with a groan.

Oh, God. This was really happening.

She didn't know it could be possible to be this hungry and nervous at the same time. She couldn't stand this level of need for much longer. Sucking in a breath, she lifted her head, needing Jake's guidance. "Jake?"

Breathing in the scent of him, she gripped him tighter and tried to sit up, but his hard arms tightened around her. "No, baby. You're okay. You're with us. We've got you." Pushing her hair back, he studied her features, his small smile of encouragement strained. "She's okay. Go ahead. Easy."

Nat's toes curled, her pussy and ass clenching in spasms. "Oh, God."

"Easy, baby." Hoyt's voice was almost unrecognizable, so harsh and clipped with tension that it sent a chill down her spine. "Nice and slow."

"Fuck slow!" More chills followed as he began to push into her, the burn of being stretched sending ripples of alarm through her. "Oh, God! Hoyt! It won't fit. Fuck. Jake, let go of me. I have to move."

She'd never felt so primitive. So wild. So out of control.

Without meaning to, she spread her legs wider and tried to fuck herself on Jake's cock, the need to move overwhelming. "It burns! Oh. Oh. Oooohhhh!"

The head of Hoyt's cock pressed into her, the tight ring of muscle giving way, the thick head of his cock forcing her puckered opening to stretch wide to accommodate him.

"Fuck! She's so fucking tight. Keep her still. Hold on to her. I don't want to hurt her."

Shaking harder, she threw her head back, amazed at the need to be filled in both openings. "Ohhh! God. So good. So good. Hurry up. I have to move. I have to move. I can't. Jake. Help me. Help me. Oh, God." She tried to rock her hips, but Jake's strong arm around her back prevented it.

Hoyt's cursing became increasingly raw and inventive, his hands tightening on her hips. "Fuck. Yeah, baby. A little more. A little more."

A fresh sheen of perspiration broke out all over her skin even as chills raced up and down her spine. Crying out, she beat against Jake in an effort to move, a sharp slap on her ass instantly subduing her struggles.

Hoyt's hands tightened on her ass, holding the heat in on the side he'd just slapped. "Be still. I don't want to hurt you."

Jake's hand fisted in her hair, holding her head in a way that allowed him to see her face. "Got your ass smacked, did you?" His hands gripped her thighs. "You're not in charge here. Behave yourself."

Nat couldn't believe the way it felt to be stuffed full of cock in both openings. "So full. Oh, God. I can't believe how full I feel."

All inhibitions melted away under their decadent assault to her senses. Awash in sensation, she cried out when Jake partially withdrew, but seconds later, another cry was ripped from her when Hoyt pushed his cock deeper.

When Hoyt withdrew, until only the head of his cock remained inside her, Jake surged deep again.

The constant stimulation of one cock withdrawing while another surged deep was like nothing she'd ever experienced.

Her mind went numb, the pleasure so intense that the shock of it made it almost impossible to move.

The slow slide of their hands both soothed and demanded, demands that her body met eagerly.

Their cocks moved inside her—so hot they burned.

"Yeah. Fucking tight. That's it, baby." Jake's hands tightened, lifting her just as Hoyt surged into her again.

Hoyt's and Jake's groans washed over her like warm honey. Being with the men she loved and trusted allowed her a freedom to lose herself in the unbelievably erotic act.

Her position left her ass spread wide, with no way to control the depth of Hoyt's thrusts. Although she trusted him, it lent an edge to sex—the kind of thrill that she reveled in.

"Oh! God, it's so good!" The tingling at her slit seemed to explode, an intense surge of pleasure unlike anything she'd ever felt before.

Instinctively clinging to Jake, she breathed in the familiar and beloved scent of him. "Oh, Jake."

Focusing on the sound of his voice, she let the pleasure roll through her, her breathing as harsh and ragged as theirs.

"That's it, Natalie. Let it have you, baby. We're here. We've got you." Hoyt's hands tightened on her hips, a low groan rumbling from his chest as he thrust into her again and stilled, his cock pulsing deep inside her. "Fuck. So fucking tight. So fucking sweet. She okay, Jake?"

"Yeah. Milk my cock, baby. Fuck. That's so good." Jake thrust into her several times, hard, quick thrusts that had another orgasm layering over the one still rippling through her. "Easy, baby. I've got you." Some of the tension in his big body eased. Loosening his hold on her waist, he caressed her—long, firm slides of his hand up and down her spine. "I love you, baby."

His lips touched her hair. "I've never been more proud of you. You're damned near fearless."

"Hmm." Nat cuddled closer, burying her face against his chest as the last ripples of pleasure washed over her. "I'm never scared when I'm with you."

"I hope you feel that way about me some day." Hoyt's lips touched her shoulder. "You okay, sweetheart?"

Nat nodded, taking another deep breath and blowing it out. "Yeah. Ohhh!" The feel of Hoyt's cock moving had her stiffening again.

Flattening a hand on her back, Hoyt rubbed her bottom and continued to ease his cock from her, holding her with gentle hands as he slid his cock free. "Easy. Yeah, that's my girl."

The heat from his body covered her back, forcing Jake to move his hands away. Hoyt's warm lips moved over her left shoulder, his hot hands caressing the outer curve of her breasts. "You just be still and rest for a minute while I go get a warm cloth." Releasing her, he straightened and started to move away.

It took a few seconds for the impact of his words to hit her. Alarmed, she struggled to sit up. "No!"

Whipping her head around, she met his dumbstruck gaze and flash of hurt in his eyes, regretting her outburst almost immediately. Shrugging, she smiled in apology, hating that she'd put that look on his face. "You don't have to do that."

Beneath her, Jake stilled. "Hoyt wants to take care of you the way that I do. You're just going to have to get used to it. Now, stop squirming, or you're gonna get fucked again." The underlying hint of steel in his gentle tone made her feel even worse.

Aware of Hoyt leaving the room, she smiled up at Jake. "If that's supposed to be a threat, it falls short."

"You've had enough for tonight." Lifting her face to his, he frowned. "Do you have a problem with Hoyt taking care of you?"

Laying her head back on Jake's chest, she sighed and stared at the doorway. "No. Of course not. I love Hoyt, but I'm not used to anyone touching me that way except you."

Chuckling softly, Jake kissed her hair as he gathered her close. "Sometimes, you say or do something that's so adorable. You're such a contrary woman." Running a hand over her bottom, he sighed. "Hoyt and I just took you together. *In the playroom.* He played with your clit, had his fingers in your pussy and your ass and then fucked your ass—and you're shy about having him use a warm cloth to wipe the lube from you and soothe you a little? You're shy with the *intimacy*? So, the sex is fine, but you're reluctant to let him close any other way? How do you think this is going to work if you accept him physically, but not emotionally? You love him, but fight it and won't let him close."

Gritting her teeth, Nat lifted her head to frown at him. "I hate when you make me sound ridiculous."

Jake grinned. "Sometimes, you make it so easy, I can't resist."

Nat poked him in the side with her nail, getting a small amount of satisfaction when he cursed and grabbed her hand. "You wouldn't understand. It's a little embarrassing. It's too new."

Easing her from his cock, Jack lifted her face to his again, his expression somber. "He *needs* this, Nat. He needs to care for you as much as I do. It's very important to a man, and especially to a man who demands submission to take care of his woman. This is a small, but very satisfying way of taking care of you and making you feel better. It's a loving and possessive gesture, Nat, not one meant to embarrass you."

Cupping her cheek, he ran his thumb back and forth over her bottom lip, his eyes dark with love and possessiveness. "You don't know what it means to have a woman that allows you to care for her. It's very satisfying to have a woman who looks to you for protection. Comfort. Support."

Nat smiled, rubbing her cheek against his hand. "You always seem to know what I need."

He pressed his thumb against the center of her bottom lip, making it tingle. "That's something Hoyt would like very much to know."

Touching her tongue to his thumb, she smiled at the glitter in his eyes. "It's different."

Jake raised a brow at that. "When you and I first got married, we had a lot of things to work through. You're going to need to do that with Hoyt as well. Talk to him, Nat. You and I used to argue things out. I don't like that you avoid talking about things with him because you're afraid of having an argument and clearing the air. We can't live like that, baby."

"I agree."

Nat spun at Hoyt's deep voice coming from right behind her. "Hoyt!"

Wrapping an arm around her waist, Hoyt lifted her back against him. "I much prefer honesty. If I do anything that you don't like, or that makes you uncomfortable, we'll talk about it and see why." His lips scraped over her shoulder, sending a shiver through her. "I certainly plan to let you know when you do something that annoys me—such as panicking at the thought of me cleaning you."

Moving her legs, Jake laughed softly and slid from under her. "It sounds as if the two of you have some things to discuss. I'm going to go take a shower."

Left alone with Hoyt, Nat leaned back against him, looking up at him over her shoulder. "I didn't mean to hurt your feelings, but it took a long time for me to get used to Jake doing that." Shrugging, she looked away. "Sometimes, it still makes me uncomfortable." A moan escaped when the warm cloth touched her puckered opening.

Holding her against him, Hoyt nuzzled her neck. "Sex is one thing, but intimacy is another. I understand you, Natalie. I've never wanted the intimacy with any other woman." Placing her facedown on the padded bench, he spread her cheeks and bent over her until his face was on eye level with hers. "I know it's going to take time, but I need it from you."

Reaching out to touch his cheek, she smiled when he caught her hand in his and raised it to his lips. "I need it from you, too. Some things are so familiar, but sometimes you seem like such a stranger to me. You can be so cold."

His eyes warmed. "I've been accused of that a time or two. I'm not cold with you, though, am I?" Holding the warm cloth against her puckered opening, he slid a hand up her back. "Unless you're misbehaving. Then, you get excited when I'm cold."

A burst of laughter escaped before she could prevent it. "Nobody likes a smart-ass."

"I do." Lifting her high against his chest, he smiled down at her. "I'm madly in love with one."

Chapter Fourteen

"Are you sure you're ready to give up your exciting life to retire and settle down in a small town like Desire?" Seated between Hoyt's thighs in the warm scented water, she rubbed the back of her head against his chest, looking up at him with eyes half-closed.

Smiling down at her, Hoyt reached for one of the shower gels arranged on the ledge of the large bathtub. "Absolutely."

He uncapped the bottle and sniffed the contents, grimacing at the lemony scent. Glancing at Natalie, he recapped the bottle and set it aside before reaching for another one. "There are all kinds of excitement, honey."

He uncapped the next, his cock stirring at the spicy-sweet scent of cinnamon and vanilla—a scent that Natalie wore often. "I've been looking forward to living here for a long time."

She shifted slightly, allowing him a flash of creamy wet thigh as she turned to lay her cheek against his chest. "I hope you're not bored here." Lifting her head, she grinned at him, her cheeks flushed from the warm water. "Aren't you going to miss having all those people to boss around?"

Pleased to see that she'd finally begun to relax, he smiled back at her and tapped her nose. "I'll just have to make do with bossing you around." Shrugging, he set the cap aside. "Besides, those young men I worked with made me feel like an old man."

Natalie's soft laughter rippled over him, the delight in her eyes enthralling him as she poked him in the stomach. "Bullshit. They were probably scared to death of you."

Dismissing what Natalie called a loofah as too rough, Hoyt felt around beneath the surface of the water for the much softer washcloth, letting his fingers slide over her bottom and thigh as he searched for it. Allowing a small smile, he bent to kiss her forehead. "Maybe just a little. I've been called things that would shock you."

She laughed again, and cuddled against him, her relaxed teasing and obvious ease with him filling him with a warm satisfaction that he'd all but forgotten. "Don't tell me they actually called you names to your face!"

Squeezing a generous amount of the scented gel onto the washcloth, he chuckled, appreciating her sense of humor. "No. They didn't have the balls for that." Taking her left hand in his, he lifted it from the water and began to wash it. "I seem to have a problem with people saying things to my face." He gave her a meaningful look. "Scaring my men was part of the job. I don't like that I scare you."

He ran the washcloth over her arm and to her shoulder. "I would die for you, Natalie. You have no reason to fear me."

"Oh, Hoyt." When she stiffened and straightened, he took advantage of her position to slide the cloth to her breast. "I'm not afraid of you." Her flush deepened, and to his relief—and delight—she arched her back and pressed her breast more firmly against his hand. "I'm not afraid of you in that way. I already told you that. I just can't wrap my head around the fact that you're back, and you actually want to build a life here. With me. With us."

She looked up at him through her lashes, making an adorable picture that he knew he wouldn't forget. "I'm sure women throw themselves at you all the time. I have stretch marks, I'm opinionated, bitchy, and set in my ways. And do you really think this place won't drive you crazy? Living in Desire is like living in a fishbowl. You're secretive and like your privacy. I know that you want to try. I love you. That won't change." Blowing out a breath, she averted her gaze. "I just don't want to argue with you and ruin the time we have together. Okay? Pitiful, I know, but I have to live with myself when you leave."

Sinking his fingers into the silky knot of her hair, he tilted her head back to look into her beautiful brown eyes. Biting back his impatience, Hoyt held her gaze, dropping the cloth into the water.

With a sigh, he squeezed more of the gel on his hands and continued to slide his hands over her, both because he needed his hands on her and because he wanted her to become accustomed to his touch in a way that had nothing to do with sex. "I've never met a woman who excited me as much as you do. The last thing on earth I'd want is someone so young that I have to explain everything to them. I love your stretch marks." He ran his hands over her stomach, his stomach clenching.

"You were so lush and beautiful when you carried Joe." Smiling, he flattened his hand on her stomach, remembering how she'd looked when she'd carried his child, and how hard it had been for him to leave her and go back to his unit.

He'd never forget getting the call from Jake to tell him that they had a son.

Tracing his finger over one of those marks. "Every time I see or feel one of your stretch marks, I get hard, thinking about you carrying my child."

He smiled when her eyes went wide and her jaw dropped, and continued before she had a chance to object. "As for living here—I want a home, Natalie. I want roots, and a sense of permanence. I want you and my son in my life every day. I want to spend the rest of my life with you. I know I can never make up for all the time I've lost, but I'm going to try my best." Kissing her hair, he breathed in the scent of his woman. "I can't live without you in my life, Natalie. Some part of me has always planned to come back for you."

Smiling, he leaned forward, running his hands over her thigh and down her back, willing his cock to behave. Keeping his touch tender instead of seductive, he rested his cheek against the top of her head. "I know how small towns work, baby. You and I grew up in a small town, didn't we?"

Stiffening in his arms, she leaned back to look up at him. "And you couldn't wait to get out."

With a hand at her back, he urged her to lean against him again. Once she did, he caressed the tight muscles there, struggling to keep the rage out of his voice. "I didn't want to get away from the town, or from you. I wanted to get away from my father. He would have made our lives miserable if we'd stayed. I could never live the kind of life I wanted to live if I stayed close to him. He was pure evil, Natalie. My mom died in an accident, trying to get away from his abuse."

Nat lifted her head, shaking it slowly and looking stunned. "Hoyt, I never knew."

Shrugging, he went back to washing her, loving the way she moved into his touch. "There was no reason for you to know. You had enough on your plate with your own father and Jesse."

Nat's chin lifted, her brow going up—both a sign of trouble. "So you were protecting me even then?"

"There was no reason for you to worry about it." Shrugging, he squeezed more of the gel on his hands and cupped her breasts, the slippery gel allowing his hands to slide over her soft, wet skin. "Besides, I wanted to make the kind of living I could never make there."

Smiling when she leaned back against him, he concentrated his attention on her breasts, massaging gently. "I found myself in love with a woman I couldn't wait to make mine, and she deserved hell of a lot more than I could give her."

Raising her arms, she linked them around her neck, giving him full access to her breasts in a trusting gesture that made his cock stir. "I didn't need anything else, Hoyt. I only needed you."

* * * *

I only needed you.

Jake paused, stopping short of knocking on the door. Dropping his hand, he stared at the door to the Master bathroom, the tight fist around his heart making it difficult to breathe.

He knew she loved Hoyt, and had for years.

At that time in their lives, Jake hadn't been able to do anything except love her from afar.

She'd belonged to Hoyt.

Of course, she'd needed him.

Jake just hadn't anticipated how much it hurt to hear it out loud.

He started to turn away, reluctant to eavesdrop on their conversation, coming to an abrupt halt when Nat spoke again.

"Hoyt, you've been an important part of my life forever, and I've loved you for so long. But, now I need Jake so much. He's a part of me now."

The fist around Jake's heart loosened, making it easier to breathe.

Hoyt chuckled. "That's how it should be, baby. He's always been there for you. I just want you to know that I plan to be there for you, too. The three of us are going to have a good life. Together."

Grinning, Jake forced himself to walk away, not wanting to interrupt their time together.

Making his way to the kitchen, he paused in front of the sink, staring unseeingly out the window above it.

He should have known better.

His wife had a heart bigger than he suspected even she realized, and he should have known there was enough love in it for both of them.

The underlying tension that he'd experienced for years seemed to melt away.

Even the only other man in her life whom she loved—her first love—couldn't diminish her love for him.

He had the answer he'd been looking for.

She belonged to him, and no one could take her away.

* * * *

Nat laughed and pushed Hoyt's hands away. "Enough! I've got so much body lotion on that I'm going to slide out of bed tonight." Knowing that she escaped his hold only because he allowed it, she grabbed her robe from the foot of the bed as she twirled and danced away from him, unable to take her eyes from Hoyt's naked, muscular body.

Hoyt stepped closer, reaching out a hand to trail his fingers down her arm. "Since you'll be sleeping between Jake and me, we won't let that happen."

Finding her gaze drawn to where his cock pressed against his gray sweatpants, she froze, her smile falling as desire beaded her nipples and made her clit stir with awareness. "Damn, you're hot."

"No." Smiling, he bent to touch his lips to hers before taking the robe from her and bundling her into it. "I'm sure Jake's waiting for you. This is hard on him, baby, and I'm sure after the way we took you in the playroom, he's anxious to hold you. Aren't you, Jake?"

"Very." Jake strolled into the room, his gaze holding hers. "How is she?"

Nat turned to frown at him. "She's right here."

Hoyt ran a hand over her hair and took a step back, his eyes never leaving hers. "She's settled, but tired. Aroused again."

Jake grinned and unbelted her robe, sliding his hands inside. "Yeah, once her motor's running, it runs for quite a while. Do you need to come again, honey?"

Grinning, she reached for him, a low moan escaping when he lifted her against him. Wrapping her legs around his waist, she pressed herself against him. "I want your hands on me."

Something about Jake seemed different—more relaxed.

There was something more confident about him, a mischievous quality that made her heart beat faster.

Silently questioning him with her eyes as he carried her to the bed, she ran her fingers through his dark hair, her pulse tripping at his ready smile.

"Oh, my hands are definitely on you. Damn, you're slippery." Placing her on the bed, he followed her down. "You trying to make it hard for me to hold on to you, darlin'?"

"Never." Wrapping her legs around his waist as the bed shifted beside her, she moaned at the feel of his hands moving on her skin. "Hoyt insisted on rubbing my lotion on me, and he went a little overboard."

From beside her, Hoyt chuckled, running a hand over her thigh. "I couldn't resist the chance to slide my hands over her skin." His eyes narrowed, a small smile of satisfaction playing at his lips. "She was afraid she was so slippery that she'd slip out of bed."

Lying beside her, Jake slid a hand down the center of her body. "We won't let that happen."

On the other side of her, Hoyt propped his head on his hand and stared down at her. "That's exactly what I said to her."

Lying between them felt like a dream. Running her hands over their chests, she smiled at each of them. "I'd forgotten how much the two of you always thought alike."

Jake smiled and nuzzled her jaw. "So, it shouldn't be surprising that we both fell in love with the same woman."

The phone rang, the shrill sound startling her.

With a groan, Jake rolled away from her, reaching out to answer it. "Hello?"

He stilled beside her and sat up abruptly. "Okay. Thanks."

Disconnecting, he rose and grabbed the television remote. "That was Clay. He said to turn on the news."

Nat sat up, surprised to see Ace's face on the screen. "What the hell?" The news report went on to the next story, but not before Nat saw that he had Debra Smith, the teller from the bank, in handcuffs. "Holy shit. He arrested her!"

Jake nodded grimly. "It looks that way. I'm going to go talk to Ace."

Hoyt had already stripped off his sweatpants and stepped into a pair of well-worn jeans. "I'll go with you. Something about this whole thing makes the hair on the back of my neck stand on end."

Chapter Fifteen

Standing at the sink, Hoyt turned when Natalie rushed into the kitchen. "Problem, baby?"

Frowning, he glanced at Jake, seeing the same worry in his friend's eyes.

She hadn't slept much, tossing and turning most of the night. The bank robbery still haunted her, and every mention of it angered her, and made her restless.

Leaning back against the counter, he attempted to appear nonchalant. "I know you were upset last night, but I told you not to worry about her. Ace is putting her on a forty-eight-hour hold while he does some more checking. That's all there is to it."

Nat gulped down the cup of coffee he'd poured for her and slammed the cup on the table. "Yeah, and if he can't find anything on her, he'll have to release her again. It pisses me off that I get nauseous at the thought of going into the bank again." Waving a hand, she plopped into the chair and started to tug on her boots. "Fuck it."

Jake reached for her. "Nat, honey—"

She finished zipping her boots and jumped to her feet. "Damn it. I can't believe I overslept. Why didn't you two wake me up? I'm gonna be late. Jesse's counting on me. I've got to fill the body butter jars and label them. I've got to cut the soaps. I need to place an order for more oils and bottles and God knows what else. I didn't finish getting the list ready yesterday."

Jake got to his feet and went to her, his arms tightening around her when she would have pulled away. "You're so outspoken most of the time, but you always try to hide it when you're afraid. I know it pisses you off and you don't want to talk about it."

Her eyes snapped at him. "Exactly. I don't want to talk about it."

He smiled down at her, but Hoyt could see the concern in his friend's eyes. Sliding his hands inside her jacket, Jake nuzzled her neck. "You smell delicious. Anything you want to talk about?"

As he poured her coffee, Hoyt looked over to see her sharing an intimate look with Jake, shaking her head in exasperation even as she fought not to smile. "Other than the fact that I have to deal with you two every day now?"

Pleased to see that Jake's teasing seemed to ease some of the tension from her shoulders, Hoyt placed a fresh cup of coffee in front of her, lifting her chin to drop a quick kiss on her dark pink lips. "Hmm. Peppermint." Straightening, he ran a hand over her hair, sharing a look of understanding with Jake over her head. "I didn't hear you bitching last night when you were filled with cock and screaming your pleasure."

Pulling a material-covered elastic from inside the sleeve of her sweater, she lifted her arms above her head. After a few deft moves, she lowered her hands again, leaving her hair pulled back in some kind of intricate knot. Smiling, she poked him in the stomach. "Just because you're good in bed doesn't mean that you're not a pain in the ass."

"Like I was last night?" Hoyt bent to nuzzle her lips with his own, delighted that her eyes danced with amusement. "I've got news for you, baby. I'm going to be a pain in *your* ass every chance I get."

Inordinately pleased that he'd managed to make her blush, he went back to the stove, glancing at her over his shoulder as she snuggled against Jake. "Stay put and I'll fix you some eggs."

Shaking her head, she grabbed the small wallet she carried and stuck it in her jacket pocket. "No time. Jake, give me some money. I'm broke, and I'm going to be too busy to go to the bank today."

Jake lifted her chin, holding it when she tried to turn away. "You don't have to be embarrassed because you're not ready to go back to the bank, and you don't have to make excuses. You'll go when you're ready, and if you want me to go with you, all you have to do is say so." Holding out his wallet with one hand, he cuddled Natalie with the other. "I want my kiss first."

Hoyt stiffened, turning slowly to see Jake grinning as he reached into his pocket. "Natalie, you know you can ask me for money." He sighed, shaking his head at the surprise widening her eyes. "I'm here for you, too, for whatever you need."

Natalie tucked the bills into her back pocket, reaching for her coffee. "Sorry. I'll try to remember."

Fighting to remember that this was new to all of them, he moved closer, touching his lips to her forehead. "I want more than just the sex, baby. I want all of it."

Shrugging, she wrapped her arms around herself, her cheeks pink. "Hoyt, I don't know. I'm sorry. I'm used to asking Jake. I never even thought about asking you."

Pushing her hair back from her forehead, he grinned. "Maybe I want a chance to earn a morning kiss, too. Maybe I can earn one by making you some breakfast."" Turning back to the stove, he began to break eggs into a bowl.

"I'm sorry, Hoyt. Look, I don't want any breakfast. I'm already late."

Regretting that he'd made her uncomfortable, he sighed. Turning in time to see her shrug into her coat, he closed the distance between them and started to button her into it, struggling to hide his frustration. "You'd better eat something or you're not going to have the energy to do what you have to do today."

Wrapping a red scarf around her neck, she paused at the doorway. "Look, Hoyt. I'm sorry. This is all still new to me. I don't mean to hurt your feelings, but I'm used to asking Jake for things."

Hoyt nodded, trying to tell himself he couldn't have expected more. "And you're not comfortable asking me. I get it. I just don't like it."

Her smile looked forced as she glanced at Jake again. "I'll work on it, okay?"

Bending close, he brushed her lips with his again, letting his hands run over her hips. "You do that."

Hiding his irritation at the quick peck on the cheek she gave him, he watched her rush out the door.

"She didn't mean anything by it, Hoyt." Jake picked up his coffee again. "It's going to take some time for us to settle down into some sort of routine."

Hoyt sighed and poured himself another cup of coffee. "I know. It just doesn't make it any easier. I'd hoped that having a physical relationship with her would automatically lead to the kind of intimacy I want." Turning with his cup, he moved to the table and dropped into a chair, staring down at his cup. "Stupid, I know, but she's got me all jumbled up. It's not the same as it was with her before. When we were younger, we could finish each other's sentences. Intimacy, I mistakenly thought, would be easy to reestablish, but it appears intimacy is harder for her."

Scrubbing a hand over his face, he looked away. "Christ, she's the only person in the world that can tie me up in knots."

"She loves hard. You know that. If she hasn't gotten over you in all this time, I don't think she ever will." Getting to his feet, Jake finished his coffee and took the cup to the sink before turning. "That's why we're in this situation, remember?"

Smiling faintly, Jake went to the row of hooks on the wall and retrieved his coat. "I knew she wouldn't let you touch her without my interference, so I initiated it, but I can't help you much with the rest. It's taken years for Nat and I to build the trust and closeness we have. That's why it's so precious." Pausing with a hand on the door, he met Hoyt's eyes. "That's why it'll be precious to you, too."

Hoyt nodded. "I'm beginning to see how much it cost you to do this."

Jake opened the door. "She loves you. I did it for her."

Sitting at the table long after Jake left, Hoyt thought about what Jake had said. He wanted Natalie to be able to relax around him.

To play.

To depend on him, and count on him to be there for her.

He knew what he wanted, and was determined to have it.

Even if it took him the rest of his life.

He got up to wash the dishes, staring out the kitchen window.

The niggling sense that something was wrong continued to plague him, causing a hard knot in his stomach that wouldn't go away.

Despite his impatience to be closer to Natalie, things between them were working out better than he could have hoped for.

She'd let him into her life again.

Jake's support meant the world to him, and other than a few minor issues, the three of them seemed to be settling into their new relationship.

Natalie was being very accepting. Reasonable.

It made him nervous as hell.

She loved his touch.

He could see it in her eyes—feel the way her muscles quivered beneath his hands.

He could hear it in her voice—in the way she breathed his name.

But, she never reached for him, or came to him for anything.

He'd known it would take time to build anything deeper. He'd known there would be compromise from all of them and a lot of adjustments.

He just hadn't anticipated how gut-wrenching it would be to have to deal with it.

The phone rang, yanking him out of his depressing thoughts, and with a sigh, he crossed the room to answer it.

"Hello?"

"Dad?"

Grinning, he leaned back against the counter, a surge of pride making his chest swell. "Of course. How's school? Did you get the check I sent you?"

"Yeah, thanks. School's good, but I called to see how everything was going at home."

Disturbed at the concern in his son's voice, Hoyt forced a chuckle. "Everything's fine here. I'm ecstatic to be back in your mother's life again. You know how much I love her."

His son had become a young man so quickly that Hoyt still found himself adjusting to it.

Joe sighed. "Yeah, I know. It's just that Mom and Dad are so happy together, and everything's been okay with you visiting—"

Hoyt's stomach clenched. "And you didn't want them to fight about this, and you didn't want them to be mad at me about it. I know, Joe. I want you to understand something. If they get mad or this doesn't work out, I don't want you to blame them. I'm the one trying to change things."

"It's working, though, right? I mean, you're living there and everything's okay?"

Not liking the concern in his son's voice, Hoyt injected a confidence in his tone he wished he had. "It's working just fine. It's slow, but your mother and I love each other very much. There are going to be a few bumps along the way, but I'm not going anywhere."

Fisting a hand at his side, Hoyt turned to stare out the window, smiling at the sight of two bright yellow flowers braving the cold weather to bloom for Natalie. "You know I had to do this. I couldn't go on without knowing if I could have your mother back in my life."

Joe sighed, his maturity and caring filling Hoyt with pride. "I know that, Dad. You always go for what you want. You always know how to handle yourself. Have I mentioned lately that I'm proud of you?"

Touched, Hoyt found he couldn't stop grinning. Swallowing a lump in his throat, he nodded. "I'm proud of you, too, son."

Damn, he never got tired of saying that.

Knowing his son well, he purposely lightened the atmosphere. "You wouldn't be saying that because you need more money, would you?"

Joe laughed as Hoyt had hoped. "I never could slip anything by you, could I? But no, Dad. I'm good." A brief silence followed before Joe spoke again. "Dad, please don't tell Mom that I was worried about this, okay? She'll get all weird about it. You know how she is. She gets upset but tries to hide it. She thinks nobody can see through that hard shell of hers."

Hoyt couldn't help but smile, pleased that he was one of the few who could. "But those of us who love her can see the marshmallow underneath. Don't worry. This conversation is our little secret."

Joe breathed a sigh of relief. "Thanks. I'm just glad the three of you are working everything out. I can't wait to get home for spring break. It'll be nice to have my mom and dads all together again."

Hoyt couldn't wait either, anxious to have his family together as a real family. "Yeah, well, we're pretty happy about it, too. Don't worry about us. Concentrate on school, and tell your cousins I said hi."

"Will do. Gotta get to class. I'll call you in a couple of days."

After the conversation with his son, Hoyt paced the house, irritated at the restlessness that didn't seem to be easing.

He couldn't get over the feeling that something was wrong, and because of his preoccupation with making things right with Natalie—he was missing it.

* * * *

Juggling the bags from the diner, Nat walked through the back door and straight to the kitchen table. Disappointed to find the kitchen empty, she set the bags on the table and listened for Hoyt, smiling at the unmistakable sound of clicking on a keyboard.

Unbuttoning her jacket, she grinned, deciding she could easily become accustomed to coming home to a man in the house. "Hoyt, I'm home!"

"Hey, babe." A grunt followed. "You son of a bitch. Oh, no, you cocksucker! I'm not falling for that again."

Pausing in the process of unwrapping her scarf from around her neck, Nat turned toward the doorway and frowned. "Hoyt?"

Another string of curses followed.

Intrigued, Nat hung up her scarf and coat before dropping into the chair closest to her. Blinking at some particularly inventive cursing, she stripped off her boots, tossing them aside and getting to her feet again.

"Hoyt?" Making her way down the hall on stockinged feet, she blinked at a particularly vulgar curse, wondering if he would wind down anytime soon.

"You piece of shit bastard. You think you've got me again, don't you. Damn it to hell. You fucker!"

Nat got to the doorway just in time to see a laptop fly across the room to join three others lying on the floor. "Um, Hoyt? I'm home."

He swiveled his chair and leaned back, the anger in his eyes dissipating as his gaze met hers. "So I see." A slow smile curved his lips. "I missed you. Did you have a nice day, baby?"

Eyeing the mess on the floor, Nat shrugged. "It was okay." She lifted her gaze to his again, smiling at the picture he made.

His relaxed pose didn't fool her for a minute. He could move faster than any man she'd ever met, but she did have to admit that he didn't seem as tense as he had on his previous visits. "You sounded pretty involved in what you were doing. I didn't know if you realized I was here."

His eyes sharpened. "I always know when you're near. You look upset. Is there something you want to talk about?"

A little unsettled that he saw something that she hadn't even acknowledged to herself, Nat shrugged and walked into the room, pointing to the mess on the floor. "What happened? Did you kill them?"

Hoyt's lips curved. "Collateral damage." Patting his thigh, he lifted a brow when she hesitated. "Problem?"

Her nipples, already beaded, tightened even more, the ache at her slit sharpening as she shook her head and crossed to him. "No. I didn't want to disturb you, but I figured you might be hungry."

Grinning, he grabbed her hand and yanked her onto his lap, wrapping one arm around her while sliding his other hand under the hem of her sweater. "You disturb me just by being in the same room. I couldn't stop thinking about you all day. Did you get everything done that you wanted to do?"

When the hand at her waist tightened, pulling her closer, she leaned into him, wrapping her arms around his neck and touching her lips to his.

Warm and firm, his lips parted against hers, drawing her in with an erotic sweep of his tongue. Pulling her closer, he deepened his kiss, swallowing her moan as he unhooked the front fastening of her bra and covered her breast with his hot hand, massaging gently.

Holding on to him, she met him kiss for kiss, losing herself in the taste—in the feel—of him.

The hard arm at her back tightened, pulling her closer as he took her mouth in a kiss meant to coerce—to seduce.

And it did—a slow seduction that warmed her and had her pressing herself against him.

Her breath caught at the friction of his callused palm against her nipple, the flood of sensation from her nipple to her slit drawing another moan from her.

Lifting his head, Hoyt stared down at her, lifting her sweater, his gaze hot on her breasts. "You are so fucking beautiful."

Arching, Nat slid her hands over his shoulders, loving the feel of solid muscle. "And you're too damned sexy for your own good."

Bending her back over his arm, Hoyt grinned, his eyes flashing with devilish amusement. "You think I'm sexy, huh?" Lowering his head, he watched her eyes as he flicked his tongue out to tease her nipple. "That's good to know. I happen to think you're sexy, too. Every time I'm near you, I'm hard."

Nat's stomach muscles quivered beneath the hand he slid lower, her breath catching when he deftly unfastened her jeans and slid a hand inside. "Oh, God. Hoyt, I—"

The slide of his finger over her clit made her forget whatever she'd been about to say. Rendered defenseless under his tender assault, Nat parted her thighs as far as her jeans allowed, desperate for more.

"Hoyt! Oh, God." Fisting her hands on his shirt, she fought to pull him closer.

He smiled indulgently. "Yeah, baby?"

"I can't wait anymore." Need clawed at her, sharpening when his head lowered and his teeth closed over her nipple. Fisting a hand in his short hair, she pulled his head up to nip at his bottom lip. "Take me."

He moved fast, as if her demand unleashed something inside him.

With a low groan, he yanked her jeans to her knees. "I want my mouth on you." Holding her close, he dropped to the floor, cursing as he shoved the laptops aside. "I want the taste of you on my tongue. I want to hear you scream my name."

His rough tone sent a thrill through her, his expression tight with tension as he stripped her jeans and panties from her with a rough jerk and tossed them aside. "Christ, you go to my head."

Supporting his weight on his elbows, he loomed over her, using his knees to shove hers wide. His hooded eyes, filled with heat, held hers. "You're in my fucking blood. You have been since the first time I held you. I can't stand that you keep parts of yourself from me. I know it's too soon, but I've been too hungry for you for years to be appeased with bits and pieces. I want it all—and, one way or another, I'll damned well have it from you."

Lowering his head, he kissed one nipple and then the other before lifting his gaze to hers again. "Even if it takes me the rest of my life."

Shaking helplessly as Hoyt parted her thighs wide, Nat squeezed her eyes closed against the pleasure, throwing her hands out in a frantic attempt to find something solid to hold on to.

The caress of Hoyts's warm breath over her already overheated slit was her only warning before his hot, decadent tongue slid over it.

Jolting at the burst of heat, and the shock of erotic electricity, she cried out and fought to escape the too-intense pleasure. Thrilling at the feel of his tight hold on her thighs, she pushed against his strong hands, lifting her hips several inches off of the floor.

He buried his face between her thighs, holding her with a firmness that made escape impossible, leaning forward slightly so that her legs fell back, leaving her completely at his mercy.

She loved it.

She loved his take-charge attitude, the confidence in his touch. The demand.

She loved the way he let her see how much he wanted her, and the way he made her feel as if nothing else mattered.

He ate at her as though starving for her, using his lips and tongue with an expertise that left her unable to do anything except hold on.

Crying out as the pleasure heightened, she threw her hands above her head, giving herself over to his mastery of her.

Trembling, she cried out his name, bowing at the sharp tingling in her clit that seemed to explode, showering her with sparks. Every nerve ending shimmered with ecstasy, spreading from her clit outward in shimmering waves of heat.

His groan of satisfaction seemed to vibrate through her slit, his firm grip controlling her body's movements with ease.

"Hoyt! Oh, God. Oh, God." The pleasure continued in delicate waves, every slow stroke of his tongue drawing it out until she shook uncontrollably.

Too much. Too intense. Too hot.

"Hoyt! It's too much. Too much."

Her clit burned, but he didn't stop, his slow strokes providing a constant, tender friction that held her in its grip.

She fought his hold, the submissive side of her delighting that she couldn't escape him. "I can't. Hoyt! I can't. Too much. Oh, God."

"It doesn't look like Hoyt's gonna be happy with just one orgasm, baby."

Nat's eyes flew open at the husky amusement in Jake's voice. Shocked to find him there, she reached for him as he knelt beside her. Even staring into his eyes, she couldn't stop crying out as Hoyt's mouth continued to work its magic. "Jake!"

Running a hand over her breast, he tugged at her nipple. "Hoyt looks like he wants to eat you alive." Smiling faintly, he rolled her nipple between his thumb and forefinger, the tug to her clit nearly driving her insane. "I can't say that I blame him. I feel that way every time I touch you."

"Jake, I can't. I can't." Her cries became more desperate when Hoyt focused his attention on her clit again. She tried to reach for him, tugging at the T-shirt covering his shoulders, unsurprised that she couldn't budge him at all.

Smiling down at her, Jake massaged her breast, moving his palm over her nipple. "You and I both know very well that you can. Put your hands over your head, let him have what he wants, and let me see those beautiful breasts."

Nat shivered as she obeyed him, the pleasure that hadn't had a chance to subside already building again.

Still massaging her breast, Jake smiled, glancing at Hoyt. "She loves not being able to close against what you're doing to her now. She loves being forced to accept it. Keep those hands up, baby."

Tugging her nipple, he searched her features as she writhed and cried out. "Good girl."

The pleasure hit her hard, and squeezing her eyes closed, she fisted her hands and rode the decadent wave. "Fuck. Oh, God. I'm so close. I'm gonna come. I can't stop it. Hoyt!" Her chest heaved in her desperate attempt to get more air into her lungs, her body shaking so hard that her teeth chattered. "Ohh! I'm coming. I'm coming! Yes. Oh, God. Oh!"

Hoyt pushed her through it, using his lips and tongue to draw it out until she couldn't bear any more.

Whimpering, she slumped. "Hoyt! Please! No more."

Lifting his head, Hoyt cursed and lowered her thighs. Gripping her shoulders, he pulled her to straddle him as he sat back on his heels, running his hands up and down her back. "Come here, baby. Damn, you taste good."

Nat dropped her head to his shoulder, slumping against him. "What the hell happened?" She took several deep breaths and turned her face to press it against his neck, smiling and closing her eyes. "I came in with dinner, which is probably cold by now." Opening her eyes, she lifted her head, frowning when she realized Jake had gone. "Where's Jake?"

Fisting a hand in her hair, Hoyt pulled her head back, his eyes glittering. "He left. Do you have a problem with spending time alone with me?"

Unnerved by his mood, Nat tried to get up, but he didn't release her as she'd expected. "Of course not. Let me up. I brought dinner home and I'm hungry."

Spreading his arms wide, Hoyt smiled coldly. "By all means."

Eyeing him warily, she got to her feet, fastening her bra and pulling her sweater back down before bending to retrieve her panties. "I don't know why you're so mad. If you want to get laid, just say so."

"If I wanted to get laid, my cock would be inside you right now." Hoyt got to his feet. "I'm fine for pleasure, but afterward, you prefer Jake. I understand it, but after being the one to pleasure you, it's a little hard to swallow."

Pulling her jeans up, she glanced at him, her stomach rolling. Trying not to show her panic, she lifted her chin, forcing her voice to remain steady, while everything inside her shook. "I don't know what the hell you're talking about, and I'm too damned tired and hungry for this conversation. I just asked where Jake was. I didn't mean that I didn't want to be with you. I don't want to argue with you, but I'm getting sick and tired of walking on eggshells to preserve your fucking ego."

Fastening her jeans, she turned away, needing a few minutes alone to settle, only to have Hoyt grip her arm and spin her back again, yanking her against his hard chest.

"My ego's just fine. Even though you're willing to walk on eggshells around me, I prefer the more direct approach. I don't like that while I'm holding you, and you're still trembling from the orgasms I just gave you, you're asking for another man."

Struggling against his hold, she almost fell when he released her unexpectedly—chilled after the heat of her recent orgasms, and shaken by the distance still between them. "I forgot what a bastard you can be when you want to be."

She had to admit that she wouldn't have liked it if the shoe had been on the other foot, and that asking for Jake while Hoyt cuddled with her might have been a little insensitive.

How the hell did Jesse do this?

Hoyt's icy smile sent a chill through her. "Baby, you have no idea what a bastard I can be. You want sex, but thwart every attempt for intimacy. If you think I'm going to let you get away with that, sweetheart, you're sadly mistaken."

Chapter Sixteen

Despite her best efforts, Nat couldn't stop glancing at Hoyt while they ate the dinner she'd brought home. Unnerved that each time she looked at him, she found him staring at her, she sent a glare in his direction and focused her attention on Jake, not even tasting the fried chicken.

She hadn't meant to hurt Hoyt's feelings, and hated feeling guilty about it, but she'd already apologized and didn't know what else to say to him.

Other women in Desire in ménage relationships seemed to handle it a hell of a lot better than she did.

Her clumsiness had already caused a good deal of hurt, making her wonder if she had what it took to handle two men.

Depressed, she toyed with her mashed potatoes and looked up at Jake. "Were you busy today?"

Swallowing his mouthful of food, Jake glanced at Hoyt. "Valentine's Day is coming. I have a lot of special orders that are going to keep me busy for the next several weeks." Sipping his sweet tea, he grinned. "Of course, there's always a market for men who are buying expensive jewelry to make up for something they did wrong."

Hoyt smiled. "Not a bad idea. I'll have to stop by to pick out some new nipple clips and a clit clip for Natalie." Meeting her glare with a smile, he leaned forward, his gaze lowering to her breasts. "Something with weights. Something to get her attention. That trip to the playroom has only whetted my appetite for more."

Sitting back, he eyed her steadily. "She doesn't seem to want anything except sex from me right now, so I might as well oblige her. Jake, do you mind very much if I have some time alone with her tonight?"

Jake glanced from her to Hoyt and back again, his eyes narrowed in speculation. "Not at all. Clay and Rio are going to the club. I'll go have a drink with them. Some of their guests arrived today, and it's useful to know who's in town for the seminar in case we run into them in town. A lot of us like stopping in when there's a seminar going on to help out if necessary, and we get a kick out of watching the subs and Doms together."

Nat knew that Jesse liked it, too, because her husbands came home aroused, and hungrier than ever.

Her pussy clenched at the thought of what kind of mood Jake would be in when he got home. Lifting her gaze to her husband's, she read the amusement in his eyes, along with erotic intent and a promise that she would be on the receiving end of the lust his visit to the club would produce.

The secret communication bolstered her confidence enough to look at Hoyt again. "I know you've been to the club several times on your visits here. Have you ever screwed any of the women there?"

Hoyt's eyes hardened. "No. I didn't just want sex, Natalie. I wanted *intimacy.*"

Grimacing, Nat looked back down at her plate, hating that her face burned. "I get it, Hoyt. I suck at it. You've made that abundantly clear."

"No, you don't. You're just not a woman who allows people in easily." Jake touched her arm. "It just takes time. Both of you are going to have to be patient."

Nodding, Nat went back to eating, her stomach rolling as she took a bite of chicken.

Hoyt was a handsome, devastatingly sexual, and compelling man, and had no doubt been with countless women over the years—women he'd dominated. Trying not to think of Hoyt in the arms of another woman, Nat shrugged. "Whenever there's a seminar, we get a lot of traffic in town. Doms and women who sign up to be submissives."

She slid another glance at Jake. "From what I hear, the submissives are all running around naked, and if any of the men in the club want them, they can have them."

Jake didn't seem surprised that she knew so much about the inner workings of the club. He probably knew that Brenna and Kelly told them what happened there. Smiling, he looked up from his plate. "It's a little more complicated than that."

Picking at her food, Nat eyed both of them. "And then there are the auctions. You can actually bid on one of the women and take them to one of the playrooms."

Hoyt inclined his head. "Blade, King, and Royce are smart businessmen. Those auctions drum up a lot of interest—and business."

Jake paused with a forkful of food halfway to his mouth. "Is there something going on that I should know about?"

Not giving her a chance to answer, Hoyt frowned and waved a hand. "Natalie's gonna have to learn how to deal with me. She and I are going to have to learn to communicate without her putting you in the middle."

Jake sighed. "I shouldn't have walked in there when you were with her."

Before he'd even finished, Hoyt started shaking his head. "No. It's not your fault. It's just something that Nat and I are going to have to work out between us. I just have to keep reminding myself to be patient. We'll get there, but I'm sure there are going to be a lot of disagreements before we do. Just don't give up on us."

* * * *

Hoyt sipped his coffee, content to sit back and watch Jake and Natalie together as he thought about the way they'd been together in the early years of their marriage.

Natalie had been restless around Jake at that time. Edgy and nervous.

Her growing love and ease with Jake had become more apparent with every one of Hoyt's visits, the closeness and intimacy between them now making Hoyt feel like an intruder.

He wanted so much to be a part of it—to share the same intimacy with her that Jake did—an intimacy even more profound and mature than what they'd shared before.

Standing at the sink, Natalie began to wash the dishes, her posture changing as soon as Jake stepped up behind her.

As his hands closed on her waist, she seemed to melt against him, her body automatically adjusting to the contours of his.

There was a rhythm to the way they moved together, a seductiveness that Hoyt saw in their lovemaking.

Sitting several feet away, he tuned out their low conversation, focusing his attention on their body language.

Natalie leaned back into Jake trustingly, as though confident that he would support her, and Jake did, taking her weight with an ease and affection of a man confident in his wife's moves.

As if in a practiced dance, as soon as Jake began to lower his head, Natalie tilted hers to the side and let it fall back to Jake's shoulder, exposing what Hoyt knew to be a particularly sensitive spot for Jake to nuzzle.

The Dominant in him admired the choreography of their dance—in the way the Master advanced and his submissive yielded to him.

Natalie gave herself over to the pleasure of his touch, reacting to the slightest shift of Jake's body even as she laughed at something he whispered in her ear.

Jake played Natalie's body like an instrument, the lightest stroke of his hand or increase in firmness eliciting a response from her—whether it was a shift in her position, an arch to her back, or a moan of delight.

The two of them flowed well together.

Jealousy reared its ugly head, along with a determination to cultivate the same kind of closeness with her.

Some of his frustration melted away as he thought about the journey in getting there.

* * * *

Nat glanced over her shoulder at Hoyt, who'd been unusually quiet since Jake left for the club. "You gonna be mad at me and sulk all night?"

Hoyt blinked as if coming out of a trance, his lips twitching. "I've never sulked in my life." Getting to his feet, he strolled closer, snagging a dish towel from the hook next to the refrigerator as he approached.

Pausing behind her back, he ran a finger down her spine, sending a chill through her. "And I'm not mad at you. I'm mad at myself. What I want with you is something very special, and very precious. Part of what makes it so special is that it takes years to get there. I tend to forget that." Smiling, he reached for one of the plates she'd washed. "I'm known for my patience, but ever since I got here, I've been rushing you, scared that you'd change your mind about us."

Nat sighed, setting the last glass in the drainer. "We're going to have to trust each other, Hoyt. You want me to trust that you'll stay. I need you to trust that I won't change my mind. We're never going to be able to relax with each other enough to make this work if we don't start trusting each other." Drying her hands, she started to turn away, a gasp escaping when he yanked her back against him.

"You're right." His lips, warm and soft, touched her neck, sending a thrill of delight down her spine. "I never even get to talk to you the way I want to. I'm always in such a hurry to have you. I've missed you so much, baby. I can't stop wanting you."

Mesmerized by the desire in his deep baritone, Nat smiled and slumped against him. "What woman could resist a man who says something like that?"

Sliding the plate onto the stack in the cabinet, he tightened his arm around her. "Hopefully, you're not one of them."

To her surprise, he kissed the top of her head and released her. "So, you like working in your sister's store?"

Smiling, Nat poured herself another cup of coffee, wondering what he was up to. "Yes, I do." She took a sip of the hot brew, eyeing him over the rim.

His faded jeans lovingly hugged his muscular thighs, drawing her attention to the bulge between them.

Letting her gaze move higher to linger on the light gray T-shirt stretched over his chest, she swallowed heavily, her throat clogged with memories.

She'd always loved his chest, and had laid her head on it several times when they'd been younger. When he wrapped his arms around her, it seemed like the safest place on earth.

"Natalie?"

Jerked from her thoughts, she lifted her gaze to his, her cheeks burning at the amusement in his eyes.

His grin flashed more readily than it had in the past, his demeanor more relaxed than it had been earlier. "You givin' me *come hither* looks, darlin'?"

"Idiot." Lifting her cup to her lips to hide her smile, she couldn't help but admire the shift of corded muscle in his arms as he slid another plate into the cabinet on top of the others. "You're a stud and you know it. You can't expect me to live with a piece of eye candy like you and not take the time to admire it."

His eyes narrowed, a small smile playing at his lips. "Eye candy? So, I'm nice to look at, good to hide behind when bullets are flying, and handy to have around when you're aroused. Is that about it?"

Nat shrugged, hiding another smile at his disgruntled tone. "Well, you make breakfast and bring me coffee in the morning, and you help with the dishes. If you're good at yard work, odds and ends around the house and killing spiders, I might just let you stay."

Hoyt's eyes danced with amusement. "Careful. If you keep throwing all that flattery around, I might think you're flirting with me."

Enjoying herself, Nat sat back and sipped her coffee. "I don't flirt. Just stating facts. There's something real sexy about a man drying dishes."

Grinning, she set her cup aside, propping her chin on her hand as he finished the last dish and tossed the towel aside. "You really want to turn me on? Clean the bathroom and run the vacuum."

Raising a brow, Hoyt leaned over the table until his nose almost touched hers. "Or, I can take you to the playroom and strap you to the table. Or, strip you out of your clothes and turn you over my knee."

His hooded gaze held hers as he reached out to circle her nipple, the pleasure sharp even through the layers of her sweater and bra. His slow caress continued, his voice lowering to silky seduction. "Or, I can just caress you, can't I?"

His eyes narrowed, flaring with heat at the shiver of delight she didn't even attempt to suppress. "Do you have any idea how much I want you?" He closed his fingers over her nipple, the light pressure creating a tug to her clit. "Do you have any idea how it makes me feel when you respond to even my lightest touch? When you lean into me?"

Struck by the wonder and emotion in his eyes, Nat lifted her arms to wrap them around his neck. "Oh, Hoyt." Lifting her face to his, she brushed her lips against his chin, breathing in the scent of him. "You don't often say something mushy, but when you do, it gets me every time."

Tears stung her eyes at the gentleness in his touch and in his voice, and she found herself falling even deeper in love with him.

He moved around the table, his eyes never leaving hers as he bent and lifted her high against his chest. "I'm not used to talking about feelings, Natalie." Nuzzling her jaw, he strode into the living room. "Just because I don't talk about how I feel about you all the time doesn't mean I don't feel it."

Sitting on the sofa, he adjusted her on his lap, sliding a hand under the hem of her sweater to caress her stomach. "I've been called cold and unfeeling my entire life because of it."

Nat lifted her arms over her head in what had become an automatic response to the upward slide of his hand, her breath catching when she felt the front clasp of her bra come undone. "You've always been a hard man, Hoyt, but I understood why."

She wanted him to touch her breasts—to give her nipples the attention they needed, but Hoyt seemed content to slide his hand from her neck to her belly without touching her breasts at all.

He smiled faintly, his eyes searching hers. "I know you did, but I was never hard or cold with you, was I?"

Smiling, she writhed on his lap, each slide of his hand arousing her more. "No, you never were."

He touched her the way he used to, with tenderness and slow, seductive quality that ripped through her defenses. The firmness in his touch, and the confidence in the way he moved his hands over her hinted at the Master he hadn't shown her then.

Smiling faintly, he lifted her higher and touched his lips to hers. "I need to be that cold, hard man in the playroom, Natalie, and I was always worried that I'd scare you away, but neither one of us was ready for that, were we?"

Leaning back, he smiled faintly. "You're a more confident woman now, and we both know what we want."

Touched and proud that he thought of her that way, she arched, offering herself to him. "So, are you going to take me, or what?"

His lips thinned. "I'm not done yet, Natalie. I'm trying to tell you something about myself because I don't want there to be any misunderstandings."

Nervous now, Nat lowered her arms and sat up. "What is it?" Burying her face in her hands, she groaned, her stomach clenching. "I'm not sure I can take any more surprises, Hoyt."

Pulling her close, he took one of her hands in his, playing with her fingers as he held it against his chest. "It's not a surprise. I just want to put all my cards on the table."

Nat nodded once. "Okay. I respect that. What is it?" She tried to pull her hand from his, but he merely tightened his hold.

"I like being in charge—no, it's more than that. I *need* to be in control." Lacing their fingers, he smiled faintly. "It was probably one of the things that made me good at my job." His smile widened, but his body tensed against hers. "It just made me lousy at relationships, and I just never cared enough to try to change."

Releasing her hand, he gripped her chin, lifting her face to his. "Just because I'm cold in the playroom, or seem distant doesn't mean I don't love you."

Amused, Nat smiled. "Hoyt, I've been submitting to Jake for years. I know that no matter what he does, he loves me."

"Yeah, well I need you to remember that I do, too."

"I will." She snuggled against him, surprised that he remained tense. "So you gonna make love to me?"

Hoyt sighed. "I can be really demanding."

"I know." She pulled him closer, nibbling at his bottom lip.

"I'm controlling, Natalie, and not just in the playroom." Smiling faintly, he slid his hand under her sweater again. "I've never had a woman who belonged to me the way you do. I've never wanted one, and most of them wouldn't have put up with it anyway. When you get mad at me for being too bossy, I want you to remember how much I love you." Leaning over her, he urged her to her back again, taking both of her wrists in one hand and raising them over her head.

Sucking in a breath at the heat glittering in his eyes, Nat pressed her heels into the sofa cushion, lifting herself into his touch. "I'll remember." Biting her lip at the feel of his warm hand closing over her breast, she struggled to focus on their conversation. "If you get too bossy, I'll j–just put you in your place. I'm not one of your men."

Pushing her sweater up, he parted the sides of her bra, smiling coldly as he exposed her breasts. "I can see that."

Watching her face, he ran his palm back and forth over her nipple, his eyes narrowing even more at her soft cry. "That doesn't mean that you're not going to obey me." Smiling, he met her look of alarm with one of amusement. "Don't look so scared. You're a mature, confident woman now." He tapped her nipple, tightening his hold on her wrists when she jolted. "My needs have sharpened and become more intense over the years. Knowing that the woman I love is the most delectable submissive I could have ever hoped for has my imagination running wild. You're perfect for me, Natalie, and I'm going to spend the rest of my life proving that I'm perfect for you."

Nat couldn't stay still, writhing on his lap as he slowly built the need inside her. She desperately wanted to explore the needs he spoke of, but a part of her still bristled at his arrogance. "Don't expect me to obey you the way your men did." She wouldn't admit to him that she was very much looking forward to having Hoyt make her, and couldn't resist daring him. "You can demand it in the playroom, but not anywhere else. Jake tries it all the time."

She didn't think it prudent to mention that Jake usually won. She didn't need two men in her life trying to boss her around.

Hoyt's grin didn't bode well for her. "Baby, every move you make is my business, and if you don't behave the way you're told, you're going to get a hell of a lot more than a lecture from me. I promise. I'm going to get a great deal of pleasure out of making you obey me." Still holding her wrists, he slid his hand down to the fastening of her jeans. "A great deal of pleasure. I know you're going to have to test your limits from time to time, and I want you to know just how much I'm looking forward to taming you."

"Taming me?" Lifting her chin, Nat snorted. "You don't scare me."

He scared the shit out of her.

He unfastened her jeans and began to work them over her hips. "Baby, I scare the hell out of you. You're not afraid that I'd hurt you, but you're scared of the way I make you feel. I can make you beg, and you and I both know you're going to submit to me in the end."

Nervous that he'd expect a submissiveness from her that she wasn't prepared to give, Nat frowned. "I won't be a doormat, Hoyt."

Scowling at her, Hoyt slid her jeans from her and tossed them aside. "What the fuck would I do with a doormat? I want *you*, Natalie. I want a woman who's going to make me earn her submission, and you sure as hell won't give it easily."

Grumbling, she tried to kick at him. "I've been pretty easy so far." She didn't like to think about how easy.

Hoyt laughed at that. "You were outnumbered and overwhelmed, and it was physical. When it comes to sex, I can control you. It's going to be getting you to submit in other things that's going to be the challenge—a challenge I'm very much looking forward to."

To her shock—and delight—he ripped her panties from her in a show of arrogance that sent her arousal soaring.

"You owe me a new pair."

"I'll buy you dozens, and rip every fucking one of them off of you."

Lifting her right leg, he braced it on his shoulder, spreading her wide. "You have no idea how much you excite me. I love your sassiness. I love your attitude. I love every fucking thing about you."

Rocking her hips, she burned everywhere as his gaze raked over her. "I don't have a fucking attitude." She struggled to adapt to his quicksilver changes in mood, from gentle lover to arrogant Master and back again.

Hoyt chuckled, his grin full of mischief, but his eyes were filled with the pride of ownership as his gaze raked over her. "Yeah, you do, and it's a constant delight to me."

Moaning at the feel of his hot hand closing on her mound, Nat fought to keep her voice steady. "Stop looking at me as if you own me, damn it!"

Without warning, Hoyt plunged his finger deep, stroking the walls of her pussy with a firm caress that drew moan after moan from her. "I own every part of you, baby. Make no mistake about that."

He'd changed from warm playfulness to cold Master in a blink of an eye.

She opened her mouth to curse at him, pausing when she saw the look in his eyes.

A need for acceptance.

A dare.

Love.

His earlier words came rushing back, and she felt some of her indignation melt away.

Allowing a whimper to escape, she forced her muscles to relax, hoping to lull him into a false sense of security. "If I'm yours, then you're mine, aren't you?"

His expression softened, his hold loosening as he bent his head toward hers. "I've been yours since the first time I kissed you." Withdrawing his finger from her pussy, he circled her wet opening, smiling faintly when she groaned in frustration and rocked her hips. "Just as you've been mine."

His softly spoken words nearly melted her resolve, but the arrogance in his eyes and his touch made her determined to teach him a lesson.

Knowing damned well that she'd never get away with it, and filled with anticipation at his reaction to her daring, Nat rolled away in a fast movement that should have earned her freedom. She yelped when his hand tightened on her wrist again, his other catching her right thigh and yanking it high against his shoulder. "Going somewhere, little sub?"

Gritting her teeth as he rolled her to her back again with insulting ease, she glared at him, secretly pleased at the flare of heat in his eyes. "You said that the element of surprise would work."

Laughing softly, he touched his lips to hers. "It does." Releasing her wrists, he cupped the back of her neck, and with an arm around her waist, pulled her closer, propping her head against his chest. "Just not with me. Your eyes are very expressive, baby. They give you away every time. Besides, I'm fast."

He worked her sweater over her head, tossing it aside before ridding her of her bra. "You did good, though."

Naked, except for her thick socks, she cuddled against him. "Not good enough."

"Oh, I think you did well enough for your purposes. You wanted to challenge me, and you did. You wanted to excite me, and you did."

Cupping her breast, he slid his thumb back and forth over her nipple. "You didn't really want to get away from me, did you?"

Hiding a smile, Nat shrugged, sucking in a breath and gripping his wrist as his touch firmed. "I knew you wouldn't let me."

The slow steady friction against her nipple kept the need growing, but he seemed to be in no hurry.

Staring down at her, he toyed with her nipple, his smile tender. "I told you that I wouldn't let you get away from me."

Lifting her hand to his chest, she pressed her fingertips into the hard muscle there. "Did you mean what you said? Did you really consider me yours since the first time we kissed?"

Fisting his hand in her hair, he tilted her head back, increasing the pressure on her nipple. "Of course." His eyes narrowed as he lowered his head and took her mouth in a slow, thorough kiss that made her head spin. "You were so sweet. So giving. I want your mouth. Open to me."

She found her mouth forced open by the pressure of his, her pussy clenching at the possessiveness and demand in his kiss. Eager to kiss him back, she wrapped her arms around his neck and tangled her tongue with his, gasping at the sharp tug to her nipple.

Hoyt lifted his head, his eyes hooded. "Be still. When Jake gets home, he wants to fuck that mouth and he doesn't want your interference."

An erotic thrill went through, her pussy clenching at the thought of how demanding her husband would be after a night at the club. "How do you know that?"

He lifted a brow at that, his eyes warm with amusement. "We talk about you. We discuss plans we have for you, things we want to do to you, and rules that you have to obey. Everything about you is discussed. It's something that I hadn't planned on, but that gives me a great deal of satisfaction. Jake wants you naked and aroused when he gets home. He plans to take your mouth, your pussy, and your ass. I'm planning to hold you, talk to you, and arouse you until he gets home. When he gets here, you're going to give him everything he wants and you're not going to hesitate at all. Now, open that mouth."

Nat shook her head. "But Jake and I both like it when I—"

"Not tonight." Hoyt pinched her nipple again. "Tonight, you're going to be the perfect submissive."

Smiling faintly, he tightened the hand in her hair. "I think we've woken a sleeping tiger. Jake seems a little more intense since I got here. You and I are both going to make sure he has what he needs."

He brushed his lips over hers again. "I know I need this time with you. We'll drive each other crazy while we wait for him."

Shivering with anticipation, she shook her head, anxious for her husband to come home aroused and masterful. Cupping his jaw, she lifted her mouth in invitation. "How do you feel about getting me ready for him?"

Hoyt smiled. "I'm hard as a rock. Now give me that fucking mouth."

His kiss, a combination of affection and brand of possession filled her with a warm feeling inside. He slid his tongue over hers and caressed the roof of her mouth with a slow thoroughness that sent her senses reeling.

He withdrew to trace her lips with his tongue, making them tingle. "That's a good girl. Just be still and let me do whatever I want to you. I want you loose. Pliant."

Each time she forgot herself and tried to kiss him back, his fingers closed over her nipple in warning. "No, Natalie. Just let me have what I want." Covering her mouth with his again, he deepened his kiss, taking her mouth with a slow seductiveness that melted her bones.

Lifting his head, he smiled. "Very good."

He paused when the phone rang, cupping her breast as he reached above her head to answer it. "Hello?" His slow smile filled her with trepidation. "Yeah." Staring down at her, he ran a hand down her body. "She's being very good. Hold on and I'll put you on speaker."

"Nat, are you being good for Hoyt?"

Nat stilled at the sound of her husband's deep voice, her pussy clenching at the cold mastery in his tone. Swallowing heavily, she met Hoyt's gaze, covering the hand at her breast and moving against him. "The two of you talk about me behind my back. Do you have a problem talking in front of me?"

"Not at all." Jake's deep chuckle had her shifting restlessly on Hoyt's lap. "You should see the action here tonight. I don't think I've ever seen so many submissives so ready to please. Since only a few of the prospective Masters have arrived for the seminar yet, the women are a little restless."

Filled with jealousy, Nat reached for the phone, but Hoyt held it out of her reach. "You'd better not be touching them!"

Jake chuckled again. "You know the rules here. Married men aren't allowed to participate. Besides, why would I want to touch one of them when I've got a hellcat like you at home waiting for me? Do you know what I'm going to do to you as soon as I get home?"

When she hesitated, Hoyt tugged her nipple, his eyes narrowing. "Answer him."

Her toes curled at the sharp pain, another rush of moisture escaping to coat her inner thighs. "Yes!"

"What did you do to her?" The sexual tension in Jake's voice told her how much he enjoyed this.

Hoyt released her nipple. "I pinched her nipple. I've been doing that every time she forgets herself. I'm going to start working on her other one soon. They should be nice and tender by the time you get home."

"I'm looking forward to it. Is she completely naked?"

Hoyt ran a hand down her body, a smile tugging at his lips. "Except for her socks. I know how much she hates it when she doesn't have her socks on." He looked inordinately pleased that he knew that.

Jake's soft laughter sent a shiver through her. "That she does. Spank her clit. I want it as sensitized as her nipples."

Nat gasped, pressing her thighs together, both alarmed and excited at the anticipation in Hoyt's eyes. "Jake!"

"Don't you even think about disobeying. Spread those thighs and let me hear Hoyt spank your clit."

Hoyt set the phone aside, staring down at her as he spoke to Jake. "I put the phone close to her so you can hear her."

"Good. Nat, what's Hoyt doing?"

Sucking in a breath, she fisted her hands at her sides, every muscle in her body tensing. "He parted my folds. Oh, God!"

The first slap to her clit had her writhing on Hoyt's lap, but she couldn't escape his hold, crying out as he delivered three more in rapid succession.

The rush of heat had her clit tingling already, making her squirm on his lap, her entire body trembling in reaction.

Jake groaned. "Hell, I'm not going to be able to wait much longer. Hoyt, how does her clit look?"

Hoyt continued to hold her open, running a finger over her burning clit. "Red. Wet. Swollen. I barely touched her and she jolted nearly off my lap."

"Perfect." Jake's voice lowered. "I'm on my way. Leave the phone on so I can listen to you get her ass ready. Nat, I want you to tell me everything Hoyt does to you. *Everything.* Do you understand me?"

Nat had never done anything like this before. They'd had phone sex too many times to count, but she'd never been dominated while he listened. She sucked in a breath, letting it out in a rush when Hoyt slid a finger over her clit again "Yes. Oh, God, Jake."

The deep sound of Jake's growl rippled over her skin. "You're doing this for me. I want you ready for me when I get home. I want you aroused and your ass lubed. I'm going to fuck your mouth, your pussy and then your ass. I'm hard as hell after watching the subs at the club and imagining the things I wanted to do to you. I don't want the pretend shit, like the way some of them here want. I want the real thing I have waiting at home."

His voice lowered even more, and through the phone, she could hear the sound of the car door closing. "That ass is mine and I want it ready for me. Now, roll over onto your belly. Hoyt, there's a tube of lube in the drawer next to the sofa. I keep them all over the house for her."

Shivering with excitement and trepidation, Nat swallowed heavily, looking up into Hoyt's eyes to see how he would react to Jake's demand.

He raised a brow at her hesitation. "You heard him, Natalie. He's on his way home and he wants that ass ready before he gets here."

"Spank her ass for hesitating."

Stunned at Jake's harsh tone, Nat rushed to roll to her stomach. "I rolled over, damn it." Crying out at the sharp slap to her bottom, Nat wiggled against the rush of heat to her pussy and clit. "Damn it!"

Several more slaps landed, making her ass hotter, and arousing her beyond belief. The warmth spread to her pussy and already hot clit, but as much as she bucked her hips, she couldn't get the relief she needed.

Jake's voice came through the phone, a possessive edge to it that seemed sharper than ever. "Nat, I want you to reach down and spread those cheeks wide for Hoyt. Wide! Give him complete access to that ass because I want it lubed good. I don't want anything in my way. My cock's hard enough to pound fucking nails. I might even have him hold you down for me."

Nat groaned, shaken by the series of mini orgasms that rippled through her. "Oh, God."

Hoyt rubbed her bottom, spreading the heat. "Another first. She's been strapped down before, but never held down, has she?"

Jake cursed. "Of course not! I wouldn't have let anyone else see her that way. Did she spread her ass?"

"Fuck." Nat rushed to obey him, spreading the cheeks of her ass and exposing her bottom hole in a way that made her feel more defenseless than anything else.

And Jake knew it.

Hoyt reached for the tube of lube, the sound of the drawer opening loud in the tense silence. "She's spread. She's being such a good girl, it's hard to believe how belligerent she can be."

"I'm not in the mood for it tonight. Tonight, I plan to use her holes for my own pleasure. I've admitted that I've been too easy on her. I've given her quite a bit, haven't I, baby? You've got another Master and lover now to take care of you."

The cold lube touched her puckered opening. "Yes! God, yes!"

His voice lowered to pure silk. "Don't you think I deserve to have what I want, baby doll?"

Shivering as cold chills went up and down her spine, Nat gulped in air, so close to coming she shook. "Yes. Anything. I want to be everything to you." Although she trusted him implicitly, she couldn't stop thinking about the naked women at the club and how eager they'd be to please her gorgeous husband. "I'll give you what you want. Don't you dare go looking for it anywhere else."

She gasped at the firm thrust of Hoyt's finger into her ass. "Oh! Oh, God. Oh, God."

"Tell me, baby. Right now. Everything." The demand in Jake's voice had her answering without hesitation.

"Hoyt pushed his finger into me. Oh, God. He's moving it in and out. Please. I can't. My clit's on fire. Oh, God, I can't stand it. I want to be fucked hard tonight, Jake, and I swear to God, if you go easy on me, I'm gonna kick your ass!" Already aroused, this new decadent assault made it difficult to even think. Knowing that Jake would come through the door in a matter of minutes with the intention of fucking her mouth, her pussy, and her ass had her on the razor sharp edge, and she didn't know how much longer she could hold off her orgasm.

"You don't have to worry about that, little sub." His cold, deep tone was right out of a fantasy.

Hoyt withdrew his finger. "Keep that ass spread. I'm just getting some more lube. Jake sounds like he might be a little rough tonight and I want your ass lubed good." Pausing with his finger and more of the cold lube pressed against her puckered opening, he groaned. "Damn, that's pretty. If there's anything more erotic than an ass glistening with lube, I don't know what it is."

"Damn. I'm almost home."

Hoyt plunged his finger into her again. "I'll have her positioned for you. Do you ever have her present herself?"

Nat stilled, wondering if they knew what their decadent conversation did to her.

Jake groaned. "Not for years."

Hoyt raised his voice to be heard over her cries. "I'll have her ready for you. Give me a couple of minutes and I'll have a surprise for you. I did a little shopping today."

Jake chuckled. "I can't wait. Keep the phone on. I want to hear everything."

Unable to hold back her whimpers, Nat dug her knees into the sofa cushion, lifting herself as Hoyt worked the lube into her ass. "W—What did you buy? What are you going to do? Oh!" The sharp slap to her upper thigh forced a primitive moan from her.

"Don't ask questions. You'll know what I want you to know when I want you to know it."

She didn't know what it was about herself that made her so contrary in nature, but she bristled at his attitude while at the same time loving the wickedness and the feminine way it made her feel.

Hoyt withdrew his finger with a speed that left her bottom clenching at emptiness. "You're so undisciplined. Jake sees that he's been too soft on you. You need a heavier hand, don't you, little sub?"

Jake's voice, raw with arousal, came through the receiver. "That she does. It'll be my pleasure to give it to her."

Hoyt gripped her wrists, pulling them away from her bottom and clasping them tightly against her lower back. "She won't give you any trouble tonight. Her holes are all available to you."

Nat shivered, excited by the things they said and their dark intentions, as if the deepest darkest hungers inside her had been unleashed.

Sliding a hand around her neck, Hoyt pressed his fingers against her jaw and arched her neck back to whisper in her ear. "You're going to give him everything he wants. You're going to submit to him as you never have before."

"Yes! Always." God, he excited her, and she found herself arching her back, lifting her head and ass even higher.

Running a hand over her ass, Hoyt bent to kiss her temple. "Very good. I like that back arched like that." Gripping her wrists again, he released her jaw and helped her to stand.

Jake groaned. "Oh, baby, you're in trouble tonight."

Nat couldn't hold back a smile. "So are you."

Hoyt drew her down the hall to the Master bedroom. "Let's get you ready for your Master."

Pausing at the foot of the bed, he released her wrists and tossed the phone onto the bed. "Don't move—and not one word out of you unless your Master asks you a question." Staring into her eyes, he tapped a nipple. "Can you steal hear us Jake?"

"Yes. Christ, all those whimpers and moans coming from her are making it hard to concentrate on my driving."

Hoyt smiled and tugged her nipple, his eyes flaring with heat at her soft cry. "Then we'll hang up. I want you to get here safe and sound, and I want you to be surprised. Drive slowly. I have a few things to take care of before you get here."

Reaching around her, Hoyt retrieved the phone and disconnected before tossing it back onto the bed. "Jake's going to be more demanding than ever now, and I want you to give him whatever he wants." He slapped her already warm ass again, sending another rush of heat to her aching clit. "I'm not going to lose the best thing that's ever happened to me because you want to prove that you're in charge."

Running a hand down her center, he stroked her clit, his eyes narrowed and steady on hers. "Believe me, we know who's in charge. Everything revolves around you. But in this, you're going to surrender, baby. You need it as much as we do, and right now, Jake needs it the most. You gonna give him what he needs, or are you going to fight it for the sake of pride?"

Nat couldn't remember ever being so excited. The warm surge of feminine power was like a shot of the strongest whiskey, making her dizzy with pleasure and confidence. "I'm going to be what both of you need. Anything." Reaching out a hand, she cupped the bulge at the front of his jeans. "Everything."

"Good. Don't move."

Nat sucked in a breath, pressing a hand to her belly as she watched him disappear into the closet.

When they learned just how much all of this excited her, they'd both be determined to push her farther.

Hoyt appeared almost immediately with what appeared to be straps of leather and chain, the sight of it nearly making her knees buckle. "I wondered if you knew the proper way to present yourself. I've never seen you do it, and tonight I want to make sure you do it properly for your Master."

Nat tried to see what was in his hand, reaching out to him as he stepped closer. "You're my Master, too, aren't you?"

Stopping directly in front of her, Hoyt thwarted her attempt to see what he held by lifting her chin. "Keep your head up."

The feel of the cold chain touching her nipple made her jolt.

Before she knew it, Hoyt began fastening a thick piece of leather around her neck. "I am." His eyes held hers as he fastened the buckle at the back of her neck. "I didn't realize, though, how Mastering you would make me fall even deeper in love with you than I already was. You're mine, Natalie, just as you're Jake's. I'll do nothing to jeopardize that. Now I know how Jake feels, and I'm going to make damned sure that you give him everything he needs tonight. You're going to do whatever he wants you to do, and you're going to open yourself to him as never before. Tonight is your chance to show him—and me—just how much you want this."

Nat tried to lower her head, shocked to find that the thick strap didn't allow it. She felt the back of Hoyt's hands brush against her breast, but she couldn't look down to see what he was doing.

Hoyt smiled, a cold smile filled with lust. "That strap will keep your head up so that both of your Masters can see your face at all times. You don't need to know what's being done to you. You can't prevent it anyway."

Rolling her nipple between his thumb and forefinger, he continued to stare into her eyes. "There'll be plenty of other times for you to assert yourself. Tonight isn't one of them." He trailed a finger down her cheek. "Let's get those hands taken care of so they don't get in the way."

He turned her, and gripped her wrists, and with the speed of long practice, enclosed them in padded handcuffs. "Very pretty. I think Jake's going to like that a lot."

Automatically struggling against the confinement, she gasped when she realized that the cuffs had been attached to the leather strap around her neck by a chain, a thick one that clinked when she moved and pulled her head back even more.

Alarmed now, she stared up at Hoyt as he turned her to face him again.

Hoyt's eyes gleamed with ownership. "Very nice. If I had my way, I'd keep you like this often." He startled her by gripping her nipple again, and without giving her a chance to adjust, clamping a nipple clip to it.

Shocked, she jolted, a cry escaping when she realized that the clips were also attached to the leather circling her neck. "Hoyt! Oh, God!"

He attached the other clip with no warning, sending another surge of pain through her, an erotic pain that turned quickly to pleasure. "Be still. Spread those thighs. I need to attach the clit clip before Jake gets here."

"Oh, God. Oh, God!"

Shaking, Nat obeyed him, listening anxiously for the sound of her husband coming through the front door. She could only imagine how she'd look to him.

In his present mood, the sight of her shackled this way would only inflame him more.

She couldn't wait.

Desperate to please Jake, she spread her thighs, sucking in a breath as she waited with breathless anticipation.

Jake always used his mouth to attach a clit clip, holding it between his teeth and sucking her clit through it to attach it. He'd told her many times that it was the best way to do it.

The thought of Hoyt using his mouth on her had her shaking with a combination of excitement and alarm.

Hoyt's touch didn't have the gracefulness that Jake's did, but it had a hunger as if he wanted to make up for all the years they'd been apart.

Crying out when he gripped her thighs, she tried to look down at him, but the thick strap around her neck prevented her from seeing him.

Every movement tugged the clips at her nipples, and when Hoyt's hot mouth closed over her clit, the jolt of shock pulled the clips hard.

"Oh, fuck! Son of a bitch. Hoyt, I'm gonna come."

With a groan, he released her just as suddenly, leaving her clit throbbing, an unfamiliar tugging sensation nearly throwing her from the edge. "You'd better not."

"Oh, God. What's there? Shit, Hoyt, what did you—oh!" The tickling sensation between her thighs threatened to drive her wild, but she couldn't look down to see it, and couldn't reach for it to try to figure out what it was. Having her head held up and her hands fastened behind her back also forced her to thrust her breasts out, the pressure on her nipples sending wave after wave of need to her slit.

His warm lips touched her thigh where he'd just slapped it. "Quiet. Not one word. You don't need to know what I do. This time, I'll tell you, but only because I want you to know. There are chains hanging from the clip on your clit—chains that will sway each time you move and tug at that beautiful clit. Now, be quiet. As soon as Jake finishes fucking that mouth, I'm gagging you."

Stepping back, he eyed her critically. "On your knees."

Nat dropped to her knees as gracefully as possible, her pulse tripping at the sound of the front door opening and closing. The tug to her nipples and clit added to her excitement, her pussy and lubed ass clenching in anticipation.

Hoyt frowned. "Spread those thighs. Your Master's going to expect to see the pussy he owns as soon as he walks through the door."

Nodding, he stepped to the side, his eyes hooded as they raked over her. "Very nice. Nice arch to that back. I want you to remember that position when you're told to assume it."

Another rush of moisture escaped as she heard Jake's slow steps coming down the hall.

She had a feeling that after tonight, some things would be changed forever.

Keeping her eyes trained on the doorway, and aware of Hoyt's scrutiny, she held her breath, anxious to see her husband's reaction.

It proved more than she could have ever hoped for.

Carrying her clothing, he stopped as if running into a brick wall, his eyes going wide for several heart-stopping moments as his gaze raked over her. His features softened briefly, his eyes filled with love and desire. "You did this for me?"

He tossed her clothing aside and started stripping out of his, unbuttoning his shirt with one hand while freeing his cock with the other.

Smiling, Nat started to nod, remembering the collar and clips at the last second. "I would do anything for you." She licked her lips, letting her gaze lower and linger on his cock before lifting it to his again. *"Master."*

The flare of heat in his eyes held an intensity that sent a thrill through her, filling her with pride that her husband got pleasure from her.

Determined to give him more, she waited expectantly while he rid himself of the rest of his clothing, tossing each item aside as he stripped out of it.

Cupping her cheek, he pressed his thumb to her bottom lip. "You're the most exciting woman I've ever known. Yes, open that mouth."

Out of the corner of her eye, she watched Hoyt move past her and disappear into the playroom. Opening her mouth wide, she shivered with delight as Jake's fingers sank into her hair.

Holding her head steady, he slipped the head of his cock past her lips.

Startled at the feel of Hoyt's hand sliding over her back, she jolted, earning a groan from Jake.

"Keep that mouth still. Jake just wants to feel that hot mouth before he fucks your pussy. As soon as he takes his cock out, I'm going to gag you. Jake looks like he's in the mood to fuck you hard, darlin', and the gag should muffle your screams."

Jake groaned again, sliding his cock deeper and fucking her mouth with slow, smooth strokes. "I love hearing her screams, but tonight a gag suits my mood."

Trembling, Nat concentrated on remaining still, focusing on nothing more than relaxing her mouth so he could take the pleasure he wanted. Jake tilted her head back as much as the collar allowed, the sharp tug to her nipples and his dark mood inflaming her. "Hmm. I like the clips on her, Hoyt. She's very nicely presented."

She could feel Hoyt's sharp gaze as he stood next to her, his arms folded across his chest as he stared down at her. It struck her suddenly that he'd adopted the role of Master, and watched over her to make sure she pleased Jake.

It excited her more than she could have imagined.

"I'm glad you think so. I'm going to enjoy buying things for her." Hoyt's voice had a gravelly tone that it hadn't before.

Nat fisted her hands behind her back as the tension inside her mounted. With her legs spread wide and the clip on her clit holding the hood back and leaving it exposed, she felt every brush of air against it.

"I want her pussy." Withdrawing from her mouth, Jake bent to lift her, his expression harder and colder than ever. Releasing her, he took a step back, running his fist up and down the length of his cock. "Very nice."

Staring into her eyes, he tugged the chain connected to first one nipple and then the other, her soft cry seeming to spur him on. "Turn around."

Rushing to obey him, she bit back a groan as the chains swayed against her thighs, the small tugs to her clit making her dizzy, and she couldn't reach out her hands to steady herself.

Jake's hands closed over her waist. "Don't move. I'll get the pillows."

He piled them high at the edge of the bed before lifting her and settling her over them. Without a word, he gripped her thighs, spread them wide and plunged into her with a firm thrust that stole her breath.

So good. So hot.

"Fuck, yeah!" Jake's grip tightened, holding her in place for his firm, quick thrusts. "That's my girl. Hell, woman, you tie me up in knots."

Each thrust took her closer to the edge, the tugs to her nipples and clit with every stroke of her husband's thick cock sending her senses spiraling out of control.

The pleasure came from everywhere, overwhelming her, and making it difficult to focus.

Feeling Hoyt's watchful gaze added another layer of eroticism that fueled her hunger.

Suddenly, Hoyt's hands tightened in her hair, and he forced her mouth open, pushing the ball gag between her lips.

He fastened it with an efficiency that stoked her jealousy, compelling her to fight him, a struggle he won with infuriating ease. When he finished attaching it, he ran his thumb over her lips, smiling down at her. "I think you should be kept this way all the time. When a cock isn't in that ass, a plug should be in there, reminding you that it belongs to us."

Jake's laugh had a hard edge to it, his thrusts coming faster. "She loves that, but won't admit it. She's. A. Naughty. Naughty. Girl."

So close.

Just when she thought she'd go over, Jake slowed his thrusts, and after another slap to her ass, he shoved a finger into her lubed bottom. "Very naughty."

Oh, God!

She cursed him—unintelligible curses that the gag muffled—so close to coming that she didn't care about anything else. Frustration made her more violent than usual, but with her hands secured behind her back and draped over several pillows with her ass in the air, she couldn't get any leverage.

She couldn't do a damned thing about her predicament, finding herself forced into whatever position they wanted to put her in.

So exciting. So decadent.

Hoyt chuckled. "She's a wild thing, isn't she?"

Jake withdrew his finger from her ass, leaving her more frustrated at the reawakened awareness there. "Yeah, she is. She's not behaving, though." Several more sharp slaps landed, heating her ass cheeks. "Be still, Nat! This pussy is mine to fuck for *my* pleasure. Not yours. This is about what *I* want. Not what *you* want."

Groaning, she blinked back tears of frustration as Hoyt tightened his hands in her hair and kept her face turned toward his.

She wanted to come. She *needed* to come.

Taking several deep breaths, she opened her eyes, looking straight into Hoyt's cold, watchful ones.

Still holding her hair, he slid a hand down her back. "Good girl. I know it's hard for you to be good, but you're just going to have to learn. I'm not going to be as easy on you as Jake's been, and it sure as hell doesn't look like he's going to let you get away with shit anymore either."

Jake thrust several more times, digging at a spot inside her that he knew well. The friction against her inner walls drove her wild, his thick cock filling her with every deep stroke.

Rougher than usual, he seemed almost primitive in his hunger for her. Even as he took, he gave, seeming determined to prove his mastery over her body, and her senses.

His sudden withdrawal shocked her, leaving her pussy clenching and her hips rocking of their own volition. "Patience, baby. As soon as I roll on this condom, I'll take your ass." He thrust a finger into her bottom once, pulling it free again just as she started to lift into it. "Oh, yeah. You want that ass filled, don't you, baby?"

Her scream of frustration behind the gag only seemed to amuse Hoyt.

"Found yourself in a predicament, haven't you?" Glancing at Jake, he rose slightly. "Too bad. Behave yourself, or I'll spank that clit again."

Nat groaned at the tingling in her clit at his threat, stilling when the head of Jake's cock pressed against her puckered opening.

Her eyes fluttered close as sensation took over.

Jake pushed the head of his cock through the tight ring of muscle and into her, the decadent feel of having her ass impaled sending her senses soaring. "So fucking tight." Gripping her thighs, he pulled them closed, leaving her legs dangling over the edge of the bed. "So good." With a hand braced on either side of her waist, he leaned over her as he sank his cock deeper.

"See, baby. Even with your legs closed, you can't keep me out. Bent over and lubed, there's nothing you can do to keep me out. Hoyt, take off the gag. I want to hear her."

Hoyt lowered his head, the fire in his eyes mesmerizing. "With pleasure." Covering her mouth and the ball gag with his, he kissed her with a raw passion and hunger that stunned her. "Hmm. Yes, baby. I want that mouth." His lips firmed and then brushed over hers, not giving her the kiss she needed.

She needed him to take her mouth. She needed the taste of him.

She didn't want anything in the way.

She needed to feel his tongue against hers.

She needed to *taste* his passion.

Frustrated, and overwhelmed at the feel of Jake's hot, steely cock forcing her ass to stretch to accommodate him, Nat whimpered in her throat.

Suddenly finding her hands free, she reached for Hoyt with a muffled cry, trembling uncontrollably at the warm tingling sensation that warned her she was about to come.

Sensation layered over sensation, hunger feeding hunger.

Hoyt lifted his head, his movements jerky as he unfastened the gag, the tension in his voice unmistakable as he gently removed it. His eyes narrowed, glittering with pride. "You're the most exciting woman I've ever known."

His mouth covered hers, letting her taste the passion she'd been desperate for.

Bracing his hands on either side of her waist, Jake leaned over her, his body hot against her back and bottom as he scraped his teeth over her shoulder. "Slick and tight."

Shivering, Nat groaned as Jake withdrew slightly and pushed his cock deep again, reveling in the hard edge to the way he took her.

Jake's hands firmed on her hips while Hoyt sank one of his in her hair, reaching under her to tug at the chains on her nipples.

Jake groaned and sank deep again, each stroke coming a little faster and with more firmness than the last, making her ass burn and clench on him. "I want to feel that ass milk my cock. Yes. Nice and tight. Hot. All bent over with that sweet ass in the air." Reaching under her, he touched his finger to her exposed clit, the jolt of electricity forcing a cry from her. "You're going to come while I'm fucking your ass, baby, and there's nothing you can do to stop it."

The arm around his waist held her steady for his quick, shallow thrusts, positioning her in a way that allowed Hoyt even better access to her breasts.

With a low growl, Jake tapped her clit. "Whose clit is this?"

"Yours!" With her feet hooked around his legs, she gripped him tighter, her breath coming out in ragged grunts with every thrust of his cock. The tingling grew stronger, every inch of her skin alive with prickling heat. "I'm yours. Please. Oh, God. I'm coming."

He thrust deep, sliding his finger faster over her clit, and the pleasure inside her exploded.

An all-consuming, tingling heat washed over her—a bliss so intense that she couldn't breathe.

She arched back as far as she could, digging her fingers into Hoyt's shoulders, thrilling at the scrape of his teeth over her nipple.

Riding the ecstasy, she sucked in a breath, and then another.

Her ass clamped down on Jake's cock, the tight burning overwhelming her senses.

The hot, tingling waves of pleasure left her breathless, cresting and rolling through her, the strength of them leaving her dizzy and weak.

Jake groaned against her ear as he sank his cock deep into her ass, his arm around her waist tightening as his cock pulsed inside her. "Yes, baby.

Let go. Come for me. Keep coming. Keep milking my cock with that tight ass. Yeah, that's my girl."

His strokes to her clit slowed, dragging out her orgasm until even the gentle friction became too much to bear.

Whimpering, she gripped his forearm. "Please. No more. Please. I'm begging." Trembling, she jolted at each slide of his finger over her clit, whimpering again when Hoyt took her hands in his and placed them on his shoulders.

Pushing her hair back, he gathered her closer. "So fucking beautiful. I love you so damned much."

His voice—a ragged whisper—washed over her as he unfastened the leather collar. "Jake, I'm gonna take off the clips on her nipples. Ready?"

"Absolutely."

Jake's strokes to her clit increased just as the blood rushed back into her nipples, sending her over again.

"Oh! Oh, God." Every inch of her body shimmered, her muscles tightening for several heart-stopping moments before going limp again.

Jake crooned to her, his voice much softer and loving than it had been a few minutes ago, all traces of cold Master replaced by warm, possessive lover. "That's it, baby. Yes, a few more little strokes. Nice and slow. Hmm. That's it."

"No more. No more. Please." She tried to lift her head, but her muscles refused to obey her.

"No more, baby." Jake's lips touched her ear as he wrapped both arms around her and slowly withdrew. "That's it. Easy, love. I've got you."

Hoyt's hands closed over her waist. "Let me have her. I need to hold her."

Jake cuddled her against him. "Yeah. I'm gonna get cleaned up and then I want to hold her, too. I'll fix a bath for her."

Taking her from Jake, Hoyt settled her against him, running a hand over her hair as she dropped her head on his shoulder. "Tub's big enough. I think I'll join you. I think she needs both of us tonight."

Nat smiled drowsily and sighed. "Yeah."

"Not so talkative anymore, huh?" Hoyt sat at the edge of the bed and settled her on his lap, chuckling softly. "Now I see why Jake spoils you rotten."

Curious, she let her head fall back against his bicep so she could look up at him, weak from pleasure. "Why?"

With a thoughtful smile, Hoyt brushed her hair back with a hand that shook. "Because you're so fucking irresistible." Bending low, he touched his lips to hers, running a hand down her side. "Every day I spend with you, I love you even more."

Chapter Seventeen

Watching his wife pace back and forth at the foot of the bed, Jake glanced at the weather forecast on the television he'd muted over ten minutes earlier to listen to Nat's unfounded complaints about Hoyt.

He didn't know what Hoyt had done to wind her up this way, but he had a feeling it had a lot more to do with her own feelings than anything Hoyt did.

It had been a week since the night he'd gone to the club, and since then, she'd been more emotional than usual.

Jake knew his wife well enough to know that having both of them in her life now had her riding an emotional roller coaster, one they'd all have to ride out until she got accustomed to having Hoyt in their lives.

The love of his life had a huge heart, and loved hard—sometimes too hard—which made her amazingly vulnerable.

God, he loved her—and had fallen even deeper at the realization of how much she was willing to give up for him, and the lengths she would go to protect him.

Those who threatened anyone she loved found themselves facing a fierce lioness, much to their regret.

He glanced at the television as she flew past it again, but didn't want to look away from his wife for long. Each time she turned, he caught an enticing glimpse of the curve of her breast, her beading nipples pressing at the soft material.

His cock seemed to get harder each time she turned, and he tormented himself with thoughts of what he planned to do to her once she wound down.

She was in a temper, and he hoped that tonight he could finally get to the bottom of whatever bothered her.

His beautiful wife, in a temper, could be very distracting.

She kept glancing toward the closed door, as though expecting Hoyt to come through it any minute, even though he'd gone to the club in order to give Jake some time alone with Nat. "He's impossible! He's so damned arrogant. He's even worse than you and I didn't think that was possible."

Jake raised a brow at that, saying nothing.

Nat didn't even glance at him as she continued to pace back and forth across the foot of the bed. "Who the hell does he think he is? Trying to tell me what to do. What to eat. How to dress."

Hiding a smile, Jake set the remote control aside. "He told you what I've told you a million times. You have to eat lunch, especially when you rush out of here in the morning without eating breakfast. He told you to make sure that you had some protein to keep your energy up, and to make sure you stay hydrated so you don't get those headaches. And he told you not to forget your scarf."

Nat waved a hand in the air negligently, and continued as if he hadn't spoken. "He's being unreasonable. He leaves money for me on the kitchen table like I'm a prostitute! How can he get mad because I didn't borrow money from him last week instead of you?"

Amused, Jake raised a brow. "You *borrow* money from me?"

Pausing only long enough to glare at him, she turned again, her breasts jiggling just enough to make his cock jump. "Why the hell would I go to *him* for money?"

"Because he wants to be family, Nat. There's nothing wrong with him making sure you have enough money on you."

With a snort, she turned to pace the other way. "Why would I ask him about the funny noise my car's making? He doesn't know my car the way you do."

"Sure." Jake didn't bother to hide his smile. "Why would you ask someone who's been taking cars apart and putting them back together ever since he was fourteen to check out the noise in your car?"

Spinning again, Nat glanced at him, looking a little more unsettled. "Okay, I could have asked him to look at it." She paced in silence past the bed two more times before shrugging again. "I could have asked him to pick up some milk and eggs from the store, but I figured he would get caught up with that virus he's working on and would forget."

Raising a brow, he turned the television off and tossed the remote aside. "Yeah, I'm sure a man responsible for leading dangerous missions and training SEALs would have trouble multitasking, and remembering something as complicated as buying milk and eggs."

Meeting her glare, Jake raised a brow, saying nothing as he waited for her impressive temper to cool.

Damn, she excited him.

A contrary woman, she'd been a joy to him since he married her.

A soft-hearted woman who did her best to show only toughness to the rest of the world.

A woman who liked to be in control, but reveled at having that control stripped from her in the bedroom.

Her steps slowed, the anger in her voice fading, and the hurt becoming more apparent with every word. "Every time Hoyt and I have sex, we fight."

Unsurprised that she blushed when telling him that, Jake eyed her steadily. "No. You don't. That's part of the problem. You don't trust him enough to fight with him. You trust him with your body, but not with your heart. You find a reason to get offended at everything he says as if you're scared to let him too close."

Nat shrugged, looking away. "He left before for something more exciting because he didn't like small-town living."

"And you're afraid he's going to do it again. I understand that, but he's already told you how important being with his family is to him. You're scared, Nat, and it's going to take time for you to trust him to stay, but he loves you." His heart ached for her.

He ached for her.

Her eyes shot sparks as she whirled and began pacing again. "Things like bills, yard work, and sitting at a computer could never hold a man like Hoyt. He's going to get bored sooner or later, and he'll be looking for a way out."

He knew his wife well—too well for her to hide her fear and hurt from him. Crossing his legs at the ankle, he folded his hands behind his head and winced when his cock jumped again. "We've talked about this, Nat. If I believed that he wasn't serious about this, or that he would leave, I'd never have agreed to this relationship. You're keeping him at a distance out of spite and fear. You want to make him pay for leaving, and hurting you, and you want to make sure he doesn't get close enough to do it again. I'm afraid it's too late for that, baby. You're in too deep already."

Nat shrugged, pausing at the foot of the bed, not meeting his gaze.

Careful to keep his expression blank, Jake crossed his arms over his chest. "So the years we've had together mean nothing to you?"

As he'd expected, she whirled to face him. "What? I never said that."

Watching her carefully, and thankful that she seemed genuinely surprised by his claim, Jake shrugged. "Well, you seem obsessed with making him pay for the fact that he wasn't here all these years as if you've been miserable since he left."

She slapped the bed close to his feet. "Don't try to put words in my mouth. I never said that!"

Holding her gaze, Jake held out a hand. "Come here."

Hesitating, she blew out a breath. "Jake, I've been happy with you. Damn it! I knew this was going to happen." She started pacing again, flashing another glimpse of the soft curve of her breast as she turned.

To his surprise, she stopped, wrapping her arms around herself in a protective gesture that ripped his heart out. "I'm not like these young girls that have two husbands. How the hell am I going to be able to hold both of you? Hoyt's probably going to leave, and I'm fucking this up so bad that I'm going to lose you, too."

Worried now, he straightened, sitting up. "Baby, come here."

Turning away, she hugged herself and walked away. "I don't need to be held, Jake."

Yes, you do.

"Too bad. I need to hold you." Gritting his teeth when she ignored him, Jake rose, taking a step toward her, purposely injecting ice into his tone. "I told you to come here." Hiding a smile at her shiver, he waited, knowing what she needed probably better than she did.

Her eyes flashed with anger and need as she approached, her nipples beaded tight and pressing against her cotton nightgown.

Anger and need—a delightful combination.

Sitting on the edge of the bed again, he drew her onto his lap, tucking her head under his chin. He ran his hand up and down her arm, and sat there with her in companionable silence, a silence he knew she needed in order to settle.

"You've got yourself really worked up tonight, don't you?" Turning his head slightly, he kissed her hair, playing with her fingers and the gold band he'd placed there over twenty years earlier. "Do you really think you're being fair to Hoyt? To yourself? To me?"

Tightening his hold in anticipation of her reaction, he held firm to prevent her from jerking away and began to rub her back.

"What?" Nat pushed at his chest, leaning back to glare at him. "How can you ask if I'm fair to Hoyt? I talk to him—"

"Barely, and when you do, you snap at him."

"I have sex with him."

"You're still trembling from your orgasm when you start pushing him away."

"Fuck you." Sitting up, she tried to jerk away from him, cursing when he unbalanced her and pressed her back against the mattress. "Let go of me. Jake, you don't know what the hell you're talking about!" She shoved at his chest, the edge of panic in her eyes telling him that he was right. "I can't push Hoyt away any more than I can push you away."

The hurt in her eyes tore at him. "No, you can't. We both love you too damned much." Smiling at her look of shock, he ran a thumb over her soft lips, amazed that after all these years, she still had the power to excite him more than any woman he'd ever known.

So soft. So sweet. So full of life.

He could spend the next hundred years with her and it wouldn't be enough.

Not nearly enough.

Pressing her thighs apart to settle into his favorite place on earth, he met her look of outrage with a smile. "Settle down."

Squirming against him, and making his cock throb with the need to plunge into her, she tried to kick at him. "You're both assholes. Let me up, damn you!"

He raised her arms above her head, gathering her wrists in one of his hands. The flare of desire that darkened her eyes gave her an unfocused look, a look that always made him feel ten feet tall. "You're trying your best to push Hoyt away because he's getting too close."

"I don't know what the hell you're talking about."

Jake cupped her breast, massaging gently. "Yes, you do. You're making excuses and that's not like you. You're afraid of letting him get close." Holding her face between his hands, he stared into her eyes. "Don't, baby. Don't do that to us. It hurts me, it's hurting Hoyt, and it's eating at you."

"I'm not doing that."

"Yes, you are." Smiling, he brushed her lips with his. "But, I know that Hoyt loves you and he only wants what's best for you. He'd die for you, Nat. *I* trust him with my most valuable possession. *You* have to trust him, too."

Releasing her face to slide his hands under her, he smiled when the door opened and her eyes went wide. Assuming it was Hoyt, he smiled, his smile falling when she stiffened, her eyes filled with horror.

She screamed his name, the fear in her voice chilling.

Spinning, he caught a glimpse of two masked men rushing toward them. "What the fuck?" He started to jump from the bed, keeping his body between hers and theirs, horrified at the sight of the guns in their hands.

He covered her body with his, desperate to protect her, and started to turn just as one of the gunmen rounded the bed and came toward him from behind.

Before he could get to his feet, pain exploded in his head.

Terrified for his wife, he silently screamed her name, reaching for her as his vision blurred.

Everything dimmed. The last thing he heard as everything went black, was the hysterical cries of his wife screaming his name.

Chapter Eighteen

Hoyt sipped his beer, watching in amusement as Hunter and Remington Ross mercilessly teased the submissive who'd spent the last hour trying to get their attention.

"You ready for another?"

Glancing at Bill Savage, the club's soft-spoken bartender, Hoyt allowed a small smile. "Not yet. Thanks."

He liked the new bartender, a quiet man, whose size alone intimidated most people. With a barrel chest, huge tattooed biceps, and a shaved head, he had a mean look about him that served him well in his new position.

Several inches taller than Hoyt, Bill doubled as a bouncer at times, and usually didn't have to do more than give a potential troublemaker a warning look in order to keep the peace. He adopted a cold, flat look in his eyes that tamed even the most belligerent badasses.

He didn't talk any more than necessary, listening more than participating, and always watchful.

Hoyt amused himself by watching him, always surprised that such a large man could move so fast without appearing to rush at all, making drinks with the ease of long practice. Once he caught up with the orders, he wandered back to where Hoyt sat just as he finished his beer.

Gesturing toward Hunter and Remington, Hoyt pushed his glass aside, smiling his thanks when Bill replaced it with another. Raising his voice slightly to be heard over the voices of the crowded bar and loud music, he leaned closer. "I don't remember ever seeing Hunter and Remington so intense before."

Bill wiped the already spotless bar. "Yeah." He glanced at the brothers before turning back to Hoyt. "I haven't been here for long—but I understand that most of the men who live here figured that the kind of women who would want to actually live in Desire were a dying breed. Not many women would put up with the old-fashioned ways."

Hoyt thought of Nat and her independent streak, and realized just how hard it must be for her at times to have not one, but two men now watching over her. He thought about the arguments he'd had with her over the last week about not coming to him when she needed something. "Yeah, we can be a little overbearing at times." Curious, he smiled. "Why did you move here?"

Bill shrugged. "I like the old-fashioned ways. I believe a man's responsible for protecting his woman, and that a woman deserves respect."

Hoyt took a sip of his fresh beer, glancing at where Hunter and Remington had a naked blonde sandwiched between them. "We only want what's best for our women. How the hell do they expect us to protect them if we don't know what they're doing, and we don't maintain some kind of control?"

Thinking of the way Nat looked at him in passion—the softness of her supple body as she melted against him—he wanted to fight demons for her.

Glancing at Bill, he shrugged. "They're so damned delicate, it scares the hell out of me."

Inclining his head, the bartender's lips twitched in the closest thing to a smile Hoyt had ever seen from him. "Yeah, but for such tiny things, they sure as hell pack a punch. I've seen grown men taken to their knees. My bosses included."

Hoyt smiled. "I'm one of them that's been taken to his knees a time or two." He took another sip of his beer, glancing toward the Ross brothers again. The woman between them cried out in pleasure, writhing under their hands.

Shaking his head, Hoyt sighed. "Man, their father sure as hell did a number on them, didn't he? How they hell can they possibly think that just because their father was an asshole, they'd be the same way?"

Bill took a long pull on his bottled water, recapped it and set it aside with more force than necessary. "I heard that their father beat their mother for years, until he finally beat her to death. That's got to be a hell of a thing to get over. I can't believe they're afraid that they're the same way. It just doesn't make sense."

Hoyt took another sip of his beer, finding it hard to believe that Hunter and Remington could still believe that. "I know that everyone's talked to them until they're blue in the face, but they won't listen to reason. Christ, look at them. They're not even undressed yet. It looks like they plan to keep her busy for a while."

Bill allowed another small smile. "Lately, they've been going through two or three at a time." His smile fell, his eyes going hard. "They seem almost desperate. I wish I could have a few minutes alone with their father, but he'll never see freedom again."

"Bastard." Hoyt took another sip as he glanced at the men again. "I know what it feels like to want like that. I sure as hell hope they find a woman they can love."

"And one who loves them."

Alerted by something in Bill's tone, Hoyt glanced up at him as he took another sip of his beer, but Bill's closed expression didn't invite questions.

Respecting the bartender's privacy, Hoyt looked at his watch, inwardly groaning to see that he still had more than an hour to kill before Jake expected him home.

As Bill walked away to serve another customer, Hoyt considered the many ways his life had changed since coming to Desire.

No one had ever been waiting for him at home before, nor had anyone ever expected him home at a certain time.

His home had never smelled like cinnamon and vanilla.

The niggling at his nape had him looking up at the mirror, a little surprised to see Lucas, Devlin, and Caleb from Desire Securities coming through the doorway and heading right toward him.

Devlin paused next to him, gesturing to Bill for three beers. "Jake told us we could find you here. Do you mind if we join you?"

Hoyt shook his head, glad for the company, but inwardly stiffened at their somber expressions. Wondering if it had anything to do with the bank robbery, he got to his feet. "Let's get a table."

Caleb glanced toward Hunter and Remington. "Christ, they're here more often than not now."

Lucas nodded, his lips thinning. "Yeah, they are. We'll all sure as hell be glad when the two of them settle down."

Devlin dropped into his seat, a beer in each hand. Handing one to Lucas, he sighed. "That'll never happen. They're too set in their ways and too scared of hurting a woman to ever allow themselves to be alone with one. They think they're just like their father because they both have tempers. They're scared to death of ever having a woman in their lives and hurting her. So, the only time they ever have sex is here. Having an audience gives them security. They know that no one here will allow them to mistreat or hurt a woman. Here, they can relax and enjoy themselves."

Thinking about Natalie, Hoyt paused with his glass halfway to his mouth. "But no intimacy."

Lucas inclined his head. "I don't know if either one of them even knows the meaning of the word."

Gripping his glass, Devlin leaned forward. "Neither one of them would get within a mile of intimacy."

With a beer in his hand, Caleb dropped into the seat next to Hoyt. "Something's got to give with them soon. Their bar fights are legendary. They have so much anger in them over what their father did."

Devlin clenched his jaw. "They're angry at their mother for taking it, and mad at themselves because they couldn't prevent it. Christ, they were just kids."

Hoyt took another sip of beer, smiling his thanks when Bill brought over a bowl of pretzels. "I have a feeling that when those two find a woman, all hell's gonna break loose." Leaning back, he met their smiles with a grin. "Same thing's gonna happen when the three of you finally meet your match."

To his surprise, their smiles fell.

Devlin sighed and glanced at the others. "I doubt very much that there's a woman out there who would put up with us."

Caleb dug into the pretzels. "We were all happy to hear that you finally decided to settle here with Nat. I have to tell you, we were also very surprised to learn that you're Joe's father."

Hoyt shrugged, once again feeling surge of pride. "I left it up to them whether to tell people or not. I wasn't here, and Jake has been his father from the very beginning. I wanted Joe to know, but Jake's the one who was there for him every day."

A scream of pleasure filled the air, interrupting their conversation, and they each turned to see the women with Hunter and Remington slump against them.

Caleb chuckled as they all turned back to the table. "They're still dressed. They don't even fuck them half the time anymore. It's getting old for them. They need a woman, and I for one, can't wait to see how they handle it."

Lucas sat forward. "I can't even imagine the kind of woman brave enough to take on those two."

Hoyt raised a brow. "You don't think there's one to take on the three of you, but I'll bet she's out there." Smiling, he thought about Natalie. "Women are remarkable creatures."

"That they are." Lucas smiled. "I saw the footage from the bank. Nice moves."

Hoyt settled back, allowing a small smile as he eyed Lucas. "I'm sure I could say the same about the three of you. You were looking for me for a reason. It can't be to tell me that."

Lucas's lips curved. "No. It's not."

Devlin sat forward, looking around to make sure they weren't overheard. "We did a little more digging. Turns out that the bank teller has two stepbrothers. Different last names. Same mother. Her first husband died. She remarried and had Debra. Her sons, Chuck and Bob Dodge were already grown by then and constantly in trouble. Debra's the apple of her stepbrothers' eyes, and she adores them. It seems that the brothers were arrested for robbery and resisting arrest a couple of weeks ago, and suddenly someone came up with bail money for them."

Sitting back, he eyed Hoyt. "Turns out John Engels, the man who led the bank robbery here in town, was the one who put up the bail."

Surprised at that, Hoyt whistled. "What a handy coincidence. Wanna bet Debra Smith is the one who put them up to it?"

Caleb nodded. "Looks that way. I can't find any other connection between them. I don't know if she really has something going on with John Engels, or if she just used them to get her stepbrothers free."

Frowning, Hoyt leaned forward. "So where are the Dodge brothers now?"

A muscle worked in Lucas's jaw. "They skipped bail and are apparently on the run."

Hoyt looked at each of them, seeing the same unease in their eyes that knotted his gut. "So, either she used them just to get her step-brothers free, or they're joining forces and that's where they got the balls to rob a bank."

Lucas leaned back, his eyes narrowed. "I think it's the first. I think she found these gullible assholes and decided to use them for her own purpose. I'll bet that she started working at the bank to get information for her stepbrothers. They went to jail, and somehow met these losers."

Devlin finished his beer. "Ace went to see her yesterday to question her about why John Engels would be bailing her stepbrothers out of jail. She went ballistic and ran."

Caleb grinned. "She panicked and began to fight him, so Ace locked her up for resisting." His smile turned cold. "It seems that our polite, shy little bank teller has quite a mouth when she's riled. She's also a little…unbalanced. Ace called in for a psychiatric evaluation when she started banging her head against the wall. Banged it good enough to bleed, and he had to have Doc Hansen come check her out."

Hoyt's stomach clenched. "I've had a bad feeling in the pit of my stomach ever since the robbery. I'd feel a hell of a lot better when we find out where the Dodge brothers are."

Lucas's eyes sharpened. "I don't like it. I've had a funny feeling ever since the robbery, too, and having her behind bars hasn't gotten rid of it."

Turning to watch the woman with Hunter and Remington throw her head back and scream with pleasure, Hoyt sighed, his arms aching to hold Natalie.

The thought of what could have happened if he hadn't been with her in the bank still made him shake. He could have lost her so easily. He hadn't seen her in years, and she could have died without knowing just what she meant to him.

Taking a sip of beer to ease his dry throat, he nodded. "I don't like this. I'm going to make some phone calls and see if I can find the Dodge brothers."

He looked at his watch again, inwardly cursing to realize only a few minutes had passed since the last time he looked at it.

"Problem?"

Meeting Devlin's hooded stare, Hoyt carefully kept his expression blank. "I want to get started on it, but I'm giving Jake and Natalie some time alone. It's late, so I'm not going to be able to make any calls tonight, but I can start doing some digging on the computer and send a few e-mails. I'm not going to be able to relax until I've done something to find these guys."

Lucas finished his beer and got to his feet. "Why don't you come to our place? We've got everything we'll need there."

Hoyt stood, nodding as Devlin and Caleb rose. "Thanks. I want to check on her first, and let the two of them know where I'll be in case they need me."

Caleb grinned. "Must be a bitch to have to check in all the time."

Smiling, Hoyt shook his head. "After being on my own for so long, it's nice to have someone to come home to, and I sure as hell want her to know where I am if she needs me."

Devlin laughed. "Thank God, we don't have to worry about that."

Lucas inclined his head, his eyes cold and empty. "Yeah. Let's go."

* * * *

As Hoyt drove the short distance home, he couldn't shake the unease that made the back of his neck itch. He parked in front of the house, and looked toward the front porch, stilling, the cold knot in his stomach turning to ice.

Light poured out from the open front door, illuminating a wide band of the small front porch and the front yard.

His senses went on full alert, adrenaline rushing through his veins. Scanning the area, he reached over the passenger seat and retrieved his gun from the glove compartment.

Terror gripped him by the throat, his mind spinning with possible scenarios and dreading what he might find inside. Swallowing heavily, he reached up to turn off his interior light and eased the door of his truck open. Slipping out, he closed the door partway, not wanting to risk anyone hearing it close.

Scanning the yard and street, he carefully stayed in the shadows as he approached the front door. Glancing down, he clenched his jaw, furious to see that the bright yellow flowers that had started to bloom—the flowers Natalie loved so much—had been trampled.

Rage and fear combined, strengthening each other.

A primitive fury nearly blinded him. Nothing mattered except getting to Natalie and Jake.

They needed him.

He couldn't afford to make a mistake.

Pausing, he took a deep breath and let the ice take over.

Holding his gun at the ready, he moved silently up the three steps and through the front door, listening for any sound that would alert him to the presence of anyone inside.

He spared a glance at the destruction, fighting the urge to rush forward screaming Natalie's name.

Lamps had been broken and lay scattered on the floor.

The overstuffed chair that Natalie liked to curl in lay on its side.

Stepping over the pillows dotting the floor and around the big screen that had been knocked to the floor, he clenched his jaw, reaching for the icy calm he needed. Despite the cool night, he broke out in a sweat, fear for his family nearly choking him.

The walls had holes in places, dents in others as though someone had slammed up against them.

Or been slammed against them.

Sign of a struggle were everywhere.

The implications of what had happened nearly took him to his knees.

He should have been here.

Natalie had needed him, and he hadn't been here for her.

He hadn't been here for either of them.

He ducked his head around the corner, making sure no one was in the hallway before plastering himself to the opposite wall and peering around the corner to the kitchen. The table had been shoved against the wall—hard—judging by the damage to the drywall, but the room was empty.

The unmistakable sound of a moan had him whipping back, stilling when he caught movement out of the corner of his eye. Spinning, he aimed in that direction, lifting his gun again when he saw Devlin paused just inside the opening—grim-faced and armed.

Holding his gun in both hands, Devlin made a hand signal to someone over his shoulder before moving soundlessly across the living room to the opposite side of the hallway across from Hoyt. Leaning to the side, he looked into the kitchen, his expression harder than Hoyt had ever seen it.

As Hoyt started down the hallway, he caught sight of Lucas coming through the back door just as Caleb came through the front.

Aware of their presence, and trusting that they had his back, Hoyt made his way down the hallway toward the Master bedroom, his heart pounding furiously at the sound of another low moan coming from that direction.

Devlin's brows went up and he shared a look with Hoyt before slipping into the room Hoyt used as an office, reappearing seconds later.

Peering into his office, Hoyt saw none of the destruction present in the living room and kitchen.

With Lucas at his back and Caleb at Devlin's, they made their way down the hallway in tense silence, following the direction of yet another moan coming from the Master bedroom.

With his heart in his throat, Hoyt paused outside the doorway, praying as he'd never prayed before, mind-numbing fear nearly choking him.

He and Devlin went through the doorway at the same time, each sweeping the room with their guns drawn. Although he didn't see anyone, he didn't relax his guard, scanning the room again and again as he moved forward.

He glanced at the tangled sheets and the comforter that lay half on the floor, scared to death that he would see Natalie's arms or legs peeking out.

The fury inside him bubbled over.

She should have been safe here.

She slept here. Made love here.

This was her sanctuary, a private place, and it had been violated.

Where was she?

Please, God.

Hoping she'd hidden and would pop out any minute, Hoyt stepped carefully around broken items all over the floor—a lamp, a statue she'd loved, a vase for her flowers—and made his way to the other side of the bed.

His gut clenched at the sight of a bloody Jake sprawled on his back among clothes, bedding and a broken lamp.

"Jake! Son of a bitch." Dropping to his knees beside his friend, he set his gun aside and checked Jake for injuries. "Where's Natalie? What happened?"

Jake moaned again, struggling to sit up. "What the fuck?" He shook his head as if trying to clear it, wincing and falling back again. "Nat? Where's Nat?"

Hoyt helped Jake to a sitting position while Lucas came forward.

Kneeling behind Jake, Lucas cursed, his eyes flat and cold. "He's bleeding badly and he's got a hell of a knot. Caleb, call an ambulance."

Devlin checked the bathroom before holstering his own gun, and returned with a towel, tossing it to Hoyt. "I'm gonna check around outside."

Jake groaned again, holding his bleeding head. "Two men came in. Knocked me out. I need to find Nat. Goddamn it. Where is she?" He pushed ineffectively against Lucas, his eyes wild with horror as he scanned the room. "Nat! Damn it, don't sit here with me. Go find her!"

Hoyt couldn't remember ever being so scared. "What the hell happened?" Dizzy with fear, Hoyt gripped Jake's arm. "Who came in here? Who did this?"

Supporting Jake's weight, Lucas helped him to his feet as Hoyt supported Jake from the other side. "Easy, Hoyt."

"No." Jake shook his head, wincing and groaning again, his movements clumsy as he grabbed for Hoyt's arm. "Find her." Lifting pain-filled eyes to Hoyt's, he groaned again as he lowered himself to the bed and ran his hands over the sheets. "We were in bed. Talking about how she's scared to let you get close. All of a sudden, she got a look on her face." Grimacing, he closed his eyes. "Surprise. Fear. Looking at the doorway. I heard the door open and thought it was you coming in. She screamed my name, but as I turned, something hit me in the back of the head. I didn't protect her." He reached for the back of his head, but Lucas pushed his hand away.

"Leave it. I'm trying to get it to stop bleeding. You have a concussion at least, probably a cracked skull. Tell us what you heard. Saw. Anything."

Jake groaned again, his face as white as the sheets on the bed. "Didn't see or hear anything except the fear in Nat's eyes." He slumped to the side, leaning heavily against Hoyt. "I'm gonna pass out again. Christ, how long have I been out? What time is it?"

Lucas frowned. "After twelve. Come on. Let's get you to the hospital."

"Hell." Jake pushed at Hoyt, his weak, clumsy effort alarming. "Let go of me. We have to find her."

Lucas helped him to his feet, his jaw clenched. "You're not in any shape to go anywhere except the hospital. Caleb and Hoyt will take you while Devlin and I call Ace and get started."

Hoyt's stomach clenched in fear for Natalie—the thought of what she could be going through at that moment making him sick to his stomach.

He couldn't think about anything but getting to her.

Jake gripped his arm again, looking at him with eyes that appeared slightly unfocused. "She needs you. Stay here with Lucas and find her." Jake shook, clenching his fists at his side, the horror and desperation in his eyes difficult to witness. "Hoyt, I need her too damned much."'

Nodding, Hoyt got to his feet and moved to the window. "I know, Jake. I do, too. I'll find her. I swear."

Natalie needed him. She was out there right now probably scared out of her mind, worried to death about Jake—and counting on Hoyt to come get her. An icy coldness came over him, sharpening his focus.

Natalie's life depended on him. She needed him.

The most important mission of his life.

Touching Jake's shoulder, he retrieved his gun from the bed. "I trusted her with you when she was carrying my child. You can trust me with her now. Go let the doctors take care of you. She's going to need you, too."

They both needed him, and he'd be damned if he let them down.

As he strode from the room, several plans of action went through his mind, some dismissed immediately, while he placed others on a mental back burner.

He had to find her as soon as possible. Every second counted.

Devlin joined Hoyt on the front porch pausing beside him as Hoyt stared down at the flowers Natalie loved so much. "Just some tracks in the front. Two men. One large. One small." He shared a look with Lucas. "Some drag marks. Nothing out back. I'll call Ace."

Burning with fury, he lowered his voice as Caleb and Lucas appeared with Jake. "No."

Devlin frowned. "Hoyt, Ace has—"

Hoyt shook off his arm, the combination of fire and ice warring inside him. "Ace will want to do everything by the book. For the first time in my life, I'm throwing the fucking book out the window."

Lifting his head, he met Devlin's eyes squarely. "I'm not playing by the rules on this one. They'll die for this."

Chapter Nineteen

Blinking back tears, Nat pulled at the duct tape they'd used to tie her hands behind her back, struggling to get free. No amount of tugging could loosen it.

She tried to look as they led her over what appeared to be an asphalt parking lot, but with the pillowcase over her head, she couldn't see a thing.

Jake!

Please, God. Let him be all right.

A door opened and they pushed her through it, and suddenly she had carpet under her feet. The pillowcase was ripped off of her head, along with several tendrils of hair, and a second later, she found herself thrown into a hardback chair.

She gritted her teeth to hold back any sounds that would have escaped through the tape over her mouth, not wanting to give them the satisfaction of seeing her fear.

Crying had given her a stuffy nose, and with her mouth taped, she hadn't been able to breathe. In a panic, she'd forced back her tears, promising herself that she wouldn't make that mistake again.

Glaring at the larger of the two men—the man who appeared to be in charge, and the one who'd hit Jake with the butt of the gun he carried—she fought the urge to jump out of the chair they'd stuck her in, not wanting to give either one of them a chance to touch her again.

She couldn't get the image of the way Jake had looked when they'd dragged her out of her bedroom out of her mind.

Even as he'd passed out, he reached for her, trying to protect her with his body.

Her protector.

Her rock.

When they'd shoved him off of her, he'd hit the floor with a thud and hadn't moved.

Please, God, let him be all right. I love him so much.

She couldn't even think about having a life without him.

"Damn it! Stay still so I can tie this." The younger, dressed in ripped jeans, a dirty T-shirt that hung on him, and a dark hooded sweatshirt, yanked her right foot hard, slamming it against the chair leg.

Squeezing her eyes closed against the sharp pain in her heel, she bit back a cry at the pain radiating up her leg. Blinking back tears, she swallowed a sob and watched the larger of the two men out of the corner of her eye as the other duct-taped her leg to the chair.

"Make sure you tie the bitch up good." The bigger man smiled—a cold smile that sent a chill up her spine. "We can't let her get away, now, can we? If she behaves herself, I might just keep her for a while."

He met her glare with a cold laugh. "She's a little older than the women I'm used to, but she sure is built, ain't she? Yeah, if she can take on those two men she's fucking, she should be able to handle me, don't you think?"

He threw his head back and laughed at the shiver of revulsion she couldn't suppress and turned away. "We'll just have to see. The men of Desire are pussies—catering to the women the way they do. They all act like they're in charge, and then let their women walk all over them. As soon as I finish my business and we get out of here, you'll find out what it's like to be with a *real* man."

Dressed in only a thin cotton nightgown that stopped several inches above her knees, she fought to keep her legs pressed together, but the man at her feet gripped her other ankle and pulled it to the other leg of the chair and began taping it. "Stop fighting me. I gotta tie you good so you don't cause no more trouble."

She flexed her sore hand, hiding a smile as she noted with no small amount of satisfaction that he had the beginning of a black eye.

Once he'd finished securing her ankle, he rose to his feet, throwing off his hooded sweatshirt and tossing it aside to reveal skinny arms almost completely covered with tattoos. Turning back, he bent, reaching out to touch her knee, letting his hand linger. "When my brother gets done with you, maybe I'll keep you for a while."

Dear God. Think, Nat. Think.

Swallowing the bile in her throat, she struggled to hide her revulsion and forced her muscles to relax.

Patting her knee, he smiled. "Hey, Chuck. I think she likes *me*."

Not if you were the last man on earth.

Lowering her eyes to hide her disgust, she jerked them up again at the unmistakable sound of someone being punched, shocked to see the smaller man fly across the room.

Picking himself off the floor, the smaller man rubbed his jaw. "Damn it, Chuck! What the hell did you do that for?"

"I swear, if you weren't my brother, and I hadn't promised ma I'd look after you, I would have cut you loose a long time ago." Chuck's jaw clenched. "How many fucking times do I have to tell you not to say my name? That's what got us locked up last time. Christ, between you and those other assholes who got themselves shot up, I think I'd be better off on my own."

The smaller man wiped the blood from his lip, his face red. "What the hell difference does it make? You said you were gonna kill her anyway."

Chuck shook his head, apparently at the end of his patience. Heading for the door, he barked instructions over his shoulder as he turned, taking a gun from the pocket of his denim jacket to tuck it into his waistband. "Stay inside. Don't do anything stupid like order a pizza. Just keep an eye on her. I'll be gone an hour or so."

Grabbing the front of Chuck's shirt, the other man snarled. "Why are you gonna be gone so long? Where are you going? You ain't thinkin' of bailing on me, are you?"

"I should. You ain't nothin' but trouble." He opened the door, turning and glancing at her. "I'm not going to make the call from here, you asshole. I'm gonna make it from out of town so that if they trace it, they'll think we're somewhere else. Just let me handle the thinking and do what I told you to do."

Nat winced at the slam of the door, shivering again at the tense silence that followed.

Pushing aside her worry for Jake, she struggled to remember the things Hoyt had taught her.

Everyone has a weakness. You just have to find it.

The man she found herself left alone had shown himself to be the weaker of the two. She had an hour alone with him.

If she was going to escape, it had to be now.

Knowing that he would relish the opportunity to feel bigger, she looked up at beseechingly and let her eyes fill with tears, whining through the tape, her mumbled words unintelligible.

Of course, he couldn't understand her, something she'd counted on. She had to get him to take the tape from her mouth, and she had to do it fast.

Moving closer, he knelt at her feet again. "What are you saying?"

She did it again, letting a whimper escape in the hopes that it would take him off guard.

He glanced toward the door and turned back. "If I take the tape off your mouth, you've got to promise you won't scream."

Nodding, she closed her eyes as if in gratitude, hoping he didn't see the triumph in her eyes. She winced at the sharp pull when he removed the tape, the pain as bad as if he'd pulled off her skin. "Thank you. Please, I'm so cold. Can you put a blanket on me? I'm so cold. Oh, God. I have to go to the bathroom." She bounced in her seat as far as her bonds allowed. "Please. Please. Please. I'm gonna wet myself."

To her amusement, he looked slightly panicked. "No. Don't do that. Hell, if I untie you, you're just gonna run."

"How?" Nat looked down at herself. "I'm dressed in a nightgown, and there's no way I could make it to the door before you caught me. As it is, I'm going to have bruises all over me from you."

Next to Jake and Hoyt, he was a wimp, but she attempted to look suitably scared of his strength. "You're so much stronger than you look. Please, I really have to go to the bathroom."

His chest puffed up, and he stood a little straighter. "Okay, but remember that I can catch you." Moving close, he pulled a knife from his pocket, sliding the flat of the blade over her throbbing cheek. "I'm good with a knife."

Nat nodded. "I believe you."

Holding as still as her trembling allowed while he cut the tape, she scanned the room for something to use as a weapon.

There are weapons everywhere, Natalie. You just have to be smart enough to recognize them and have the courage to use them.

She glanced down at him as he worked the knife between her calf and the leg of the chair, weighing her chances of getting the knife. "Your brother said he was going to go make a call. How the hell do you expect my husband to pay, or even answer the phone? You knocked him out."

The way he held the knife, she doubted she could get it from his hand. She had to find something else.

Her voice shook, but she didn't bother to try to hide her fear. "I just hope he's all right."

"He's a fucking pussy." With a jerk, he sliced the tape—nicking her calf in the process. "Scowling, he sat back on his heel. We don't want anything from your fucking husband—or from that other guy you're sleeping with. All we want is our sister. Thanks to your lover, my sister's in jail. No one would have suspected her of anything. It was a great plan, but those assholes didn't want to wait for us. If your lover hadn't been there, everything would have turned out just fine."

When he bent again to focus on her other leg, Nat glanced at the heavy, ceramic lamp on the bedside table, and tried to stall. "Your sister?"

"Yeah. Debbie. She's sitting in the fucking jail right now. Ch—my brother went to call the sheriff. When he lets Debbie go, we'll let you go. She never would have gotten into trouble if that dickhead hadn't been trying to impress her—to show her that he was as good as us."

Nat knew they had no intention of ever letting her go. Her kidnapper had already admitted as much, and they hadn't worn masks, so she could easily identify them.

She also knew enough about Ace Tyler to know that he wouldn't negotiate with kidnappers.

She also knew that he would be furious, and the men of Desire would be frantically searching for her.

With Hoyt leading the way.

Allowing herself a moment to imagine what Hoyt would do to these men, she eyed the lamp again, jerking her head back when her kidnapper freed her other leg and stood. "So, your brother's going to call the sheriff?"

"Yeah, that's what I said, isn't it. You talk too much." He moved behind her, slicing the tape at her wrists. "Hurry up and use the bathroom. There's no windows in there, so don't try anything stupid."

Straightening, he moved to stand in front of her again, his wide smile showing several missing teeth. "Your sheriff has six hours to give our sister back. If not, you die, and we grab someone else from Desire. My sister told me how the men in your town feel about protecting their women. Pussies."

Dear God!

Her horror must have shown on her face because he burst out laughing.

"Yep. Chuck says the men of Desire won't allow the sheriff and his deputies to put their women in danger. Before you know it, they'll take over and let Debbie go."

Shrugging, he smiled again. "That sheriff needs to go anyway, and then the entire town will be different. In the meantime, they can all worry about what we're doing to you."

Since she already knew what they planned to do to her, she kept silent.

Nat swallowed heavily and nodded, worried about Jake and looking forward to Hoyt and Ace showing up to kick their asses.

Her kidnapper went to a backpack she hadn't noticed before and pulled out a bottle of whiskey. "You said you had to go to the bathroom. Hurry up and go so that I can tie you again before Chuck gets back."

Nat sighed and nodded. "Of course. I really appreciate this and I wouldn't want you to get into trouble."

Escaping into the bathroom, she hurriedly locked the door behind her, jolting when he started banging on it. "Hey! I'm not scared of Chuck. We're equals in this, and I don't get into *trouble*. Unlock this damned door."

"I'm using the bathroom. I'll be out in a minute."

Frantically searching for anything she could use as a weapon, she started to pull the remaining tape from her wrists and then decided to leave it, hoping it would protect her if he got a chance to tie her up again.

Nothing.

Little soaps. Little bottles of shampoo. Toilet paper. Towels. Shower curtain.

"Hurry up in there. I'm giving you two minutes and I'm breaking the door down."

Running the water so he couldn't hear her, she yanked a towel from the rack. "Please. I'm already scared. Now I have to go again. I'll be out in a few minutes. I promise."

She'd bet Hoyt would be able to look around the room and find fifteen different things to use as a weapon, but she couldn't find one.

He'd probably be able to strangle her kidnapper with a towel, but she knew she'd never be strong enough.

Your mind is your best weapon.

She could almost hear Hoyt in her head.

She couldn't allow herself to worry about Jake, knowing it would only mess up her head.

He was probably fine and worried about her, and would be mad as hell if she didn't do everything in her power to get free.

Thinking of her men gave her the boost she needed to turn off the water and open the door. Finding her kidnapper right outside, still drinking, she forced a smile. "Thank you. I really had to go." Walking back toward the room, she casually made her way toward the lamp on the nightstand between the bed and the chair they'd forced her into.

"Chuck isn't the boss, you know. We came up with this plan together."

Noting that he slurred his words, Nat braced herself, knowing that now he would be highly unpredictable. "I'm sure you did. He must be the brawn, but you're the brains."

Puffing out his chest, he nodded. "That's right. Now, get back in the chair."

Judging the distance, she stood less than an arm's length away from the lamp. "Okay. Um, do you think it would be okay if I had a sip of that first? Maybe, it'll calm my nerves."

He lowered the bottle, his eyes wild. "Is that why you think I'm drinking? I don't need to—"

Forcing back the panic, she reached for the lamp and slammed it over his head, watching incredulously as he crumbled to the floor.

Shaking, she froze, shocked at what she'd done. "Oh, hell, I've killed him."

Move, Nat, move!

She would swear she could hear Hoyt's words in her head.

Stepping around the largest pieces of the broken lamp, she hurried to secure him with the duct tape, watching the door at the same time. She had no idea how much time had passed, and she didn't plan to be here when Chuck got back, but she couldn't leave until she made a call.

* * * *

Hoyt rubbed his burning eyes and poured yet another cup of coffee.

Where the hell was she?

He and the others had set up the equipment in his new home, wanting to be here in case they got a kidnapping demand.

Lucas sat bent over a laptop, the same position he and Hoyt had been in for the last few hours.

Caleb had called just a short while ago to tell them that Jake had a concussion and he had to stay in the hospital overnight.

While setting up everything, Hoyt had called Clay and explained what had happened, fighting to keep his head clear.

Clay, enraged and frantic, had raced to the hospital with Rio and Jesse, who'd become hysterical when she'd heard that her sister had been kidnapped.

She'd grabbed the phone from Clay, her voice choked with sobs—but she'd made her demand perfectly clear. "Hoyt, do whatever you have to do to get my sister back. *Anything*!"

"I will."

"Promise me! If anyone can do this, you can. I know the kind of things you did. You can do this. I'm begging you, Hoyt. Get my sister back."

Hoyt swallowed the lump in his throat, humbled by her trust in him. "I will, honey. I promise. Just go look after Jake for me so I can concentrate on this."

"We'll take care of Jake. You don't think about anything except getting Nat back." Her voice broke, ripping his heart to shreds. "Please!"

Caleb had stayed with Jake until the others got there, and had returned to Desire, and even now, woke store owners and anyone else who had surveillance cameras.

Lucas leaned back and rubbed his eyes. "Damn it. I keep getting bits and pieces, trying to eliminate the cars and trucks that are familiar from those that aren't."

Hoyt swallowed heavily, went back to the laptop he'd been using, and loaded yet another disk. "Yeah. Something's gotta be on one of these. We'll find something. Caleb and Devlin should be back with more disks soon."

A knock at the door had both Hoyt and Lucas on their feet, their guns drawn.

Glancing at Hoyt, Lucas moved toward the door, waiting until Hoyt got into position on the other side of it before yanking it open.

Ace's eyes widened at the sight of two guns aimed at him, pausing with his hand on his own, his expression grim. "There's better be a hell of an explanation as to why I didn't get a fucking phone call from any of you."

Hoyt turned away, and went back to the kitchen, setting his gun on the counter. "Because we don't need your help."

"I'm the goddamned sheriff in this town!"

Spinning back, and shocked at Ace's rare show of temper, Hoyt glanced at Lucas. Seeing the same shock on his face, Hoyt straightened, meeting the sheriff's fury with his own.

"And it's my woman who's been kidnapped. If I have to buck the rules to get her back, I will, and I don't want any of your fucking laws getting in my way." At the flash of hurt in Ace's eyes and the censuring look in Lucas's, Hoyt sighed and scrubbed a hand over his neck. "Lucas and the others wanted to call you, and I told them that I would do this myself if they did. Look, Ace. I'll do whatever I have to do to get Natalie back, and I don't want to get you into any trouble. The less you know, the better."

Lucas frowned. "How the hell did you know about this anyway? We asked Clay and Rio not to say anything, and I know Jesse's out for blood."

"We all are." With his hands on his hips, Ace surveyed all the disks and laptops. "I just got a call. I'm almost positive it was one of the Dodge brothers."

Hoyt stilled, his stomach clenching. "Ransom?"

Ace's jaw clenched. "Of a sort. They want me to release Debra Smith to them in exchange for Nat."

An icy rage settled over Hoyt. "Are you going to do it?"

Ace's eyes narrowed. "No. What are you doing here?"

Lucas got up to pour two cups of coffee, and handed one to Ace. "Caleb and Devlin are going around town collecting surveillance tapes from all the homes and businesses that have them."

Ace shook his head. "And did you give them a reason."

Lucas sipped from his cup and frowned. "We asked them not to ask. So, they didn't."

Hoyt dropped into his seat again and started the disk. "It's a hell of a town you've got here. Not many people would do such a thing."

Lucas dropped into his own seat again. "Desire isn't like most towns, and the people here stick together."

Ace reached into his shirt pocket. "I assume that you already have photos of the brothers."

Hoyt nodded. "We do."

Ace sighed. "I thought as much, but I brought their mug shots. I forwarded the calls to the station to my cell phone. Give me a laptop."

Hoyt felt like a caged animal, but knew that the best chance of finding her would be the videos.

He looked at grainy disks until he thought his eyes would fall out, and didn't even look up as Devlin and Caleb came through the door.

Devlin dropped four disks on the kitchen table. "This is the last of them."

Hoyt couldn't believe what he saw on the computer screen. "Son of a bitch. Here it is!"

Adrenaline rushed through his veins as the others cursed and gathered around him, watching the screen over his shoulders.

Lucas leaned closer. "That's them. Damn, I can't see the license on the truck. They're going past Logan's Leathers and Beau's Adult Toy Store at eleven thirty-eight, only minutes before they'd burst into the house."

Glancing at the time noted on the screen, Hoyt gritted his teeth. At that time, he'd been in the club with Lucas, Devlin, and Caleb, instead of at home protecting his family. "Maybe we'll get a chance to see the license when they leave."

A tense silence followed as they all watched the screen while Hoyt slowly fast-forwarded it, his breath catching when he saw the truck driving in the opposite direction seven minutes later.

Natalie sat in the front seat between them, and she appeared to be struggling. The oldest brother drove while the other did his best to subdue Nat, who didn't stop struggling until the driver backhanded her, knocking her against the other man.

She didn't move after that.

The rage inside Hoyt exploded and he actually saw red.

Turning to Ace, Hoyt jumped to his feet, knocking his chair over in the process. "If I get to him first, he's dead."

"I understand how you feel." Inclining his head, Ace glanced at the others. "But, you're not alone in this. None of us will stop until we get her safely home. You're not going to do her any good from a prison cell."

"I know." He'd been part of a team for years, but this felt different.

It was personal—for all of them.

Moving away from the others, he braced a hand on the counter on either side of the sink, his eyes closed as he bent his head. "He hit her."

Gritting his teeth, he clenched his hands into fists, struggling to control his rage at the image that would haunt him forever. "Jake said she was only wearing her cotton nightgown."

Lifting his head, he opened his eyes, staring at their reflections in the dark window. "Her robe was on the bedroom floor. She must be freezing."

He couldn't remember ever being so scared, or feeling so impotent.

He wanted her here.

He wanted to wrap her in warmth and shield her from the rest of the world.

Turning to look at Ace over his shoulder, he sighed. "It made me feel good to know that Natalie was watched over here, but I always thought all of you were a little overprotective of your women. I thought it was fucking amusing. Not so funny now. Once I get her home, I'm never letting her out of my sight again."

Caleb touched his shoulder. "We're going to find her."

Turning his head, Hoyt nodded and glanced at Ace. "Yes, we will, and I'm going to take great pleasure in doing a little hitting of my own."

From behind him, Lucas cursed. "I can't clear the image enough to see the damned license plate."

Sitting back, Ace folded his arms across his chest, staring thoughtfully at the computer screen. "I haven't been able to find any records of property they might own, but I'll bet they've been here before. The way they drove straight here tells me that they knew exactly where they were going."

Devlin stiffened. "I'll bet they've been to the jail and tried to figure out a way to break her out."

With a curse, Lucas grabbed the stack of disks they'd marked, ejecting the one in the laptop to insert another. "And if they were targeting Nat because of what happened at the bank, I'll bet they watched her. We should get some images of them around Jesse and Kelly's store. They'd want to get a good look at her during the day, so maybe we can get a good look at them in the daytime and make sure that's who we're dealing with."

He glanced at Hoyt. "They probably followed her home."

Hoyt groaned, furious at himself for missing it. "I should have thought of that. Damn it!" He slammed his hand on the countertop. "I've done this shit for years—planned out everything—and now when it's most important, my fucking brain's scrambled."

Leaning forward, his eyes narrowed on the computer screen, Ace shot him a glance. "I can't say that I blame you. I love Nat, but I have to say—if it was Hope—I'd be out for blood, and I'd be a little—off."

Shrugging, he looked back at the screen. "I'd also appreciate every damned bit of help I could get, and would count on my friends to catch something I'd missed, and to keep me from doing something stupid."

Lucas sat back, allowing the others to see the computer screen. "Look at this." He tapped several keys. "Let me see—yeah, there they are. Broad daylight, too. It's them. Let me see if I can get a clear look at the license plate."

Hoyt studied the screen, ice forming in the pit of his stomach.

The image had been taken the previous afternoon, and because it had been shot in the daytime, the Dodge brothers faces could be seen clearly.

A quick check showed that the truck had been reported as stolen.

Hoyt straightened. "From where?"

A muscle worked in Ace's jaw. "From Cushing. Close to where Debra was staying. I want to keep my line clear. Give me a phone. I want to get Linc to put out an APB on the truck."

Hoyt began to pace, too restless to sit still. "I can't fucking just sit here and wait." He ran a hand through his hair, so frustrated, he wanted to punch something. "Christ, on a mission, I could sit for hours and wait. I can't now. I've got to go look for her."

Devlin laid a hand on his arm, his eyes filled with concern and compassion. "Where? Where are you going to look? You could be headed in the wrong direction. You're not thinking clearly, and I get that. It's Nat. We're all scared for her, and we're all furious. Christ, she's got more spunk that almost every woman I know, but she's still just a little thing."

Lucas shot Devlin a warning look. "We saw the way the house looked. She fought. There's no reason to believe she's going to quit fighting."

"If she can still fight." Hoyt pushed aside the thought of Nat lying hurt somewhere, knowing that it would only mess up his head even more. "Over the years, I've tried to teach her a little about self-defense. I don't know how much she remembers." Cursing, he rubbed a hand over the back of his neck. "I should have taught her more. I haven't been around in years. I loved her too much to come around until I'd worked things out with Jake."

Ace disconnected from his call with Linc. "Nat seems able to take care of herself, and she'll use whatever you taught her."

Hoyt grimaced, sick to his stomach. "If she gets hurt trying to do what I taught her, I'll never forgive myself."

He was so focused on his thoughts, that he jumped when his cell phone rang. Not recognizing the number, he frowned. "Must be someone calling from the hospital." Dreading hearing that something was wrong with Jake, he accepted the call. "Campbell."

"Hoyt? Can you come get me?"

The sound of Natalie's wobbly voice had to be the sweetest sound he'd ever heard.

His knees turned to rubber. "Natalie? Baby, is that you?"

Dizzy from the rush of adrenaline, he glanced at the others, who'd all jumped up and rushed to him.

Lucas ran to another laptop and began hitting the keys. "I'm tracing it. Keep her talking."

Hoyt ran a hand through his hair, wishing he could reach through the phone and wrap his arms around her. "Where are you? Are you okay?" His voice shook with emotion, his entire body trembling.

"I'm okay. Just cold. Look, I can't talk long. Chuck is going to come through the door any minute. Oh, God. I can't stop shaking. They hurt Jake, Hoyt. They hurt him real bad. Please tell me he's not dead." Her voice shook so badly that he had trouble understanding her.

She needed his strength now, and he was damned well going to give it to her. Firming his voice, he straightened, struggling to push emotion aside and be the ice cold soldier she needed. "Jake's fine. He's in the hospital with a concussion. Tell me where you are and we'll come get you and go to him."

"Promise me he's okay. Please, Hoyt. Don't let him be dead."

Hoyt purposely injected anger into his voice, desperate to shake her out of her fear so that she could help him find her. "I don't lie." He put the phone on speaker so the others could hear. "What motel? Where? Are you safe? Where are the men who took you?"

"Chuck went to call Ace, and the other one's tied up. I want to get out of here. He's unconscious, but I'm afraid he'll wake up. I tied him with duct tape, but I don't know if I did a good job or not. Hell, I might have killed him. Oh, Hoyt. Chuck's going to come back any minute. I have to get out of here. Please come get me." A sob broke free, ripping his heart to shreds. "I don't know where the hell I am."

"Go to the window. Tell me everything you see."

"Okay. There's a diner across the street. There's a sign! It's called the Day and Night Motel." Her voice still shook, and he knew it must be costing her dearly to hang on.

Clenching his fist at his side, Hoyt struggled to keep his voice calm and even. "Can you go outside? Wrap a blanket around yourself and get out of that room before Chuck gets back."

She grunted, cursing as a sob escaped. "I have it. I have the blanket. To go outside, I have to hang up."

"Not yet! Don't hang up yet."

Lucas jumped to his feet. "Got it. Tell her to get the hell out of there and hide. We'll be there in fifteen minutes."

Ace grabbed his phone, rattling off an address to Linc.

Hoyt gripped the phone tighter as they all ran out of the house. "Hang up and go find a place to hide. We'll be there in fifteen minutes."

"Okay. Hoyt?"

Hoyt paused. "Yeah, baby?"

"Please hurry."

"Like lightning. Hide, baby. I'll be there soon."

Sitting in the passenger seat, he grimaced when she hung up.

He should have told her he loved her.

Chapter Twenty

Pulling the blanket more tightly around herself, Nat eyed her handiwork, hoping that the tape held until she could escape. Alarmed at the amount of blood covering his face and dripping onto the carpet, she swallowed heavily and stepped cautiously around him.

He hadn't moved since she'd hit him, but had moaned a few times, and she didn't want to take the chance that he would somehow get loose and reach for her.

He moaned again, and tried to open one eye. "Bitch."

"Fuck you." Nat kicked him in the thigh, instantly regretting it as pain radiated up her leg. "Asshole."

Rushing to the door, she eased it up a few inches, fighting the urge to throw it open and run outside. The beat of her heart sounded loud in the ominous silence as she peered through the small opening.

She scanned the dark and deserted parking lot before looking across the street to the diner. She could see several cars in the parking lot, and a few dark pickup trucks, and didn't want to take the chance that one of them belonged to Chuck.

She had to find a place to hide.

With a last glance at her captor, she slipped out the door, closing it quietly behind her.

Staying close to the building, and in the shadows, she made her way to the left, heading for the opposite end of the parking lot from the entrance.

A hedge bordered the parking lot, one high enough for her to duck behind, but low enough to enable her to peek out so she could see Hoyt.

Scanning the area, she raced toward the opening in the hedge, wincing at the pain of stones digging into her feet. She didn't slow down, though, scared that Chuck would appear any minute.

She didn't know how long he'd been gone, but the fifteen minutes she'd have to wait for Hoyt seemed like forever.

She pushed her way through the small opening in the hedge, ignoring the scratches on her hands and hurriedly ducked behind it. Uneasy at the open yard she found herself in, she wrapped the blanket more securely around herself and moved back several feet and to the right, plastering herself against the base of a large tree trunk.

Hoping that the ugly brown blanket allowed her to blend in with her surroundings, she squatted next to the tree—and waited.

Shaking with the combination of cold and nerves, she stiffened at every sound, her breath catching when she heard the slam of a car door from across the street. Pressing herself against the side of the tree, she raised herself just enough to see over the hedge, her stomach clenching when she saw a dark pickup pull out of the parking lot and cross the street to the motel.

Where are you, Hoyt? Please, hurry. Please, hurry.

Her heart pounded furiously when the truck pulled in right in front of the room where they'd taken her, and holding her breath, she watched Chuck emerge.

Carrying takeout bags, he glanced from side to side as he made his way to the door.

With her heart in her throat, she ducked down again, knowing it would only be a few seconds before he realized she was gone.

She only hoped he wouldn't leave and head back to Desire for another hostage before Hoyt arrived.

No.

He would have to find her first. She could identify them.

What if they didn't care?

Oh, God! Hoyt, where are you?

"Son of a bitch! Bob! What the hell happened? Where the fuck is she?"

Huddled against the tree, she listened to Chuck curse. An angry tirade ensued. She couldn't make out the words, but the message was clear.

Chuck was mad as hell.

Stiffening at the sound of running footsteps, she hugged the tree trunk tighter, searching the street frantically for any sign of Hoyt's truck.

She froze as the sound of squealing tires echoed in the night.

Please be Hoyt. Please be Hoyt.

"Where are you, you fucking bitch?"

Nat blinked at Chuck's furious demand, wondering if he really expected her to jump out and wave her arms in the air, yelling "I'm over here."

Idiot.

Another squeal of tires made her pulse leap, and brimming with excitement and relief, she straightened, grinning at the sight of a big black SUV squealing to a stop behind Chuck's truck.

All four doors opened—Hoyt emerging from the front passenger seat and heading straight for a clearly shocked Chuck. "You son of a bitch! Where's Natalie?"

To her surprise, Caleb and Devlin shot out of the backseat, while Lucas jumped from the driver's seat.

As the man she now knew as Bob staggered from the doorway to lean heavily against their truck, Chuck took off in the opposite direction of the four men—straight toward her.

Shit.

She knew the moment her kidnapper saw her, his evil smile sending a chill through her. Shifting her gaze to Hoyt's, she realized the moment he saw her, too, and the flare of panic on his face when he saw that her kidnapper was between them.

Caleb and Devlin split up—Devlin going to Bob as Caleb circled the hedge from her left. Lucas stayed with Hoyt, both men gaining on Chuck with every stride.

Something inside her settled at the icy rage on Hoyt's face, and confident that her kidnapper wouldn't stand a chance against him, she threw the blanket off and ran.

Going left, she headed toward Caleb, who called out to her, watching over her shoulder as Chuck gained on her.

And Hoyt gained on him.

Turning to look back at Caleb, she stumbled at the sight of the gun in his hand, letting out a cry as she struggled to regain her balance—afraid that her kidnapper would reach her before Hoyt reached him.

She'd barely managed to regain her balance before Caleb caught her, just as a thud and harsh cry sounded behind her.

Pointing the gun at his shoulder toward the sky, Caleb cursed as he yanked Nat behind him. "Damn it, Hoyt."

She had to struggle to see around him, and when she did, it was to see that Hoyt had tackled her beefy kidnapper to the ground. "Let go, Caleb. I want to see Hoyt kick his ass."

Lucas, who stopped just short of the men fighting on the ground, cursed and holstered his own gun, gesturing toward her. "Get her to the truck where it's warm, and check her over."

Despite being cold, Nat pushed against Caleb's hold. "No."

Hoyt moved like lightning, delivering blow after blow to her kidnapper, making the other man look clumsy and slow. Struck by the fury lining his features, Nat called out to him just as the bigger, heavier man fell to the ground with a thud.

Hoyt still wasn't finished, and with a growl of rage, started toward him again.

Shaken, Nat called out to him again, just as Lucas grabbed him from behind.

Holding him, Lucas said something in a voice too low for Nat to hear, something that had Hoyt's head whipping around, his eyes still wild as they met hers.

Hoyt didn't even appear winded as he started toward her, catching her securely when she ran to him. "God, baby. I've never been so fucking scared. You okay?" He removed his jacket without releasing her, tucking her into it and lifting her face to his.

Enveloped in the warmth of his body, Nat leaned into him, blinking when a grim-faced Ace appeared with another uniformed officer. "I am now." She gestured toward the man on the ground as the other officer placed him in handcuffs. "That's Chuck. The other one's name is Bob. They're the bank teller's brothers. How's Jake?"

"He's got a concussion and has to stay in the hospital overnight for observation. Clay, Rio, and Jesse are with him." Hoyt eased her back, lifting her face and eyeing her critically. "We know who these guys are. You're going to have quite a shiner. We'll get you checked out at the hospital and you can go see Jake." Despite his light tone, his eyes glittered with anger as he ran a finger lightly over her upper cheek where Chuck had hit her as they rode out of town.

Nat smiled up at him, hoping to relieve some of the concern in his eyes. "I don't even feel it."

Lucas came up to her from behind with the blanket she'd dropped and wrapped it around her shoulders. "You will."

Nat gripped Hoyt's shoulders, swallowing a sob. "Hoyt?" Her voice broke, and she had to swallow another one that threatened to choke her.

His hand moved over her hair, cupping the back of her head. "Yeah, baby?"

Conscious of the men talking around them, she buried her face against his neck. "I think I'm going to cry."

Hoyt hugged her closer. "Go ahead, baby. I've got you. God knows you have every right to cry."

"I don't want them to see."

"Then they won't." He started moving, through the hedge and back to the parking lot. "Go ahead, baby. It's just you and me."

The first sob broke free without warning, and before she knew it, she started crying hysterically. It was as if a torrent broke free, the fear of the last few hours all coming out in a rush. Keeping her face against Hoyt's neck, she struggled to speak. "I c–couldn't b–breathe."

Hoyt's arms tightened, his hand moving up and down her back. "What do you mean, you couldn't breathe?"

Now that she'd started crying, she couldn't seem to stop. "I started c–crying before, but my m–mouth was t–taped and I c–couldn't breathe."

The horror of the night continued to wash over her, and as soon as she thought she could calm down, it all came rushing back. "They c–came into the house. The h–hit Jake. They hurt him. I w–want to s–see him."

"We'll go right now, honey." His voice, so calm and soothing, wrapped around her.

"Okay. Okay." Nat nodded, wiping her face on his jacket. "I'm okay now." The hiccups in her voice irritated her, and she accepted the bottle of water Hoyt offered to her, knowing that either Lucas, Devlin, or Caleb had given it to him.

After taking several small sips, she felt steadier. Lifting her gaze to his, she smiled and sniffed. "Sorry about that. Thanks."

Hoyt smiled faintly, but his features looked as if they'd been carved in stone. "Thanks for the call."

Nat shrugged, more of the tension escaping on a giggle. "I figured you might be looking for me."

"Fucking bitch." Her kidnapper's voice came from somewhere behind Hoyt, who turned. A bloodied and battered Chuck started to struggle, but Ace, who towered over him, tightened his grip and gave him a warning look.

She knew Ace would be right in the thick of things.

"Careful." Ace smiled coldly. "You're talking about his woman, and if I let him, he'd tear you limb from limb."

Caleb's usual smile was conspicuously absent. "And enjoy doing it. Hell, I wouldn't mind having a few minutes alone with you."

Looking up at Hoyt, Nat grinned, feeling a little better. "He called you a pussy."

Hoyt's slow smile warmed her all the way through. "Did he?" He didn't seem at all concerned by the insult.

"Yep." She turned her head as Devlin appeared with the other man. "Said all the men in Desire are pussies because of the way they coddle the women."

Held against Hoyt's muscular chest, and drawing strength from him, Nat tilted her head back to smile up at him. "I hate to admit it, but I needed a bit of coddling."

Devlin smiled, but she suspected it was for her benefit. "Then he picked a hell of a way to test that theory." He grinned and winked at her. "Doesn't appear that the women are too soft, either. What the hell did you do to Bob, Nat? He can barely stand." He turned him over to the other officer, who demanded a statement.

Blinking at the other officer's tone, Nat leaned her head against Hoyt's wide chest. "I did the same thing to him that he did to Jake, but instead of the butt of a gun, I used a lamp. Asshole." Lifting her gaze to Hoyt's she smiled and cupped his jaw. "I remembered what you said about looking for a weapon."

Hoyt grinned. "Good girl." Bending low, he touched his lips to hers. "I'm proud of you, baby, but I'm never letting you out of my sight again."

Lucas leaned close, running a hand over her hair as he pulled out a flashlight and pointed it at her face. "We may coddle our women, but they're our greatest strength."

Without a backward glance, Hoyt turned and started toward the truck with Lucas, Devlin, and Caleb. "And our greatest weakness. Christ, I've never been so scared." Raising his voice, he turned to glance at Ace. "Tell your friend that if he wants a statement, we'll be at the hospital."

Chapter Twenty-One

Still tense, and watching Natalie carefully, Hoyt smiled as she fussed over Jake.

She'd been checked over, and other than a few bruises, including the beginning of a black eye, some cuts on her feet, and some soreness, she appeared to be fine.

He'd been furious to see the duct tape still remaining on her wrists and ankles, and even more furious to see the red marks and broken skin left behind when they removed it.

She'd been treated, the marks wrapped with gauze. Dressed in hospital scrubs and non-slip socks, she looked adorable, and somehow even smaller and more delicate, and he couldn't stop hovering over her.

Jesse had cried when she'd seen her, and looked like hell.

Clay and Rio didn't look much better, but now that the crisis had passed, they did their best to lighten the atmosphere and try to get Jesse to settle, but when neither of the women was looking, their eyes glittered with anger and concern.

As Natalie leaned over Jake, Hoyt reached out to rub her back, unable to stop touching her. He knew the muscles there were sore by the way she moved, but she wouldn't admit it.

Jake didn't seem able to stop touching her, either. Holding her hand, he smiled drowsily. "Tell me again."

Natalie bent to kiss him, seeming steadier now that she was with Jake. "No. You have to sleep. I'll tell you the whole story again when we get home."

Jake's brow went up. "Just because I'm lying in this bed doesn't mean that you're in charge, little one. I want to hear how you got away again."

Lucas, Devlin, and Caleb came through the door with food and coffee. Devlin grinned. "Hey, we're just in time. I want to hear all the details, too."

With a look at Jake, Hoyt moved to one of the reclining chairs the hospital staff had provided, settling Natalie on his lap. "Eat while you talk."

Accepting the cup of coffee from Lucas, Hoyt watched as Jesse fussed over her sister, making sure she had orange juice and coffee, while Caleb urged both women to take breakfast sandwiches.

Sipping his coffee, Hoyt listened to Natalie tell her story, watching her attentively for any signs of pain.

She looked exhausted, but she couldn't seem to sit still for long. Her pale features made the dark circles under her eyes, and the bruise forming around her right one even more pronounced. When she finished her sandwich and juice and set her coffee aside, he pulled her back against him, where she slumped without protest.

"I swear I could hear Hoyt in my head telling me to look for a weapon, and I knew that if I did something stupid, Jake would kick my ass."

"You're damned right I would." Jake smiled, but didn't open his eyes, obviously under the effects of the pain medication.

Caleb bent to kiss Natalie's hair. "Our tough girl. We're all very proud of you, honey."

Ace walked through the door, smiling gratefully as he accepted a cup of steaming coffee from Devlin. "Both men have had medical attention and are on their way to jail."

"Pity." Hoyt finished his coffee and set his cup aside, gathering Natalie closer. "I wish I'd had the chance to strangle both of them with my bare hands."

Clay nodded. "I can imagine, but I have a feeling that getting to Nat was more important."

Ace sipped his coffee, eyeing Natalie over the rim. "You did a hell of a job of escaping, and word's already spreading around town. The sun's coming up. Why don't you try to get some sleep? You look beat, honey."

Jake stirred. "Why don't you and Hoyt go home and get some sleep? Everyone's been up all night."

Natalie stiffened. "No. I'm not leaving until you do. If you sleep, I will."

Clay got to his feet. "Come on. Let's clear out of here. No, Jesse. Don't bother arguing. You need to go home to get some sleep, and Nat needs to be alone with Jake and Hoyt."

Within minutes, everyone had gone, leaving the three of them alone. Before he could say anything, a nurse came in, handing him a blanket with a smile.

"I didn't think you'd be leaving with the others. Everyone's talking about what happened, and we're all so thankful that you're all okay."

"Thank you." Accepting the blanket, Hoyt covered Natalie before easing the chair back to a reclining position, settling Natalie as he watched the nurse take Jake's vital signs.

He waited until the nurse left and closed the door behind her before kissing Natalie's hair. "Go to sleep, baby. You're safe now."

God, it felt good to have her in his arms again.

* * * *

God, it felt good to be in his arms again.

He'd held her all the way to the hospital, checking her for injuries as she spoke on the phone to Jake.

Once they got to the hospital, he carried her inside, meeting her demand to go straight to Jake with a steely glare, and continued to the desk.

Remembering the look on the nurse's face, she smiled, knowing that if she hadn't been used to it, the sight of Hoyt would have been enough to make her take a second look.

But, with Lucas and Devlin striding confidently on either side of him, and Ace and Caleb bringing up the rear, she could understand the woman's dumbstruck expression.

Living in Desire, she'd seen it often enough, but she always got a kick out of it.

The men of Desire had a presence that others seemed to lack.

To her relief, Hoyt stayed close while the police got her statement, and seemed to know when her strength waned, somehow ending the interview and clearing the room.

He'd helped her dress in the scrubs the kind nurse had given her to wear, and despite her objection, carried her to Jake's room where the others waited.

He hadn't been more than an arm's length away from her, giving her the strength she needed to put on a brave face for the others.

She'd never been so scared—for herself and for Jake—and now that it was over, she couldn't seem to stop shaking.

It had been a struggle to hide it from Jesse, and it was a relief to finally be able to relax.

She watched Jake until her eyes began to droop, struggling to stay awake until he fell asleep.

Grateful for the dim light, she leaned against Hoyt, pressing her face against his chest. She didn't want Jake to see how badly it shook her to see him lying in a hospital bed, his face almost as white as the bandage wrapped around his head.

His hair, so dark against the white sheets, had been washed clean of blood, but she still saw it. The image—imprinted on her mind—refused to go away.

Even hurt, his concern had been for her.

According to Jesse, it had taken both Clay and Rio to keep him from leaving the hospital, and even though Hoyt had called him and let him speak to Nat on the phone, Jake hadn't settled until she walked into the room.

Even through the relief in his eyes, the concern couldn't be mistaken. He'd gripped her hand like a lifeline, and hadn't looked away from her as if trying to convince himself that she was all right.

He'd had his eyes closed for several minutes and started to doze, suddenly jerking. "Nat?"

"I'm right here." She started to get up, pausing when he waved a hand and closed his eyes again.

"No, don't get up."

Hoyt settled her back against him again, his eyes narrowed. "Do you need something, Jake?"

Opening his eyes again, Jake glanced at Hoyt before his gaze settled on hers. "Is she really all right?"

Nat blinked, stiffening. "I already told you—"

A dark brow went up, his arrogant look making her feel a little better. "You told me what I want to hear. Hoyt will tell me the truth."

The concern and love for her shining in his eyes made it impossible for her to get angry with him for not believing her. Shaking her head, she smiled and leaned back against Hoyt, hoping to allay her husband's fear. "If you're accusing me of lying, I'm going to kick your ass when we get home."

He didn't smile as she expected, his expression hard as he held her gaze while adjusting his pillow. "You're not fooling me, Nat. I see the worry in your eyes. Seeing me in this hospital bed scares you, and you've already been scared enough. It makes me sick to my stomach that I couldn't protect you, but it doesn't make me fragile or weak, and I won't be treated that way. I want the fucking truth."

"Jake, don't get upset." Afraid that getting worked up would only make his head hurt worse, she tried to go to him, but Hoyt tightened the hand around her waist, pulling her back against him.

"He's got every right to be upset. I'd be pissed off, too, if you tried to hide something from me, or treated me like a child." Closing his hand over her arm, he massaged gently, facing Jake. "Her wrists and ankles are raw from the duct tape. Her jaw isn't broken, but it's swollen and she's got the beginning of a black eye from where she was backhanded."

"Backhanded?"

Nat shivered at the ice in Jake's tone. "Jake, I'm—"

"Quiet." Lifting his head, Jake looked at Hoyt. "One of them backhanded her?"

"Yeah." Staring down at her, Hoyt ran a finger lightly down her sore cheek. "He paid for it, but not enough. It's still swollen, but not as much. They put an ice pack on it down in the emergency room, but she didn't want to walk in here with it because she didn't want you to worry."

Nat pushed his hand away. "You weren't supposed to tell him that."

Hoyt smiled, bending to touch his lips to her cheek. "I'd want to know." Lifting her chin, he studied her features as he continued to speak to Jake. "She's also sore, especially her back—probably from wrenching it, and being pulled around."

His lips twitched at her look of surprise, and he turned back to Jake. "She's been trying to hide it. The doctor wants her to take it easy for a couple of days. He gave her a muscle relaxer, and I have a prescription for more. Between being up all night, the adrenaline crash you both have to be feeling, and the medicine they've given you, I think both of you should settle down and go to sleep. I know I could use some. I'm getting too old for this."

With a sigh, he dropped his head back and closed his eyes. "Christ, Jake, I don't know how you do it." Lifting his head again, he smiled down at her. "One week with her and I'm exhausted."

Jake grinned, looking so much like his old self that she wanted to cry, and she squeezed Hoyt's hand in gratitude. Reaching up, Jake turned off one of the lights, leaving only a very dim one to bathe the room in a soft glow. "She's always been a handful. Keeps me on my toes—that's for sure."

Looking a little more relaxed, Jake closed his eyes and settled back. "I'm glad you're here to watch over her tonight. As soon as I get a few hours sleep and get rid of this headache, we'll go home, and I can check her over myself."

His faint smile held a hint of sadness that ripped a piece of Nat's heart. "This'll be the first night since we got married that we haven't slept together, won't it?"

Swallowing the lump in her throat, Nat nodded, blinking back tears. "Yeah." It was a silly thing, she supposed, but one that saddened her. Forcing a smile, she met his gaze squarely. "We're together, though, and that's what's important."

Hoyt lifted his head again, looking from one to another. "Except for the night Joe was born—right? Wait a minute." He frowned at Jake. "I thought you said you didn't have sex for a while after you got married."

Grinning, Jake dropped his head back again. "Even though we didn't have sex, I wasn't about to start married life sleeping in separate beds. That kind of thing could become a habit, and that's not what I wanted. Besides, she didn't need to be alone and I wanted to hold her. She was a restless sleeper when she was pregnant."

Smiling, Nat shared an intimate look with Jake as memories of the night she'd given birth to Joe came rushing back. "Despite the dirty looks from the nurse, Jake crawled into bed with me and held me all night. She tried to kick him out. Hoyt! What are you doing?"

Standing with her in his arms, Hoyt carried her across the room and lowered her to the hospital bed. Holding on to her as Jake smiled and made room for her, he smiled. "I'm not surprised Jake didn't let the nurse kick him out. I know that once I'm in bed with you, I certainly don't want to leave." He touched his lips to her forehead before straightening, tucking the blanket around her. "You two need each other tonight. Get some sleep."

Searching his features for any signs of jealousy, Nat gripped his hand. "What about you?" Relieved to see only love and concern in his eyes, she lifted his hand to her lips. "You're not leaving, are you?"

The flare of pleasure in his eyes humbled her. "I'm not going anywhere. Get some sleep so I can take you both home."

* * * *

Lying in the recliner, Hoyt found it nearly impossible not to go to Natalie when she started to cry, but knew that she and Jake needed some time together.

She'd needed him, not only to rescue her, but to hold her—to hide her from the other—so she could cry.

She'd trusted him enough to let go in his arms, and despite the turmoil, it had been the most precious moment of his life.

The surge of love for her made him dizzy, the intimacy he'd craved even more potent to his senses—more overwhelming—than he ever could have anticipated.

Jake murmured to her, holding her close as he comforted her. "I'm fine, honey. Just a headache. How many times have you accused me of being hardheaded?" Settling her against his shoulder, he kissed her hair. "I was scared for you. Your poor face. Does it hurt? Maybe I should call the nurse for more ice."

"No way."

Hoyt kept his head back and eyes closed, smiling at the determination in her voice.

She still sounded tired, and a little shaky,

He knew it would be difficult to get her to take it easy for a few days, but he'd tie her to the bed, if necessary.

Cuddling closer to Jake, she sighed. "I thought I'd never get warm again, and now that I am, I plan to stay that way. Jake, just hold me." Her voice broke, tightening the fist around Hoyt's heart.

Jake rubbed her back, wrapping himself around her. "Always."

"Poor Hoyt. I cried all over him."

"Did you?"

"Yeah. It was pitiful. He didn't let the others see me, but they knew."

"Don't worry about it. Nobody's going to be talking about anything except how you smashed a lamp over your kidnapper's head and called Hoyt to come get you." Jake kissed her hair, sharing a look with Hoyt. "Our tough girl."

"Don't feel so tough now."

Her words slurred, and Hoyt knew that between the adrenaline crash and pain medication, she wouldn't be able to stay awake for long.

Jake rubbed a hand over her back. "Just rest, baby. It's all over."

Hoyt started to relax as the silence lengthened, making himself comfortable in the recliner. He'd slept in a lot worse places over the years, but now missed the warmth of having Natalie's body nestled against his.

He'd just started to doze when Natalie's voice reached him.

"Jake, you should have seen Hoyt. Damn, he's fast. That guy was big, and he didn't even get to land a punch. Hoyt kicked his ass real good."

Jake chuckled. "And I'll bet he enjoyed every second of it. I keep missing the action. I heard that the other guy didn't fare so well either."

"I was scared, but not as much as I could have been. I knew Hoyt would come."

Hoyt stilled, his chest swelling, her words warming him all the way through.

She'd depended on him, and had trusted him to save her.

As much as she needed Jake, she'd needed *him*.

Tonight, she'd clung to him as they made their way to the hospital. Shaken after her ordeal, she'd struggled to put on a brave front, but she hadn't let him out of her sight once they got to the emergency room—reaching for him often as the doctor examined her.

It was a heady feeling—to be needed by the woman he loved.

Addictive. Intoxicating.

It left him feeling as if he'd just drunk whiskey.

It heated his blood and made his head swim.

His chest swelled even more as he settled back to watch over his family, the realization that he'd already begun to make a place for himself here, leaving him feeling better than he could have ever imagined.

He'd always been an adrenaline junkie, and found loving Natalie an adrenaline rush more potent than any other.

Listening to their breathing even out, Hoyt couldn't help but smile in the darkness.

Nothing he'd ever done in his life gave him the satisfaction he got from earning Natalie's love, but also her trust.

And an intimacy he treasured.

Chapter Twenty-Two

Hiding a smile, Hoyt watched the woman he loved shamelessly maneuvering his best friend just where she wanted him.

He couldn't help but admire how damned good she was at it.

She actually reverted to pouting in an attempt to keep Jake from going to work. "But, Jake, I think you should stay home. Your head could start hurting again. You got your brain rattled good. Another day at home would be good for you. If you go to work, I'm going to spend all day worrying about you."

They'd come home from the hospital early the previous afternoon to find Clay, Rio, and Jesse waiting for them with a hot meal.

Jesse still hadn't settled, fluttering around the house as if afraid the kidnappers would burst through the door any minute.

Clay and Rio didn't smile as often, hovering over Jesse as she hovered over her Natalie and Jake.

The number of visitors and phone calls staggered Hoyt, and it became glaringly obvious that the residents of Desire took watching out for each other *very* seriously.

One after another arrived—with food, offers to help with whatever needed to be done—even helping Hoyt repair the damage to the walls, and promises to come back to help repaint.

They'd included Hoyt in their conversations, treating him as if he'd lived there for years.

Still amazed, he mentally shook his head, sitting back and enjoying the interaction between Natalie and Jake.

Jake sipped his coffee, his eyes dancing with amusement. "I spent all day yesterday relaxing after you nagged me to death."

"Nagged?" Her chin went up, her eyes narrowing—a clear sign of trouble—and fisted her hands on her hips. "Are you calling me a nag?"

Frowning, Jake glanced at Hoyt and with a gentle brush of his fingers, pushed her hair aside, his gaze narrowing on the bruise around her eye. "I wouldn't dare."

Gripping her chin, he turned her face toward the light streaming in from the kitchen window. Raising a brow in challenge, he ran his finger lightly over her cheek. "You're hurt and you're going to work, aren't you?"

Intrigued at the way Jake handled her, Hoyt hid another smile behind the rim of his coffee cup, and settled back to wait for his friend to close the trap.

Natalie pursed her full lips, and Hoyt could almost hear her thinking—probably realizing that Jake had maneuvered her to a position she couldn't escape.

"Jesse needs me there, but you have people to take care of the store. I'll be worried about you all day, and probably mess things up so I have to work late." Smiling, she laid her head on his chest, clearly convinced that she'd get her way. "If I don't have to worry about you, I'll get my work done sooner and won't have to stay late to finish."

Smiling over her head, Jake rubbed her back and shared a conspiratorial look with Hoyt. "Jesse already told me that Brenna and Kelly are both going in today, and she's already placed an ad for more help." With a shrug, he wrapped his arms around her. "Besides, if you're not here, there's really no reason for me to stay home to do paperwork. I can do it at the store and check out a few things while I'm there."

Stepping back, Natalie frowned up at him. "You're going to do too much."

Jake took another sip from his cup, raising a brow again. "No more than you will." Turning away, he set his cup in the sink and dropped a kiss on her forehead. "Have a nice day."

If Hoyt hadn't been watching closely, he would have missed the flash of panic that crossed her features. "Jake!"

Jake paused at the doorway and turned. "Yes?"

Shifting from one foot to the other, Natalie sighed. "My back really does hurt a little. I was hoping that you'd stay home and massage it for me. My cheek hurts, too. I didn't want you to worry, but I think I'd feel better if I stayed home with you."

Frowning, Jake closed the distance between them. "Of course, baby. If you need me, I'll stay here with you."

Over her head, Jake grinned. "Strip out of your clothes and get back in bed while I change out of my suit."

Understanding that she wanted Jake to stay home and relax another day, Hoyt got to his feet, unable to resist confronting her and curious to see how far she'd go. "Natalie, you know I'm perfectly capable of taking care of you."

Whipping her head around, she glanced meaningfully at Jake. "I know, but I don't feel good. Is there something wrong with wanting both of you here?"

"Of course not." Gesturing toward the hallway, he inclined his head. "Do what Jake says. It doesn't make sense for you to get dressed today. You might as well be comfortable. We'll both take care of you today."

Looking a little disconcerted at how she'd been manipulated, Natalie scowled, looking from him to Jake and back again. "Um, sure." Holding her head, she sighed, alarming him. "I think I need to go back to bed for a while, and I'll feel better with both of you beside me."

Hoyt smiled as he watched her go. "I was going to congratulate you on maneuvering her, but she turned the tables on both of us. She's a master manipulator, isn't she? She not only got you to stay home from work, but somehow made it impossible for me to turn down going to bed."

With a chuckle, Jake shrugged out of his suit jacket. "Yeah. You look tired, and she knows you didn't get much sleep. Did you really think she'd miss that?"

Jake laughed softly as he bent to take off his shoes. "Being part of a family like ours is a little different from the family you had in the SEALs, Hoyt, and navigating the emotional minefield of having a wife is a hell of a lot different than planning a mission."

Hoyt stilled, a lump forming in his throat. "She's not my wife, though, is she?"

Jake's smile fell. "That's up to you. In Desire, you can marry her, and even though it wouldn't be legal anywhere else, it is here. It also shows the rest of the town that you take this seriously."

Hoyt stiffened. "Of course I take this seriously."

Jake grinned. "Then marry her."

* * * *

Nat spread a thick towel over the bed, unable to stop smiling.

Her darling husband thought he'd outsmarted her, but she'd already talked to Jesse, who'd told her that Rio would be spending the day at the store with her, along with Brenna and Kelly, and that if Nat showed her face before tomorrow, she'd be escorted home.

Knowing that Rio would take great pleasure in doing it, she hadn't intended to go to the store anyway, and had allowed Jake to talk her out of it, but only if he would also stay home.

Another day of rest would help him heal faster.

As a bonus, she also got Hoyt's promise to lie down when she did. She didn't like the dark circles under his eyes, or the pinched look around his lips.

He hadn't slept much at all in the last two nights, and had been awake every time she woke during the night.

Twice, she'd even caught him standing at the window and staring out, brushing off her questions and climbing into bed again as if nothing was wrong.

Shrugging off her robe, she lay facedown on the bed, biting back her irritation that the muscles in her upper back pulled.

Slamming a heavy lamp down on someone's head took a lot more effort than she'd expected, and her shoulders ached from being yanked around by Chuck.

Seeing a movement out of the corner of her eye, she turned her head, wincing when her muscles protested. Expecting to see Jake, she smiled, her smile falling when she saw a very serious-looking Hoyt. Turning, she sat up, pulling the edges of the towel around her to cover herself. "Is something wrong?"

"Don't." Moving closer, he sat on the edge of the bed, frowning as he pulled the towel away. "I hate when you do that. You cover yourself up as if you're embarrassed and afraid I'll find you unattractive."

Nat's face burned, and she wanted to deny it, but knew he'd catch her in the lie.

He shook his head, touching a finger to her lips when she would have apologized. "It pisses me off." Stretching out next to her, he rolled to his side to face her, his eyes hooded as they raked over her. "From the minute I met you, I thought you were the most beautiful and exciting woman I'd ever met." Running his fingers through her hair, he stared down at her. "Not once have I ever changed my mind about that. You're still the most beautiful and exciting woman I'd ever known."

Incredibly moved, Nat blinked back tears and reached up to cup his cheek. "For a man who doesn't like to use pretty words, you're sure as hell good at it."

Hoyt smiled and slid a hand down her body, igniting every nerve ending in his path as he bent closer. "Yeah, well just don't expect it every day."

Nat met the love and hunger in his kiss with her own, pouring herself into it.

Passion flared, and gripping his shoulders, she pressed herself against him, loving the feel of his hands moving over her nakedness.

His touch became more familiar by the day, and even more exciting.

Firm in some places, a gentle caress in others, Hoyt's touch left her awash in sensation, his fingers sliding with expert precision over her.

Slow, gentle slides of his fingertips over the underside of her breast had her gripping his shoulders in desperation and writhing against him.

Her nipples ached with the need for his touch, a touch he refused her. "Hoyt, please!"

Lifting his head, he smiled, his eyes flaring at her whimper. "We're getting married."

"Married?" A sob escaped before she could prevent it, the last wall of defense crumbling all around her. "You're really staying?"

Frowning down at her, he slid his hand into her hair. "You and I are really going to have to work on your trust issues. Once we're married, maybe you'll realize I have no intention of going anywhere."

She couldn't imagine anything better than spending the rest of her life with the two men she loved.

Swallowing the lump in her throat, she ran a hand over his chest, arching into the hand at her breast. "Are you asking me—or telling me?"

His smile—pure sin—sent a shiver of delight through her. "Let's put it this way." Bending his head, he nuzzled her jaw, zeroing in on a particularly sensitive spot. "After spending all these years wanting you—loving you—I have no intention of taking *no* for an answer."

Moaning as the pleasure took over, Nat slid her hand into his short hair, throwing her head back to give him better access. "I'll tell you what." Lifting her right leg, she hooked it over his, her inner thighs already slick with her juices. "I'll give you an hour to convince me."

Lifting his head, he grinned down at her, his eyes flaring at the challenge. "Baby, I can fulfill my mission in half that time." His eyes narrowed as he closed his fingers over her nipple. "Then, I can spend the rest of my allotted time making you pay for the way you manipulated Jake and me a little while ago."

Whimpering at the rush of pleasure that shot straight to her clit, she slid her hands to the hem of his T-shirt and struggled to rid him of the soft fabric. "I don't—oh, God—know what you're talking about. Damn it, Hoyt. I want you naked."

Leaning back slightly, he yanked his shirt over his head and tossed it aside before rolling her to her stomach. "Yes, you do. You know exactly what I'm talking about."

Reaching for the bottle of oil he'd placed on the bedside table, he ran a hand down her back. "Now, for my first mission."

Bracing herself for a decadent onslaught, she fisted her hands in the pillow, her entire body tight and tingling with anticipation.

Instead of the erotic assault she'd expected, Hoyt leaned over her, running his lips over her shoulder. "I want to sleep beside you every night, and see that beautiful face every morning while you're running around getting ready for work."

The slide of his lips over her back drew a moan from her, the warm hands on the outer curves of her breasts drawing another.

"I want to be there for you when you need me. You love me, don't you?"

Mesmerized by his slow, silky drawl, Nat lifted her head, turning it to look into his eyes. "You know I do."

His hands slid to her waist and back again, while his lips continued to move over her back and shoulders, his gentle touch inflaming her. "And I know that you want me. I'm barely touching you, and you're aroused. Why don't we work on those muscles in your back and see if I can't loosen you up a little more?"

"Hmm. I'm already loose."

Hoyt chuckled and sat up. "You seem pretty tense to me. When you're aroused and loose at the same time, you'll be putty in my hands."

Turning his head to kiss her forearm, he smiled down at her. "Say it. Tell me you love me. Tell me you've missed me."

Blinking back tears she'd promised herself she wouldn't shed, Nat nodded. "I love you so much, and I never dreamed I could actually have you back in my life." She slapped at his shoulder, meeting his cocky grin with a glare. "And yes, you shit, I've missed you. You know that. You don't have to look so smug about it. You missed me, too."

"More than you'll ever know." Sliding his hand under her, he cupped her breasts. "I love the taste of you. The feel of you."

Hissing at the sharp pleasure of his fingers closing over her nipples, she writhed against him. "Hoyt!"

Hoyt scraped his teeth over her shoulder. "Christ, you excite me. You think I'll get bored here because I'm an adrenaline junkie. Loving you is a rush that I can't get anywhere else."

Nat moaned at the feel of his hands on the outer curve of her breast, thrilling when he parted her thighs and settled between them. "Hoyt. Oh, God. That means so much to me. I would die if you got bored with me."

His hands slid down her sides, his breath warm against her neck. "Bored with *you*? You've got to be joking."

"We've had a lot of excitement this week."

Hoyt chuckled and ran a hand down her back to her bottom. "I know. It's about to get exciting again."

A giggle escaped before she could stop it. "That's not the type of excitement I was talking about. The bank robbery. The kidnapping. That stuff doesn't happen around here."

"Good." Hoyt straightened and a few seconds later, she felt oil dribble over her back. "Without that stuff getting in the way, we can get to the really exciting stuff."

Grinning, she buried her face in the pillow. "Idiot. Hmmm. That feels good."

Sliding his hands over her back, he spread the oil. "Idiot? Is that any way to talk to your future husband and Master?"

"Nope. I'm bad." God, the feel if his hands drove her wild. "Maybe you should spank me."

Hoyt's chuckle vibrated over her skin. "I'll take a rain check. Right now, I'm working on something else—or did you forget? Are you going to accept my proposal?"

Nat hid a smile. "If you think I'm going to give in so easily, you're sadly mistaken. You need to convince me a little longer."

Chuckling again, Hoyt continued the long, smooth strokes over her back, loosening her sore muscles with every slide of his hands. "You do know that I'm skilled in the art of torture, don't you?" His strokes lengthened, his strong, firm hands sliding lower with each pass.

Another moan escaped when his caress included her bottom cheeks. "I believe it. You gonna torture me?"

"Of course. I have to get the answer I want, don't I?"

Tingling with anticipation, Nat lifted her arms above her head, stretching out completely. "Do your worst. I don't break easily."

Hoyt's oily hands slid to the outer curves of her breasts. "That's what I'm counting on."

Nat melted under his hands, moan after moan escaping as he added more oil and worked it into her sore muscles. She found herself drifting more and more, so drowsy that she couldn't even open her eyes.

Hoyt didn't speak, keeping his hands moving in a slow, lulling rhythm over her back, down her sides, and lower to her bottom.

Gradually, she became aware that his hands continued to work their way lower on her bottom, until he began to focus his attention there. She stiffened slightly, too relaxed and loose to do more than moan, a groan escaping when his hands went to her back again.

Over and over, he focused his attention to her back and shoulders before moving to her bottom again, melting every muscle along the way.

Pliant under his hands, she couldn't even work up the energy to tighten against him when he began to work on her thighs.

Her thigh muscles were no match for his firm massage, and before she knew it, she'd become so relaxed that she couldn't move.

His hands kept moving, and he occasionally added more oil, allowing his strong fingers to slide over her skin.

Rubbing more of the oil into her ass cheeks, he kept massaging, working the muscle there until it became so pliable that she couldn't seem to tighten it anymore.

Her entire body melted under his hands, and when he began spreading her cheeks as he massaged them, she didn't even think about objecting.

Even the sensation of more of the scented oil being drizzled down the crease of her ass didn't alarm her.

When his fingers followed the trail of oil, brushing over her puckered opening, she moaned at the faint stirring of arousal.

Too loose and drowsy to tighten against him, she let herself go, her arousal growing with every pass of his finger.

His fingers slid easily from just above her bottom hole to her pussy, back and forth, each pass arousing her more, but so nonthreatening and rhythmic that she found herself lifting into them.

Her body had become so slack, that even when a slide of his fingers took them into her pussy, she did nothing more than moan.

"You're all mine now, aren't you, baby? Nice and loose." Sliding his finger upward again, he pressed at her puckered opening as his fingers slid over it. "Even your ass is nice and relaxed. Pliant."

Working his fingers over her, he pressed into her pussy and against her puckered opening with each pass. "That's my girl." His voice, so low and even, washed over her, adding to the delicious sensations swirling through her.

"So beautiful. So sweet."

Nat couldn't work up the energy to answer him, unable to move a single muscle. Her only response to his delicious ministrations were the weak moans that poured out of her.

Another moan escaped when he slowly, gently worked her cheeks wider, drizzling more of the oil to run inside her. "So beautiful. That's my baby. So loose. Glistening with oil."

His finger massaged her puckered opening, forcing the muscle to loosen even more as his other hand slid lower, rubbing the oil over her pussy and clit. "You're already wet here, but the oil feels good, doesn't it, baby?"

Nat moaned, unable to work up the energy to lift into him.

He seemed to know what she needed, though, sliding his thighs under hers to lift her several inches from the towel. "Yes, that's my girl. Just relax and let me take care of you."

The slow slide of his fingers over her bottom hole made her want more, and she moaned in relief when he increased the pressure there. "I know, baby. I know what you need."

The tip of his finger pressed into her bottom, increasing the sense of awareness there. The slide of his fingers over her clit sent a riot of sensation through her, making every inch of her body sizzle with arousal.

She needed more, but was too relaxed and weak to fight for it.

So good.

A slowly building arousal that left her warm and languid under his hands, even as her body screamed for release.

She needed the fingers at her clit to move faster, moaning with the need to have her ass filled with the fingers teasing her.

A groan of frustration escaped. "Hoyt! Please."

The finger at her ass slid deep. "Are you going to marry me? One word, sweetheart, and I'll give you what you need. Just say yes."

"Yes!"

"Good girl. Nice and easy, baby."

He slid his hands over her clit again and again, the slow slide of them building her hunger and taking her closer and closer to the edge.

At the same time, he worked his finger in and out of her ass, the tight ring of muscle there so relaxed that he had no trouble adding another finger.

"Yeah, that's my girl. Doesn't that feel good?"

Nat could only moan, so overwhelmed that tears stung her eyes. "So good."

Her clit felt so swollen, the erotic slide of his fingers increasing the burning sensation with every stroke. The oil kept the friction light, dragging out the pleasure.

With his fingers moving slowly in her ass and over her clit, Nat gripped the slats in the headboard, crying out when her orgasm hit her. Riding the delicious wave, she moaned again as Hoyt slowed his strokes, keeping the incredible feeling washing over her.

"Oh, God."

The wave crested and slowed, the fingers in her ass and on her clit dragging it out with mind-numbing slowness. She rode it on and on, her entire body warming as the heat spread through her.

"We're getting married tomorrow."

Nat moaned again at the feel of his fingers sliding from her bottom. "Can't."

"Yes, you can. Jake's setting it up right now." Moving from between her thighs, he stretched out next to her. "And now we have to address your punishment for manipulating Jake and me."

Turning her head, Nat forced her eyes open. "What kind of punishment?" Her words came out slurred, and she had to struggle to focus.

Hoyt grinned. "When we get married, you're going to be wearing a clip on that pretty clit."

He scraped his teeth over her shoulder, chuckling at her gasp. "And nipple clips, and a nice thick plug up your ass."

Her bottom clenched, and she found the energy to push herself up to face him, her body still trembling. "Hoyt! I can't have a butt plug inside me on my wedding day! And a dress. Oh, God. I need a dress. I can't plan for a wedding in one day."

Hoyt slid a hand under her to tease her nipple. "I don't give a damn what you wear. I've waited long enough for you, and I'm not waiting another day. Joe already knows. We'll have a party when he comes home."

Not about to risk losing an opportunity to negotiate, Nat pretended to consider that. "Only if I can have a new dress for the party."

Hoyt grinned, his eyes dancing. "Of course. Any dress you want."

"And new shoes?"

"Of course."

"I'll need a new purse to match the shoes."

Chuckling, he nodded. "Whatever you want, baby. Just remember that you're penchant for manipulation is what got you into trouble in the first place."

Hoyt stared down at her for several long seconds, a muscle working in his jaw. "I love you, baby."

Nat could see the truth of his words in his eyes, an adoration that tore through her defenses like no threat or dark look ever could. "Oh, Hoyt. I love you so damned much."

"We have a lot of time to make up for, don't we?"

"Take her on a honeymoon. You two need some time alone." Jake smiled as he approached, running a hand over her back as he sat on the other side of her."

Staring down into her eyes, Hoyt smiled. "We're going to go out and spend some time together tomorrow, but she's slept with you every night since you got married. I won't interfere with that."

"No. You deserve the time alone with her."

"We'll be here."

Nat reached for Jake, her movements clumsy as sleep tried to claim her. "Can we talk about this later? Hoyt wore me out. Lie down. You promised to rest, and Hoyt promised to sleep next to me."

Jake smiled. "As soon as you fall asleep, I'll crawl into bed next to you."

Nat smiled, sighing in contentment. "Good. I sleep better when you're beside me." Knowing Jake wouldn't lie to her, she sighed again. "Hoyt's not going to keep his promise, is he?"

Jake ran his hands over her shoulders, massaging gently. "Why don't you ask him?"

Aware of the pause of Hoyt's hands before they started moving again, and that he listened attentively, she fought the lethargy and struggled to keep her voice even. "Because he would tell me what I want to hear, instead of the truth. He did it when I caught him at the window at night, and wouldn't tell me what was wrong. He'll do the same thing with this."

"Shit." Hoyt's hands firmed. "I just didn't want you to worry. I just had some things to work out in my head."

"If that's all it was, why didn't you tell me?"

His pause didn't surprise her. Neither did the frustration in his voice.

"I told you. I didn't want you to worry. There was no need to upset you."

Nat forced a smile, gathering the energy to lift her head to turn and look at him. "And there's no reason to risk pissing me off, so you promise me that you will, and then you'll do whatever you want to do."

Hoyt's eyes narrowed. "Are you saying that you don't trust me?"

Dropping her head back onto the pillow, Nat hid her face against her upper arm. "Can I? Are you going to do what you promised, or are you going to wait for me to fall asleep and disappear?"

He looked so tired, and the stress of the last few days showed. He hadn't slept much, and had watched over her and Jake, making sure they ate, and were comfortable, and kept a sharp vigil as if expecting someone to burst through the door at any time.

Hoyt passed a hand over her bottom, squeezing lightly. "You wouldn't be trying to manipulate me again, would you?"

Nat shrugged, attempting nonchalance. "Nope. Just asking. Honesty is a big deal for a woman, and it would be nice to know if I can depend on you to tell me the truth before I marry you tomorrow."

After a pregnant pause, Hoyt laughed and started to massage her thighs again. "You know, I think you missed your calling." His warm lips brushed over her shoulder, followed by a sharp nip. "You're sneaky, devious, and too damned adorable to resist."

"Yep." Nat sighed, struggling to stay awake. "Your last chance to escape."

"Not a chance." To her surprise, Hoyt stretched out beside her. "I'm not going anywhere. Tomorrow, my ring will be on your finger next to Jake's."

Unable to resist, Nat used the last reserve of energy she possessed to face him again, opening one eye. "I want you to wear one, too. I want to make sure all the women you run into know that you're taken." Pleased that she'd managed to keep the neediness out of her voice, she let her eye close again, not wanting him to see too much.

She hated feeling so damned insecure.

Brushing her hair back from her face, Hoyt nuzzled her shoulder, his breath warm against her skin. "Believe me, baby. Everyone will know that I've found the woman I want to spend the rest of my life with."

Nodding, Nat tried to turn her head as tears stung her eyes, her eyes flying open when Hoyt's hand tightened in her hair, preventing it.

Running a thumb over her cheek, he smiled, a smile filled with so much tenderness that her eyes welled with tears she hadn't wanted to shed. "You don't need to hide from me anymore, remember?"

Pushing his hand away, she wiped away a tear and sniffed. "I hate feeling so damned needy. I feel like ever since you got here, all I do is cry.

You're turning me into a wuss." She knew that Jake listened to their conversation, another aspect of having two men in her life that she'd have to get used to.

Bending to touch his lips to her cheek, Hoyt groaned. "Don't apologize for that. I love knowing that you need me. It makes me feel ten feet tall."

* * * *

Pleased that Nat had finally gone to sleep, Jake glanced at Hoyt, amused to see that his friend seemed a little unsettled. He pulled his sleeping wife closer and tucked the blanket around her bare shoulder, smiling with satisfaction when she moaned and buried her face against his chest. "That's it. Sleep, baby."

Hoyt rolled toward her, his expression thoughtful as he rubbed her back. "Sometimes, it hits me—just how close the two of you are. It reminds me that I've got a long way to go, but if I could earn half of what she feels for you, I'd die a happy man."

With a sigh, he toyed with the ends of her hair, his smile self-deprecating. "I was cocky enough to think that getting her to admit that she loves me and accepting me as her lover would be enough."

Meeting Jake's gaze over Nat's sleeping form, Hoyt frowned. "Not even close. You know what she's thinking. What she's feeling. You know how to get around her, and she goes to you for comfort." Staring at the curl he wrapped around his finger, he sighed. "You know her so well—in ways I've never even thought about knowing a woman. In ways I've never cared to."

With a sigh, he rolled to his back, dropping his arm over his forehead as he stared at the ceiling. "I never wanted to know everything about a woman the way I want to know Natalie."

Amused at Hoyt's obvious confusion, Jake smiled. "I don't think I've ever seen you look so baffled. You're always so controlled and confident."

Lifting his arm, Hoyt turned his head to frown at him. "I've never felt so out of my element in my life."

Lifting her hand, he ran his finger over the ring he'd placed there years earlier. "You love her. At times, it really hits me, too."

Glancing at Hoyt, he smiled at his friend's look of surprise. "Sometimes, I just look at her and can't believe she's really mine. You're getting more than you bargained for, though, aren't you?"

Shaking his head, Hoyt rolled toward her again, plastering his chest against her back. "If that's not a fucking understatement, I don't know what is."

Loving the feel of his wife's warm, limp body against his, Jake caressed her hip under the covers. "What you felt for her when you got here was only the tip of the iceberg. I knew that once you were with her again, you'd realize that."

"Is that why you objected to me coming back here?"

Jake smiled. "Yes. I knew the same thing would happen to her. The more time the two of you spend together, the deeper your feelings will be for each other."

After several long seconds, Hoyt spoke again. "And that doesn't bother you anymore?"

"Nope." Shifting to a more comfortable position, he smiled as his wife moved with him, attuned to him even in sleep. "As a matter of fact, your decision to come here has made us even closer. I know now what she's willing to give up for me. You were always the greatest threat to our marriage."

Hoyt grimaced. "I'm sorry for that."

"Not your fault. Besides, we faced it and came out even stronger."

"Glad I could help."

Hoyt's sarcasm wasn't lost on Jake.

Jake chuckled softly, not wanting to wake his wife. "You did. That's why I can afford to be generous. Take Nat on a honeymoon. Go away somewhere so the two of you can be alone."

"No." Hoyt bent to kiss Nat's shoulder, smiling when she moaned in her sleep. "It's clear that it means a lot to her to sleep with you every night. Besides, she's going to be unsettled, and nervous about your reaction to our marriage, and she's already a little anxious about Joe coming home and seeing the three of us together. I'd like to take her out to dinner so we can talk, and maybe stop at a hotel somewhere for a few hours, but we'll be back here tomorrow night. I want her to be comfortable, and the sooner we settle into a routine, the better."

Jake grinned. "See, you know her better already." Blowing out a breath, he frowned. "I can't believe she's so nervous about Joe."

"To be honest, I am, too."

Jake blinked. "Why? Joe sounds thrilled."

"Yeah, but it's gonna be different for him, and he's going to be watching Natalie and I closely. He'll be curious, and he's very protective of his mother. I have you to thank for that."

Smiling, Jake glanced at him. "I think we're both responsible for that." Closing his eyes, he started to doze, surprised when Hoyt spoke again.

"I wanted to kill him. I could have done it with no regrets at all."

Jake didn't need to ask, already knowing that Hoyt referred to Nat's kidnapper. "That's understandable under the circumstances."

"No, it's not. Not for me. I've been teaching men for years not to let their emotions interfere with what had to be done."

Another silence followed, but Jake knew that Hoyt hadn't finished.

Hoyt sighed. "Lucas saw it."

"Oh?" Jake didn't doubt it for a second.

Very little got past Lucas.

With a curse, Hoyt rolled to his back again. "I've been accused of having ice water in my veins, but I swear, when I saw him running after her, I actually saw red. I didn't care about getting him into custody. I wanted to make him pay for what he'd done to her. I wanted him *dead*."

Jake glanced in his friend's direction. "I can't imagine it would have been too difficult for you to kill him. So, why didn't you?"

"I looked at her." Cursing, Hoyt stared at the ceiling. "She knew I wanted to. Her eyes were huge, and her face was so white—I thought she was going to pass out."

Rolling toward her again, Hoyt passed a hand over her hair. "And that fucking mark on her cheek. Christ, I could have killed him just for that."

Jake fisted his hand at his side, and only when Nat moaned in protest in her sleep did he realize he'd tightened his grip on her. Relaxing his hold, he glanced at Hoyt again. "But you wanted to go to her."

Hoyt sighed. "She was trying to look so brave and unaffected, but you could see it in her eyes. She was scared. Terrified. How the hell could any man ignore that?"

"No man who really loves a woman could." The mental image of his wife—cold, scared, and injured—raced through his mind. "The others were there to take care of him. She needed *you*, and I'm glad you were there for her."

"I love her so damned much."

"You'll love her even more."

"I don't think that's possible."

Jake smiled at that. "That's what I thought—for the first ten years or so—and every day, I love her more than the day before. Now, I just accept it. Anticipate it."

"Christ, I'm a goner. She's going to lead me around by the nose, isn't she?"

Amused, Jake couldn't hold back a chuckle. "Yep. You might as well learn to accept that, too. It's a big responsibility, but you know there's nothing that she won't do for you."

"Maybe I need to be a little firmer with her."

Smothering a smile, Jake bent to touch his lips to his wife's hair, breathing in the scent of her. "I used to believe that, too. She's in charge, Hoyt. Once you accept that, you'll get along just fine."

Chapter Twenty-Three

Nat hissed, slapping her husband's shoulders. "You're enjoying this too damned much." She stood in the middle of the Master bedroom, every inch of her body trembling with desire. "I knew I shouldn't have let you help me get ready."

Releasing her clit, Jake grinned and leaned back, looking up at her from where he knelt in front of her. "I didn't give you any choice. You're still mine, Nat. Besides, it's not every day a man gets his wife ready to marry another man."

He ran a finger over her clit, tapping the clip he'd just attached, eyeing her critically as he rose to his feet. "Beautiful."

Dressed in a dark suit, he looked both powerful and devilishly handsome.

Standing naked in front of him, she felt delightfully exposed, erotically vulnerable, and incredibly desirable.

Tapping the chain dangling from one nipple clip, and then the other, he circled her, bending to touch his lips to her shoulder as he pushed against the base of the plug in her ass. "Hoyt isn't going to know what hit him. Be still. I have some chains to attach to the plug. You won't be wearing any bra and panties today. Bend over for me, baby."

Shivering, she leaned back into him, lifting her hands to his hair. "You really are enjoying this, aren't you?"

With a chuckle, he tugged at the clips on her nipples and slid a hand down her body to her slit, running his finger over her slick pussy opening. "Apparently, so are you. Bend over so I can attach the chains. Hoyt wants them to brush against your inner thighs every time you take a step. It seems he wants to torture you a little today." Taking her hands from his hair, he put them in front of her and pressed at her back.

Bending, she kept her knees straight the way she knew he expected, another rush of moisture escaping. "So do you." She moaned at the pressure against the plug, gasping at the feel of several small chains against her inner thighs. "Hell, I'm never going to be able to walk around like this."

Straightening again, Jake wrapped an arm around her waist and pulled her back against him. "You're going to have to. You're accepting another man into your life now, one you're going to belong to as much as you belong to me. Behave yourself." He released her and moved to stand in front of her again, his eyes raking over her. "Very nice."

She'd been watching him all morning for a sign of unease or jealousy, but so far had found none. Before she saw Hoyt again, though, she had to make sure. Stepping closer to him, she smiled when his arms automatically came around her. Flattening her hands on his chest, she studied his handsome features and dark, glittering eyes. "Are you sure about this?"

The flare of love in his eyes weakened her knees, his hands clenching on her waist. "I'm sure, baby." Bending, he touched his lips to hers, wrapping his arms around her to pull her close, the feel of his suit jacket brushing against her nipples sending another wave of hunger through her. "I'm happy that there aren't any secrets between us anymore. Your feelings for Hoyt were like a wall between us."

Her stomach clenched, her face burning. She hated that she'd made him insecure, or made him think that she didn't love him enough. Gripping his lapels, she rose to her toes, desperate to make him believe her. "Jake, we've been so happy together. I wouldn't have given that up for anything—or anyone. You're my world. I've been closer to you than I thought I could ever be with anyone."

A hand slid to her back, steadying her, while the other cupped her jaw, lifting her chin. "But there was still something there, wasn't there? A shadow that you felt you had to hide from me."

She thought about how anxious she'd been when Hoyt was due, and how nervous she'd been during his visits. She'd been so afraid that Jake would see what she felt for Hoyt, and that she fell deeper in love with the man he'd become every time she saw him.

Running her hands over Jake's chest, she swallowed the lump in her throat, blinking back tears of self-disgust. "Jake, I love you so damned much! You're everything to me. You're my rock. I couldn't even imagine not having you in my life. It's all my fault that you felt that way. I'm so sorry."

Sniffing, she swiped at a tear, while Jake used his thumb to catch another. "I swear, I tried to stop loving Hoyt. I never wanted to hurt you. I hated that I couldn't stop loving him. You're everything I ever wanted. I hated myself for wanting more."

Gathering her close, Jake rocked her, running a hand up and down her back—comforting her the way he had hundreds of times before. "Shh, baby. No crying. You have no reason to hate yourself. I knew you'd never betray me. You can't help how you feel, only what you do about it. I know how much you love me, and I'm humbled by what you'd be willing to give up for me." Leaning back, he smiled down at her. "Your heart's just too big to turn love off that way. That's one of the things I love most about you. So, I know there's no way you're ever going to be able to stop loving me."

Tapping her chin, he grinned. "I'm in your blood, baby, the way you're in mine. "You're never getting away from me."

Relief made her dizzy. Rubbing her nipples against his chest, she gasped at the friction and looked up at him through her lashes. "Does that mean that I'm your prisoner?"

"Absolutely." Gripping her shoulders, he turned her and slapped her ass. "Complete with a dungeon to chain you up in when you're misbehaving. Now, move it. Get dressed so we can go meet Hoyt. Once the two of you get married, maybe you'll both be able to settle down and we can get back to normal."

Pausing with her hand on the closet door, Nat sniffed again, grateful for his attempt to lighten the mood. "I love you so much it hurts."

Jake's slow smile warmed her all the way to her bones. "I know. I no longer have a single doubt."

* * * *

Standing in front of the Justice of the Peace, Nat glanced at Jake as Hoyt slipped a gold band on her finger to join the other. "I can't believe this is real."

Hoyt, masculine and incredibly handsome in a navy blue suit stared into her eyes, fingering the ring. "It's very real."

Despite their audience, he raised her hand to his lips, smiling encouragingly. "And very forever." Releasing her hand, he lifted his. "I want *my* ring."

She knew he used a playful tone to lighten the atmosphere, while making it clear that he knew how important it was to her, and that he took wearing a wedding band seriously. Nodding, she blinked back tears and turned to take the ring from Jesse, who stood crying next to her.

Turning back, she glanced at Jake again, silently thanking him with her eyes for helping her pick out the ring from his jewelry store.

Inclining his head, Jake smiled, acknowledging her thanks.

Taking a deep breath, she shifted her gaze to Hoyt's, her breath catching at the love gleaming in his eyes, and began to slide the ring onto his finger. "With this ring…"

* * * *

Even the smallest bump in the road shifted the plug in her ass, and increased her awareness of the clips attached to her nipples and clit. "I'm glad Jake didn't put the clips on tight. You're evil. You know that, don't you?"

Turning his head, he grinned. "Yeah, but you love me."

Smiling, Nat looked down, struck by the difference in the two gold bands that rested side by side on her ring finger. Scratches marred the surface of one, the years of wear clearly visible.

She hardly ever felt it there anymore and rarely took it off.

Next to it, a shiny band that felt strange—not quite as comfortable.

One had become almost a part of her. The other shiny and new—a sign of promise.

Dividing his attention between watching her and driving, Hoyt took her hand in his, running his thumb over the band he'd slid onto her ring finger almost two hours earlier. "Is something wrong, baby?"

Turning toward him, she dropped her head back against the headrest and smiled. "Other than the fact that I have a plug up my ass and clips that are driving me crazy—no. I was just thinking."

"About?"

Struck by the contrast of his arrogant tone and uncertainty in his eyes, she gripped his hand. "I was thinking about the day I married Jake. I was so scared. I was sure that he'd realized he made a mistake and find he didn't want to be tied to a woman who loved someone else, *and* another man's baby."

"Christ, I never even thought of that. I left you, thinking you were safe and being taken care of, and you were scared and insecure."

Nat smiled. "It wasn't that bad, Hoyt. Jake was great. I should have known he would be, but I was a mess." Holding his hand, she rubbed his forearm. "I just meant that today, I wasn't scared at all. I had to marry you. I couldn't fall out of love with you if I tried—and believe me, I've tried."

Grinning, he turned to pull into the parking lot of an upscale hotel he'd driven to. "You can't shake me off any more than I can shake you off."

"Face it, baby." He pulled into a parking space, cutting the engine before turning in his seat. "You and I are stuck with each other for life."

Grinning, Nat sat back as he undid their seat belts. "Don't tell me the pragmatic Navy SEAL believes in fate."

Laughing, he pulled her close. "I believe in making my own destiny, honey, but some things are just written in stone. Come on. Let's get to our room so I can ravage my *wife*."

My wife.

The possessiveness in his tone, and the way he'd emphasized the word wasn't lost on her.

Pressing a hand to her stomach to quell the butterflies, Nat couldn't help but smile at the satisfaction he'd managed to convey in that word, a satisfaction that matched her own.

Walking out of the elevator, she glanced up at him, trying to come to grips with the fact that the man she'd loved for so many years was now her husband.

Tall, muscular, and with straight, broad shoulders, he led her down the hallway, holding her hand securely in his, his gaze not missing a thing as they made their way to a door at the end.

The small plaque next to the entrance caught her attention. Blinking, she turned to him. "The honeymoon suite?"

Hoyt shrugged and inserted the key card into the slot. "Even though we're only going to be here a few hours, it still qualifies." His tone held a hint of defensiveness as he shoved the door open. "If you don't like it, I can ask for another room." After slinging the backpack over his shoulder, he reached for her, lifting her high against his chest.

Touched by his thoughtfulness, and stunned that he actually blushed, she wrapped her arms around his neck and nuzzled his jaw. "It's perfect. You know, I like when you get all manly and carry me."

Shooting her a look, his eyes narrowed in suspicion, he carried her through the doorway in a romantic gesture that surprised her even more. His gaze never left hers as he kicked the door closed behind them and turned, locking it while still holding her in his arms. "Do you?"

Unable to resist, she ran a hand over his chest, hiding a smile. "Yep. Makes me go all girly inside." Pleased that she'd managed to surprise him, she smiled at his skeptical look and cuddled closer. "Don't expect me to say things like that all the time. It's just that there's something about being held that turns me to mush."

"Hmm." Hoyt's lips twitched before he bent and touched them to hers. "I'll remember that. Something tells me that when dealing with you, I'm going to need all the help I can get."

Lowering her to her feet, he studied her features, his smile falling. The silence lengthened, the look he gave her unlike any he'd ever given her before.

She swallowed heavily, her smile falling. "Hoyt?"

His fingertips moved over her hair, his eyes darkening as he continued to stare down at her. "Sometimes I'm stunned by just how beautiful you are."

With trembling hands, she gripped the lapels of his jacket. "Back atcha. When I look at you sometimes, I want you so much it makes me dizzy." She rose to her toes, pulling him closer. "For someone who doesn't always say the right thing, you're getting pretty damned good at it."

Wrapping her arms around his neck, she pressed her lips to his. "I love you so damned much."

He met her passionate kiss with his own demanding one, taking all the hunger and love she poured into it, giving it back to her while demanding even more.

One kiss blended into another, their harsh breathing and frantic efforts to undress each other leaving her breathless.

324   Leah Brooke

Her dress puddled at her feet, leaving her naked except for the clips, pale thigh-high stockings, and lavender pumps that matched her dress.

His jacket hit the floor seconds later, and she reached for his tie, growling in protest when he gripped her wrists, pulling her hands away as he broke off his kiss.

"Hoyt, damn it! Let go. I want you naked."

Overcoming her struggle to get closer, he held her at arm's length, his heated gaze raking over her. "Damn, baby." Gathering her wrists in one hand, he lifted them above her head. "Look at you."

Struck by the awe in his voice, and the wonder in his eyes, she arched toward him. "They've been driving me crazy. I hope you plan to do something about it besides stand there and stare."

Hoyt grinned, shaking her just enough to send the chains swaying. "Don't be such a baby. Those clips aren't tight at all. They're just for decoration." Reaching out, he tugged at one of the chains attached to her left nipple, grinning again at her cry of pleasure. "Let me see that fine ass."

Still holding her wrists above her head, he circled her, the brush of his trousers against her hip a sharp reminder of her nakedness. Bending close, he nuzzled her neck, running a hand over her bottom, emphasizing her nakedness even more.

"I was hoping that wearing the plug and the clips would distract you. I was afraid that you would be nervous today." Closing in behind her, he pressed his body against hers. "Were you?"

Nat shivered at the feel of his body against hers, the warmth against her back making the front of her body feel cold and tightening her nipples even more. "Hmm. A little but Jake and I talked. That's why you insisted I wear this stuff?"

"It was one of the reasons." Taking her hands in his, he lifted them higher and placed them around his neck. "Keep them there. I like having your body accessible."

Trembling, she leaned back against him, letting her eyes flutter closed, a moan escaping at the sharp awareness in every erogenous zone. "What were the other reasons?" Her voice came out as a breathless whisper as his hands moved over her, igniting pleasure in every nerve ending. Her position left her breasts lifted and exposed, something Hoyt used to his advantage.

The slide of his hands over her breasts made it nearly impossible to concentrate, the friction against her sensitized nipples sending sharp stabs of pleasure racing through her.

His breath, warm on her neck as he nuzzled her ear, sent another shiver through her. "Because I wanted to see you this way. Because I wanted you to feel as desirable as you are. Because I wanted you to feel me even when I wasn't with you."

His hands closed over her breasts. "Because I wanted you to think about *this*."

"God, that feels so good."

"Hmm." Hoyt tugged at the chains on her nipples. "Now that I'm here, we don't need these any more. I want my mouth on you."

"Yes!" Crying out when he removed the small clips and tossed them aside, she arched, pushing her breasts more firmly into his hands.

Turning her, he slid a hand behind her back to support her as he lowered her to the bed. "Keep those hands above your head and out of my way."

Nat obeyed him with a groan of protest, her breath catching when he sucked a nipple into his mouth. "I want to touch you."

Lifting his head, he glanced up at her, his expression hard and lined with tension. "Later. Right now, I plan to devour you, and I don't want to be distracted."

Gathering fistfuls of the silky bedspread, she writhed beneath him, crying out at the feel of his mouth on her sensitized nipples.

Each tug, each pull sent an answering pull to her slit, making her clit throb even harder, and with the clip holding the hood back, the sensitivity there became almost unbearable.

"Please, Hoyt. My clit's on fire."

"Good." Trailing his lips lower, he nipped at the underside of her breasts. "Just the way I like it." Brushing his lips over her belly, he worked his way down her body, closing his hands over her thighs to push them wider. "I love the stockings, baby. Very sexy. Kick those shoes off. I don't want one of those heels stabbing me in the back when I use my mouth on you." He moved lower, brushing his lips against her mound. "So soft."

She'd already lost one shoe, so she kicked the other off, the soft thud of it hitting the carpet almost as loud as the thudding of her heart. Sucking in a breath, and then another, she tightened her fists on the bedding, a moan escaping as Hoyt draped her thighs over his wide shoulders.

Flattening a hand on her stomach, he blew softly on her exposed clit, his hold tightening when she pushed her thighs down, using his shoulders for leverage to lift herself. "No way, baby. I've been thinking about having the taste of my wife on my tongue all day."

Her clit was so sensitive that even the feel of his warm breath moving over it sent her senses reeling. Writhing against him, she sucked in another breath when his other hand flattened on her stomach, and he leaned forward, using his shoulders to push her thighs higher and wider, effectively taking away her leverage.

With a groan, he lowered his head.

Squeezing her eyes closed, Nat screamed his name, jolting at the too-sharp pleasure of his tongue against her swollen and throbbing clit. "Hoyt! It's too much. Oh, God. My clit. Please, Hoyt! Oh, God!"

The pleasure exploded, sending hot, tingling sparks of pleasure washing over her. The tingling travelled up and down her body, making the throbbing in her clit even worse. Clamping down on the small plug in her ass made it feel even larger. Her orgasm crested, and crying out, she fought his hold, her inability to escape it exciting her even more.

His tongue continued to slide over it, slow, gentle strokes that kept the pleasure rolling through her. "That's a girl. Just enough to take the edge off before I fuck this sweet pussy."

His tongue flicked over her clit several times in rapid succession, drawing her orgasm out even longer. "So good." Removing the clip, he plunged his tongue into her pussy, fucking her with it—the quick thrusts of his tongue against her inner walls making it impossible to come all the way down, and arousing her all over again.

"Please, Hoyt. Oh, God. I need to come again."

"You will." Rising to stand between her thighs, he shrugged off his clothes and reached into the duffel bag packed with a change of clothing for both of them. He retrieved a condom, rolling it on before running a hand down her body from just below her breasts to her mound, his gaze following the movement of his hand. "I can't believe you're finally mine."

"Believe it." Lifting her arms, she reached for him, smiling as he hooked her knees over his arms and braced himself with a hand on either side of her. "You're mine, too."

"Yes, I am." With a groan, he thrust into her. "And I have a hell of a lot of time to make up for."

Nat gripped his shoulders, moaning with every thrust, each one filled with a possessiveness and hunger that thrilled her. "Yes! God, Hoyt, it feels so good." Each stroke shifted the plug in her ass, making it feel as if she was being taken in both openings.

"Yes, it does. That pussy's so wet and hot. I swear, baby, it's like it was made for my cock."

He pumped into her, the friction against her inner walls and the depth of his thrusts quickly driving her to the edge again. "Mine, damn it. Mine." He shortened his thrusts, his eyes sharp on hers as he dug at a place inside her that sent her senses reeling.

Crying out, she threw her hands over her head again, fisting her hands in the bedspread as a kaleidoscope of colors burst behind her eyes. "Yes, Oh, Hoyt." Her body gathered, the warning tingling sensation growing stronger with every thrust of his cock.

"No, you don't." Withdrawing with a speed that left her pussy clenching at emptiness, he released her and flung her to her stomach. Covering her body with his, he scraped his teeth over her shoulder as he gripped the base of the plug. "Let's get rid of this little piece of rubber and fill your ass with a real cock, okay, baby?"

"God, yes!" Gulping in air, she rocked her hips as he drew the plug from her ass and shoved two pillows under her hips.

He seemed determined to imprint himself on every part of her, and the hunger he'd created made it impossible to refuse him anything. "We're both on the edge, aren't we, honey?"

Nat cried out as the head of his cock began to push into her, his body pressing hers to the mattress.

With a curse, he worked his cock into her, each shallow stroke pushing his cock deeper. "That's it. Christ, your ass is tight."

To her surprise, he wrapped his arms around hers, flattening his hand on each of hers and lacing their fingers. "My wife. Every part of you belongs to me now."

Gripping his hands, she used her knees to move into his thrust as much as she could, her body tightening with each inch he gained. "Yes. Oh, God, Hoyt. Fuck me. Fuck me hard."

Almost before she finished speaking, he began to move faster, fucking her ass with the quick, shallow thrusts he'd used when fucking her pussy. "Yes. Fuck. So fucking good. So fucking tight. Oh, fuck."

He groaned when she came, growling against her neck when her orgasm tightened her ass on his cock. "That's it. Yeah, baby. Come. Fuck, yeah."

Crying out, Nat threw her head back against his shoulder, tightening her hands on his with a whimper. "Oh, God."

Her ass milked his cock, each ripple making his cock feeling even bigger, thicker, and unbelievably harder inside her.

With a groan, he sank deeper, his cock pulsing inside her. "My God, Natalie. I can't get enough of you."

"I'd die if you ever did."

With a sigh of satisfaction, he groaned again, bracing his weight on one arm to look down at her, rubbing her arm at her shiver when he slid his cock free. "Never." Pushing her hair back from her face with a gentleness that sent a warm surge of love through her, he smiled. "I'll want you on my deathbed. Even when we're both too old to be doing this, I'll want you with me. I want to see your smile every morning, and feel you against me every night. I want to hold you while you're sleeping and listen to you breathe. I've lost too much, Natalie—more than I can get back. I've hurt you—and I'm going to spend the rest of my life making it up to you, and making sure you're never hurt again."

Stunned, Nat smiled tremulously, blinking back tears. "I love you so much. I couldn't bear it if this isn't everything you hope for."

Hoyt's smile transformed his features, a relaxed smile so filled with love and tenderness, it brought a lump to her throat. "I've got everything I ever hoped for right here in my arms. Just being with you is more than I ever thought I'd have again, baby. We've got the rest of our lives together, and I'm determined to make every day count."

Epilogue

Nat sat back, sipping her iced tea, and enjoyed the view, trying to remember if she'd ever been as happy as she was at that moment. Turning her head, she smiled at her sister, who sat in the folding chair next to her. "You know, people pay good money to see stuff like this."

Jesse didn't take her eyes from the sight in front of them. "Umm. That's their problem. Damn, are you sure you don't have any more flowers? It looks like they're running out."

Nat turned back, watching four shirtless, sweaty men working in her flower garden. "No. Unfortunately, that's the last of them. Jake and Hoyt look sexy as hell all sweaty and covered with dirt. Maybe I should get the hose and hose them down."

Jesse giggled. "As long as I get to hose down Clay and Rio. Damn, I never get tired of looking at them. All that muscle—bunching and shifting. Gets a girl real hot and bothered, doesn't it?"

Nat didn't want to mention that her panties had been soaked for the last hour. "It sure as hell does."

Jesse glanced at her. "So, you need any advice about handling two of them? You've only been married to Hoyt a little over a month, so I figure you've still got a lot to learn."

Nat lowered her glass. "Cute. Nope. I think I've got this all figured out, or haven't you noticed that both of them have spent the entire day working on my flower bed?" Grinning, Nat lifted her glass again. "I even got yours over here."

"I think I had a little something to do with that." Jesse giggled again. "I asked *real* nice."

* * * *

Hoyt paused and glanced at the women. "Do you have the feeling they're talking about us?"

Rio grinned and looked toward his wife. "I'd bet on it. They've been ogling us ever since we came out here. The two of them, sitting there sipping iced tea, and giggling like girls."

Clay straightened, leaning on the shovel. "It's about damned time. They've both been out of sorts ever since Nat was kidnapped. Jesse just fell apart. It's not something I ever want to see again."

Jake wiped his brow, smiling indulgently at Nat. "If this is what it takes to get them to relax, I'll stand here and do this all fucking day."

Hoyt looked over toward where the bright yellow flowers that had been trampled, had started to bloom again. "She loves these damned flowers. Seeing the destruction those two assholes made of them seemed to remind her of it."

Jake nodded grimly. "Yeah, and I couldn't even get her out here to do anything about them. She kept saying she just wasn't interested anymore."

Clay dug another hole. "This should cheer her up. I'm just glad they have each other."

Hoyt placed the flower in the hole that Clay had just dug. "Well, this is it. I guess the show's over. We don't have any more to plant."

Jake looked around. "You're kidding. There was a shit load of them. It took her all day to pick them out."

Hoyt looked up at the sound of a car pulling into the driveway. "Look. Joe's here." Straightening, he brushed off his hands and went to greet his son. He glanced at Natalie, knowing how nervous she'd been about him seeing them together, and held out a hand for her as he passed. "Our son's home, baby."

Watching his wife throw herself at Joe, Hoyt grinned with pride for both of them.

Wiping away tears, Nat grinned. "I'm so glad you're home, honey."

Joe adopted one of his mother's stern looks, but the twinkle in his eye was unmistakable. "It looks like you've been putting my dads to work."

Natalie crossed her arms over her chest, lifting her chin. "You wouldn't want them to get fat and lazy, would you?"

Joe threw his head back and laughed. "With you around? Not likely." Wrapping his arm around his mother, he faced Hoyt. "So Dad, how does it feel to be married to Mom?"

Hoyt couldn't miss the way Natalie tensed, or the concern in his son's eyes. Shaking his head, he grinned. "Unbelievable." He slid his gaze to hers. "I've never been happier in my life. Are you ready for the party tomorrow?"

"I can't wait." Joe grinned. "So, Mom, how does it feel to have two husbands?"

To Hoyt's surprise, and alarm, Natalie's eyes filled with tears. "Hey!" Going to her side, he wrapped his arm around her and pulled her close. "What's all this, baby?"

Joe backed away, obviously shaken. "Mom, please don't cry. Please don't cry." He looked up at Hoyt, his eyes dark with panic. "She never cries. Make her stop."

Hoyt lifted Natalie's face to his, searching her features. "You're scaring your son. Having two husbands is that good? Or that bad?"

As he'd hoped, she laughed through her tears. "That good."

As if by some unspoken agreement, the others gave them a few minutes alone with Joe before coming over. When they approached, Jake moved in on the other side of Natalie, speaking in low tones while the others made a fuss over Joe. "Problem, baby?"

With Hoyt on one side and Jake on the other, Natalie lifted her head, looking at each of them. "No. I just love both of you so damned much. I was sitting over there a few minutes ago, wondering if I'd ever been this happy. Her eyes shimmered. "Now that Joe's here, I'm even happier."

"Good." Jake touched his lips to hers, lifting his head when Jesse squealed. "What the hell?"

Hoyt laughed, following the movement of the flatbed that pulled up out front, and the tarp that covered his cherry red Mustang.

Joe's eyes went wide. "I gotta go call Alex, Will, and Kyle."

* * * *

Sitting in the chair Natalie had been sitting in earlier, Hoyt held her on his lap, lazily running a hand up and down her arm. "You okay, baby."

Flattening a hand on his chest, she grinned up at him. "Yes, but starving. Do you think they'll ever get back with the steaks, or have they all run off with your car?"

Hoyt chuckled. "If your sister gets her way, they're long gone, but I have a feeling they'll be back. I still can't figure out how all of them got in there."

Jake plopped into the chair next to him. "They're squeezed in there like sardines. The grill's hot and the potatoes are on."

Nat giggled and slumped against him. "I have a feeling we're all going to be eating potatoes and salad for dinner." Stiffening, she sat up. "Hoyt, you don't think something happened, do you?"

"They're fine, honey. They're probably just showing off the car."

Biting her lip, she leaned against him again. "I hope they don't scratch it."

Taking her hand in his, Hoyt kissed the band he'd placed there weeks earlier. "It's just a car."

"You love that car!"

Hoyt smiled down at her. "The last few years have shown me what's really important."

Looking up as the Mustang pulled up in the driveway, he watched everyone pile out, all of them smiling and talking at once.

Holding his wife in his arms, he looked at Jake, unsurprised to see that his friend had taken her other hand in his.

Family.

Touching his lips to Natalie's hair, he breathed in the scent of her and sighed, happier than he'd ever thought he could be—happier than he could have ever hoped for. Watching the others come toward them, all talking excitedly, he pulled Natalie closer and looked at his son. "I've got my family. The woman I love. My best friend. My son. Nothing's as important as that."

THE END

WWW.LEAHBROOKE.NET

ABOUT THE AUTHOR

Leah spends most of her time with family and friends, and the rest of her time creating new ones.

For all titles by Leah Brooke, please visit
www.bookstrand.com/leah-brooke

Siren Publishing, Inc.
www.SirenPublishing.com

CPSIA information can be obtained at www.ICGtesting.com
Printed in the USA
LVOW06s1440301114

416285LV00032B/1611/P